W9-BLT-773

THE CARDBOARD KINGDOM

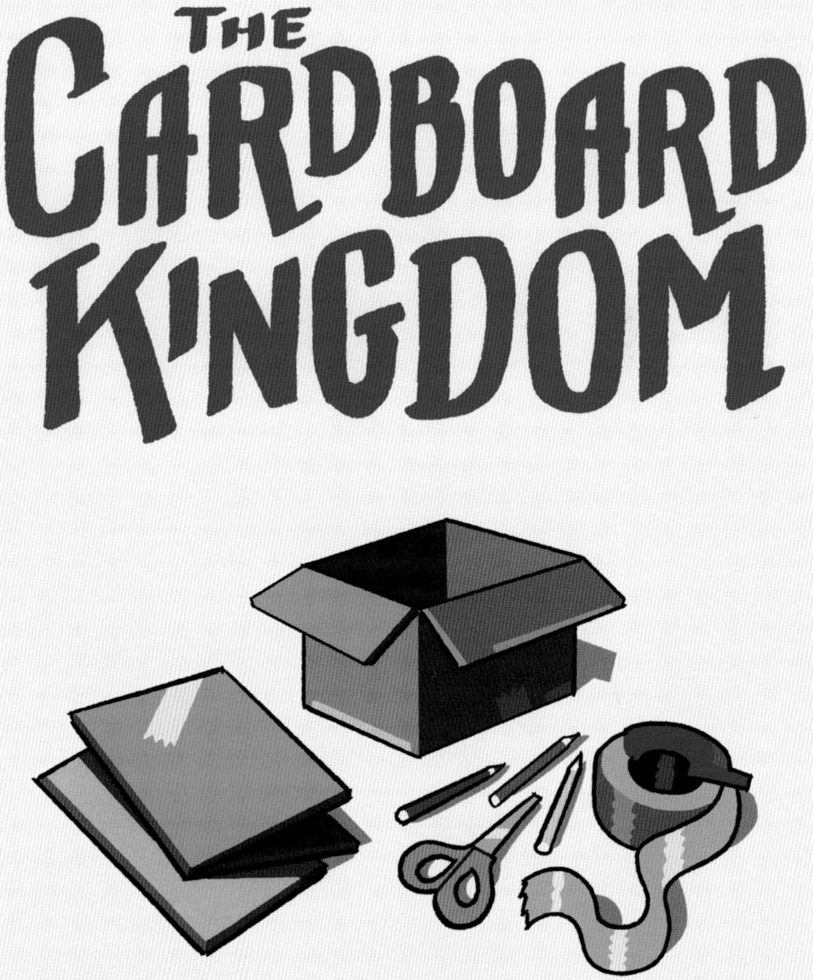

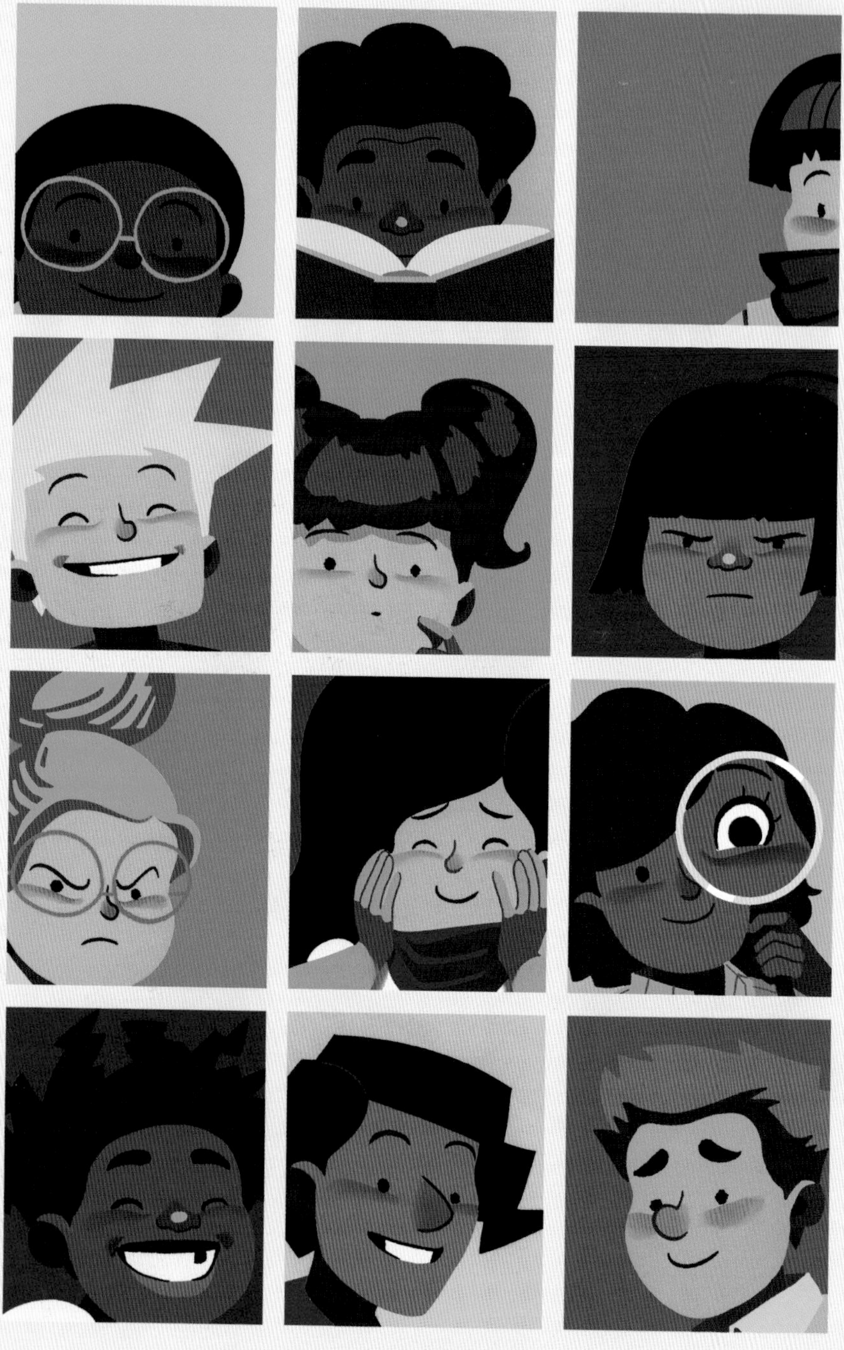

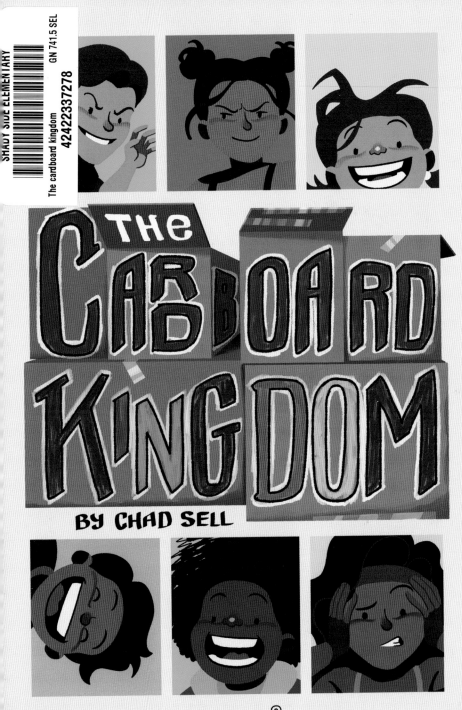

THE CARDBOARD KINGDOM

BY CHAD SELL

SHADY SIDE ELEMENTARY

GN 741.5 SEL

424 2233 7278

The cardboard kingdom

ALFRED A. KNOPF · NEW YORK

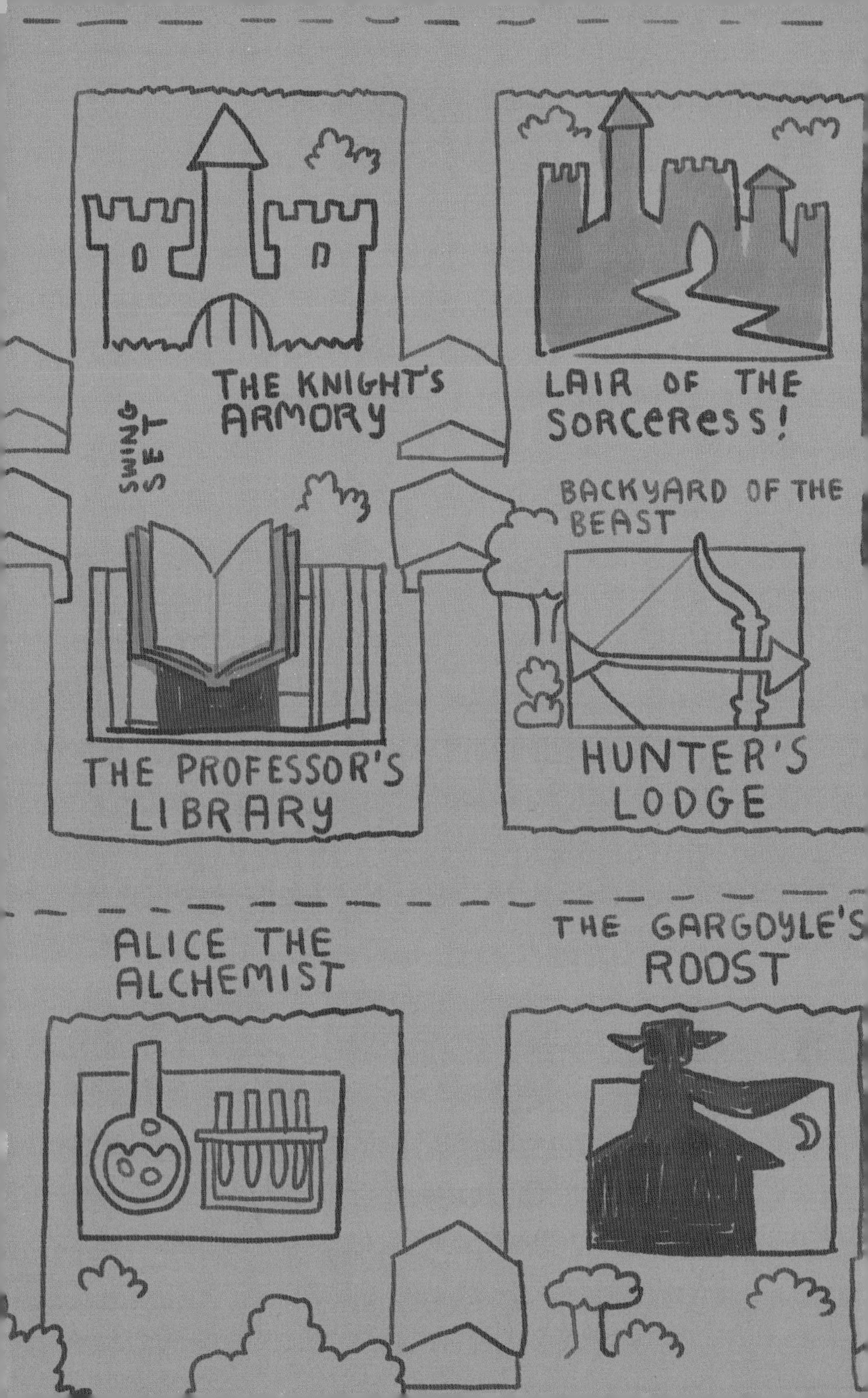
THE KNIGHT'S ARMORY
LAIR OF THE SORCERESS!
SWING SET
BACKYARD OF THE BEAST
THE PROFESSOR'S LIBRARY
HUNTER'S LODGE
ALICE THE ALCHEMIST
THE GARGOYLE'S ROOST

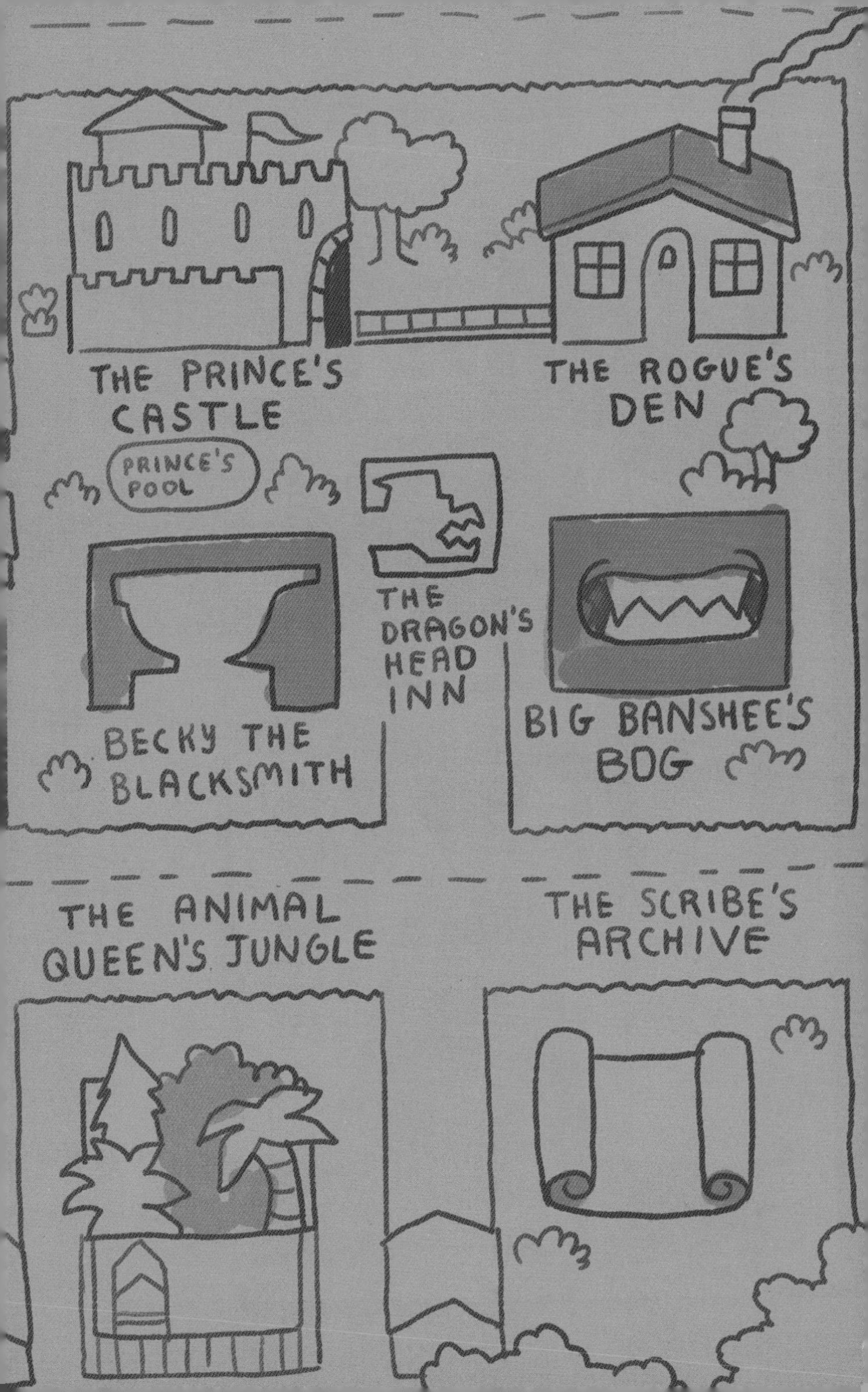
THE PRINCE'S CASTLE
PRINCE'S POOL
THE ROGUE'S DEN
THE DRAGON'S HEAD INN
BECKY THE BLACKSMITH
BIG BANSHEE'S BOG
THE ANIMAL QUEEN'S JUNGLE
THE SCRIBE'S ARCHIVE

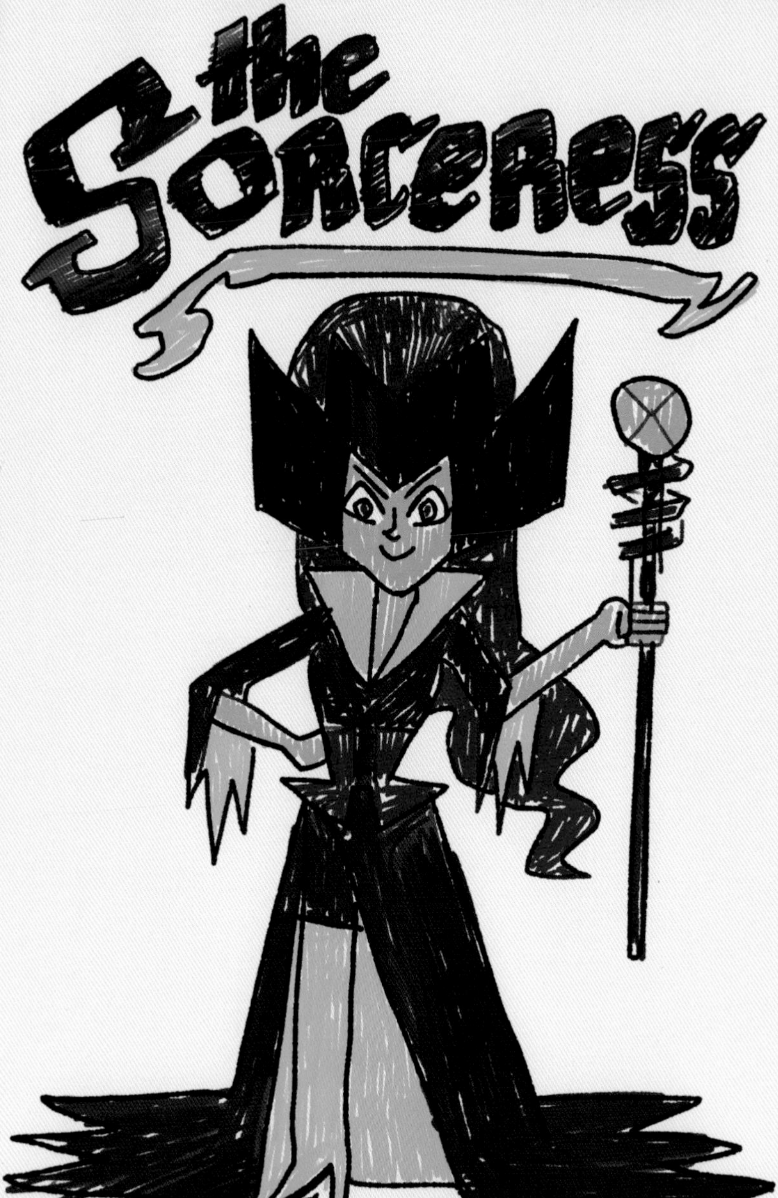

the Sorceress

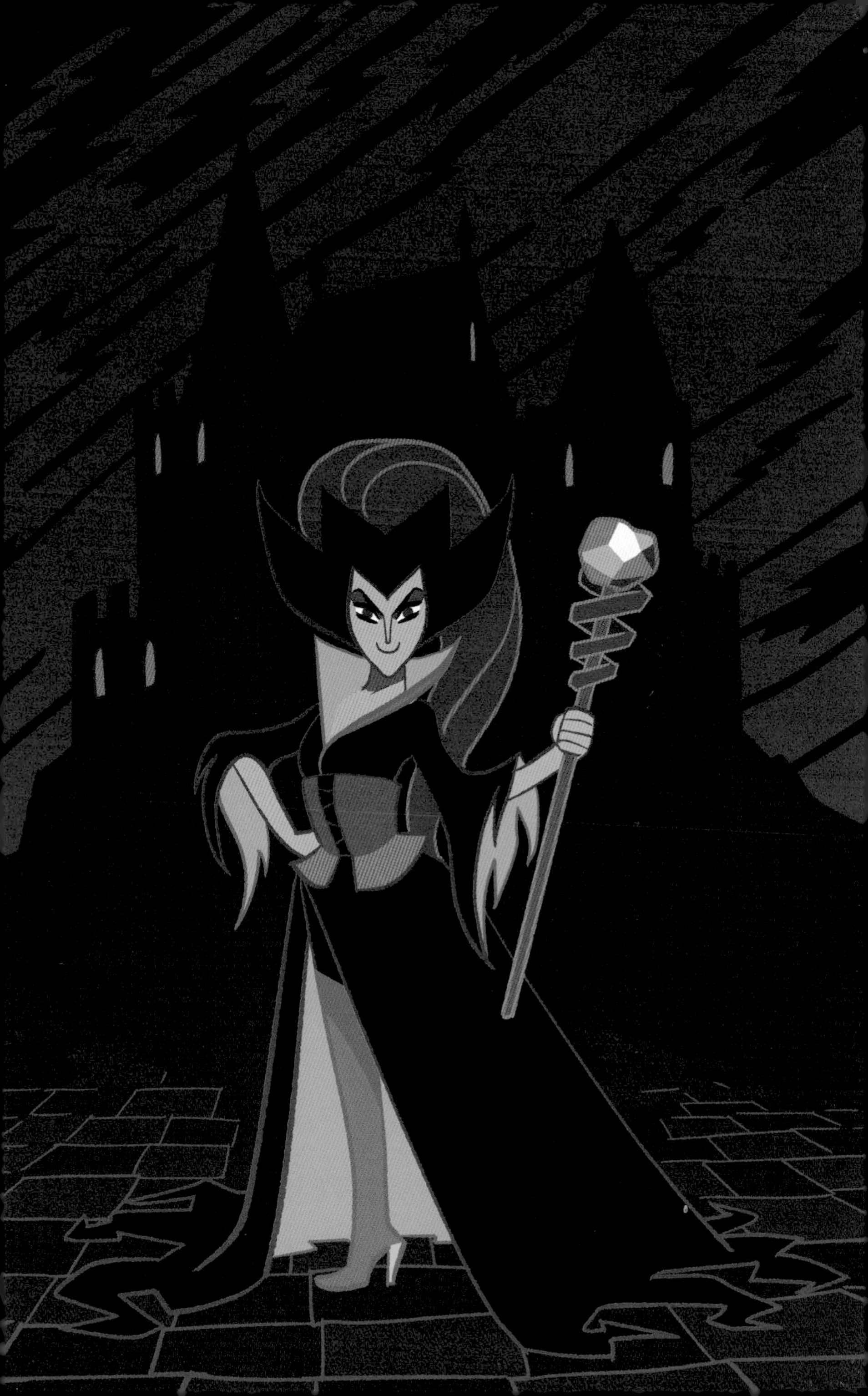

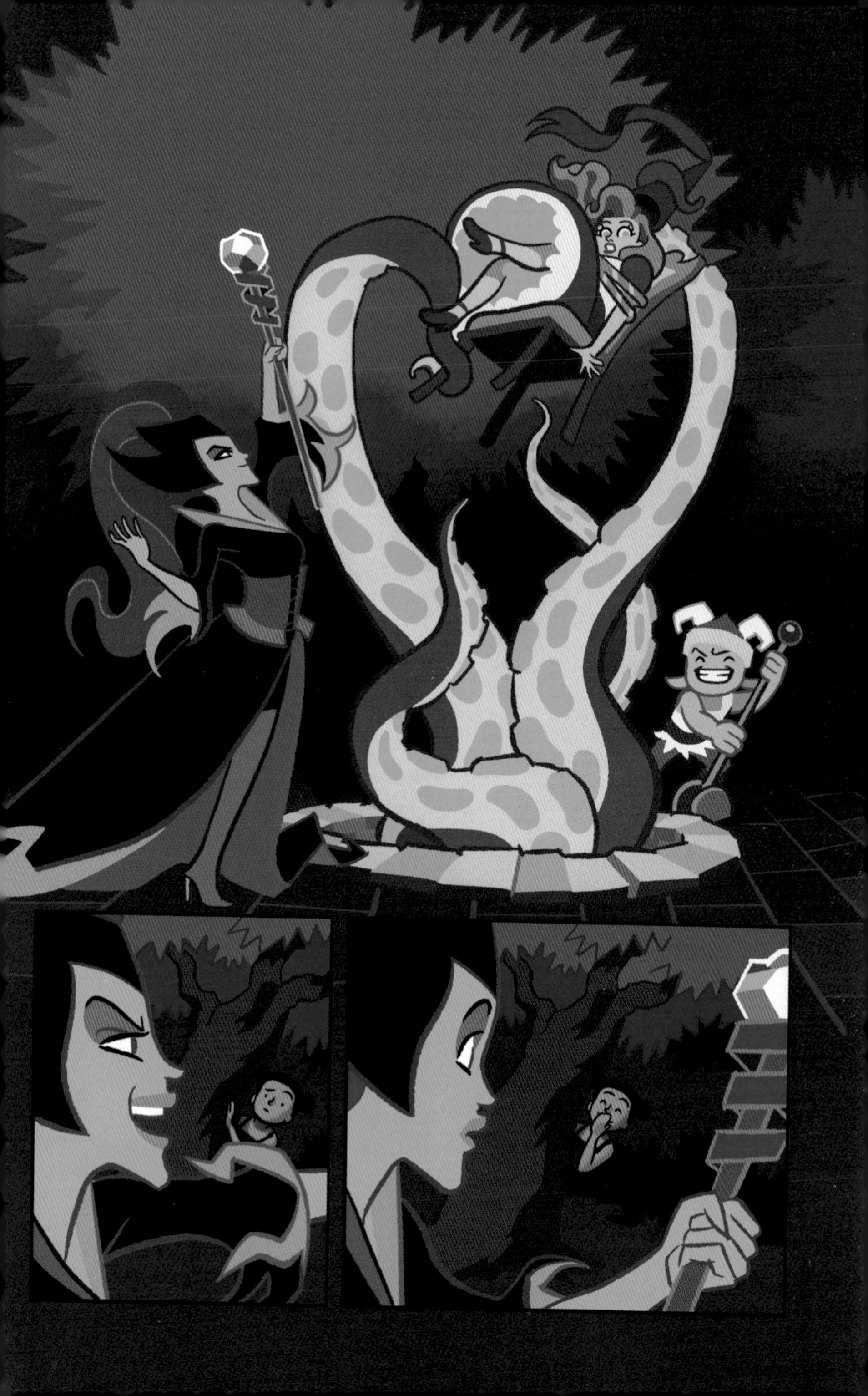

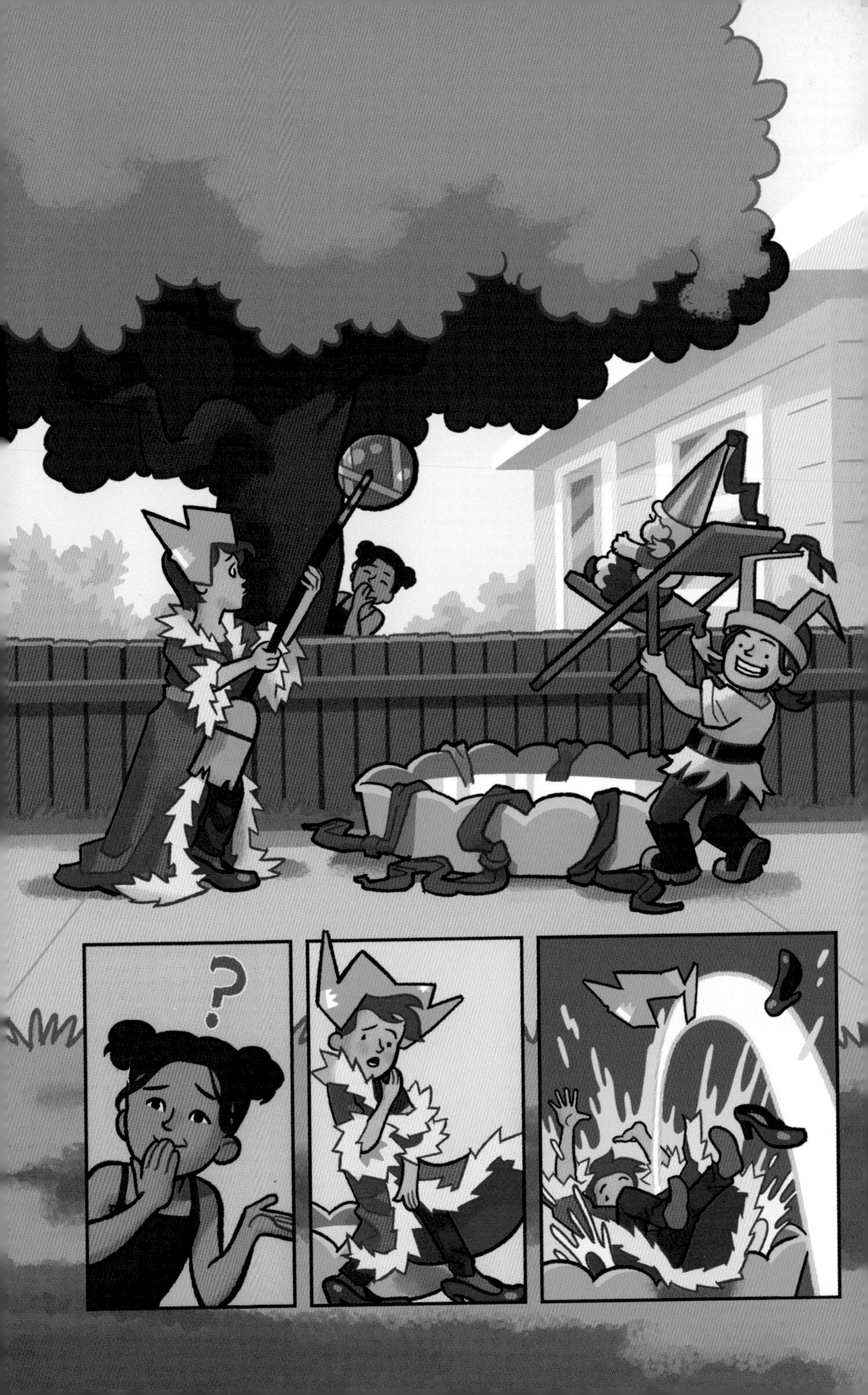

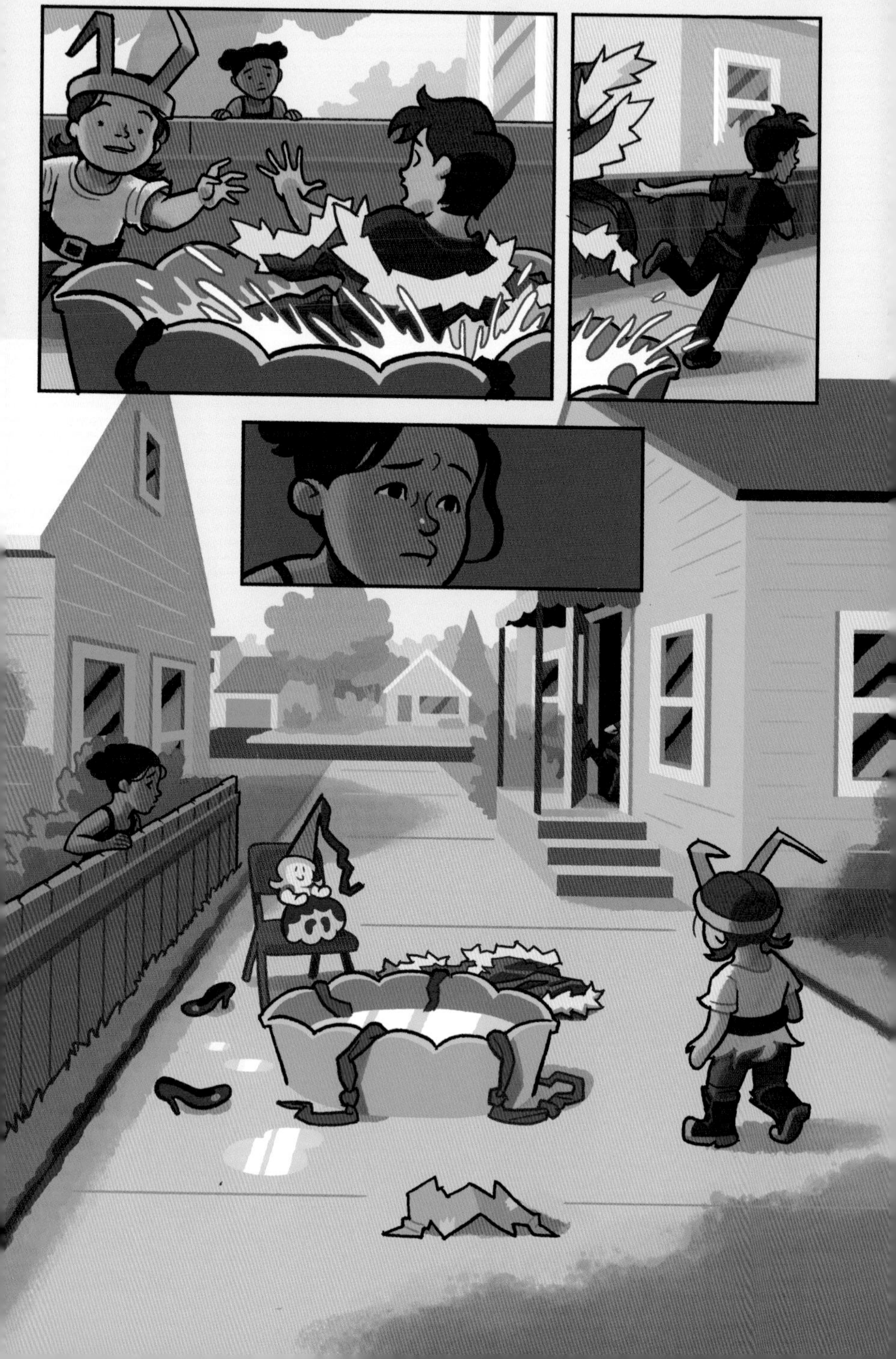

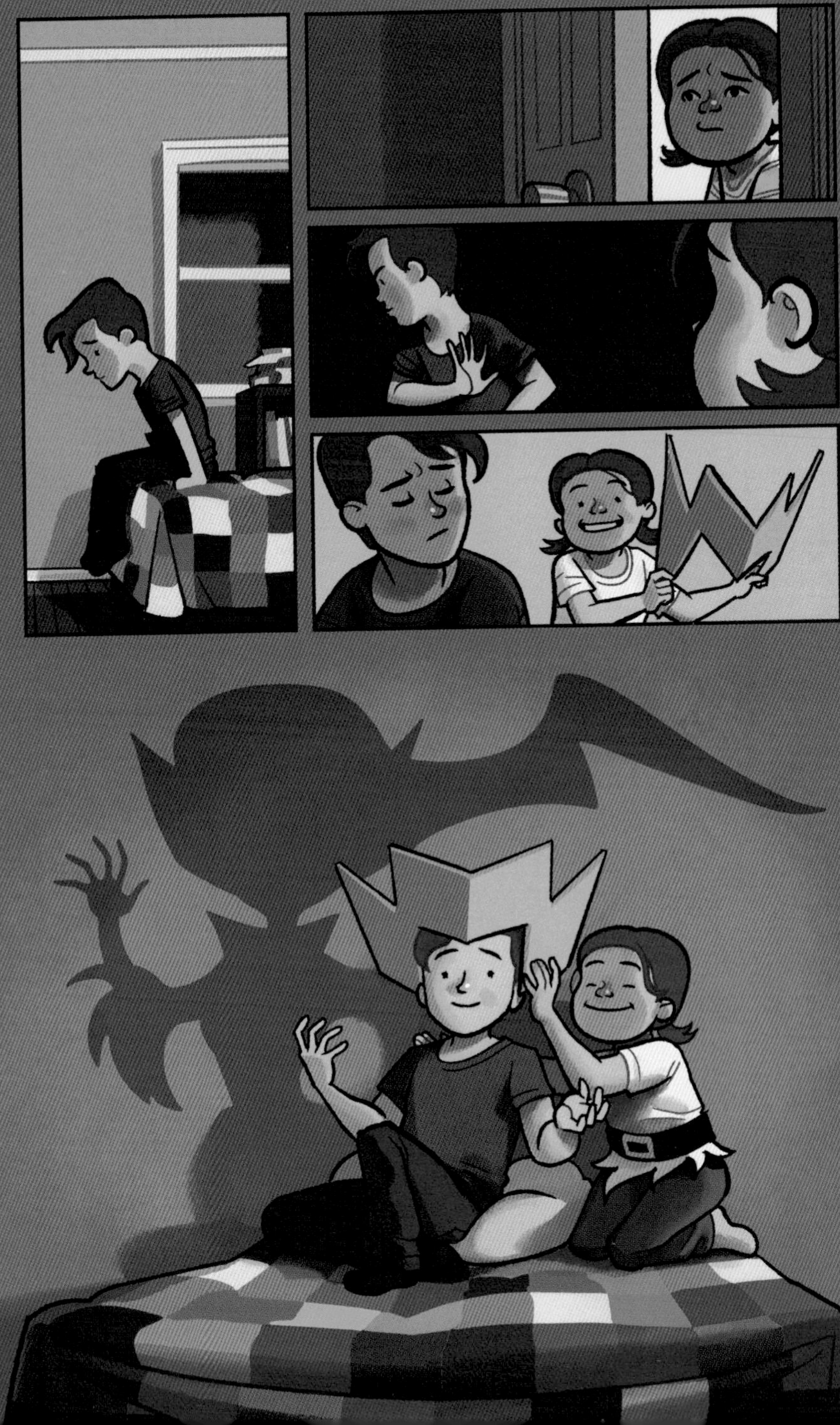

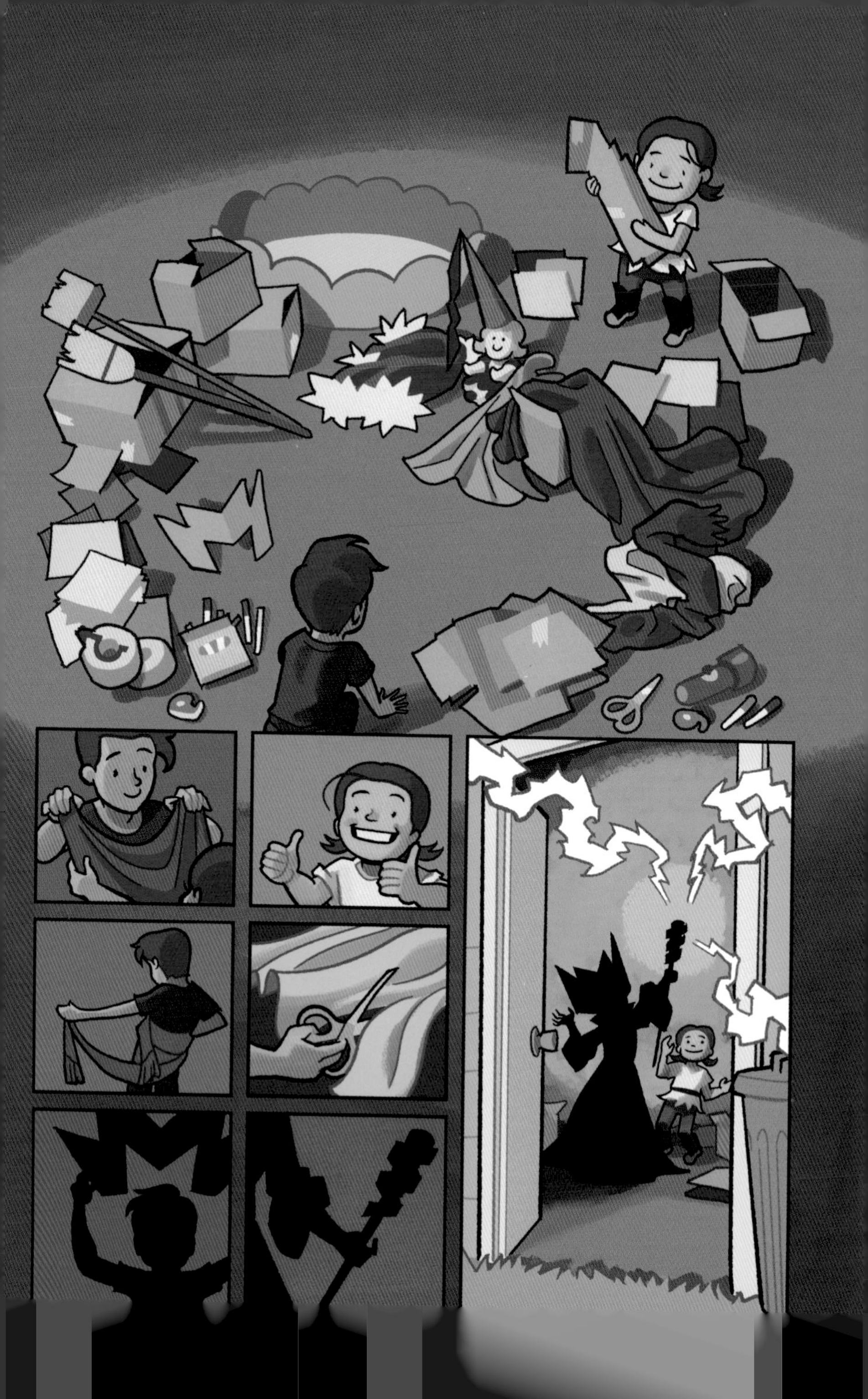

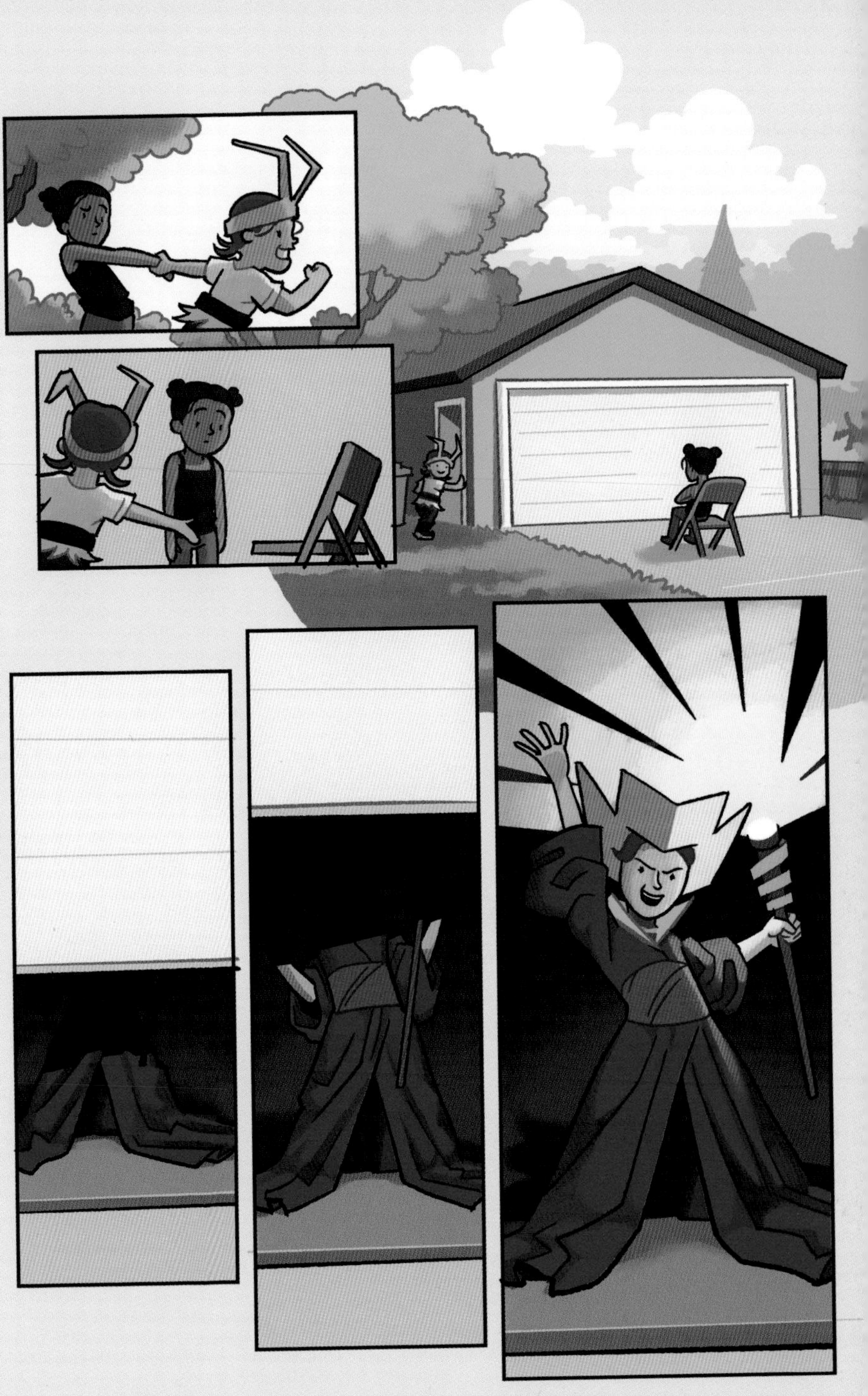

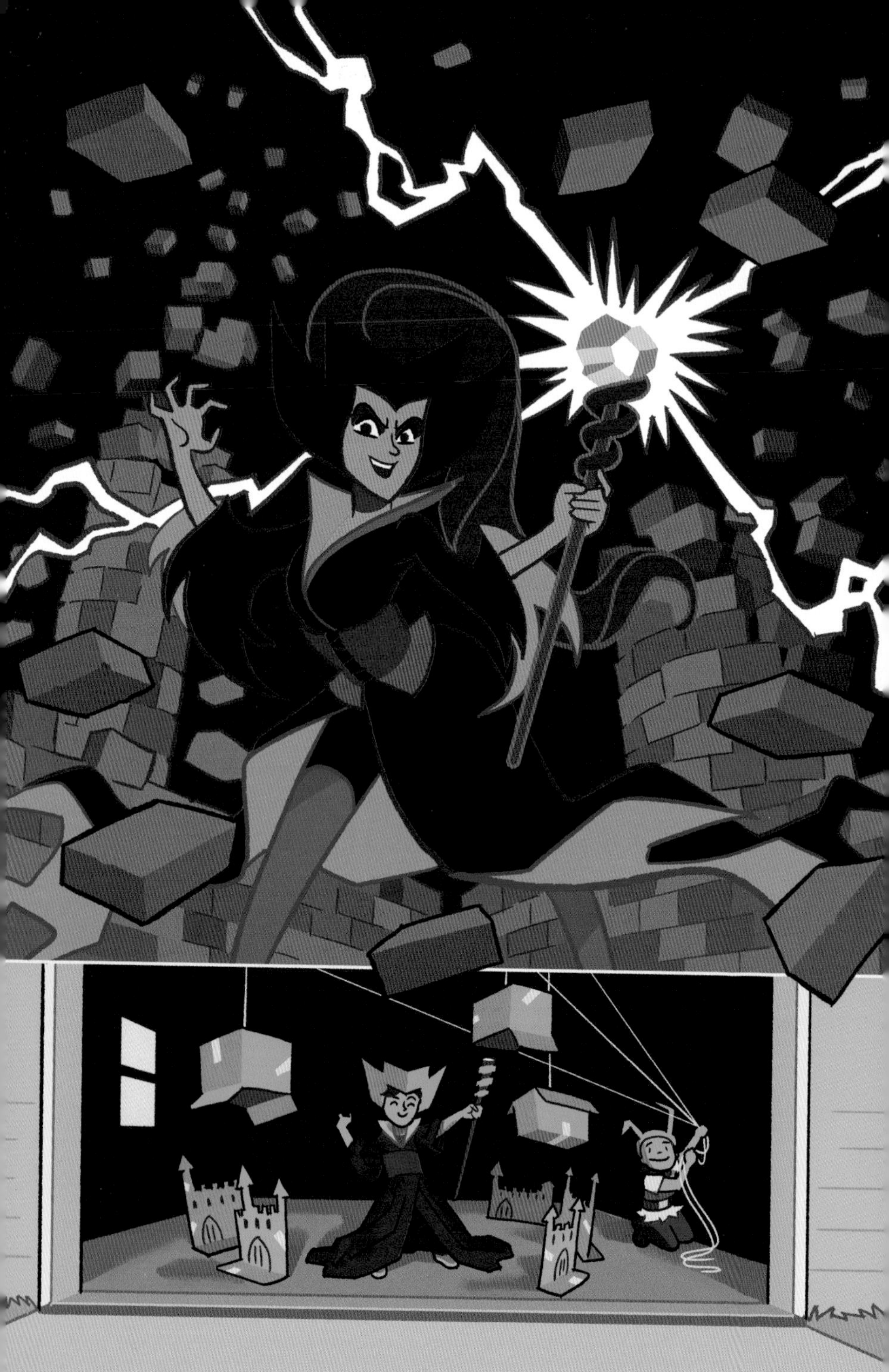

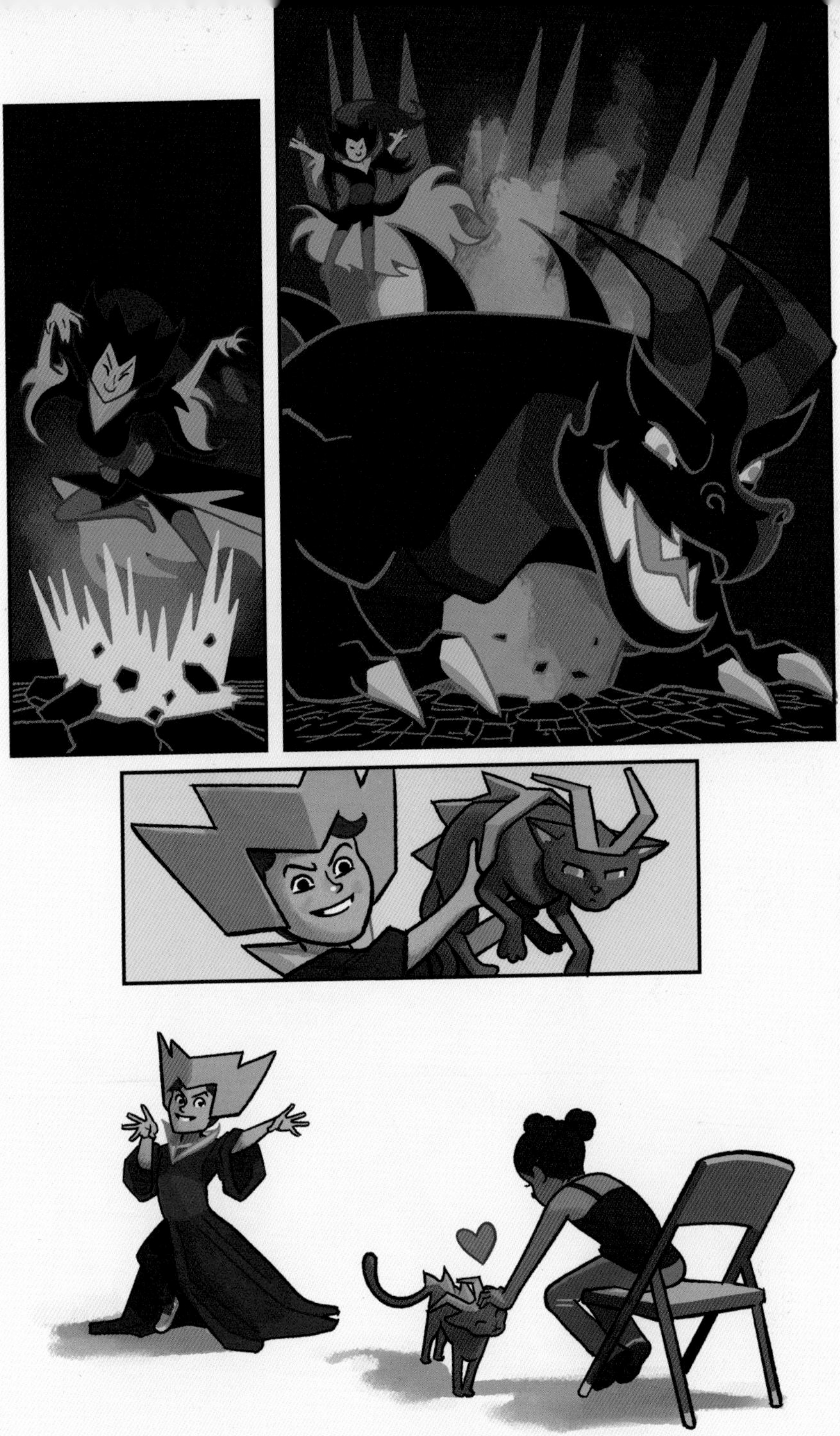

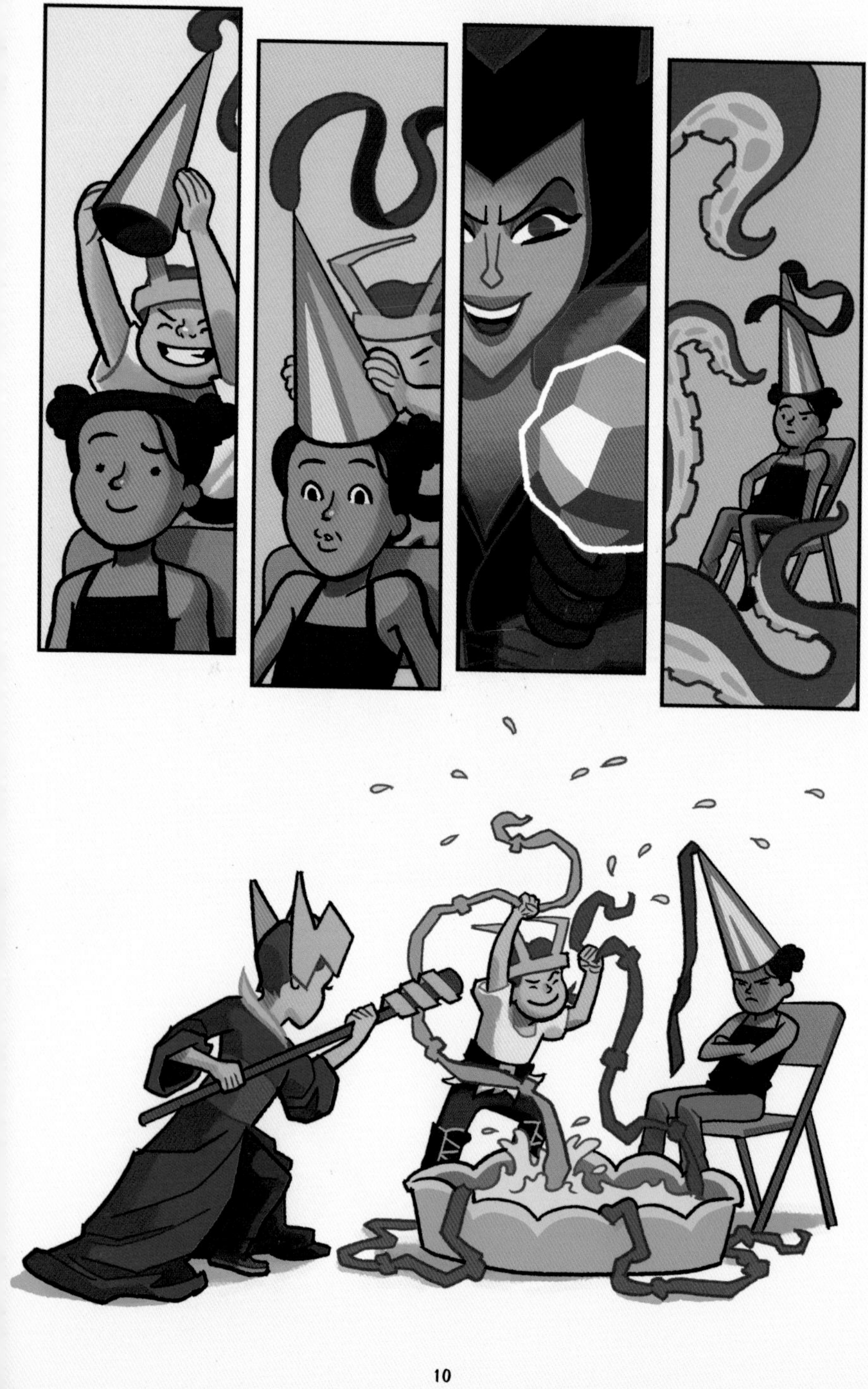

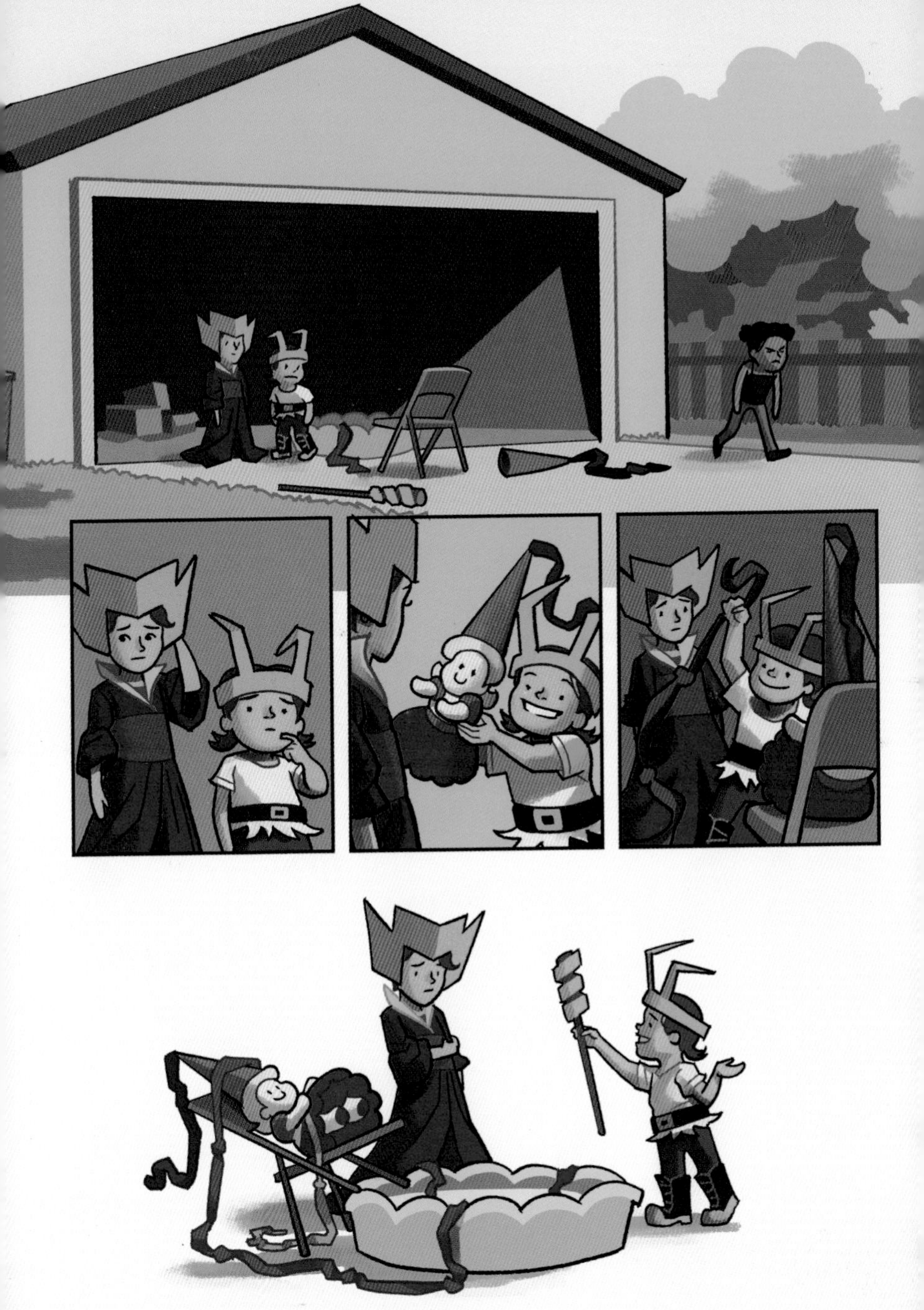

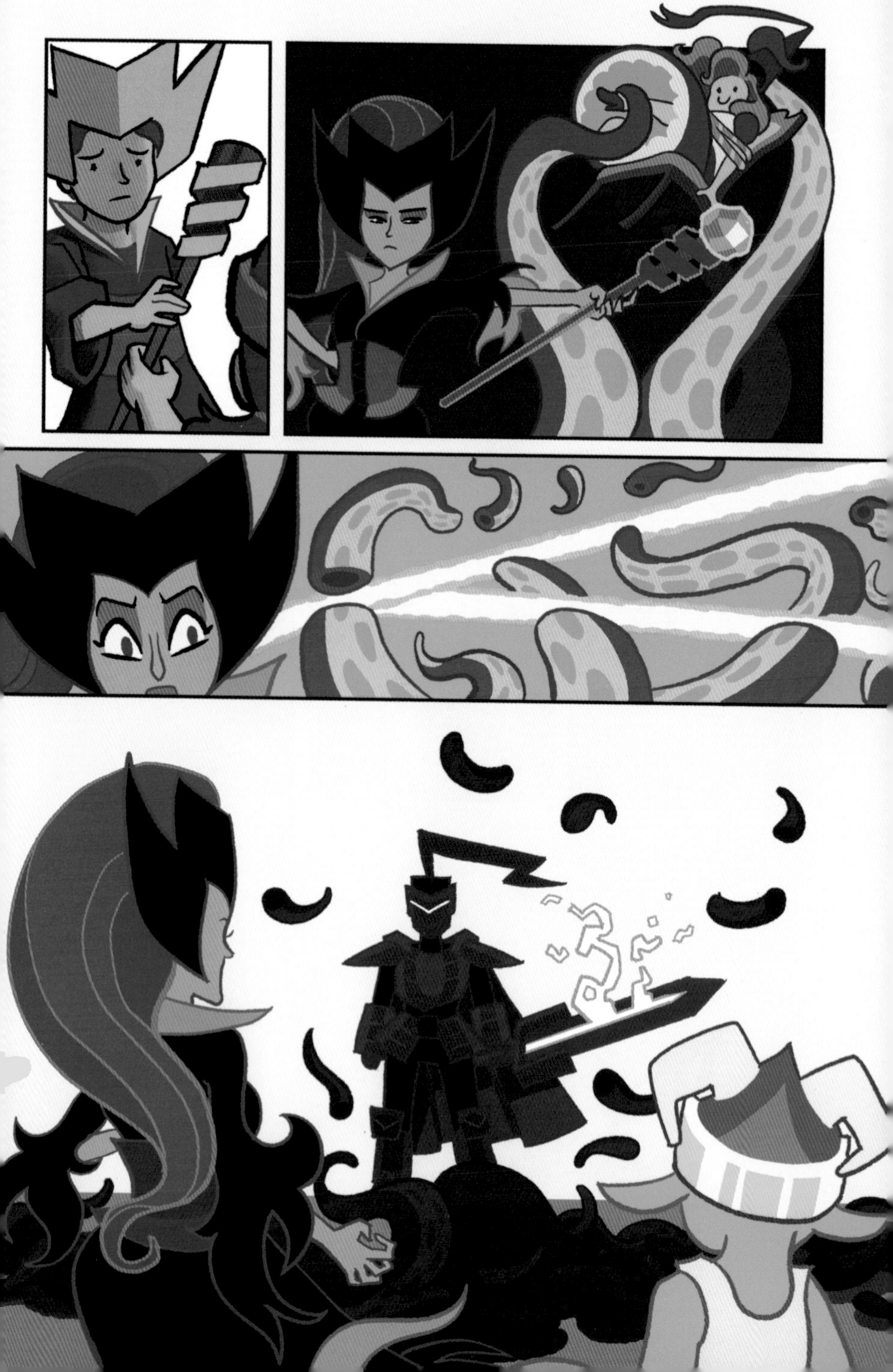

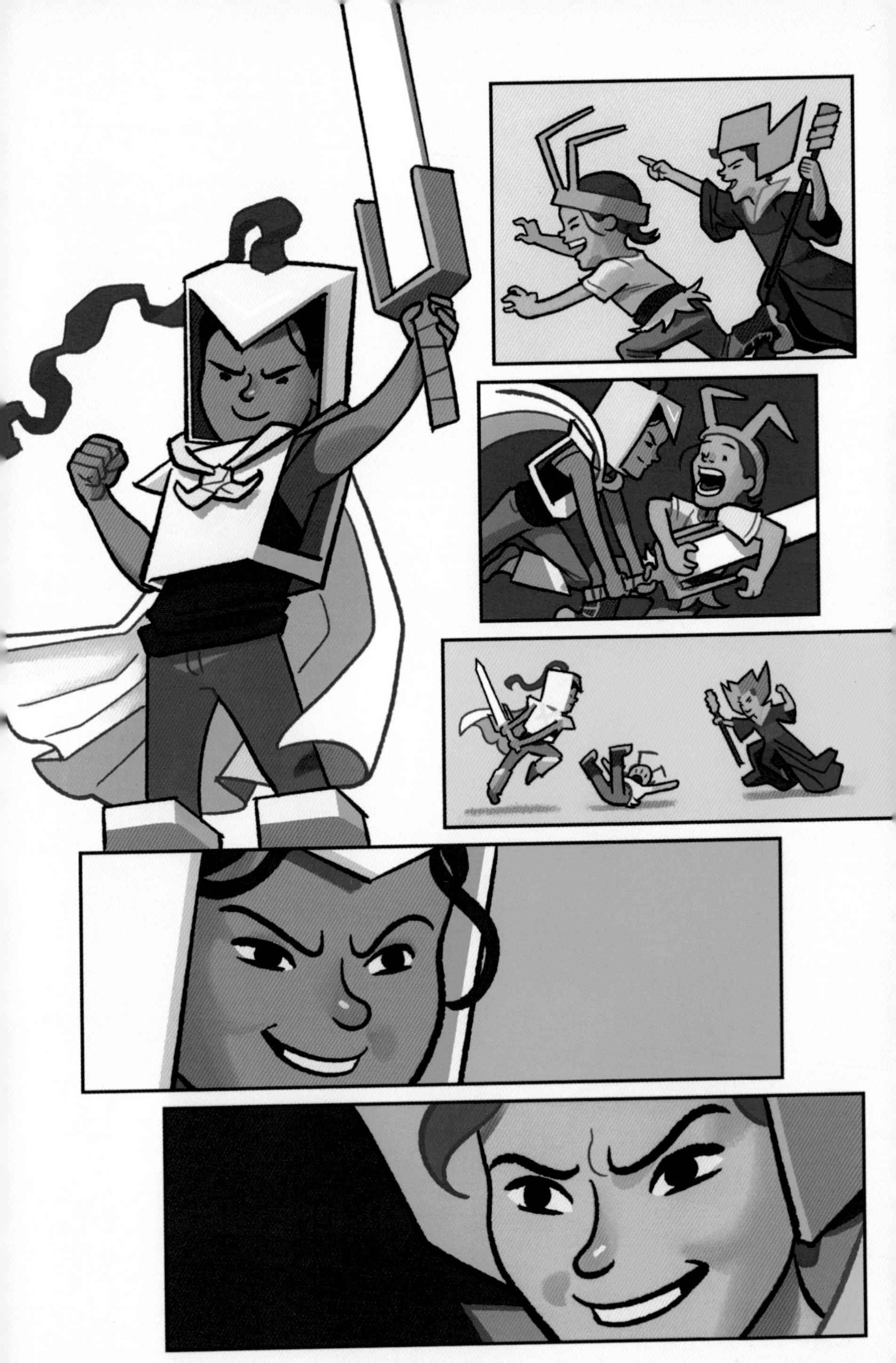

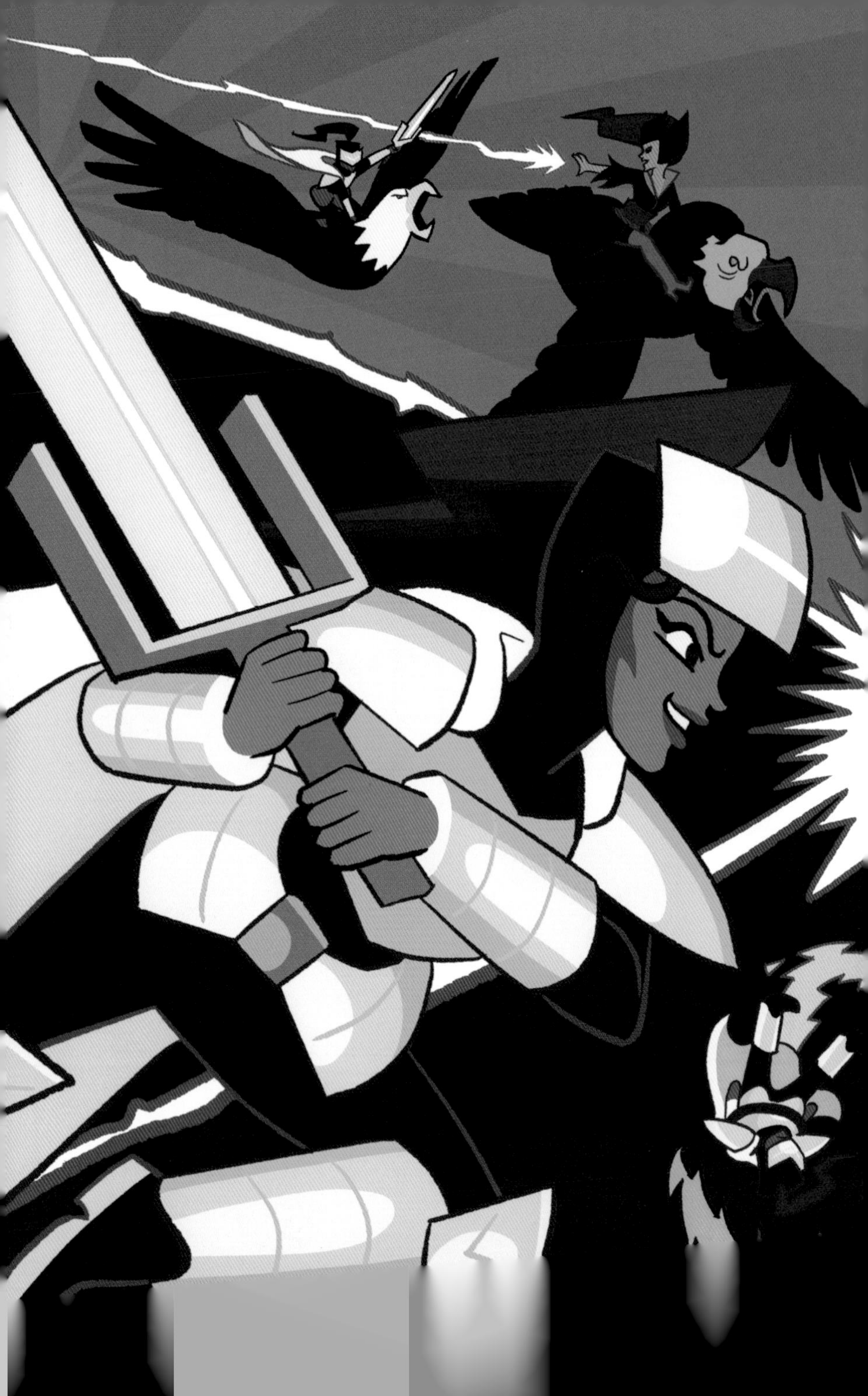

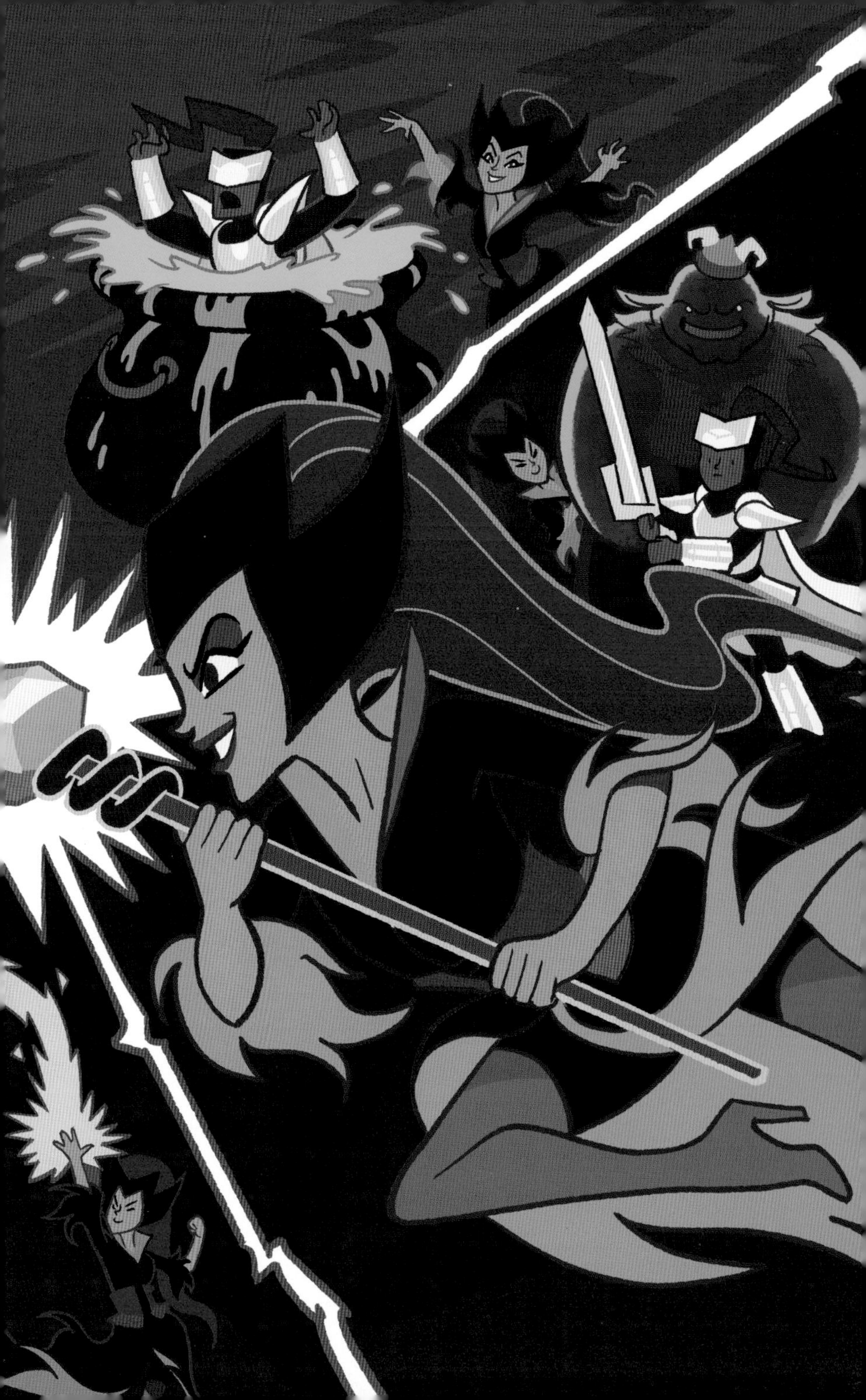

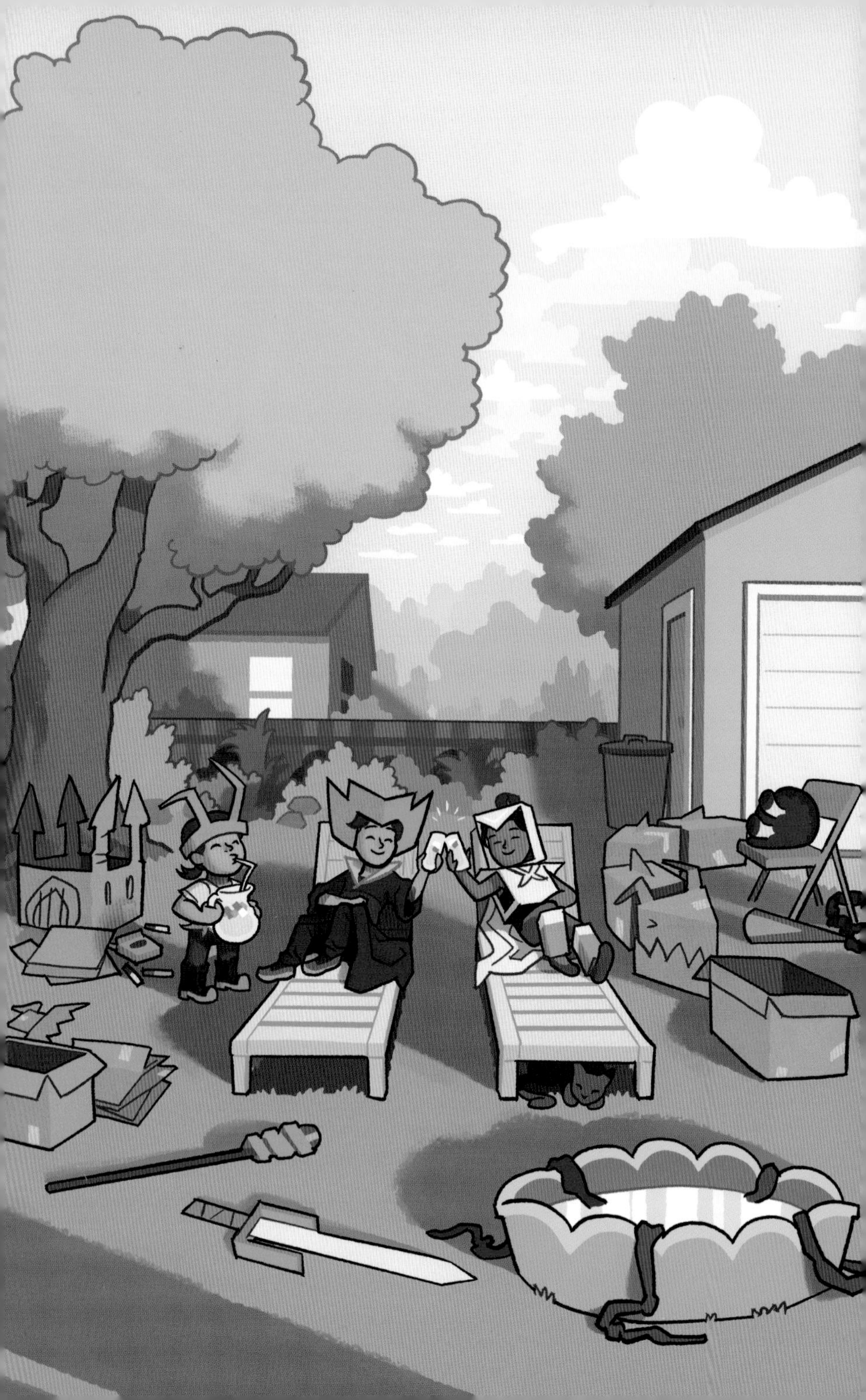

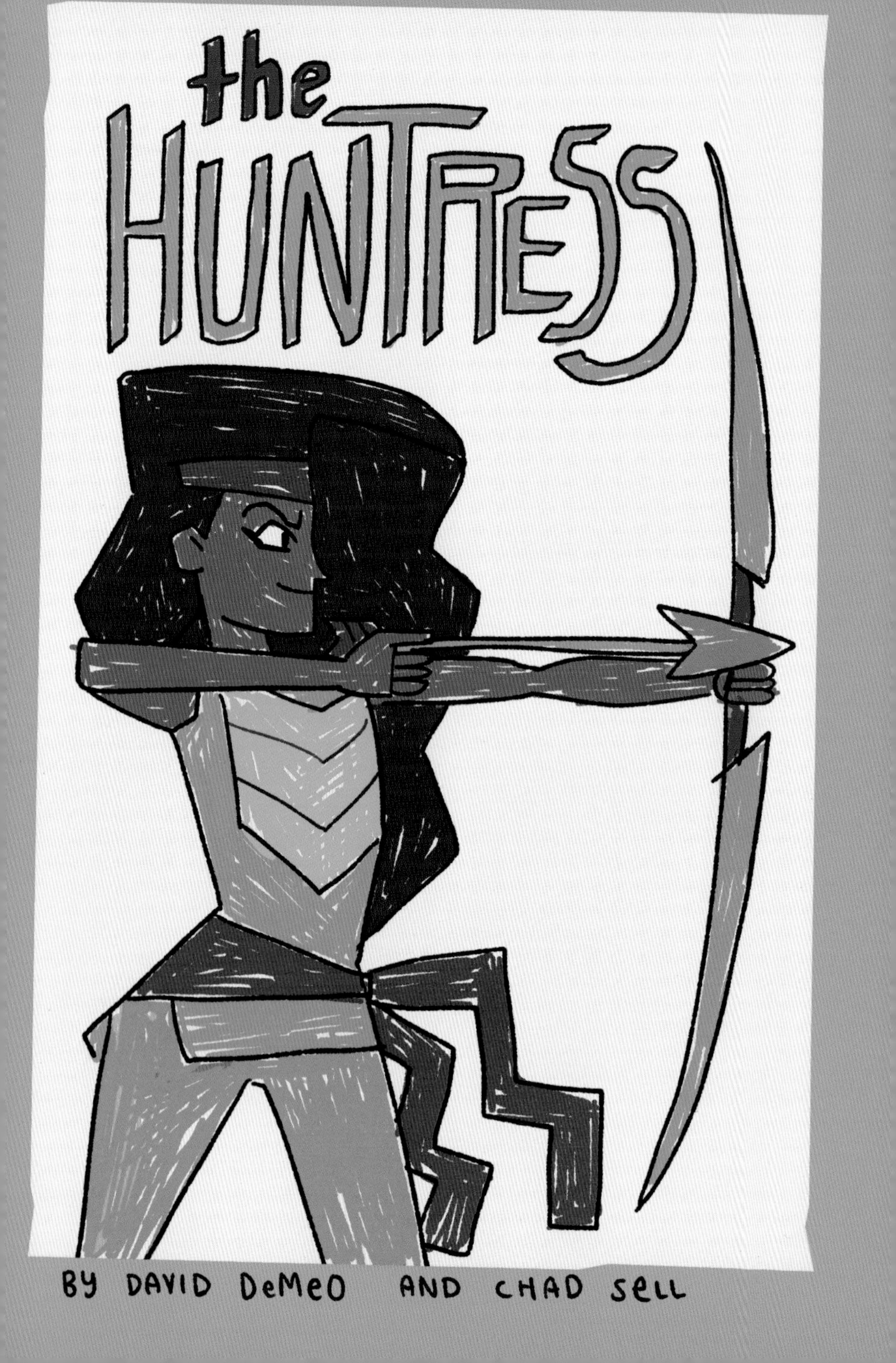
the HUNTRESS

BY DAVID DeMeO AND CHAD SELL

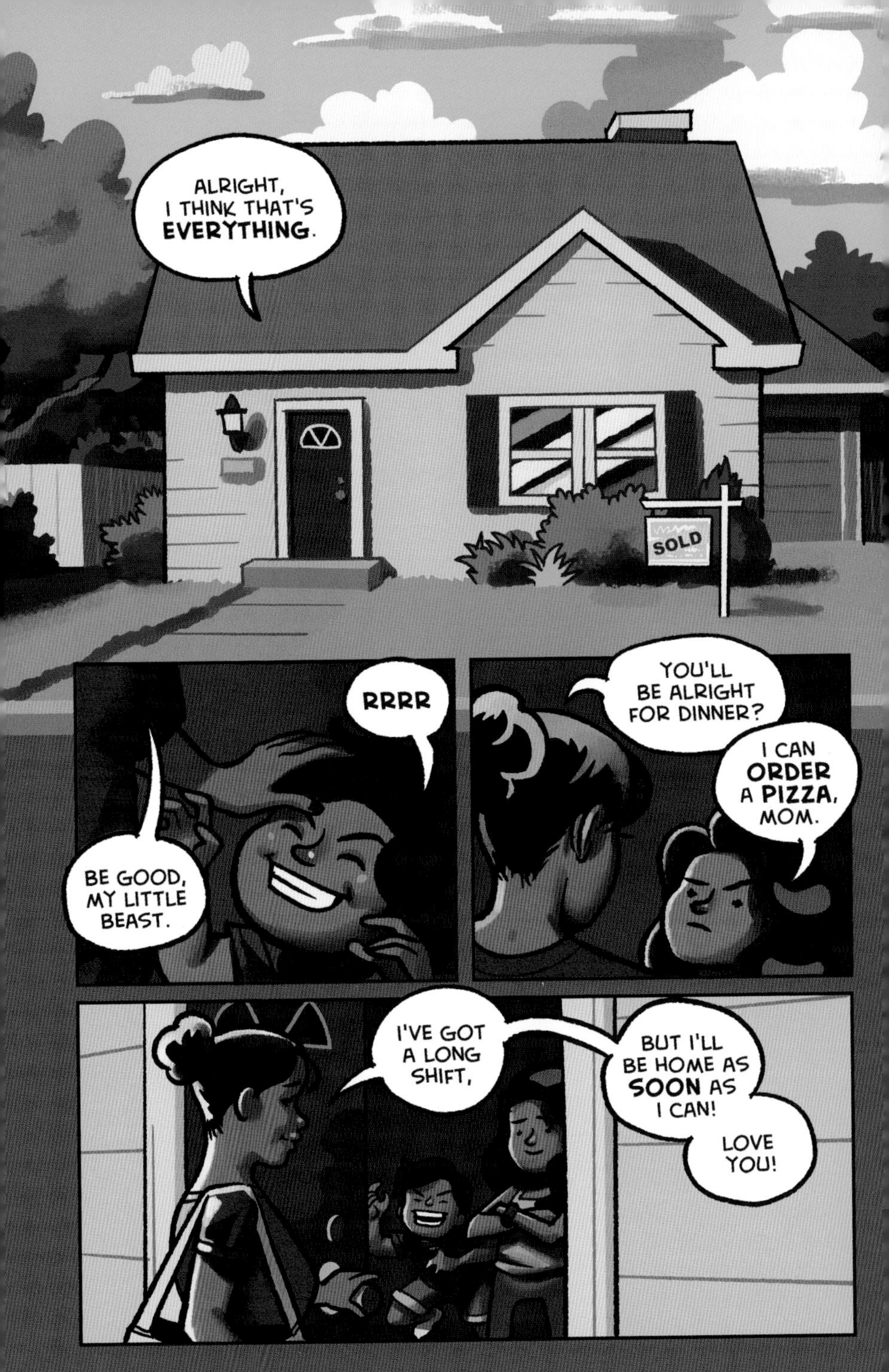
ALRIGHT, I THINK THAT'S EVERYTHING.
SOLD
RRRR
BE GOOD, MY LITTLE BEAST.
YOU'LL BE ALRIGHT FOR DINNER?
I CAN ORDER A PIZZA, MOM.
I'VE GOT A LONG SHIFT,
BUT I'LL BE HOME AS SOON AS I CAN!
LOVE YOU!

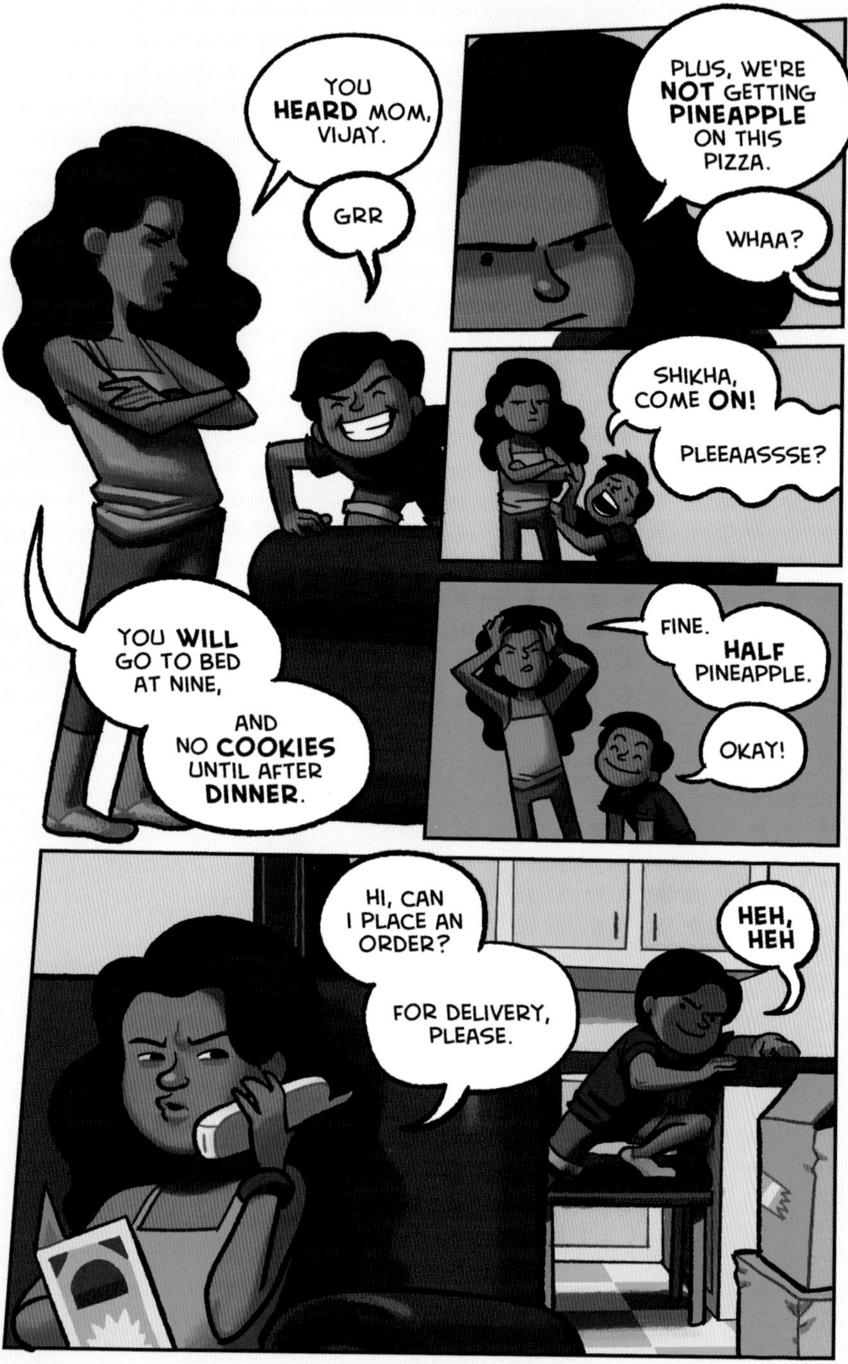
YOU **HEARD** MOM, VIJAY.
GRR
PLUS, WE'RE **NOT** GETTING **PINEAPPLE** ON THIS PIZZA.
WHAA?
SHIKHA, COME **ON**!
PLEEAASSSE?
YOU **WILL** GO TO BED AT NINE,
AND NO **COOKIES** UNTIL AFTER **DINNER**.
FINE. **HALF** PINEAPPLE.
OKAY!
HI, CAN I PLACE AN ORDER?
FOR DELIVERY, PLEASE.
HEH, HEH

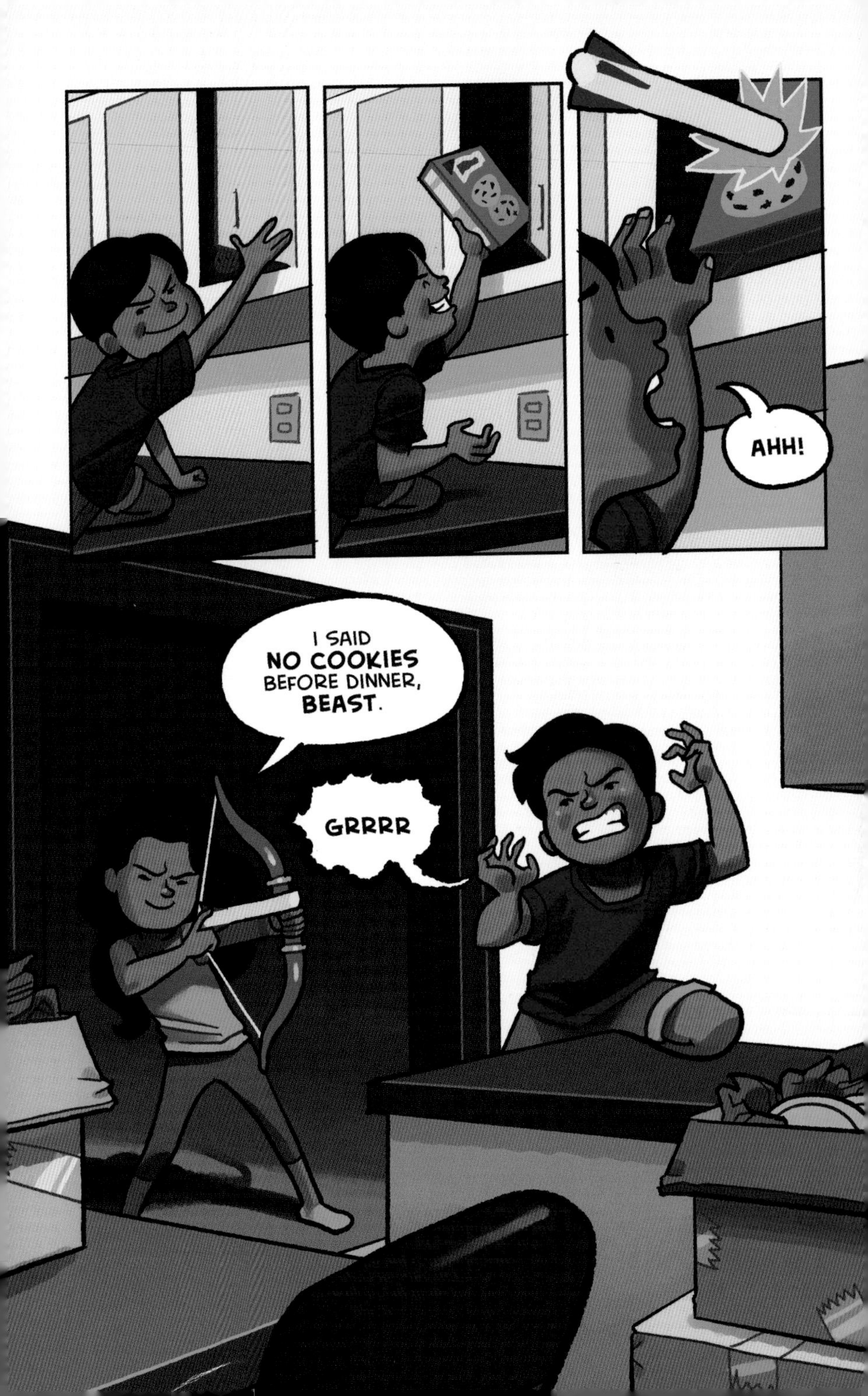
AHH!
I SAID NO COOKIES BEFORE DINNER, BEAST.
GRRRR

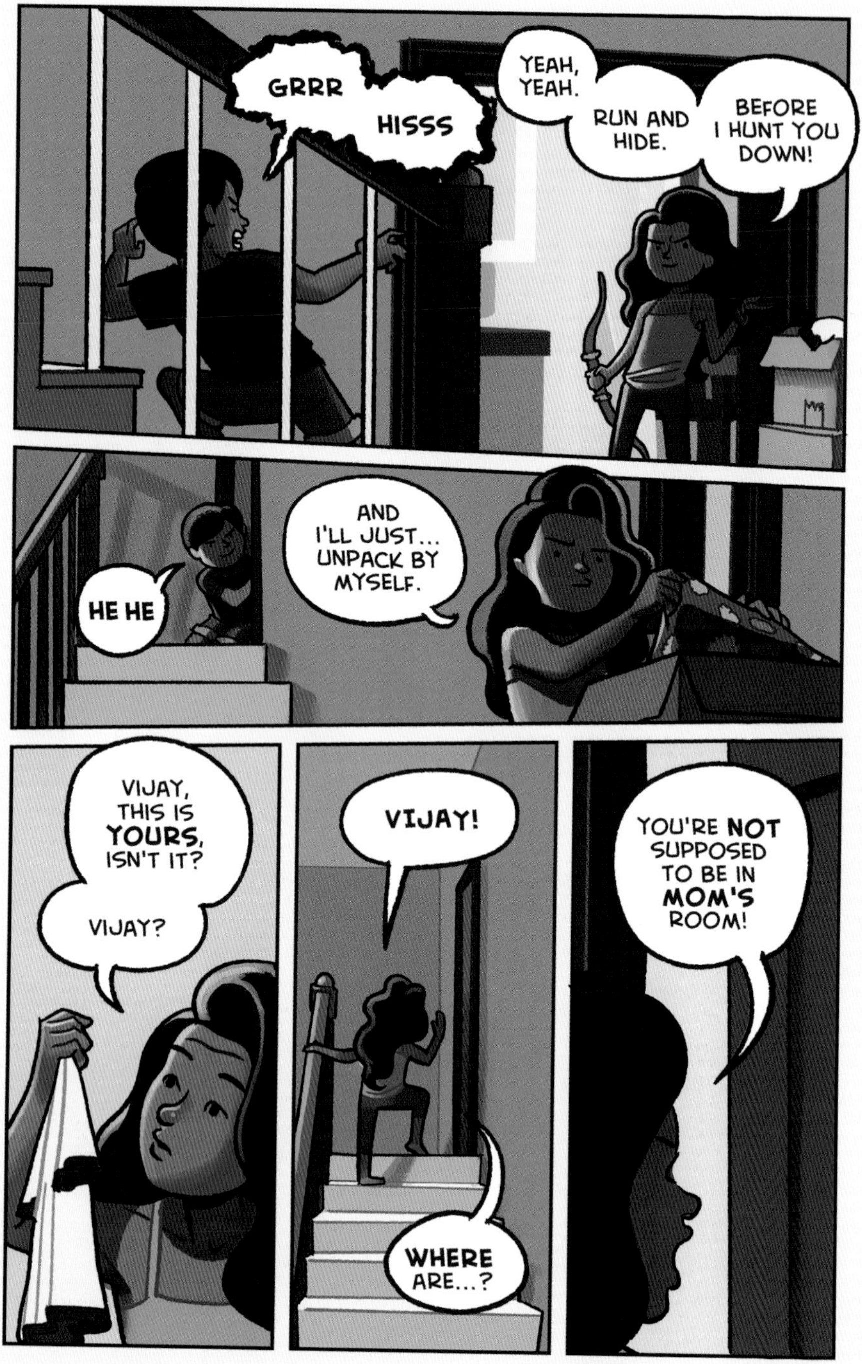
GRRR
HISSS
YEAH, YEAH.
RUN AND HIDE.
BEFORE I HUNT YOU DOWN!
HE HE
AND I'LL JUST... UNPACK BY MYSELF.
VIJAY, THIS IS **YOURS**, ISN'T IT?
VIJAY?
VIJAY!
WHERE ARE...?
YOU'RE **NOT** SUPPOSED TO BE IN **MOM'S** ROOM!

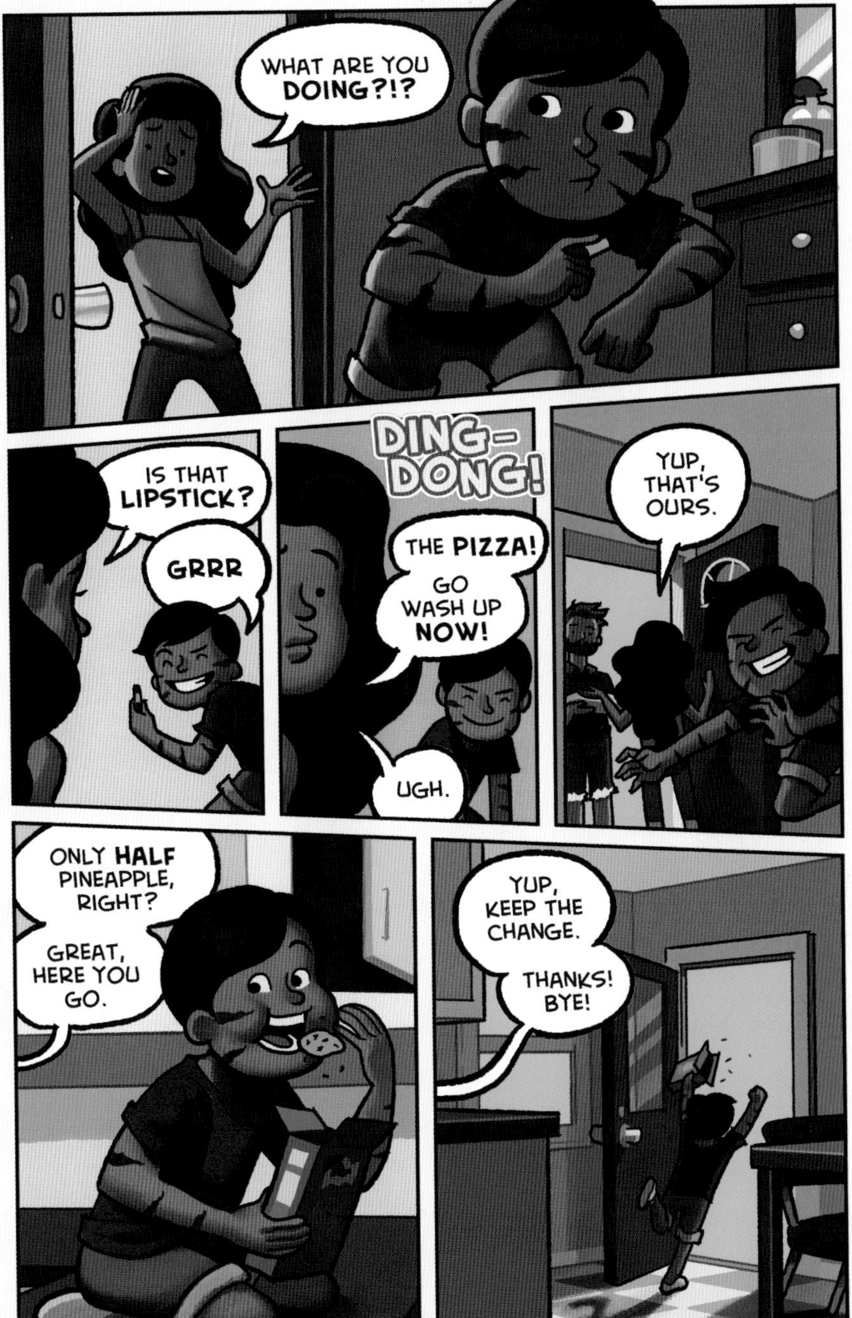
WHAT ARE YOU DOING?!?
IS THAT LIPSTICK?
GRRR
DING-DONG!
THE PIZZA!
GO WASH UP NOW!
UGH.
YUP, THAT'S OURS.
ONLY HALF PINEAPPLE, RIGHT?
GREAT, HERE YOU GO.
YUP, KEEP THE CHANGE.
THANKS! BYE!

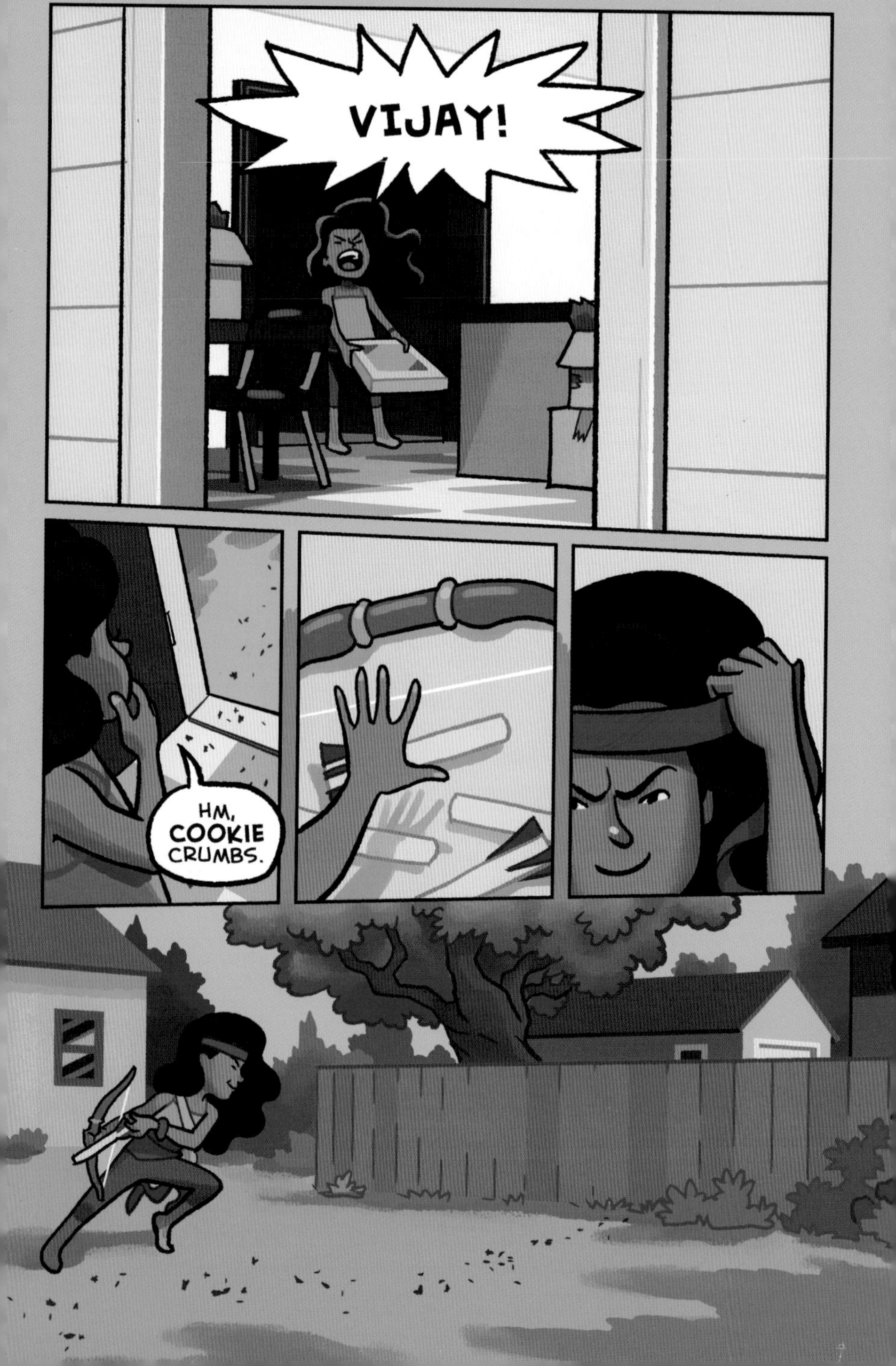
VIJAY!
HM, COOKIE CRUMBS.

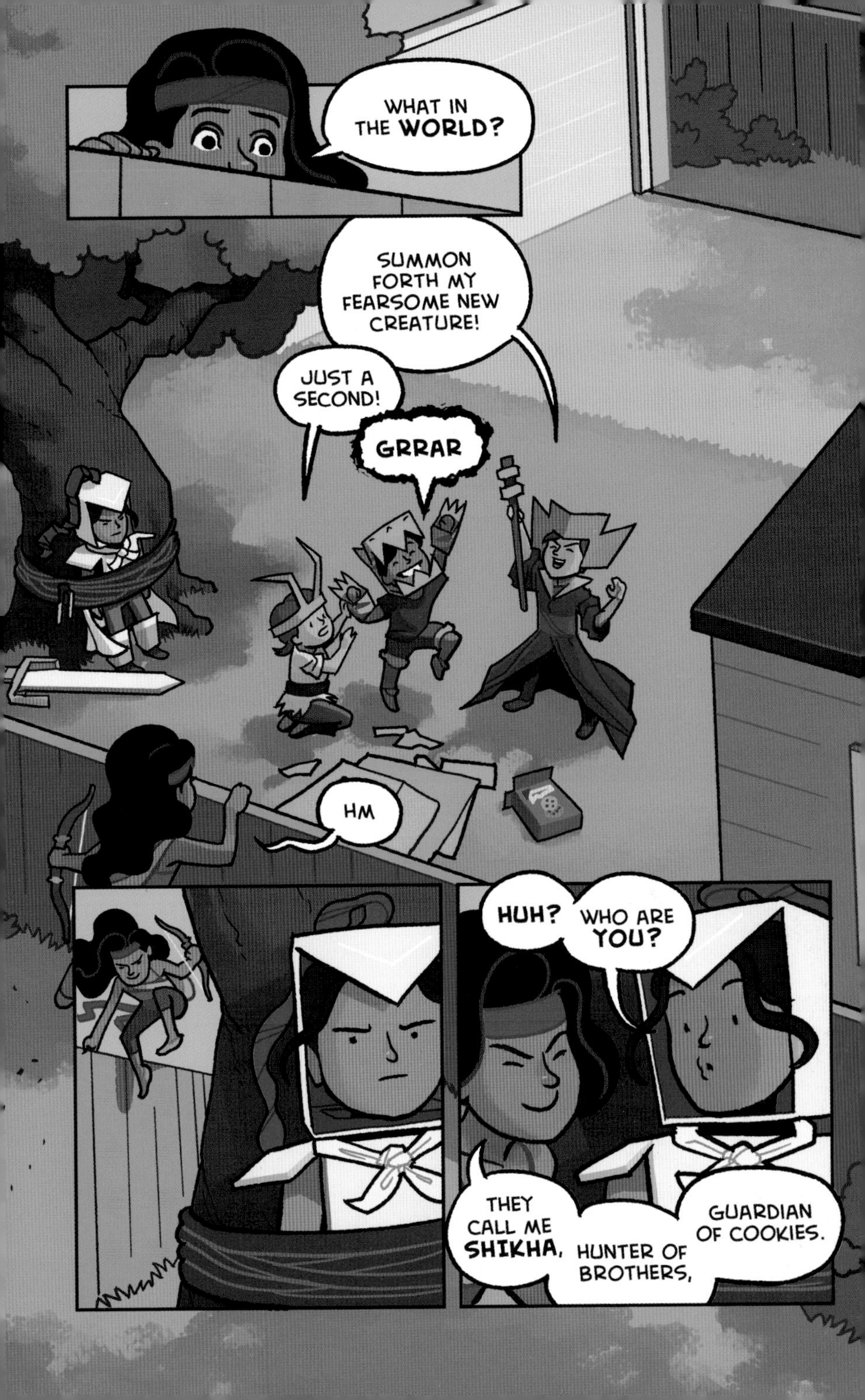
WHAT IN THE **WORLD**?
SUMMON FORTH MY FEARSOME NEW CREATURE!
JUST A SECOND!
GRRAR
HM
HUH?
WHO ARE **YOU**?
THEY CALL ME **SHIKHA**,
HUNTER OF BROTHERS,
GUARDIAN OF COOKIES.

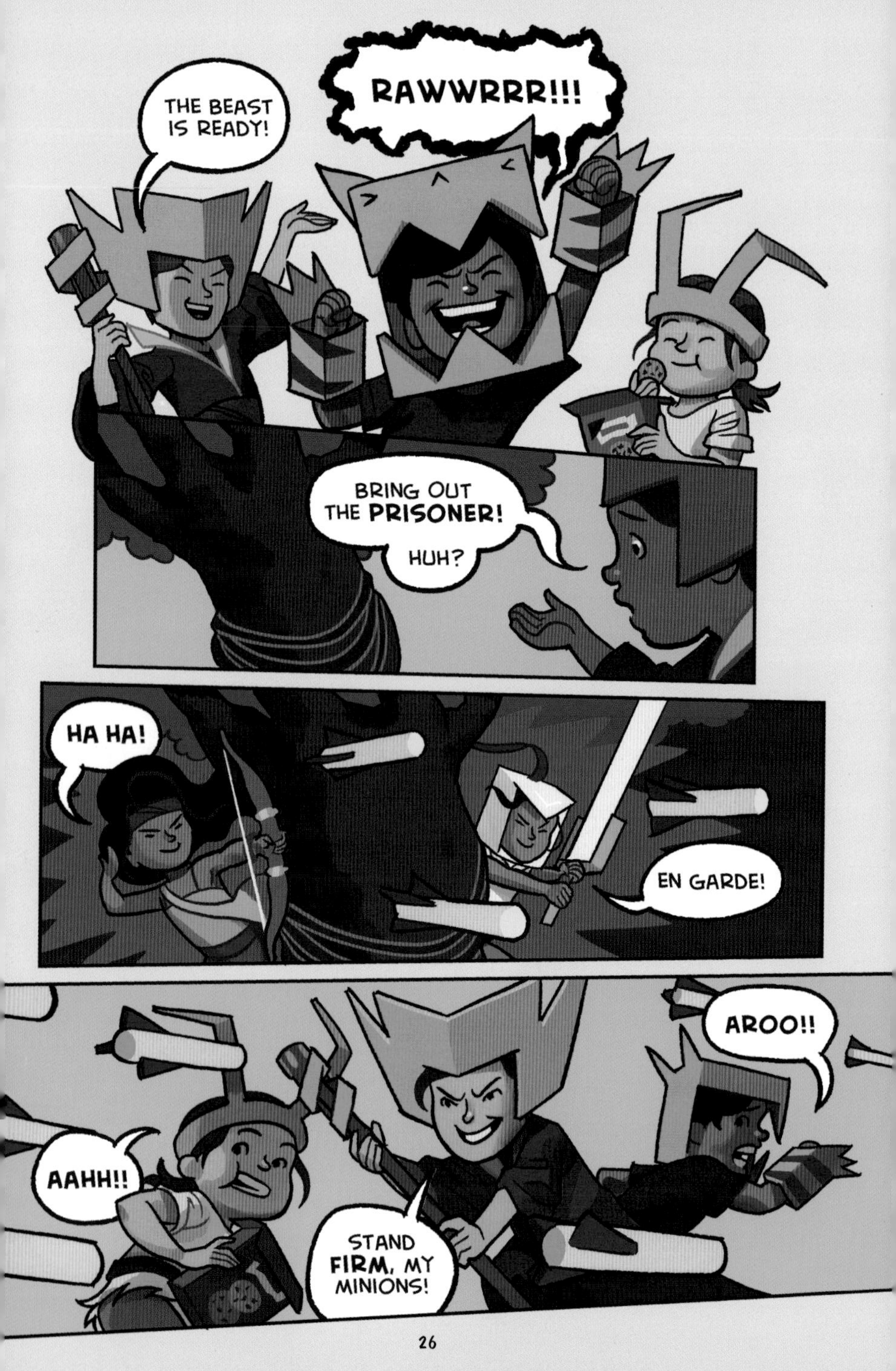
THE BEAST IS READY!
RAWWRRR!!!
BRING OUT THE **PRISONER!**
HUH?
HA HA!
EN GARDE!
AROO!!
AAHH!!
STAND **FIRM,** MY MINIONS!

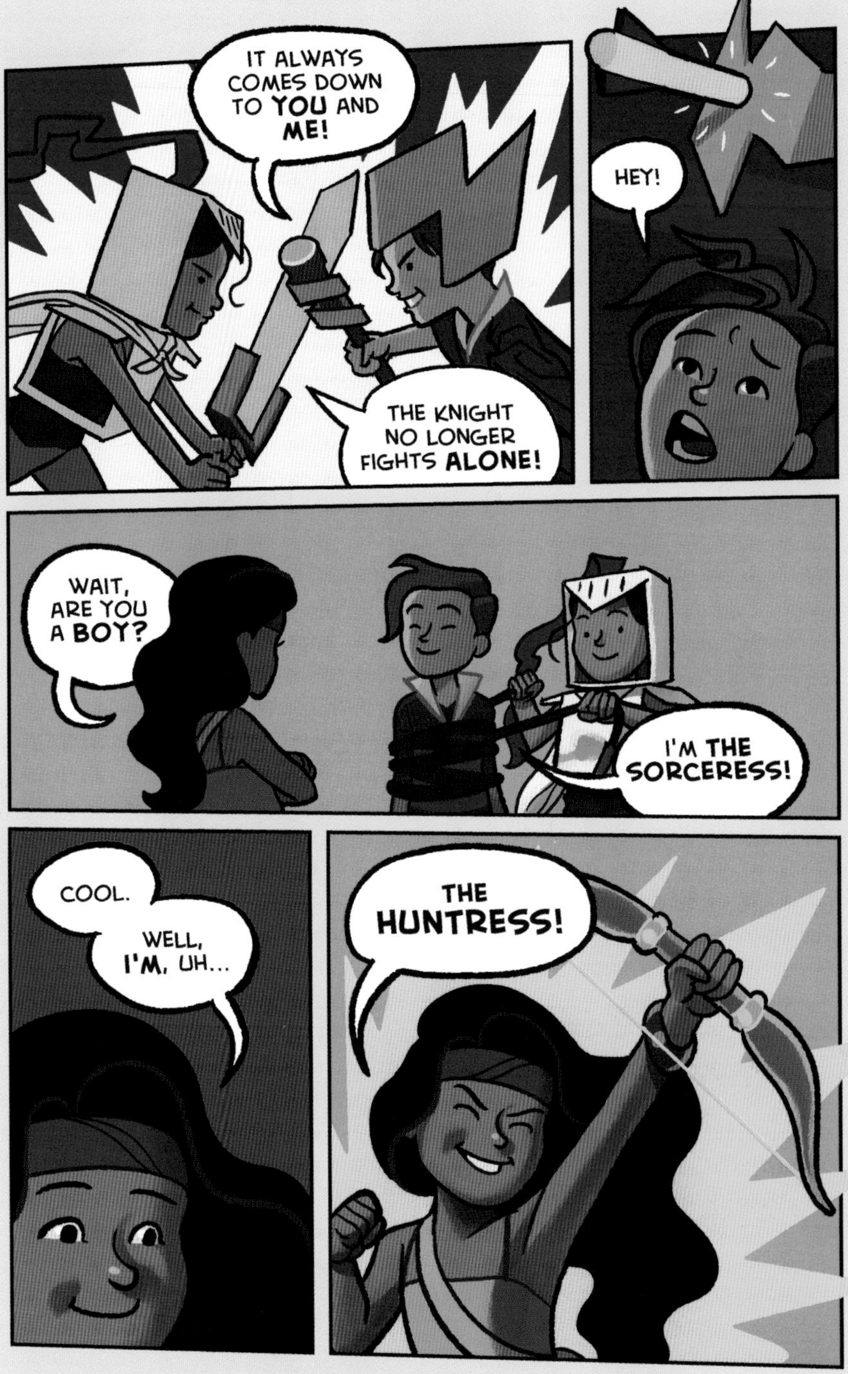
IT ALWAYS COMES DOWN TO YOU AND ME!
THE KNIGHT NO LONGER FIGHTS ALONE!
HEY!
WAIT, ARE YOU A BOY?
I'M THE SORCERESS!
COOL.
WELL, I'M, UH...
THE HUNTRESS!

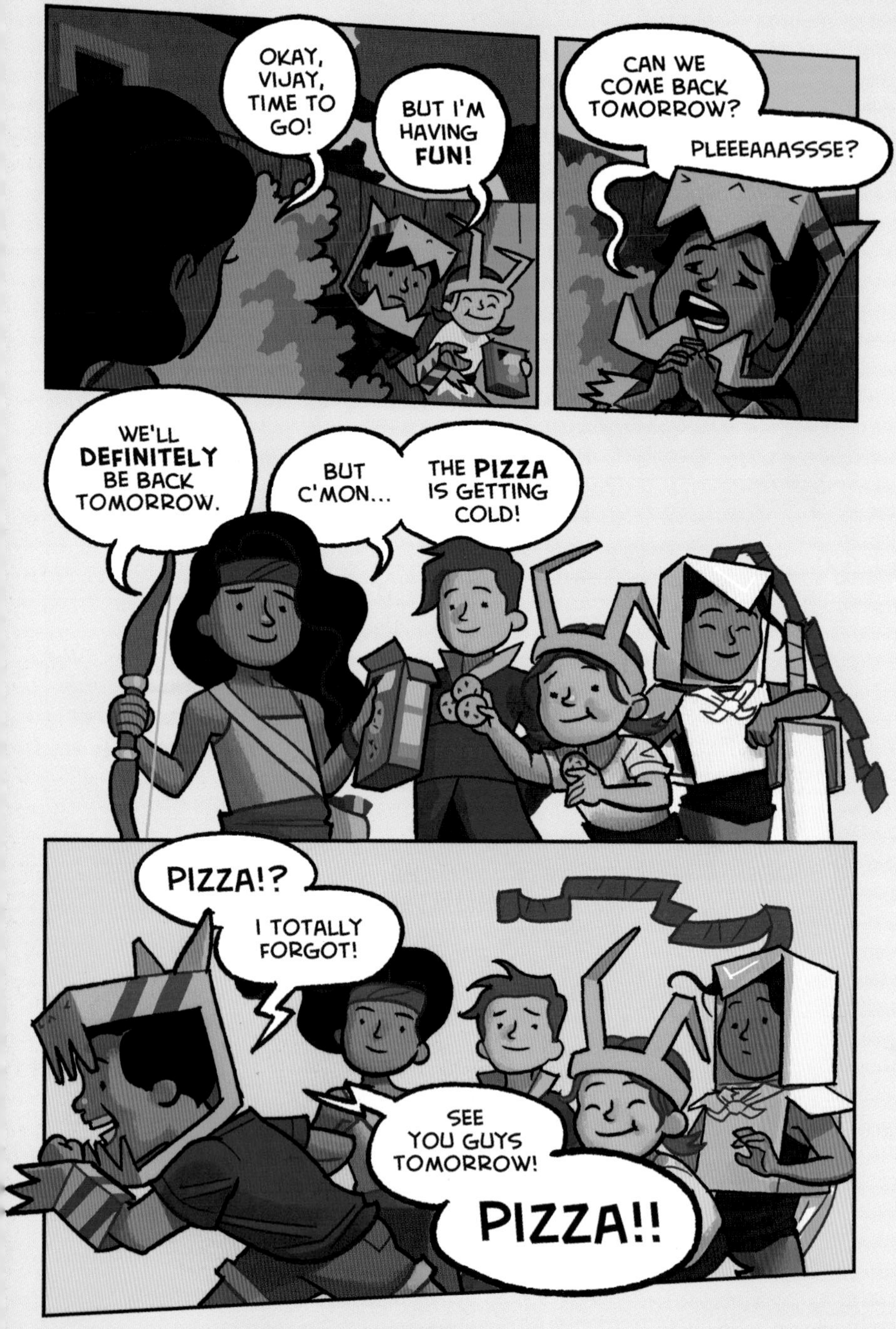
OKAY, VIJAY, TIME TO GO!
BUT I'M HAVING **FUN!**
CAN WE COME BACK TOMORROW?
PLEEEAAASSSE?
WE'LL **DEFINITELY** BE BACK TOMORROW.
BUT C'MON...
THE **PIZZA** IS GETTING COLD!
PIZZA!?
I TOTALLY FORGOT!
SEE YOU GUYS TOMORROW!
PIZZA!!

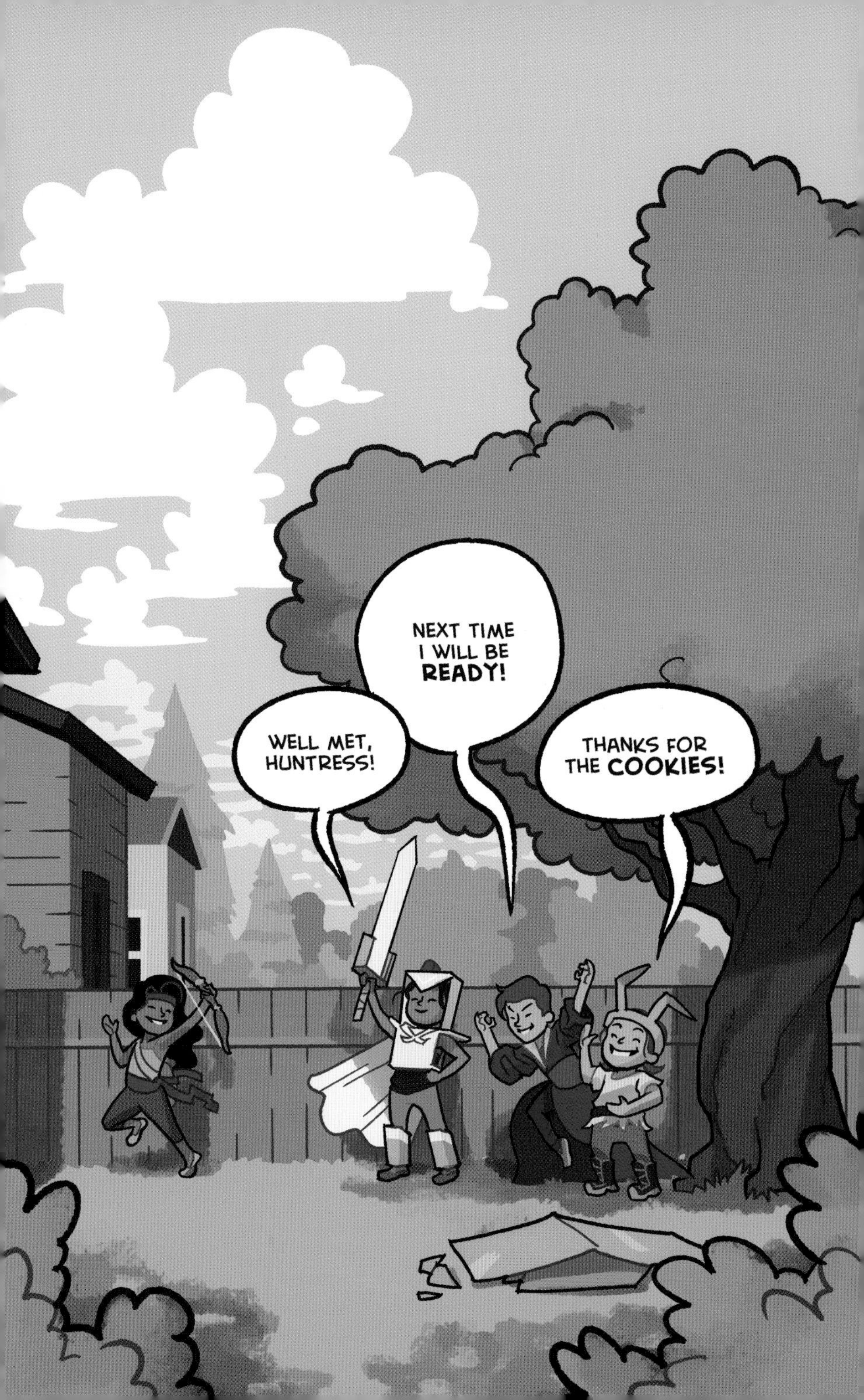
WELL MET, HUNTRESS!
NEXT TIME I WILL BE READY!
THANKS FOR THE COOKIES!

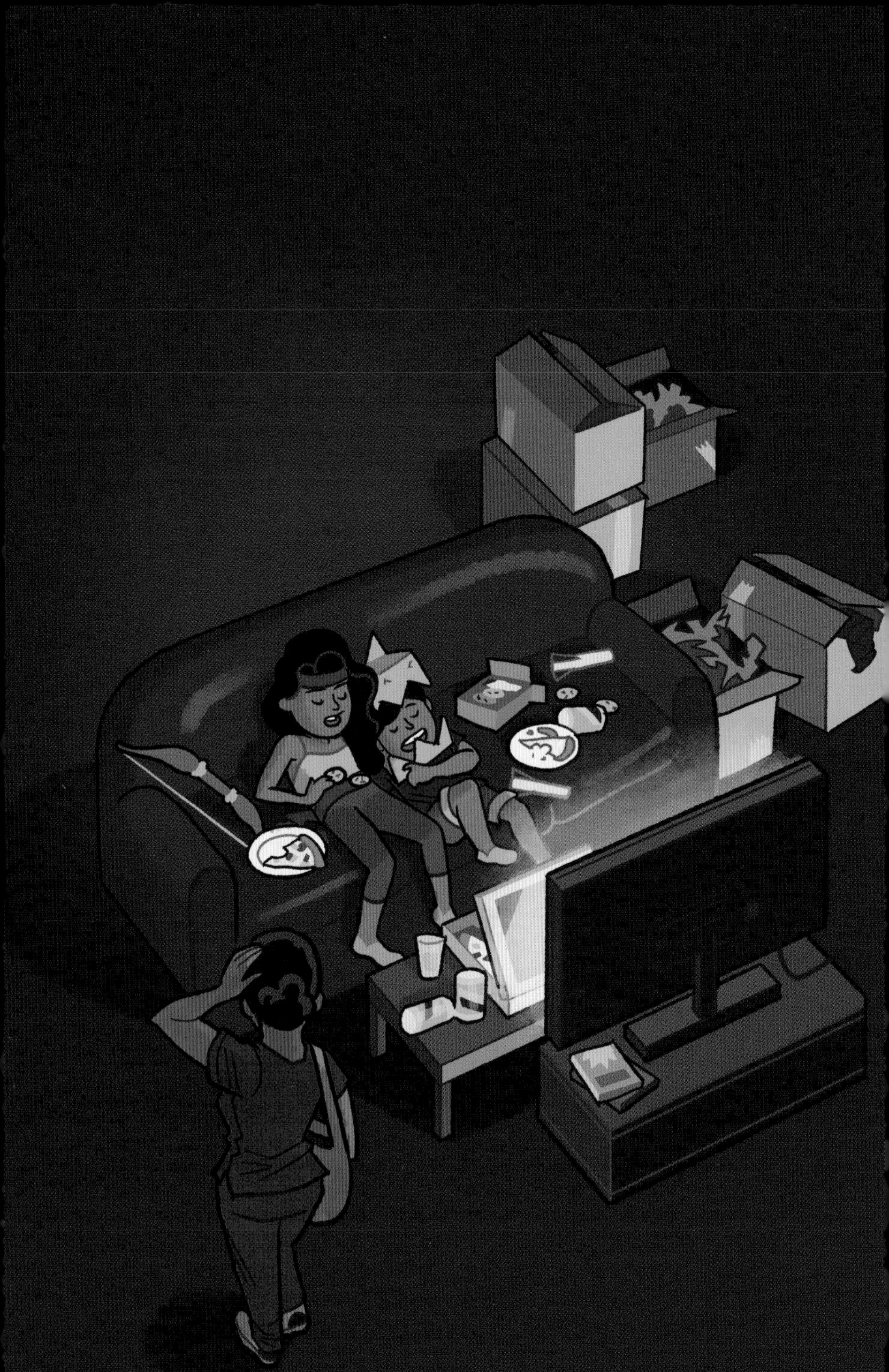

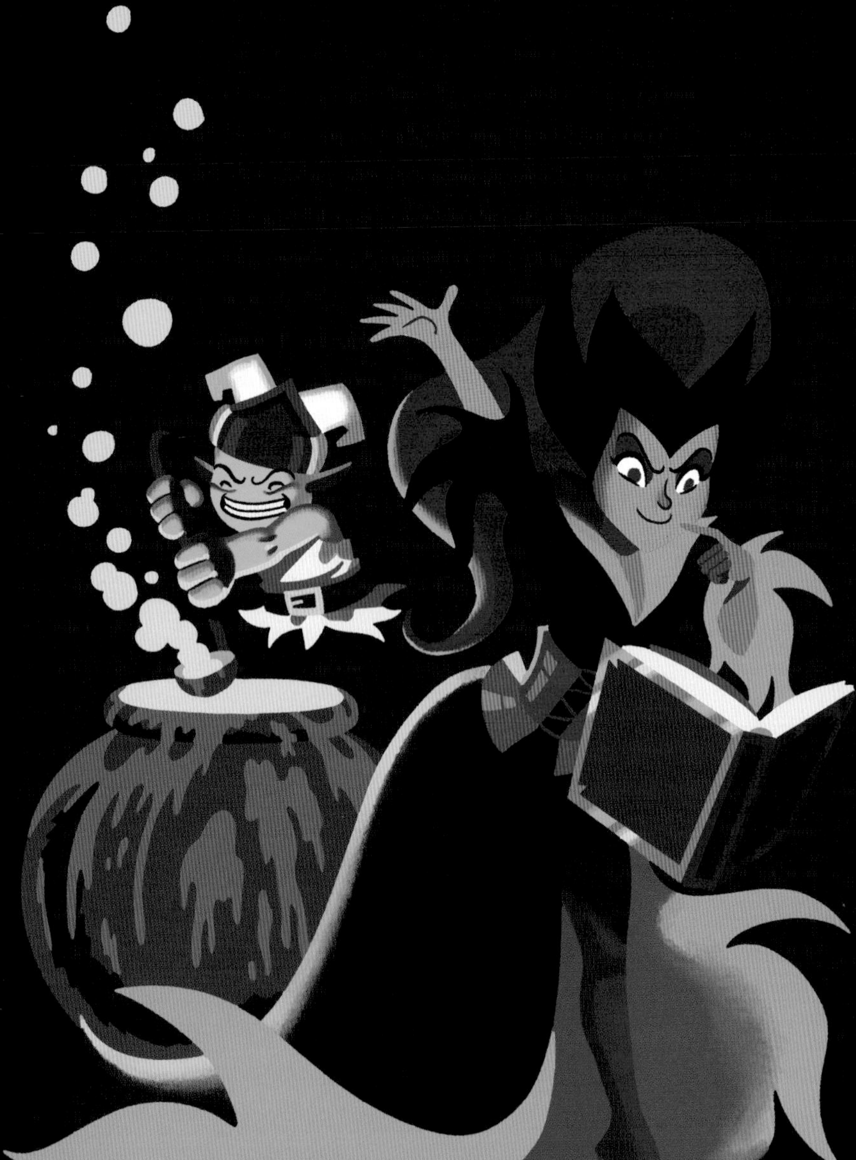

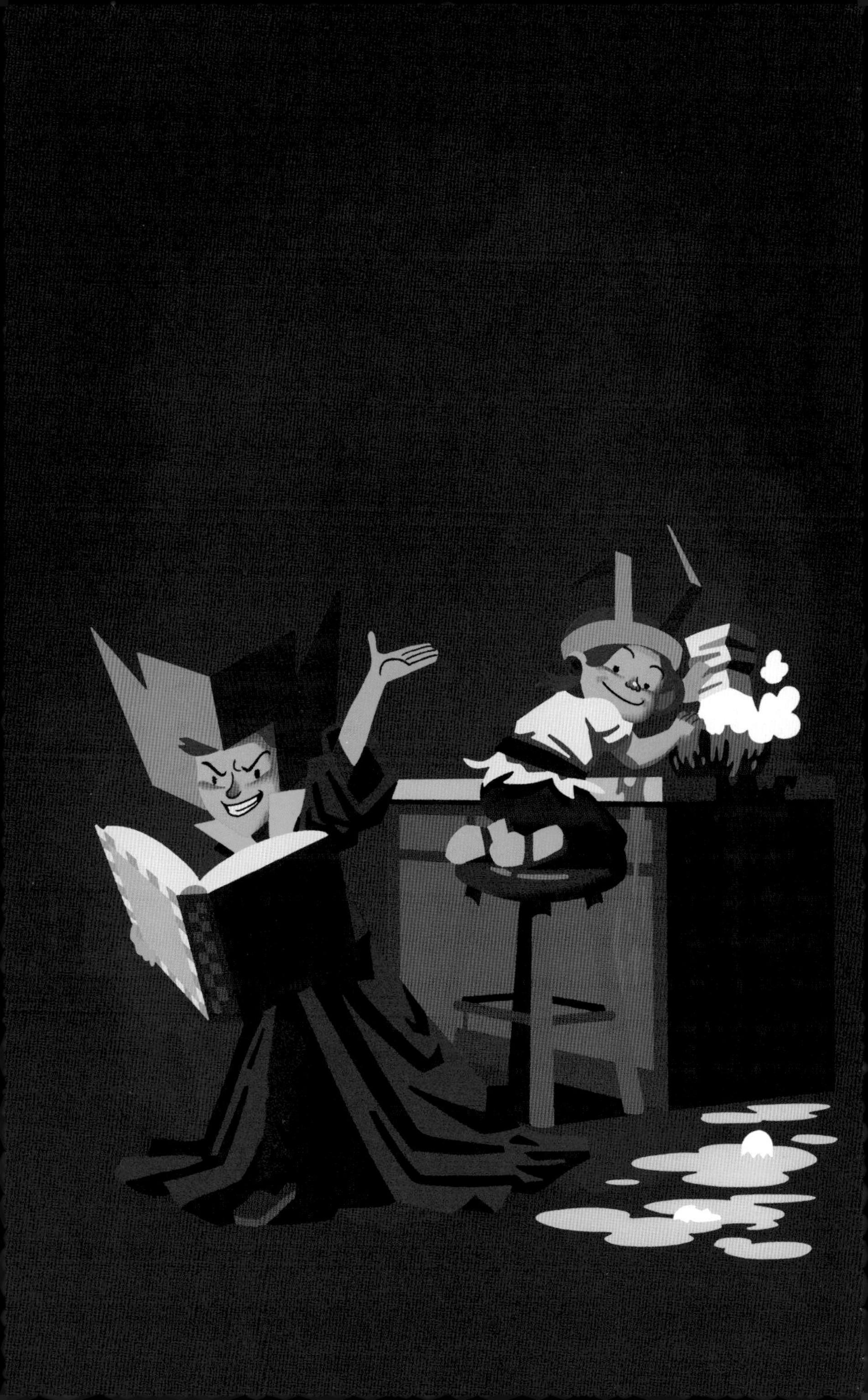

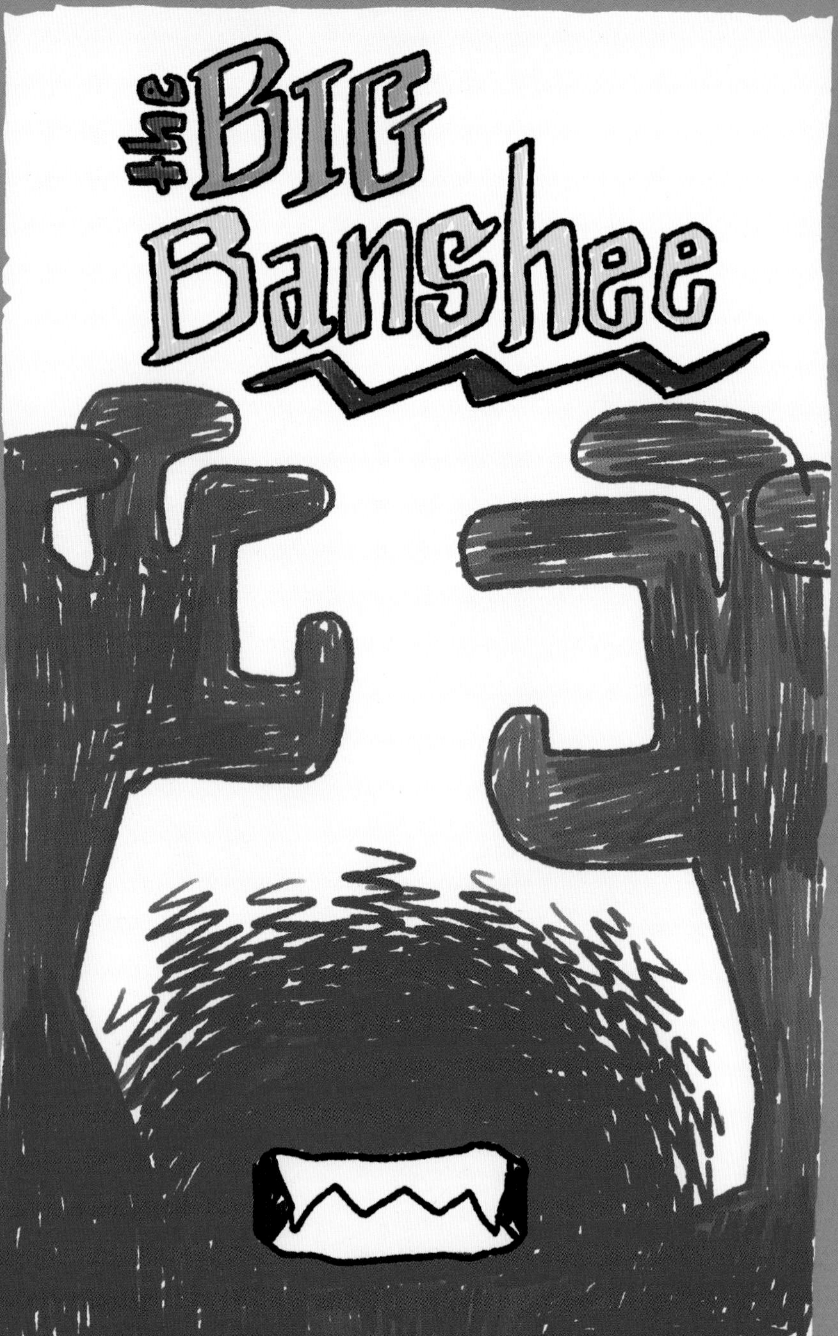
the BIG Banshee

BY KATIE SCHENKEL AND CHAD SELL

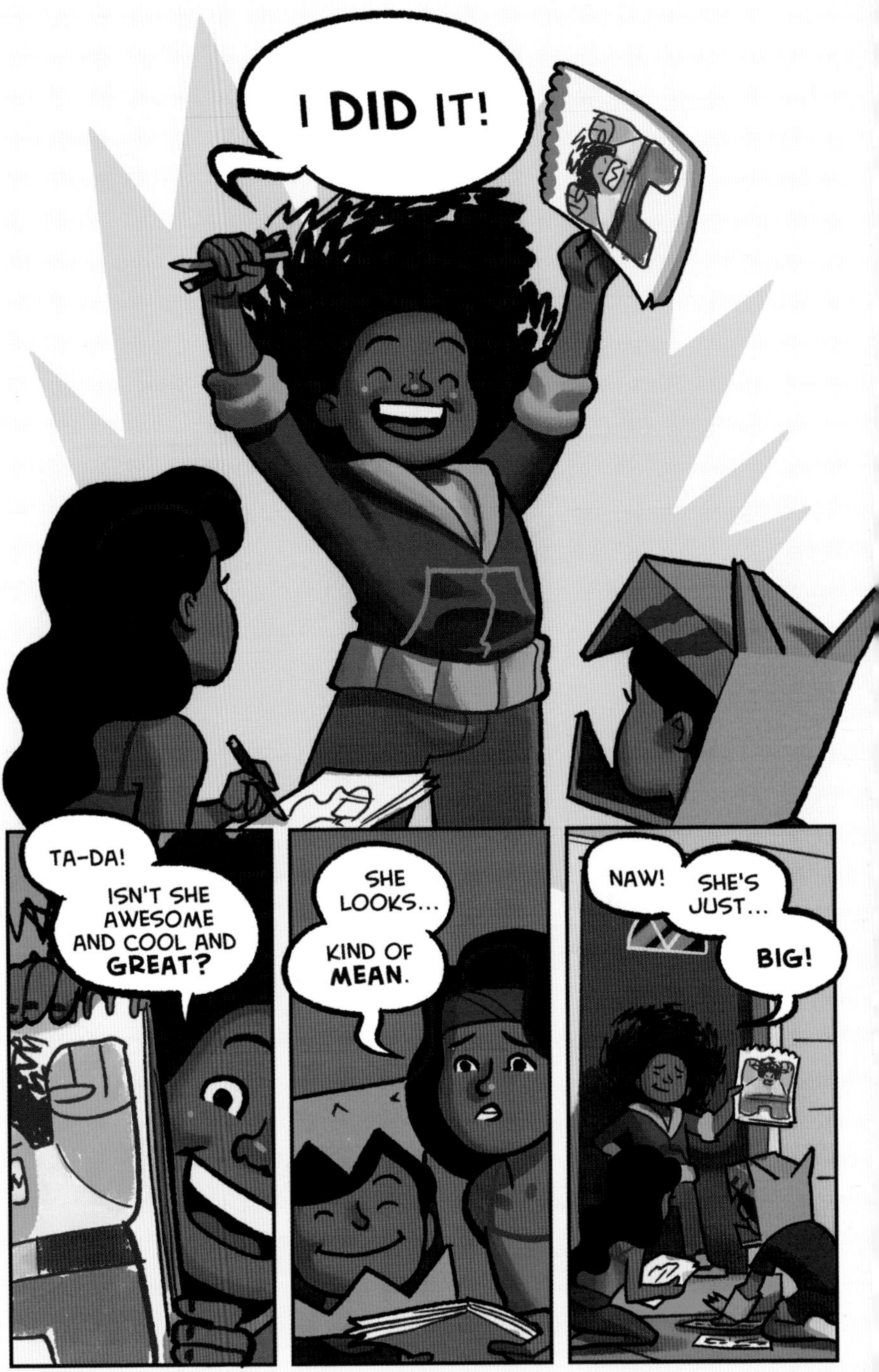
I DID IT!
TA-DA!
ISN'T SHE AWESOME AND COOL AND GREAT?
SHE LOOKS...
KIND OF MEAN.
NAW!
SHE'S JUST...
BIG!

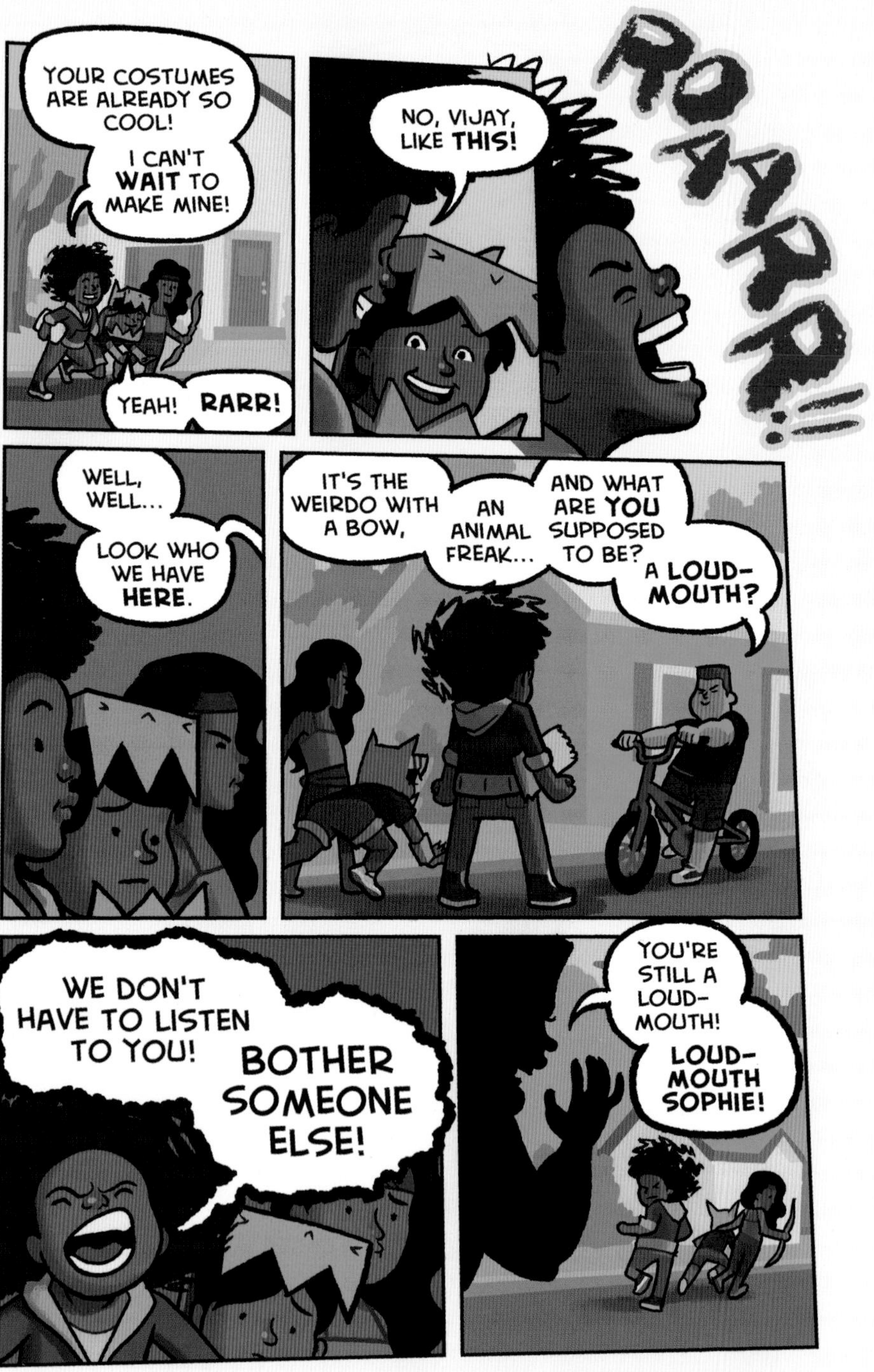
YOUR COSTUMES ARE ALREADY SO COOL!
I CAN'T WAIT TO MAKE MINE!
YEAH!
RARR!
NO, VIJAY, LIKE THIS!
ROAAAR!!!
WELL, WELL...
LOOK WHO WE HAVE HERE.
IT'S THE WEIRDO WITH A BOW,
AN ANIMAL FREAK...
AND WHAT ARE YOU SUPPOSED TO BE?
A LOUD-MOUTH?
WE DON'T HAVE TO LISTEN TO YOU!
BOTHER SOMEONE ELSE!
YOU'RE STILL A LOUD-MOUTH!
LOUD-MOUTH SOPHIE!

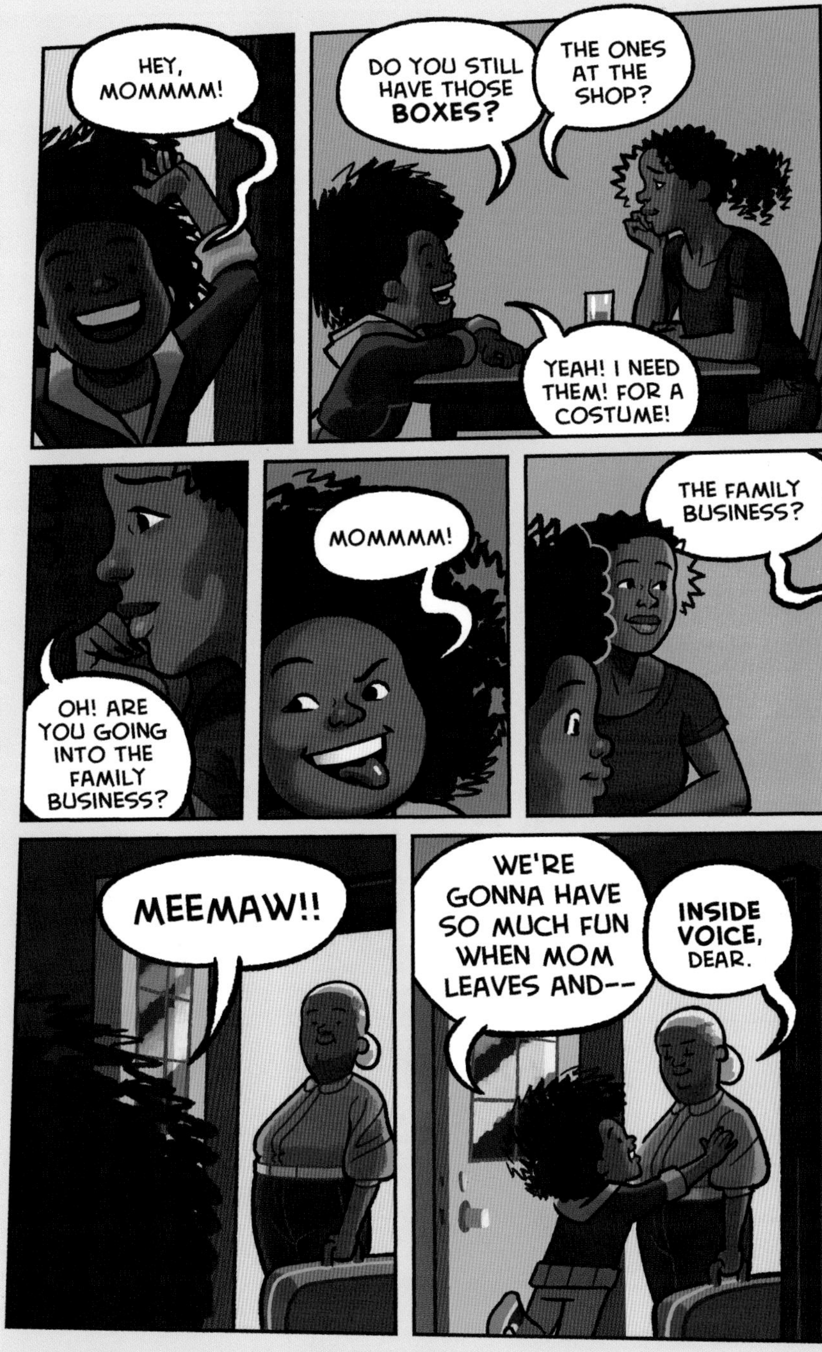
HEY, MOMMMM!
DO YOU STILL HAVE THOSE BOXES?
THE ONES AT THE SHOP?
YEAH! I NEED THEM! FOR A COSTUME!
OH! ARE YOU GOING INTO THE FAMILY BUSINESS?
MOMMMM!
THE FAMILY BUSINESS?
MEEMAW!!
WE'RE GONNA HAVE SO MUCH FUN WHEN MOM LEAVES AND--
INSIDE VOICE, DEAR.

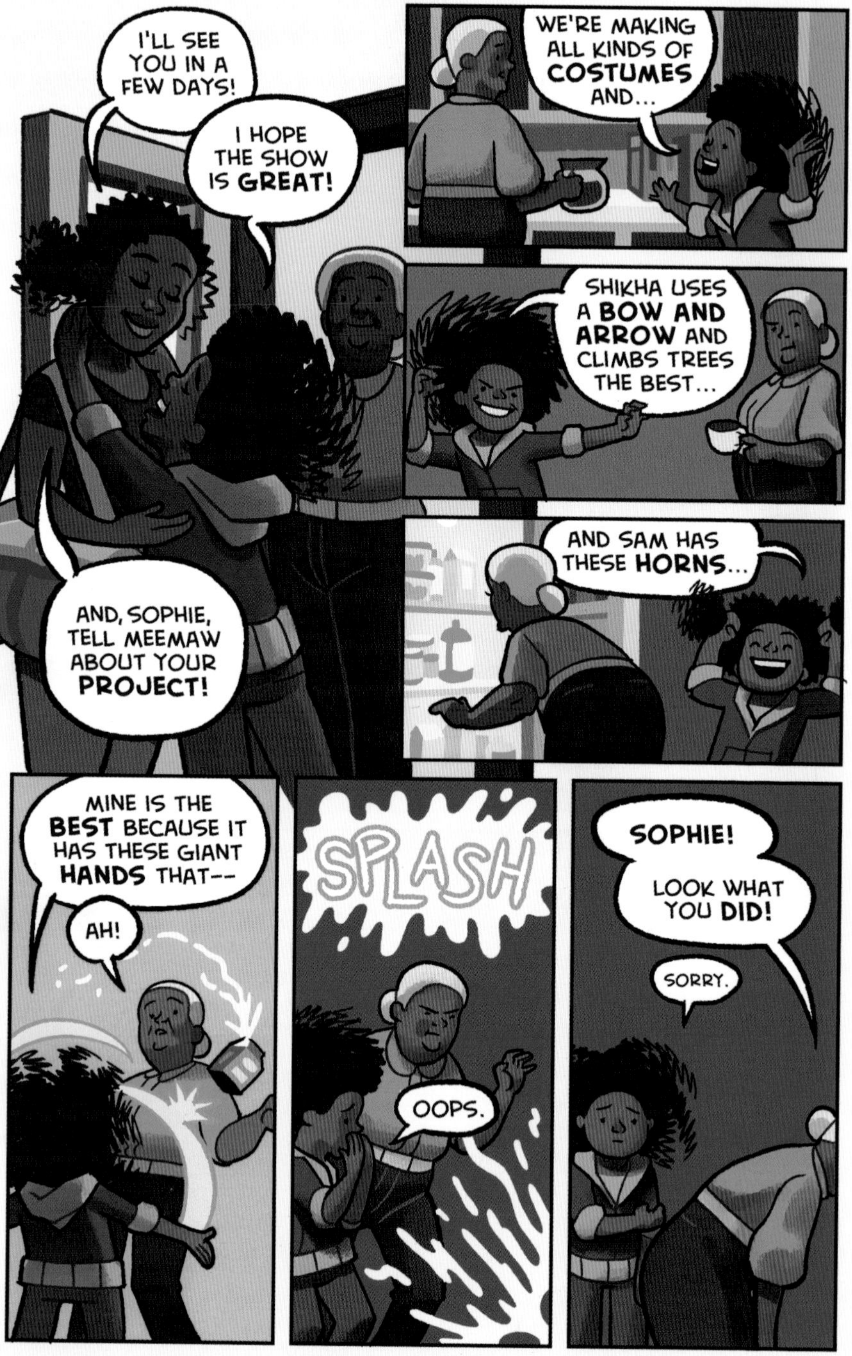

I'LL SEE YOU IN A FEW DAYS!
I HOPE THE SHOW IS GREAT!
WE'RE MAKING ALL KINDS OF COSTUMES AND...
SHIKHA USES A BOW AND ARROW AND CLIMBS TREES THE BEST...
AND, SOPHIE, TELL MEEMAW ABOUT YOUR PROJECT!
AND SAM HAS THESE HORNS...
MINE IS THE BEST BECAUSE IT HAS THESE GIANT HANDS THAT--
AH!
SPLASH
OOPS.
SOPHIE!
LOOK WHAT YOU DID!
SORRY.

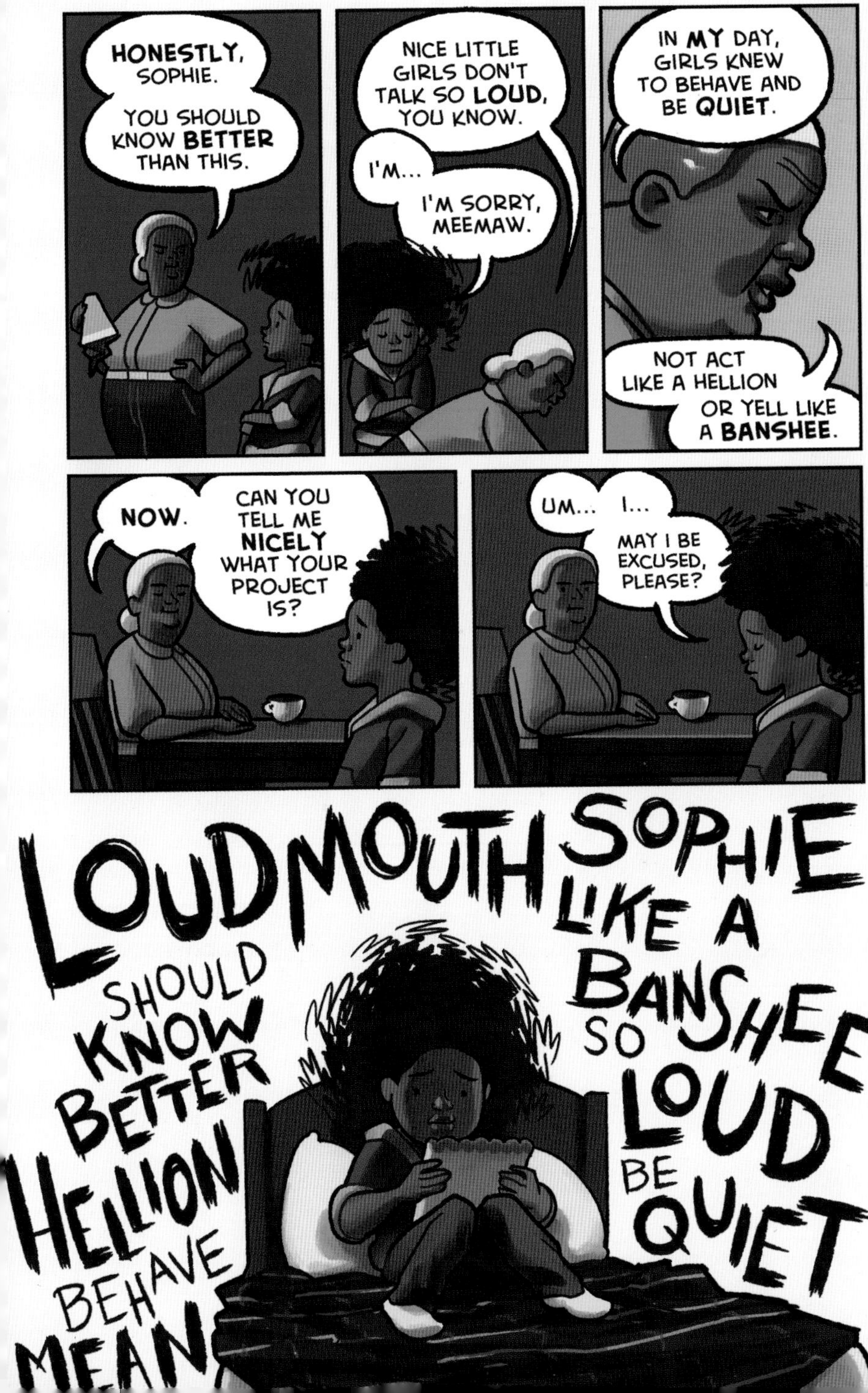
HONESTLY, SOPHIE.
YOU SHOULD KNOW BETTER THAN THIS.
NICE LITTLE GIRLS DON'T TALK SO LOUD, YOU KNOW.
I'M...
I'M SORRY, MEEMAW.
IN MY DAY, GIRLS KNEW TO BEHAVE AND BE QUIET.
NOT ACT LIKE A HELLION
OR YELL LIKE A BANSHEE.
NOW.
CAN YOU TELL ME NICELY WHAT YOUR PROJECT IS?
UM...
I...
MAY I BE EXCUSED, PLEASE?
LOUDMOUTH
SOPHIE
LIKE A BANSHEE
SHOULD KNOW BETTER
SO LOUD
HELLION
BE QUIET
BEHAVE
MEAN

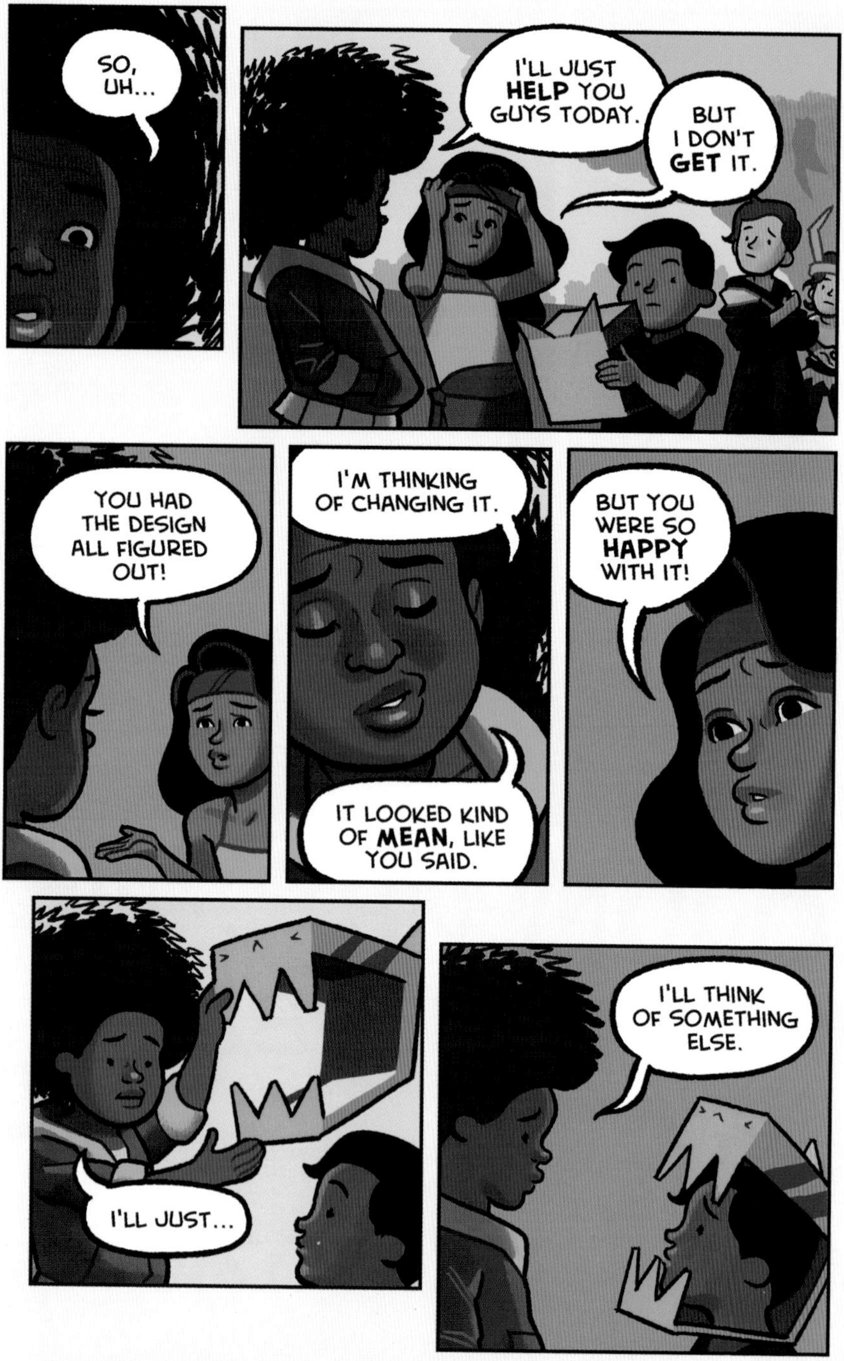
SO, UH...
I'LL JUST HELP YOU GUYS TODAY.
BUT I DON'T GET IT.
YOU HAD THE DESIGN ALL FIGURED OUT!
I'M THINKING OF CHANGING IT.
IT LOOKED KIND OF MEAN, LIKE YOU SAID.
BUT YOU WERE SO HAPPY WITH IT!
I'LL JUST...
I'LL THINK OF SOMETHING ELSE.

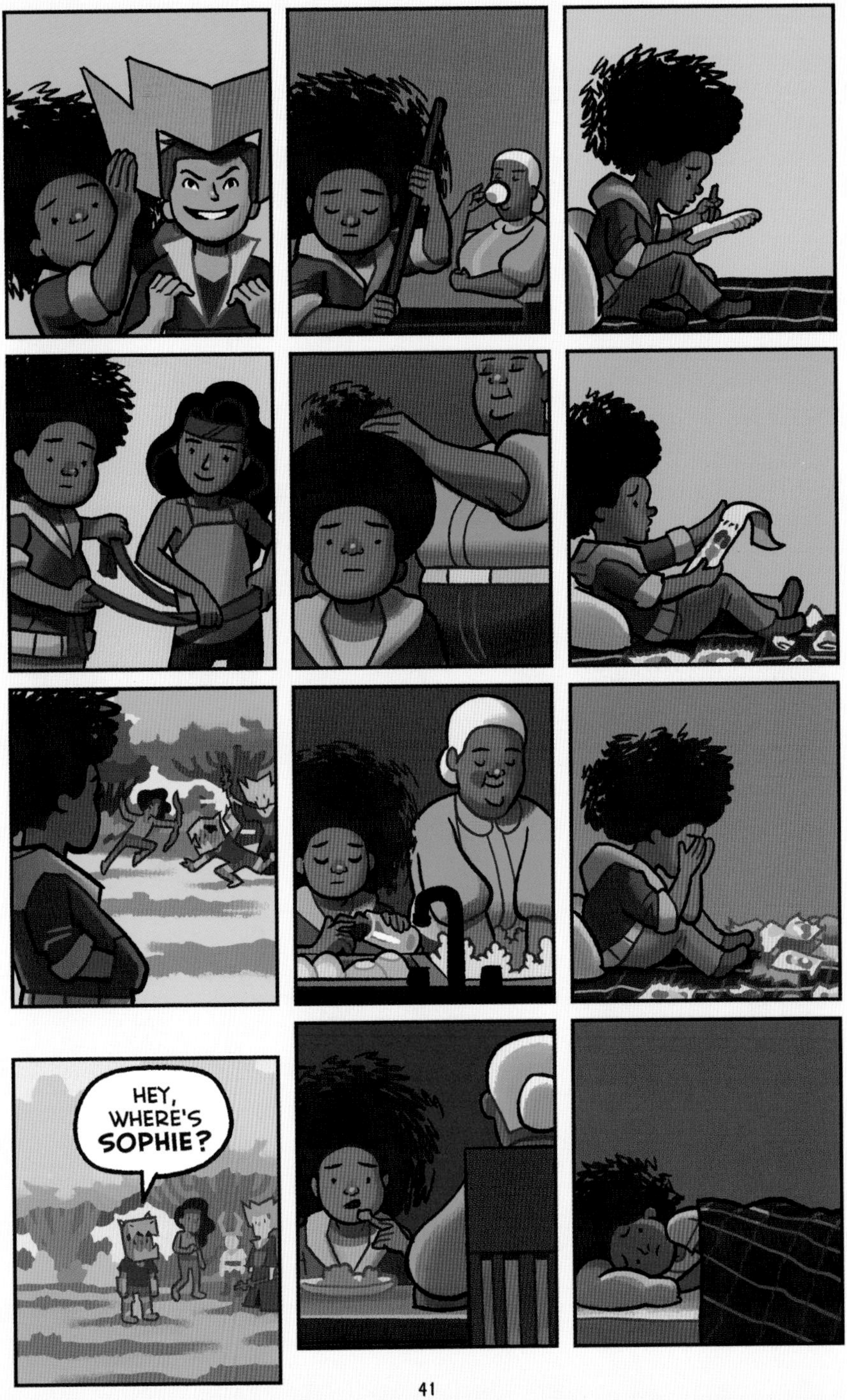
HEY, WHERE'S SOPHIE?

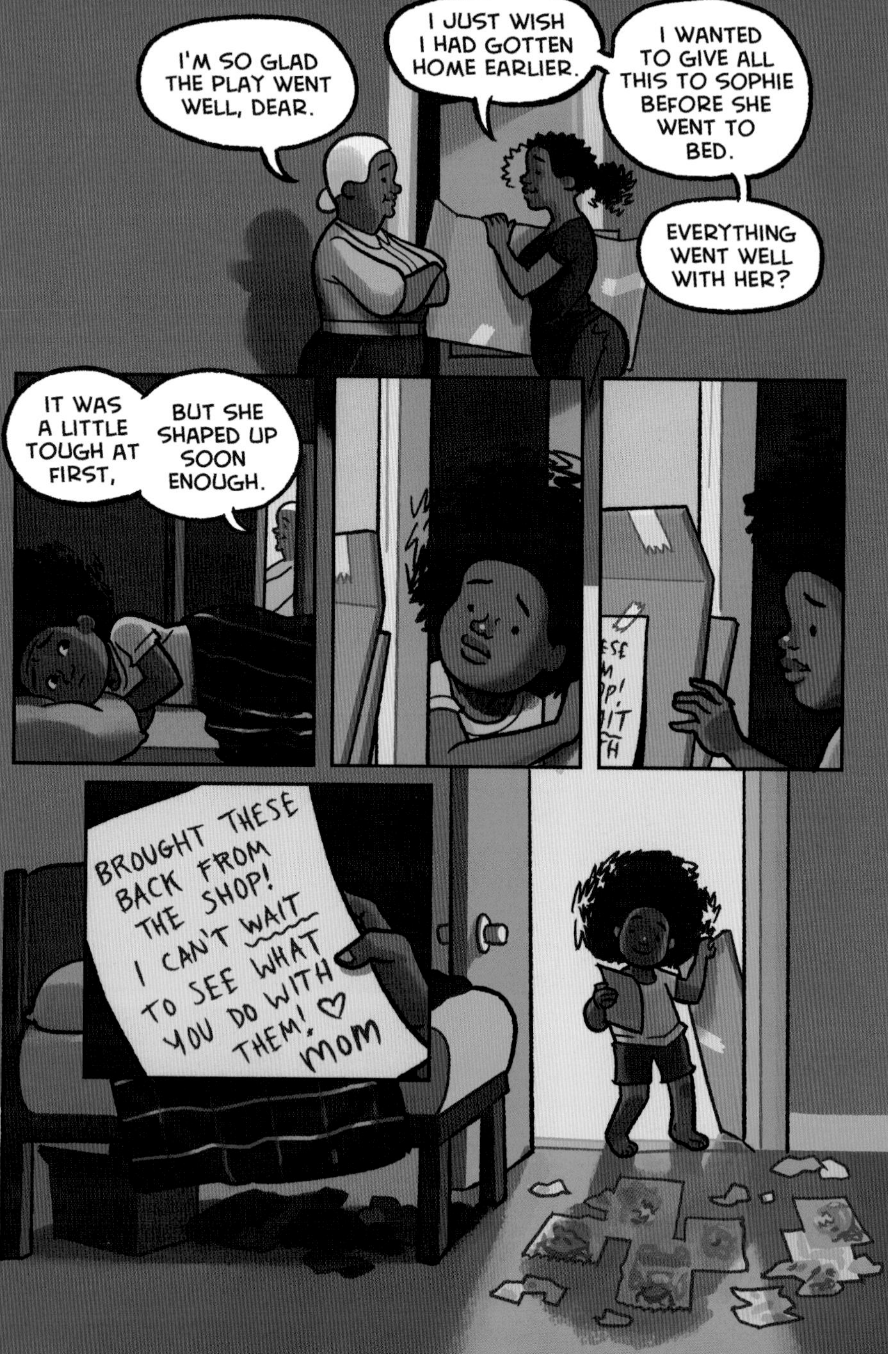
I'M SO GLAD THE PLAY WENT WELL, DEAR.
I JUST WISH I HAD GOTTEN HOME EARLIER.
I WANTED TO GIVE ALL THIS TO SOPHIE BEFORE SHE WENT TO BED.
EVERYTHING WENT WELL WITH HER?
IT WAS A LITTLE TOUGH AT FIRST,
BUT SHE SHAPED UP SOON ENOUGH.
BROUGHT THESE BACK FROM THE SHOP! I CAN'T WAIT TO SEE WHAT YOU DO WITH THEM! ♡ MOM

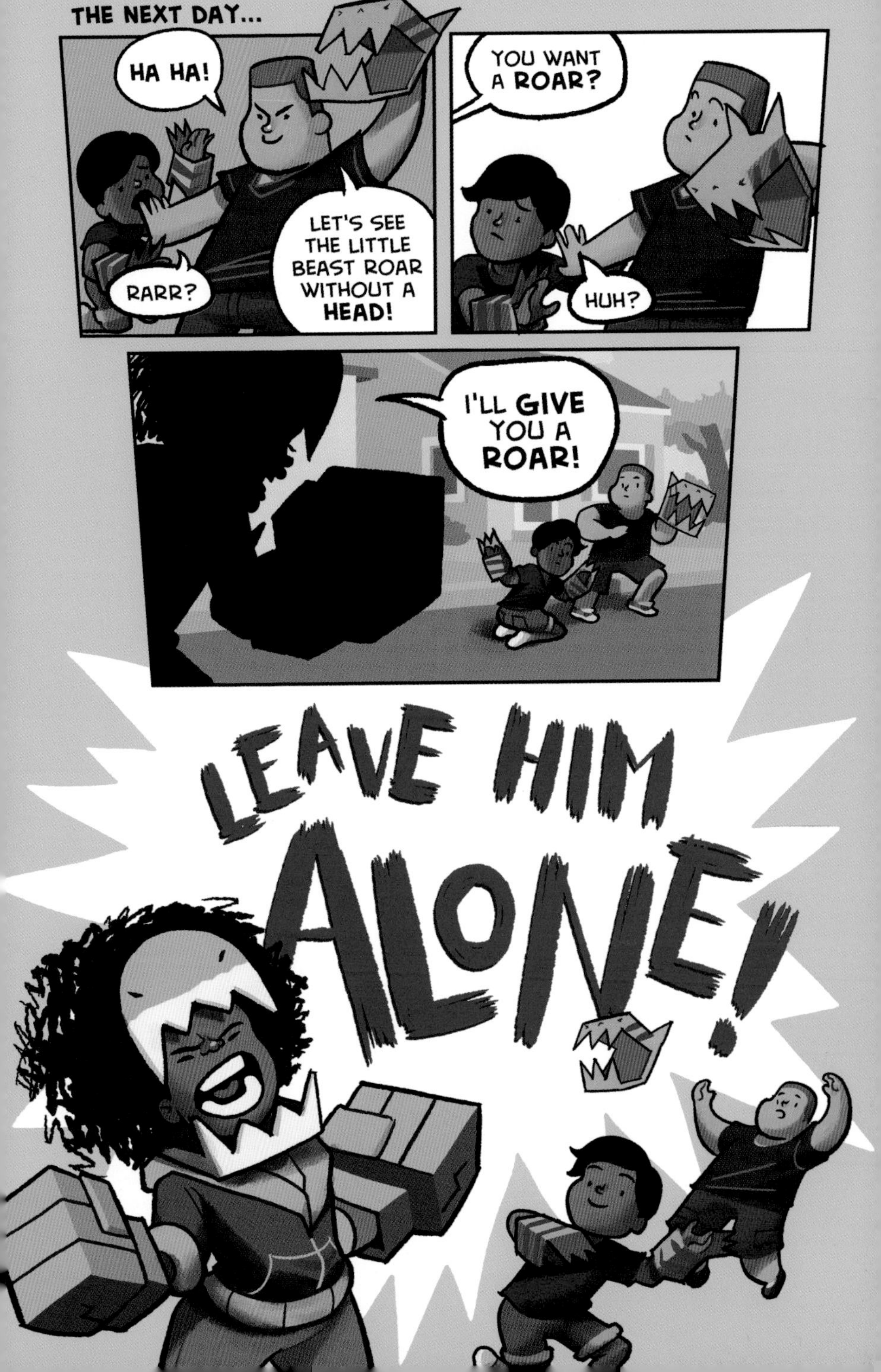
THE NEXT DAY...
HA HA!
RARR?
LET'S SEE THE LITTLE BEAST ROAR WITHOUT A HEAD!
YOU WANT A ROAR?
HUH?
I'LL GIVE YOU A ROAR!
LEAVE HIM ALONE!

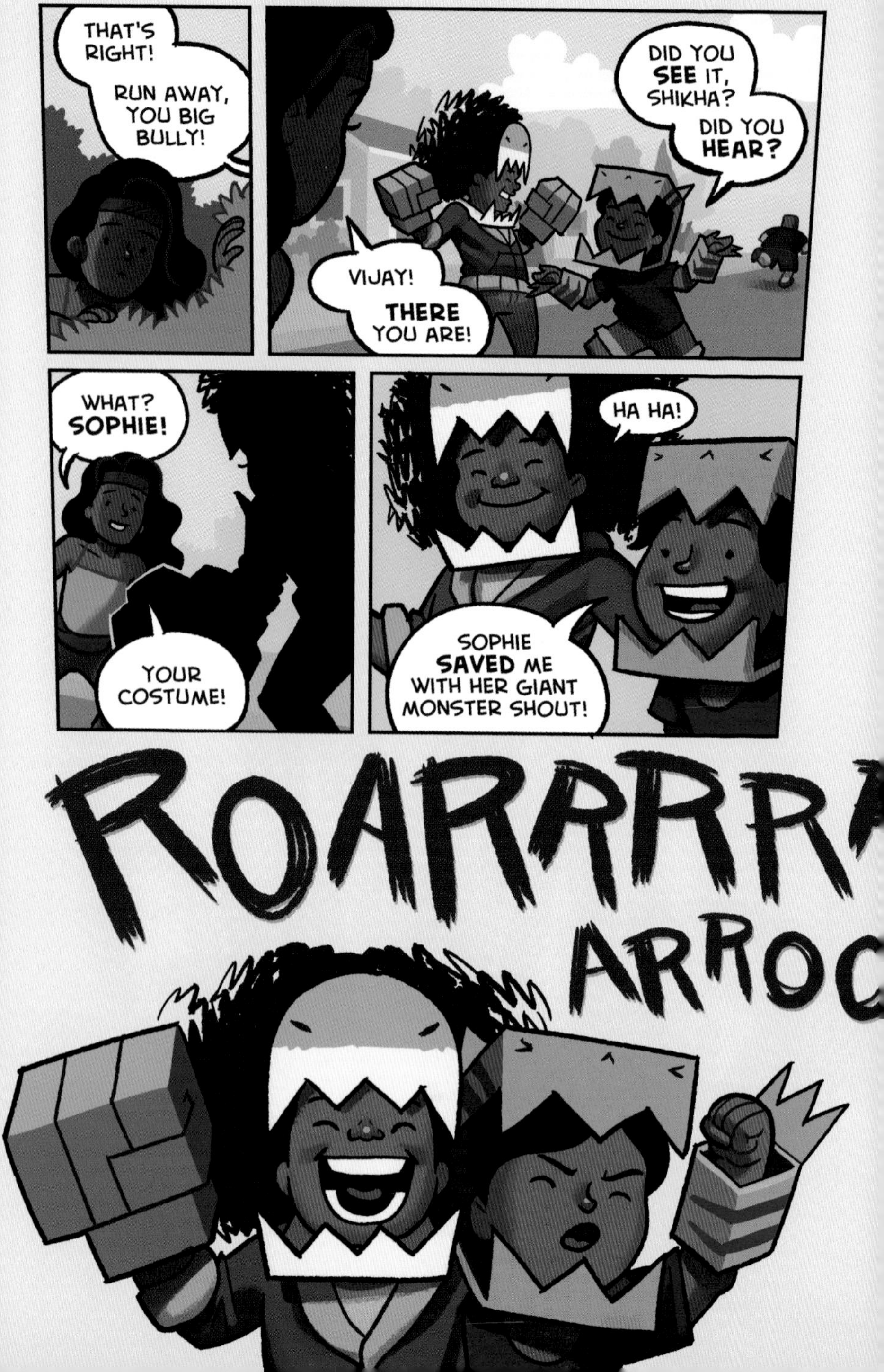
THAT'S RIGHT!
RUN AWAY, YOU BIG BULLY!
DID YOU SEE IT, SHIKHA?
DID YOU HEAR?
VIJAY!
THERE YOU ARE!
WHAT? SOPHIE!
YOUR COSTUME!
HA HA!
SOPHIE SAVED ME WITH HER GIANT MONSTER SHOUT!
ROARRRRA
ARROO

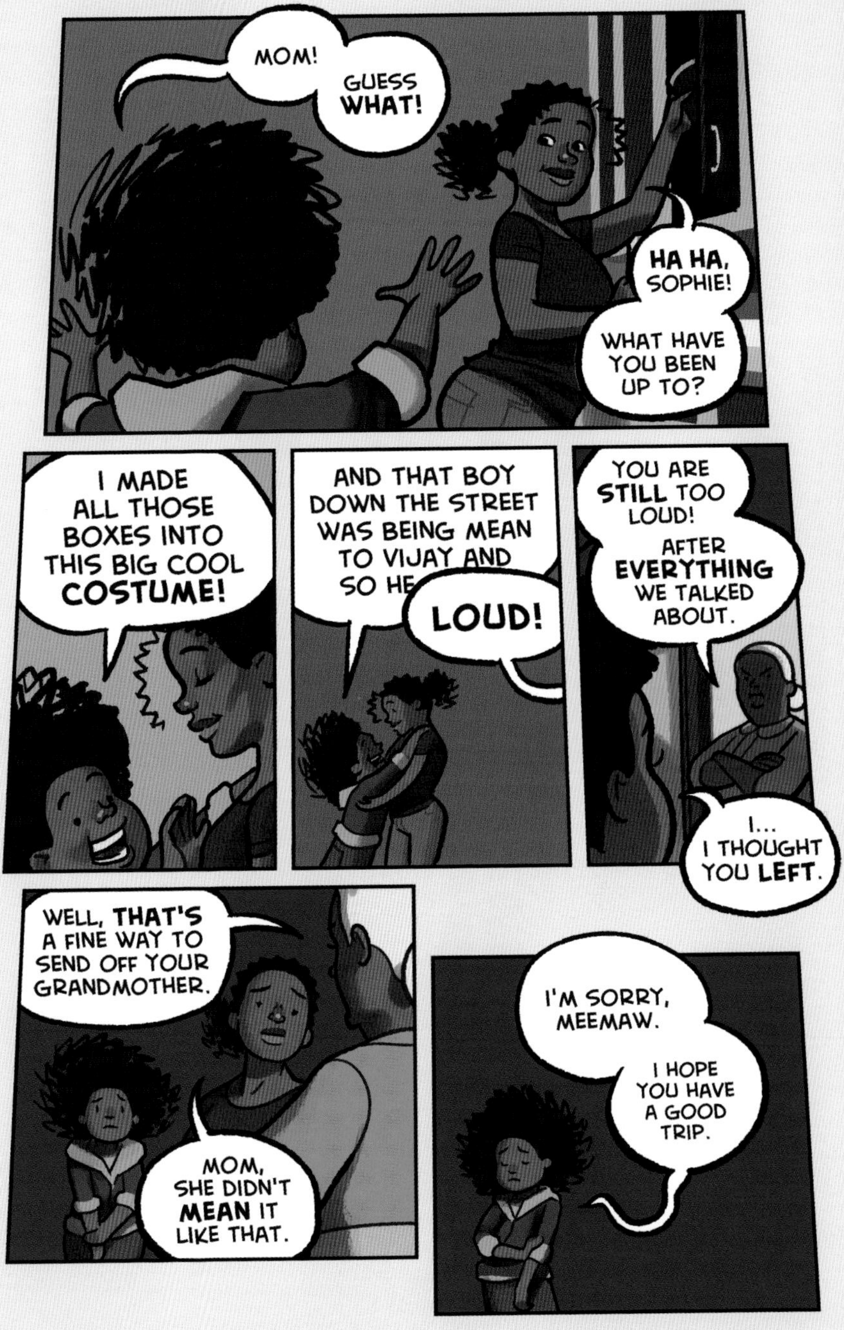
MOM!
GUESS **WHAT!**
HA HA, SOPHIE!
WHAT HAVE YOU BEEN UP TO?
I MADE ALL THOSE BOXES INTO THIS BIG COOL **COSTUME!**
AND THAT BOY DOWN THE STREET WAS BEING MEAN TO VIJAY AND SO HE
LOUD!
YOU ARE **STILL** TOO LOUD!
AFTER **EVERYTHING** WE TALKED ABOUT.
I... I THOUGHT YOU **LEFT**.
WELL, **THAT'S** A FINE WAY TO SEND OFF YOUR GRANDMOTHER.
MOM, SHE DIDN'T **MEAN** IT LIKE THAT.
I'M SORRY, MEEMAW.
I HOPE YOU HAVE A GOOD TRIP.

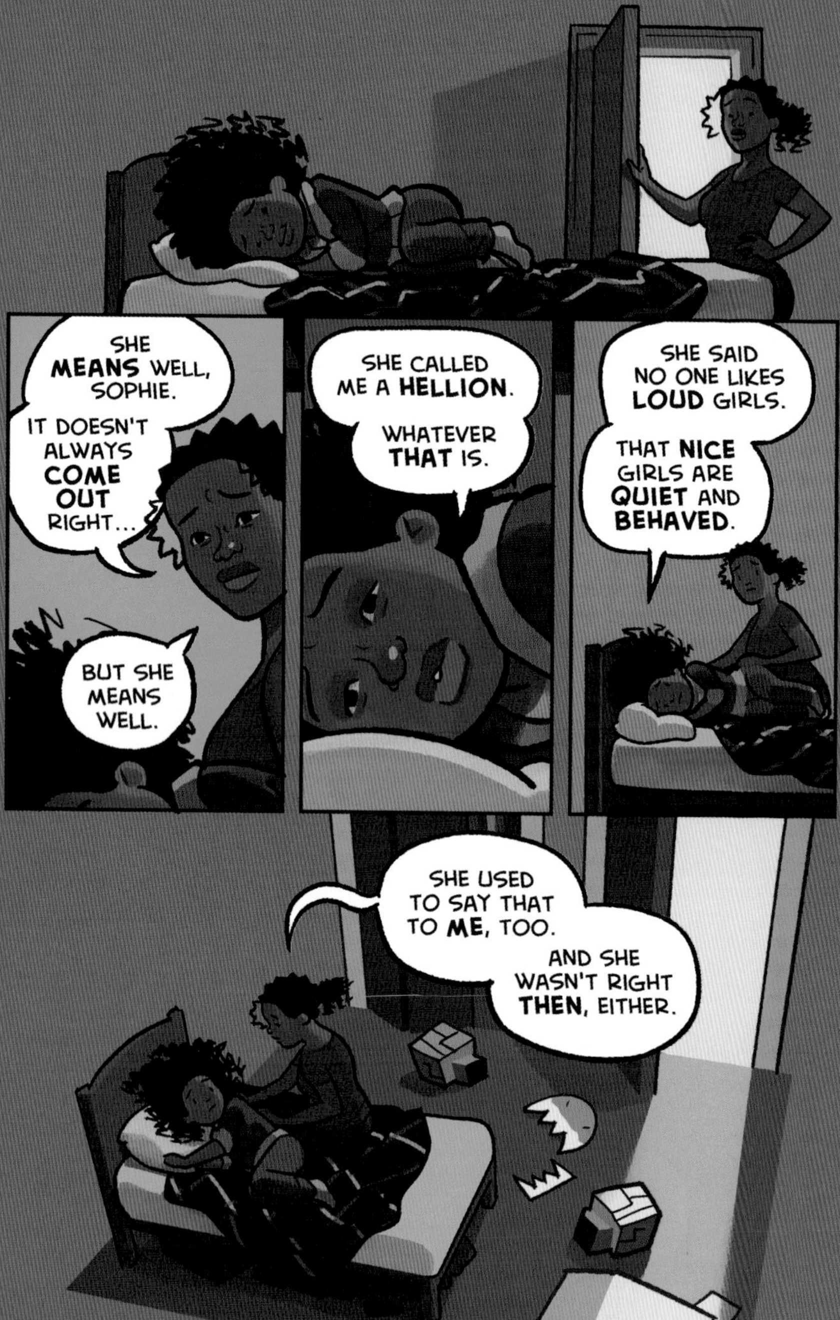
SHE **MEANS** WELL, SOPHIE.
IT DOESN'T ALWAYS **COME OUT** RIGHT...
BUT SHE MEANS WELL.
SHE CALLED ME A **HELLION**.
WHATEVER **THAT** IS.
SHE SAID NO ONE LIKES **LOUD** GIRLS.
THAT **NICE** GIRLS ARE **QUIET** AND **BEHAVED**.
SHE USED TO SAY THAT TO **ME**, TOO.
AND SHE WASN'T RIGHT **THEN**, EITHER.

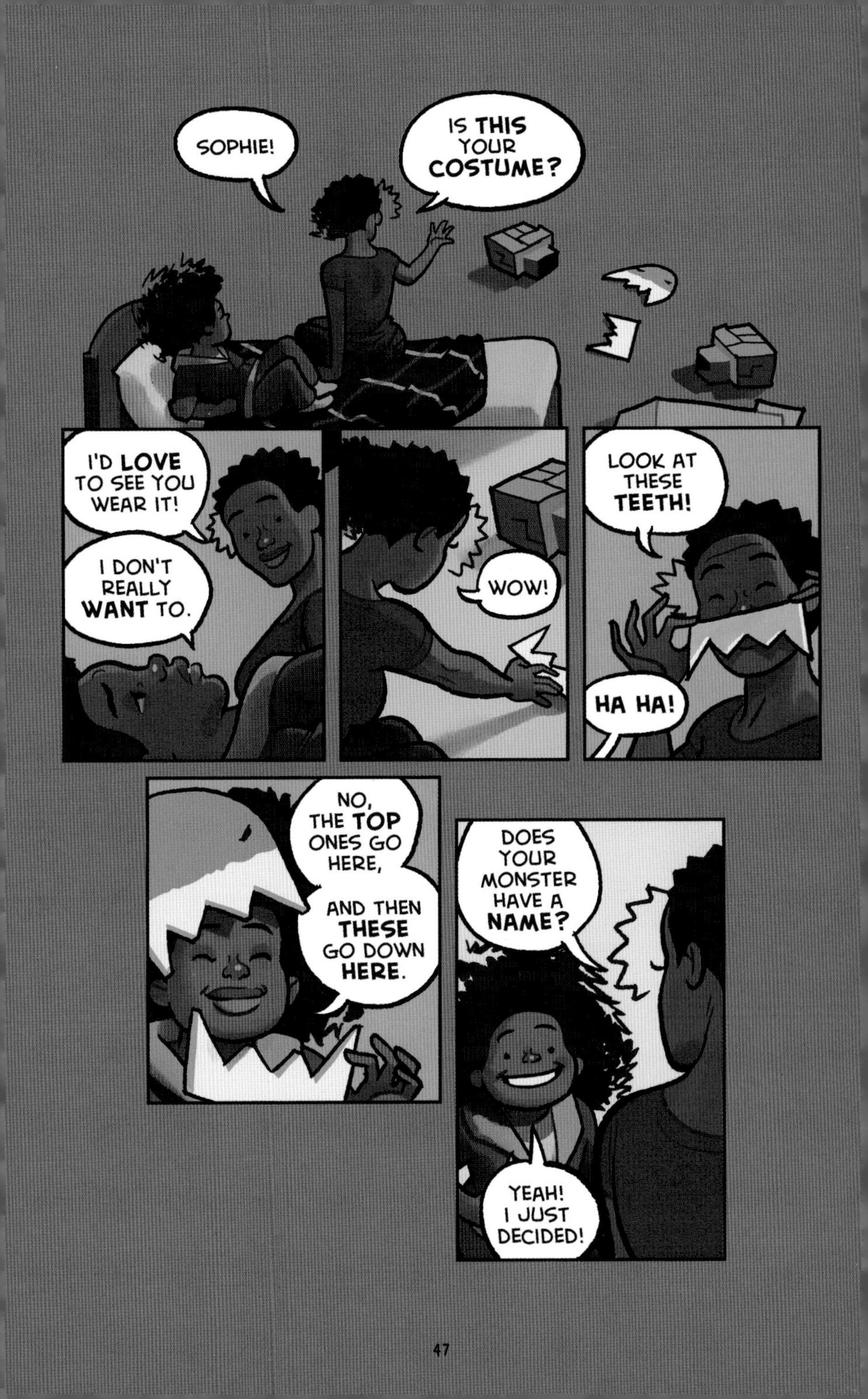
SOPHIE!
IS THIS YOUR COSTUME?
I'D LOVE TO SEE YOU WEAR IT!
I DON'T REALLY WANT TO.
WOW!
LOOK AT THESE TEETH!
HA HA!
NO, THE TOP ONES GO HERE,
AND THEN THESE GO DOWN HERE.
DOES YOUR MONSTER HAVE A NAME?
YEAH! I JUST DECIDED!

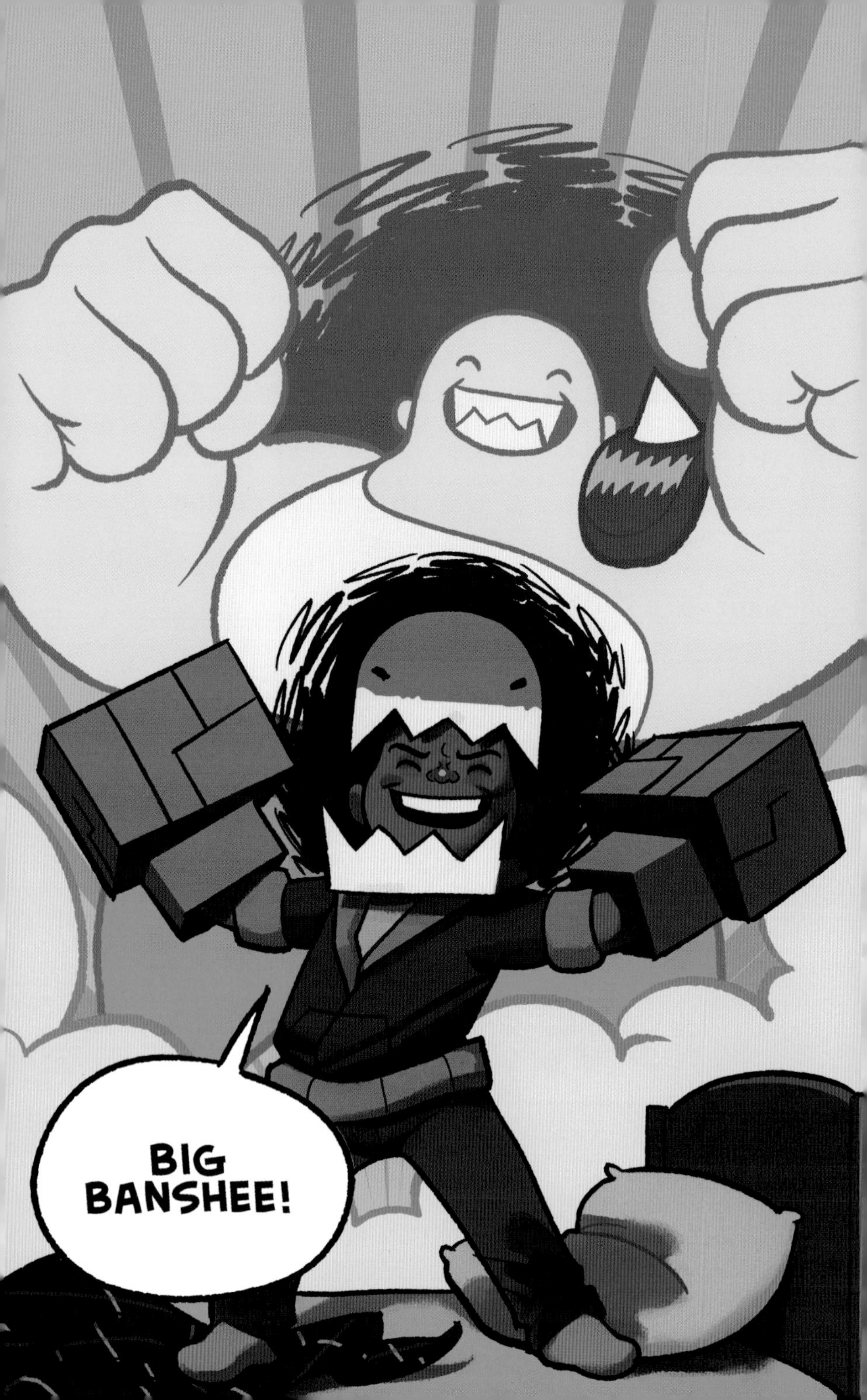
BIG BANSHEE!

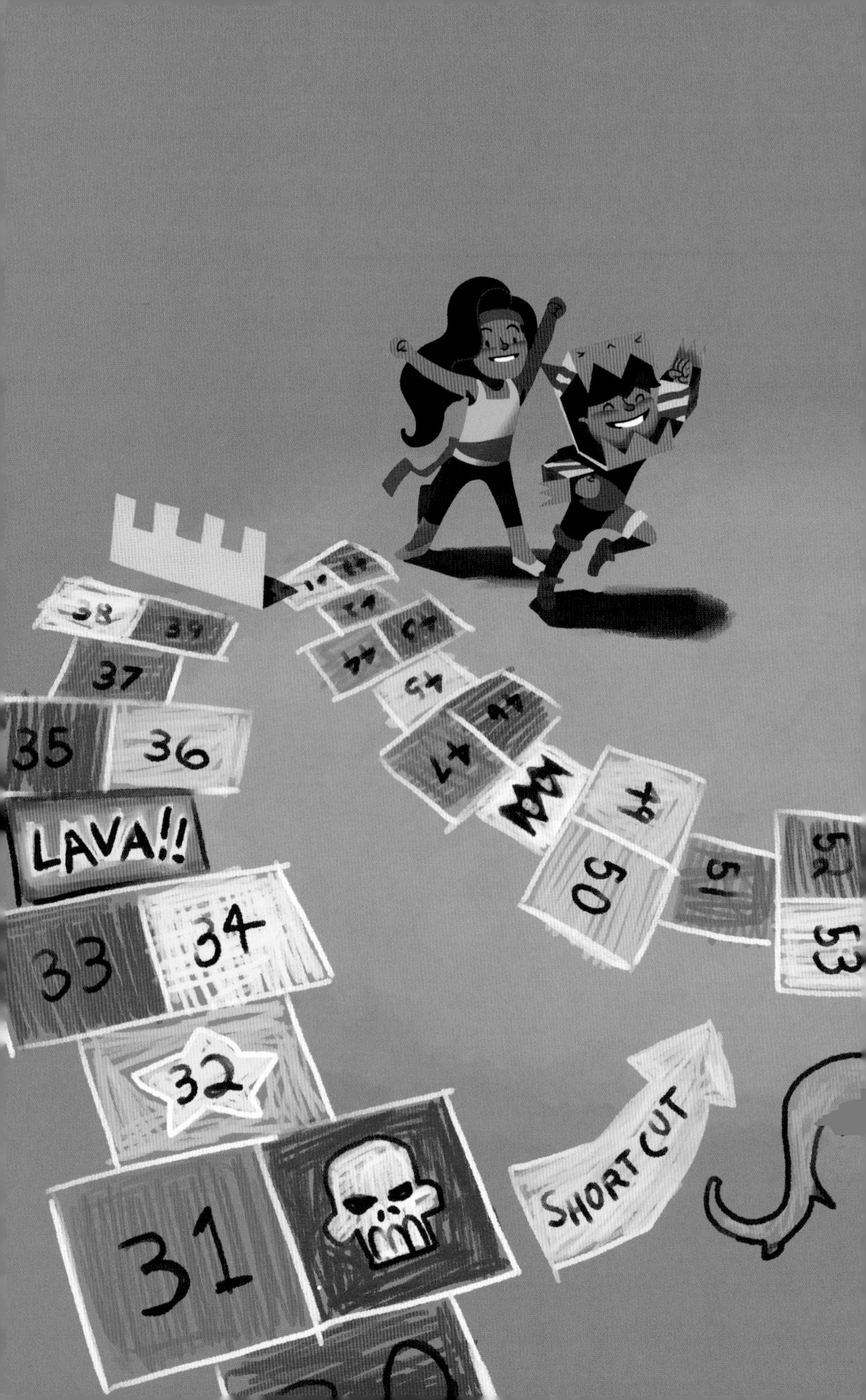

31
32
33
34
LAVA!!
35
36
37
38
39
44
45
47
49
50
51
52
53
SHORT CUT

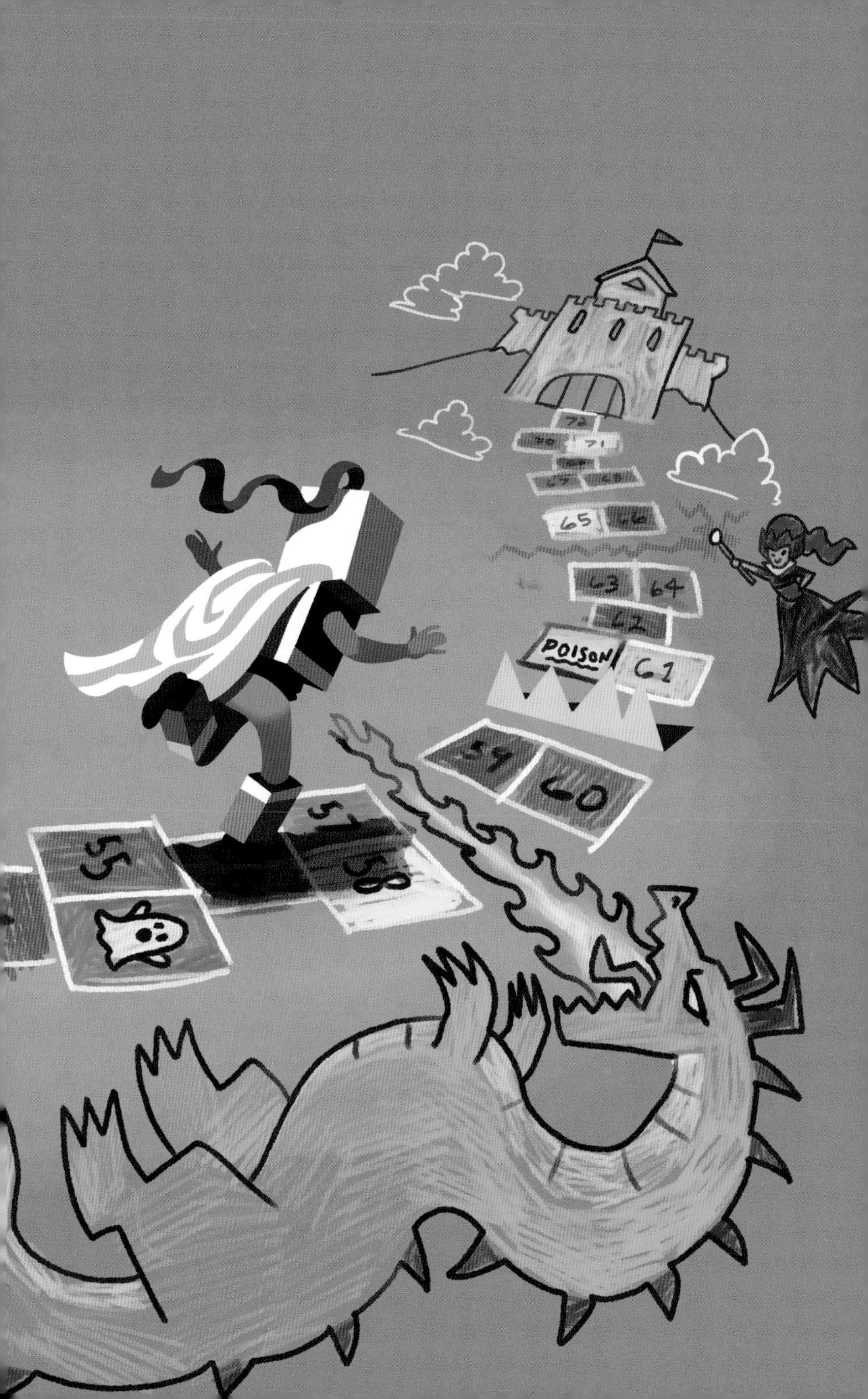

65
63
64
62
POISON
61
60
57
55
58

the ALCHEMIST AND THE BLACKSMITH

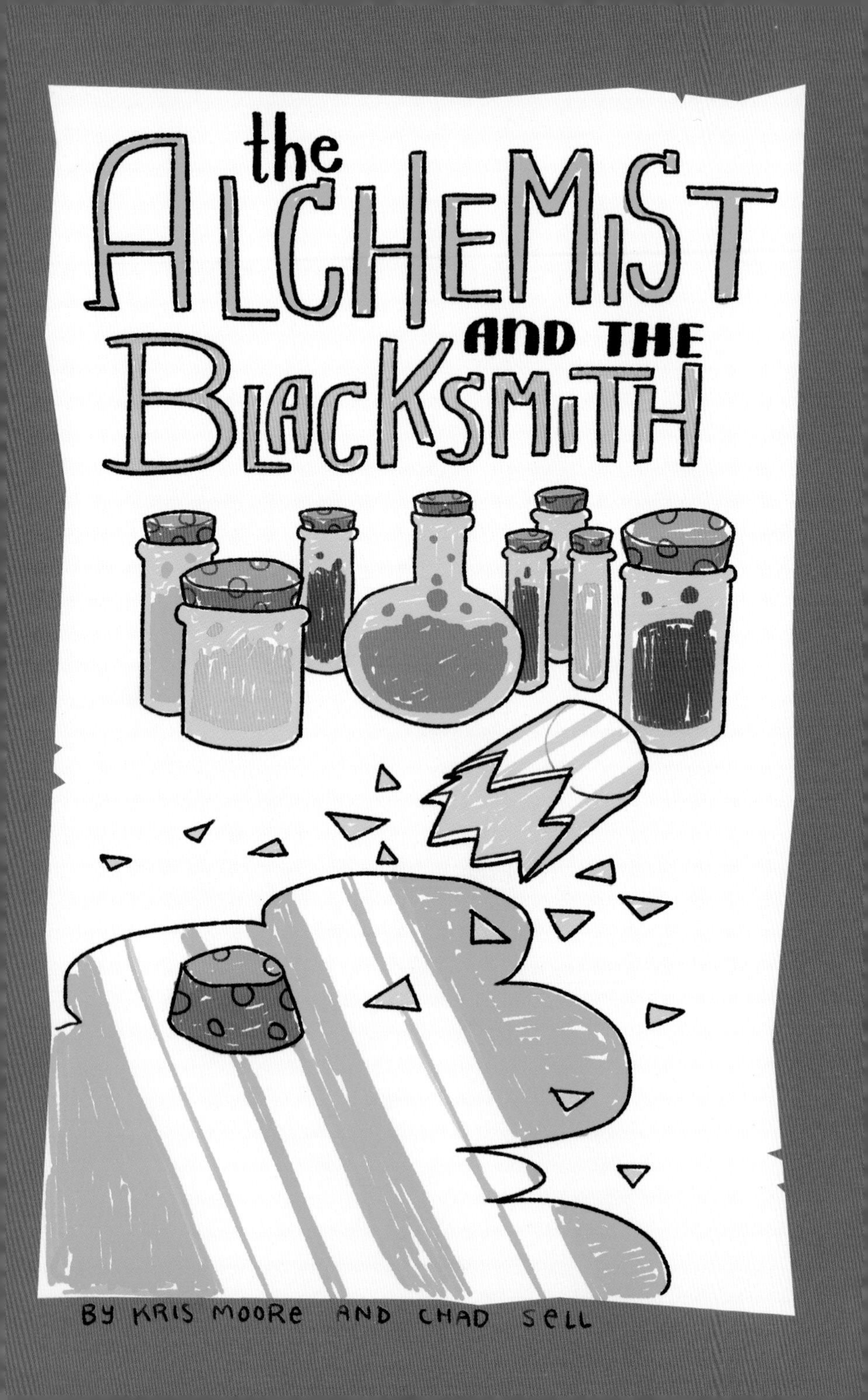

BY KRIS MOORE AND CHAD SELL

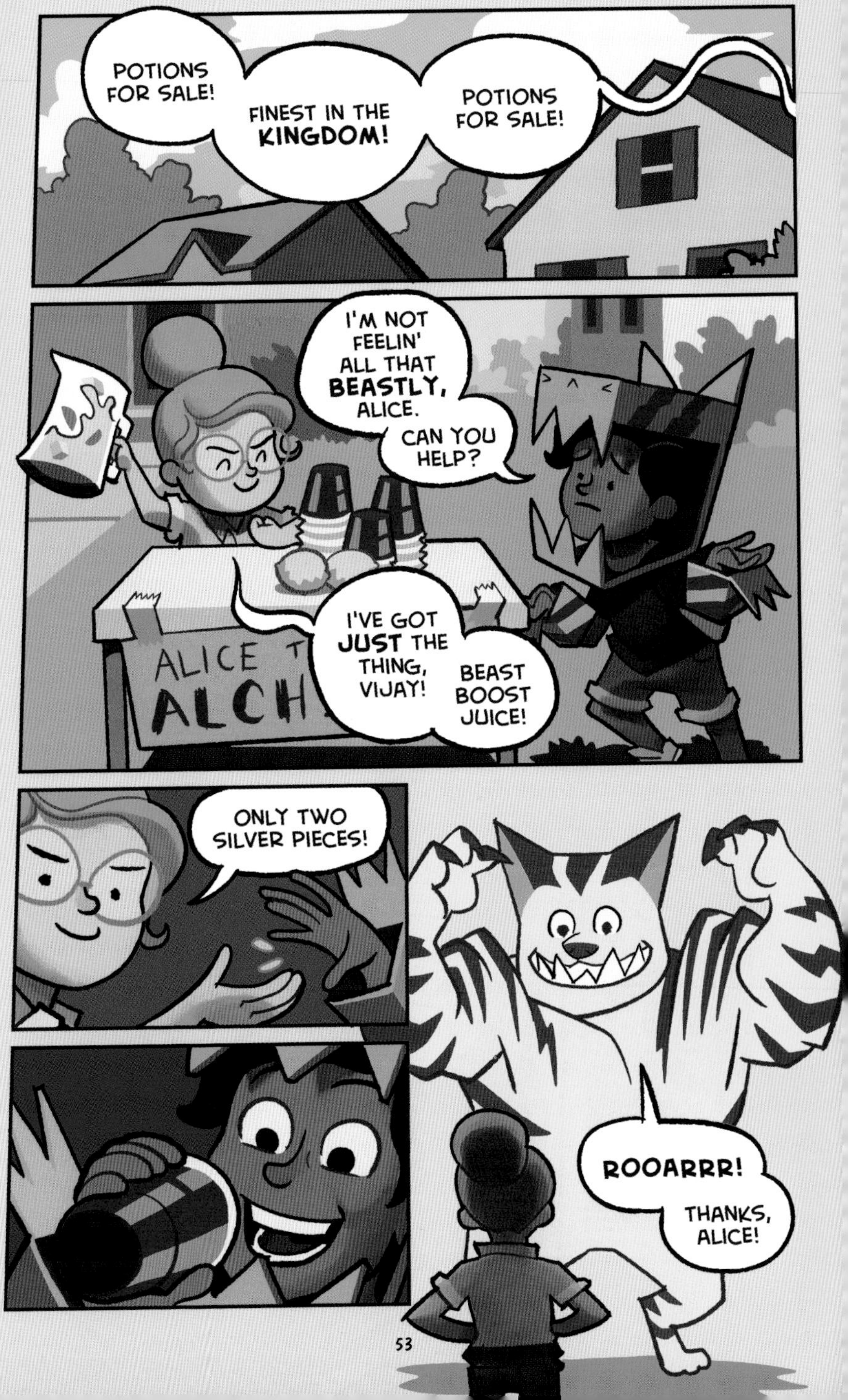
POTIONS FOR SALE!
FINEST IN THE **KINGDOM!**
POTIONS FOR SALE!
I'M NOT FEELIN' ALL THAT **BEASTLY,** ALICE.
CAN YOU HELP?
I'VE GOT **JUST** THE THING, VIJAY!
BEAST BOOST JUICE!
ONLY TWO SILVER PIECES!
ROOARRR!
THANKS, ALICE!

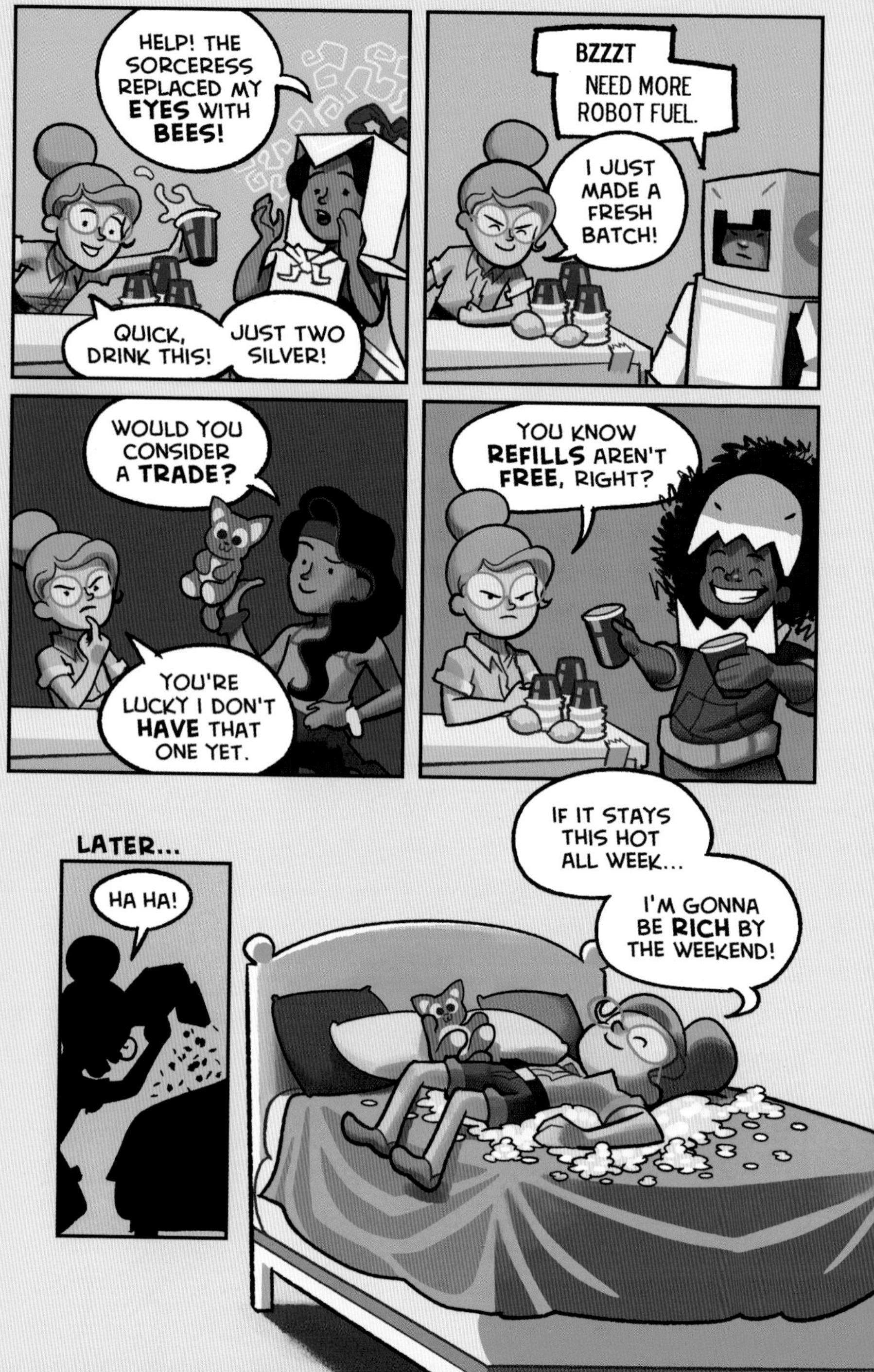
HELP! THE SORCERESS REPLACED MY EYES WITH BEES!
QUICK, DRINK THIS!
JUST TWO SILVER!
BZZZT NEED MORE ROBOT FUEL.
I JUST MADE A FRESH BATCH!
WOULD YOU CONSIDER A TRADE?
YOU'RE LUCKY I DON'T HAVE THAT ONE YET.
YOU KNOW REFILLS AREN'T FREE, RIGHT?
LATER...
HA HA!
IF IT STAYS THIS HOT ALL WEEK...
I'M GONNA BE RICH BY THE WEEKEND!

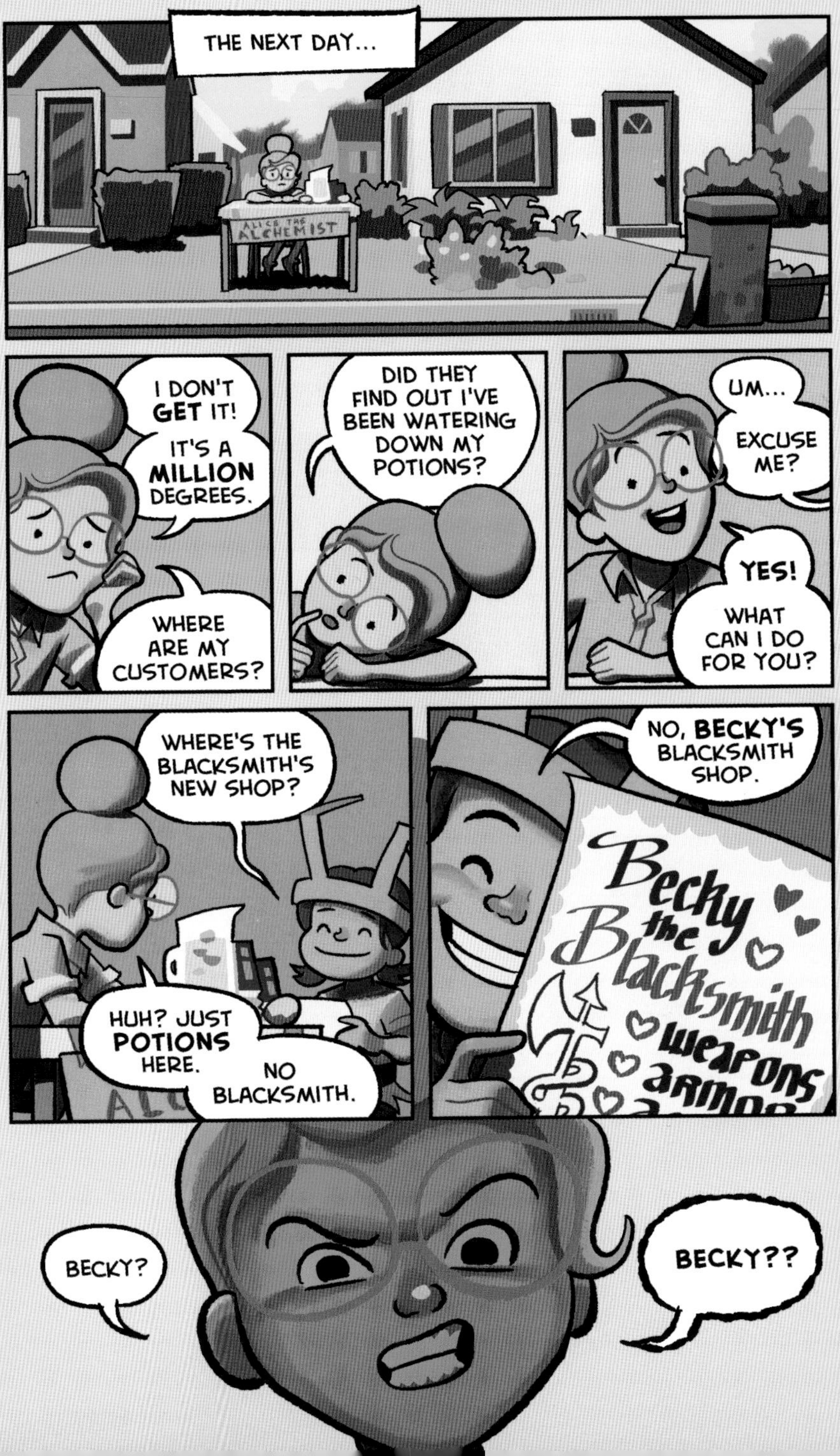
THE NEXT DAY...
ALICE THE ALCHEMIST
I DON'T **GET** IT!
IT'S A **MILLION** DEGREES.
WHERE ARE MY CUSTOMERS?
DID THEY FIND OUT I'VE BEEN WATERING DOWN MY POTIONS?
UM...
EXCUSE ME?
YES!
WHAT CAN I DO FOR YOU?
WHERE'S THE BLACKSMITH'S NEW SHOP?
HUH? JUST **POTIONS** HERE.
NO BLACKSMITH.
NO, **BECKY'S** BLACKSMITH SHOP.
Becky the Blacksmith
WEAPONS
BECKY?
BECKY??

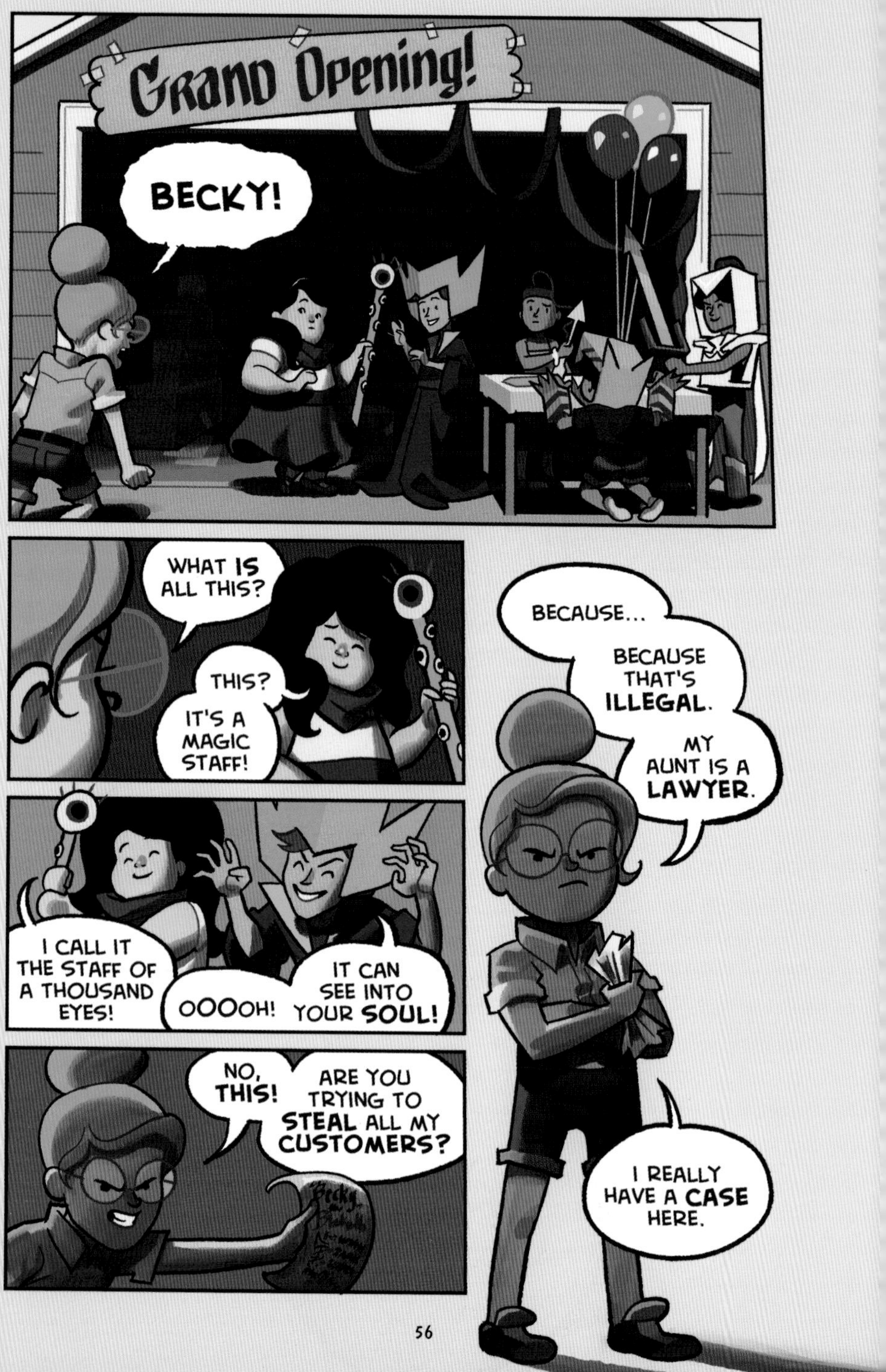
Grand Opening!
BECKY!
WHAT IS ALL THIS?
THIS?
IT'S A MAGIC STAFF!
I CALL IT THE STAFF OF A THOUSAND EYES!
OOOOH!
IT CAN SEE INTO YOUR SOUL!
NO, THIS!
ARE YOU TRYING TO STEAL ALL MY CUSTOMERS?
BECAUSE...
BECAUSE THAT'S ILLEGAL.
MY AUNT IS A LAWYER.
I REALLY HAVE A CASE HERE.

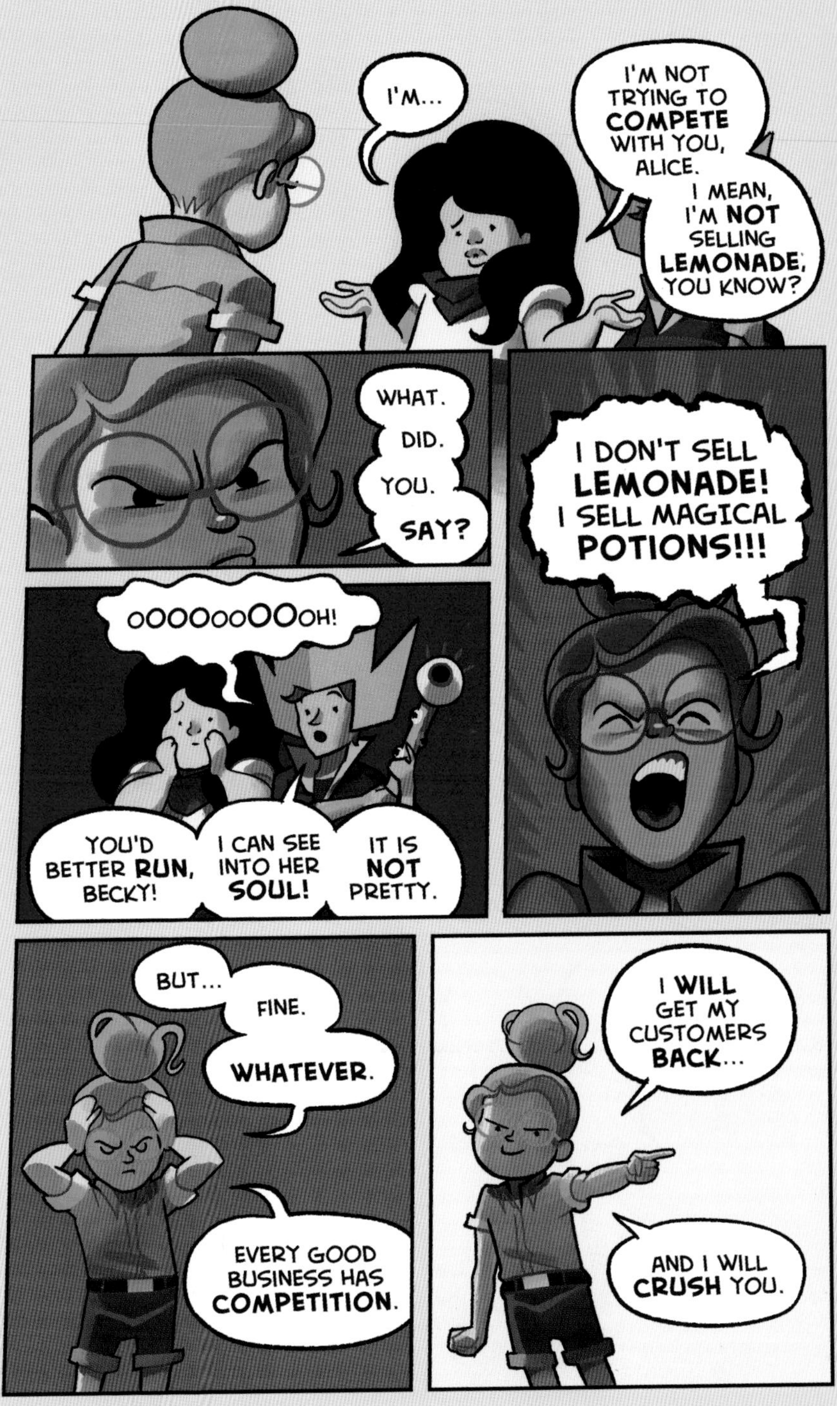
I'M...
I'M NOT TRYING TO COMPETE WITH YOU, ALICE.
I MEAN, I'M NOT SELLING LEMONADE, YOU KNOW?
WHAT. DID. YOU. SAY?
I DON'T SELL LEMONADE! I SELL MAGICAL POTIONS!!!
OOOOOOOOOOH!
YOU'D BETTER RUN, BECKY!
I CAN SEE INTO HER SOUL!
IT IS NOT PRETTY.
BUT... FINE.
WHATEVER.
EVERY GOOD BUSINESS HAS COMPETITION.
I WILL GET MY CUSTOMERS BACK...
AND I WILL CRUSH YOU.

LATER THAT DAY...

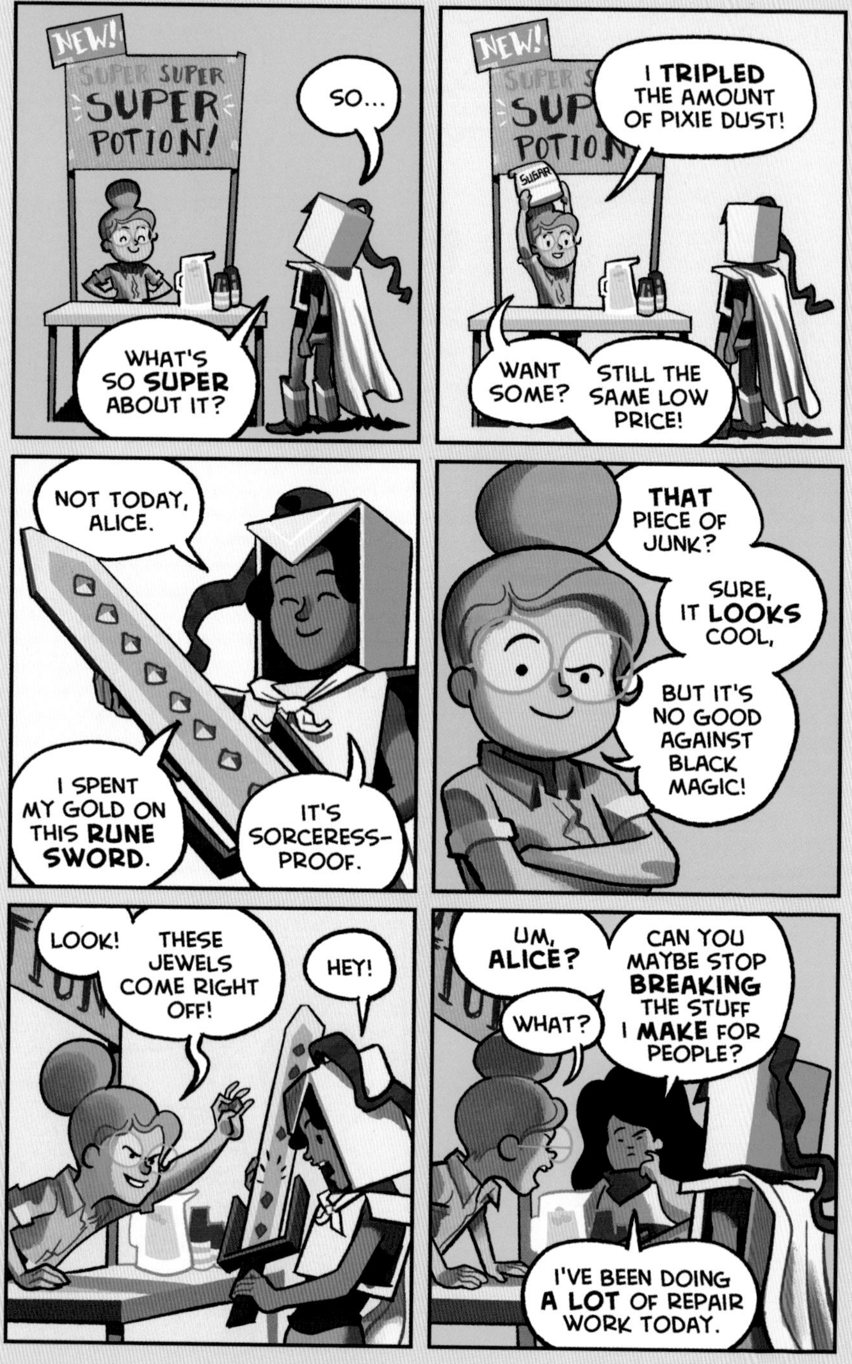
NEW!
SUPER SUPER SUPER POTION!
SO...
WHAT'S SO **SUPER** ABOUT IT?
I **TRIPLED** THE AMOUNT OF PIXIE DUST!
SUGAR
WANT SOME?
STILL THE SAME LOW PRICE!
NOT TODAY, ALICE.
I SPENT MY GOLD ON THIS **RUNE SWORD**.
IT'S SORCERESS-PROOF.
THAT PIECE OF JUNK?
SURE, IT **LOOKS** COOL,
BUT IT'S NO GOOD AGAINST BLACK MAGIC!
LOOK!
THESE JEWELS COME RIGHT OFF!
HEY!
UM, **ALICE?**
WHAT?
CAN YOU MAYBE STOP **BREAKING** THE STUFF I **MAKE** FOR PEOPLE?
I'VE BEEN DOING **A LOT** OF REPAIR WORK TODAY.

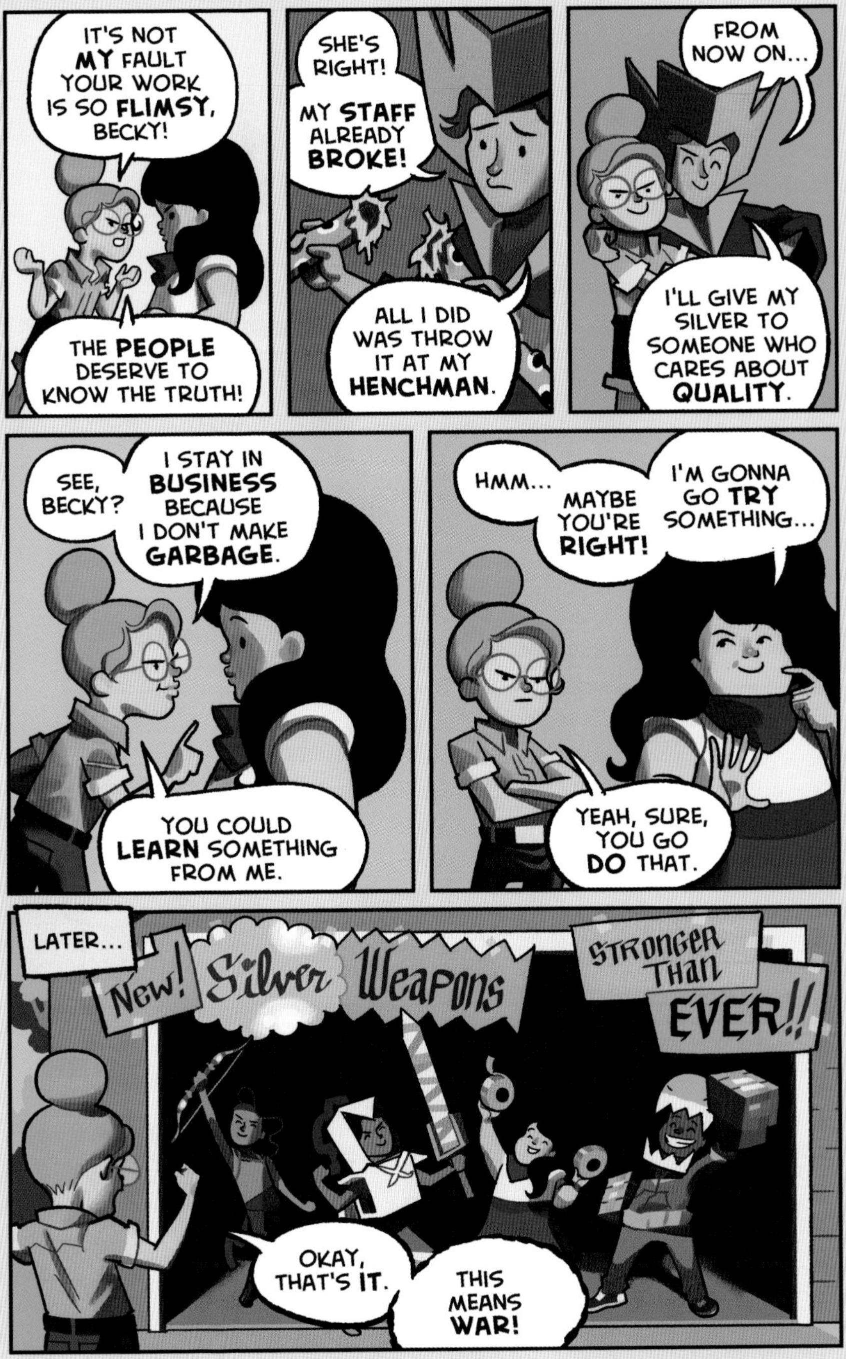
IT'S NOT MY FAULT YOUR WORK IS SO FLIMSY, BECKY!
THE PEOPLE DESERVE TO KNOW THE TRUTH!
SHE'S RIGHT!
MY STAFF ALREADY BROKE!
ALL I DID WAS THROW IT AT MY HENCHMAN.
FROM NOW ON...
I'LL GIVE MY SILVER TO SOMEONE WHO CARES ABOUT QUALITY.
SEE, BECKY?
I STAY IN BUSINESS BECAUSE I DON'T MAKE GARBAGE.
YOU COULD LEARN SOMETHING FROM ME.
HMM...
MAYBE YOU'RE RIGHT!
I'M GONNA GO TRY SOMETHING...
YEAH, SURE, YOU GO DO THAT.
LATER...
New! Silver Weapons
Stronger Than EVER!!
OKAY, THAT'S IT.
THIS MEANS WAR!

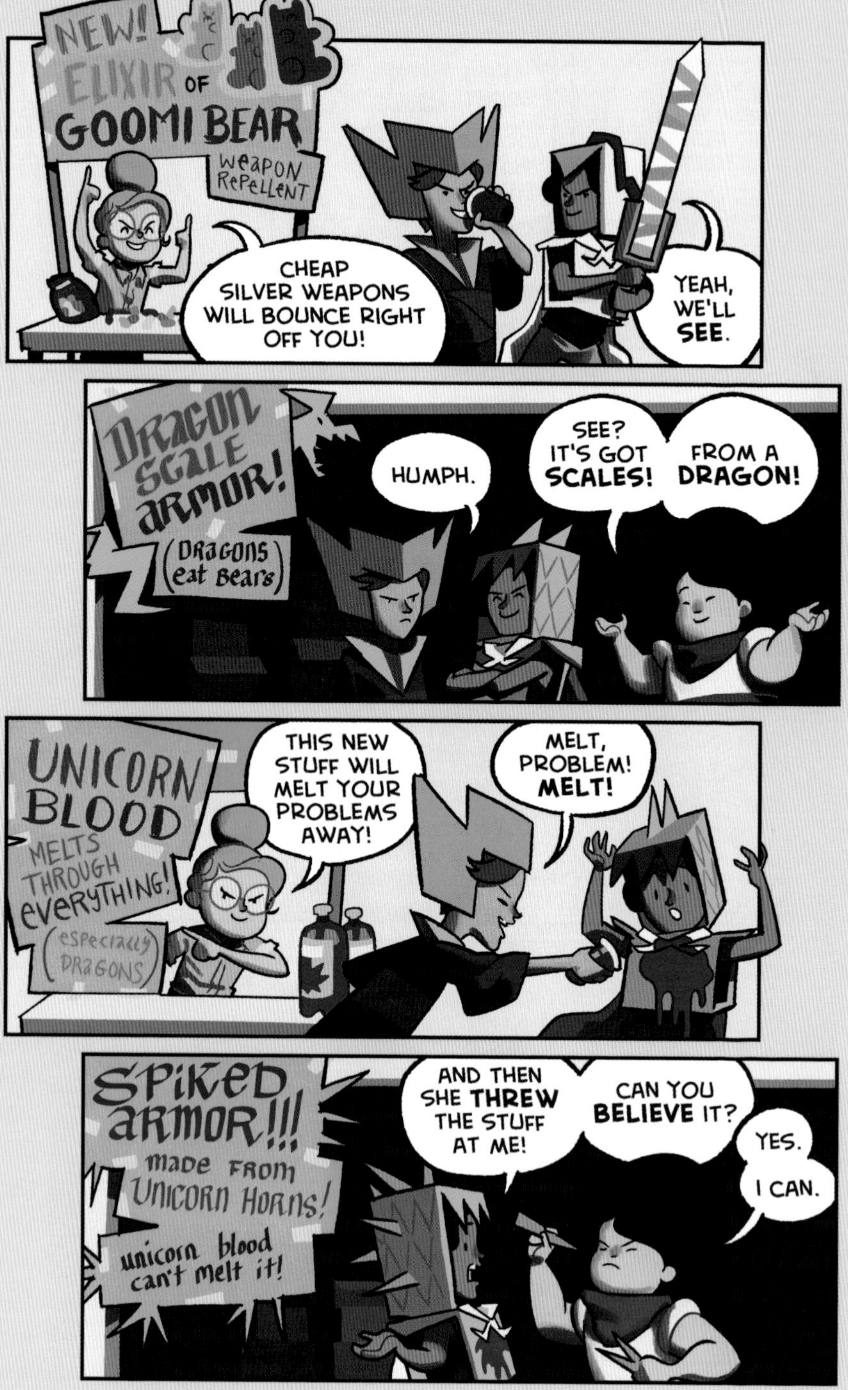
NEW!! ELIXIR OF GOOMI BEAR
WEAPON REPELLENT
CHEAP SILVER WEAPONS WILL BOUNCE RIGHT OFF YOU!
YEAH, WE'LL SEE.
DRAGON SCALE ARMOR!
(DRAGONS eat Bears)
HUMPH.
SEE? IT'S GOT SCALES!
FROM A DRAGON!
UNICORN BLOOD
MELTS THROUGH EVERYTHING!
(especially DRAGONS)
THIS NEW STUFF WILL MELT YOUR PROBLEMS AWAY!
MELT, PROBLEM! MELT!
SPIKED ARMOR!!!
made from UNICORN HORNS!
unicorn blood can't melt it!
AND THEN SHE THREW THE STUFF AT ME!
CAN YOU BELIEVE IT?
YES.
I CAN.

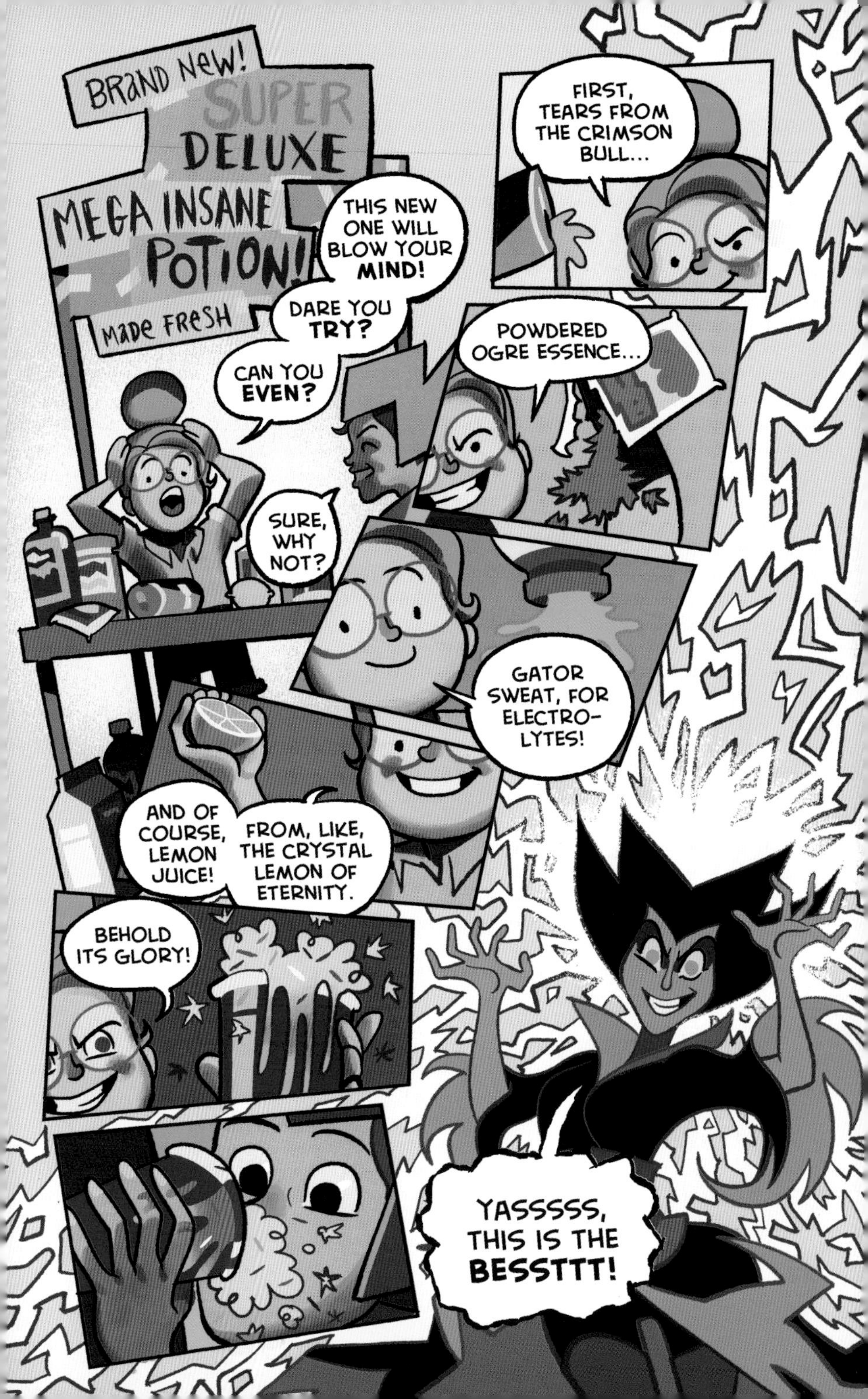
BRAND NEW! SUPER DELUXE MEGA INSANE POTION!
MADE FRESH
THIS NEW ONE WILL BLOW YOUR **MIND!**
DARE YOU **TRY?**
CAN YOU **EVEN?**
SURE, WHY NOT?
FIRST, TEARS FROM THE CRIMSON BULL...
POWDERED OGRE ESSENCE...
GATOR SWEAT, FOR ELECTRO- LYTES!
AND OF COURSE, LEMON JUICE!
FROM, LIKE, THE CRYSTAL LEMON OF ETERNITY.
BEHOLD ITS GLORY!
YASSSSS, THIS IS THE **BESSTTT!**

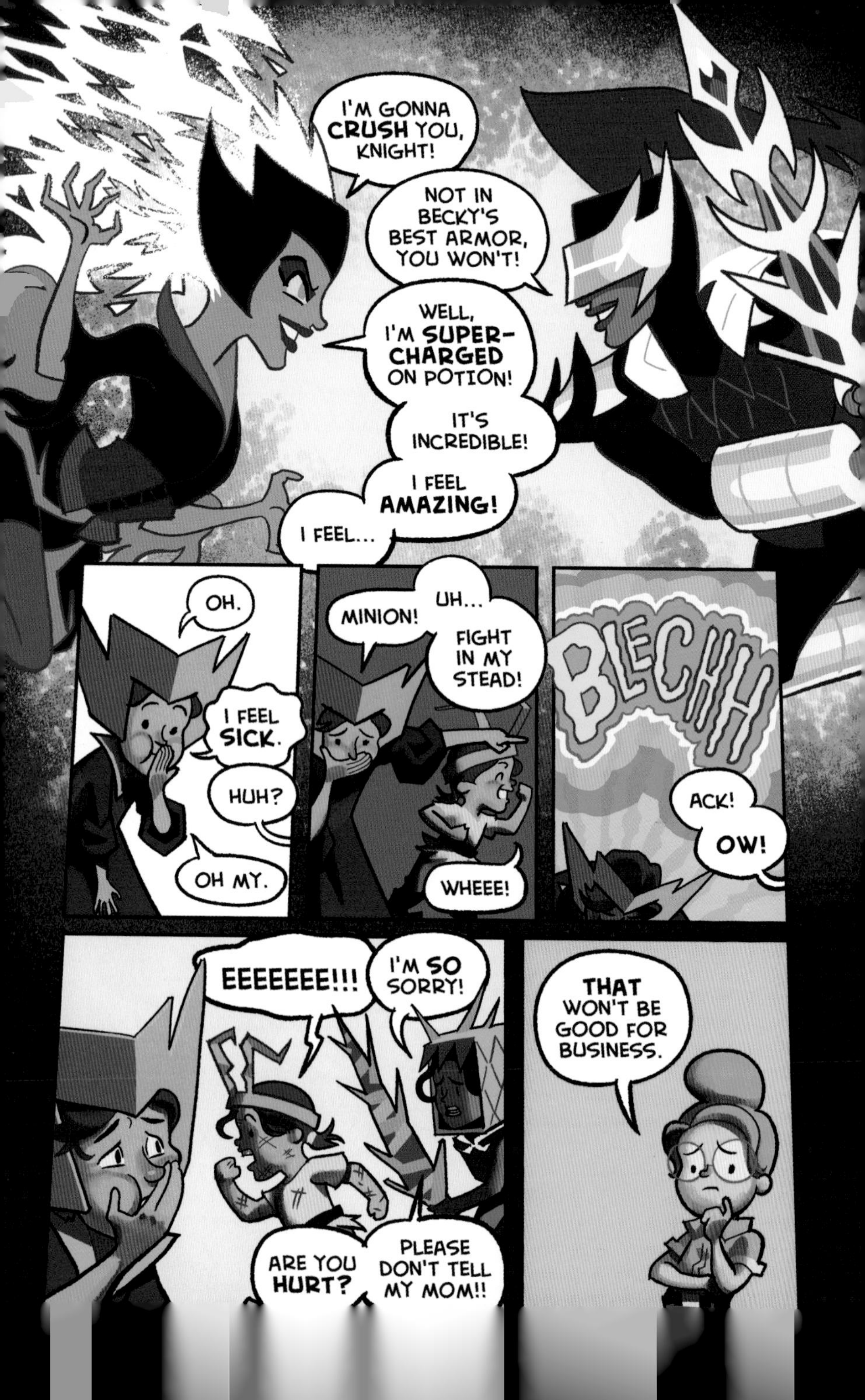
I'M GONNA CRUSH YOU, KNIGHT!
NOT IN BECKY'S BEST ARMOR, YOU WON'T!
WELL, I'M SUPER-CHARGED ON POTION!
IT'S INCREDIBLE!
I FEEL AMAZING!
I FEEL...
OH.
I FEEL SICK.
HUH?
OH MY.
MINION!
UH...
FIGHT IN MY STEAD!
WHEEE!
BLECHH
ACK!
OW!
EEEEEEE!!!
I'M SO SORRY!
ARE YOU HURT?
PLEASE DON'T TELL MY MOM!!
THAT WON'T BE GOOD FOR BUSINESS.

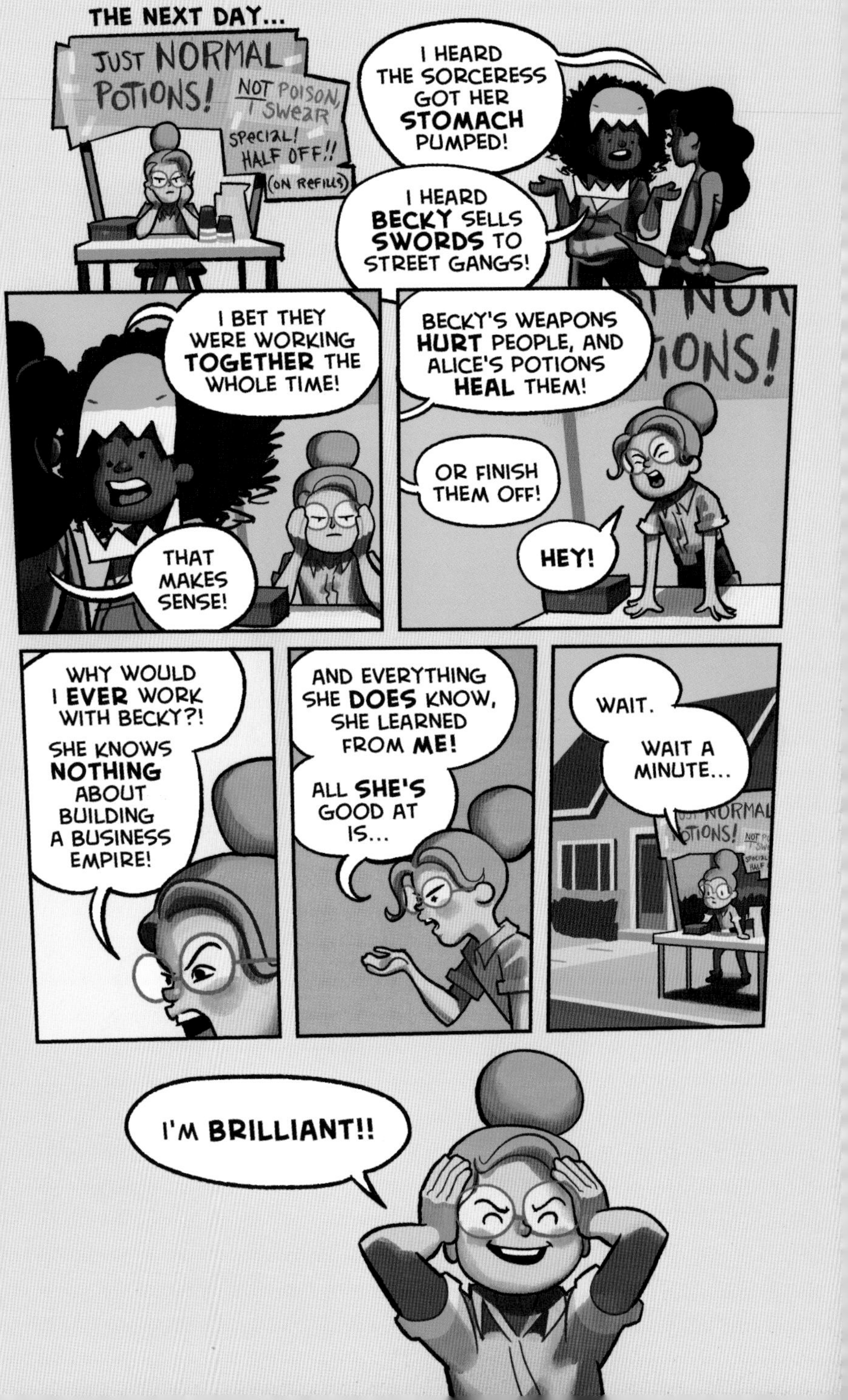
THE NEXT DAY...
JUST NORMAL POTIONS!
NOT POISON, I SWEAR
SPECIAL! HALF OFF!!
(ON REFILLS)
I HEARD THE SORCERESS GOT HER STOMACH PUMPED!
I HEARD BECKY SELLS SWORDS TO STREET GANGS!
I BET THEY WERE WORKING TOGETHER THE WHOLE TIME!
THAT MAKES SENSE!
BECKY'S WEAPONS HURT PEOPLE, AND ALICE'S POTIONS HEAL THEM!
OR FINISH THEM OFF!
HEY!
WHY WOULD I EVER WORK WITH BECKY?!
SHE KNOWS NOTHING ABOUT BUILDING A BUSINESS EMPIRE!
AND EVERYTHING SHE DOES KNOW, SHE LEARNED FROM ME!
ALL SHE'S GOOD AT IS...
WAIT.
WAIT A MINUTE...
I'M BRILLIANT!!

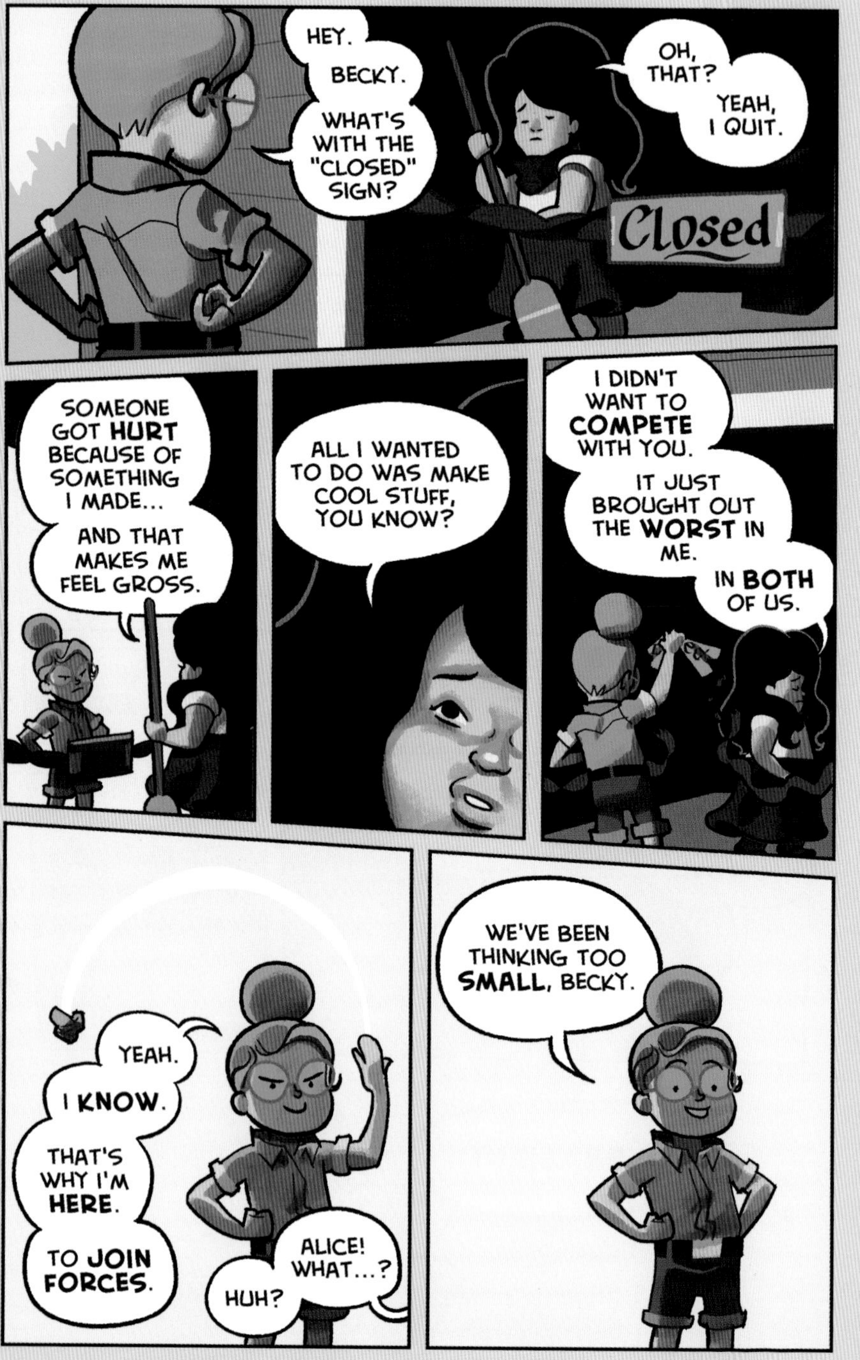
HEY.
BECKY.
WHAT'S WITH THE "CLOSED" SIGN?
OH, THAT?
YEAH, I QUIT.
Closed
SOMEONE GOT HURT BECAUSE OF SOMETHING I MADE...
AND THAT MAKES ME FEEL GROSS.
ALL I WANTED TO DO WAS MAKE COOL STUFF, YOU KNOW?
I DIDN'T WANT TO COMPETE WITH YOU.
IT JUST BROUGHT OUT THE WORST IN ME.
IN BOTH OF US.
YEAH.
I KNOW.
THAT'S WHY I'M HERE.
TO JOIN FORCES.
HUH?
ALICE! WHAT...?
WE'VE BEEN THINKING TOO SMALL, BECKY.

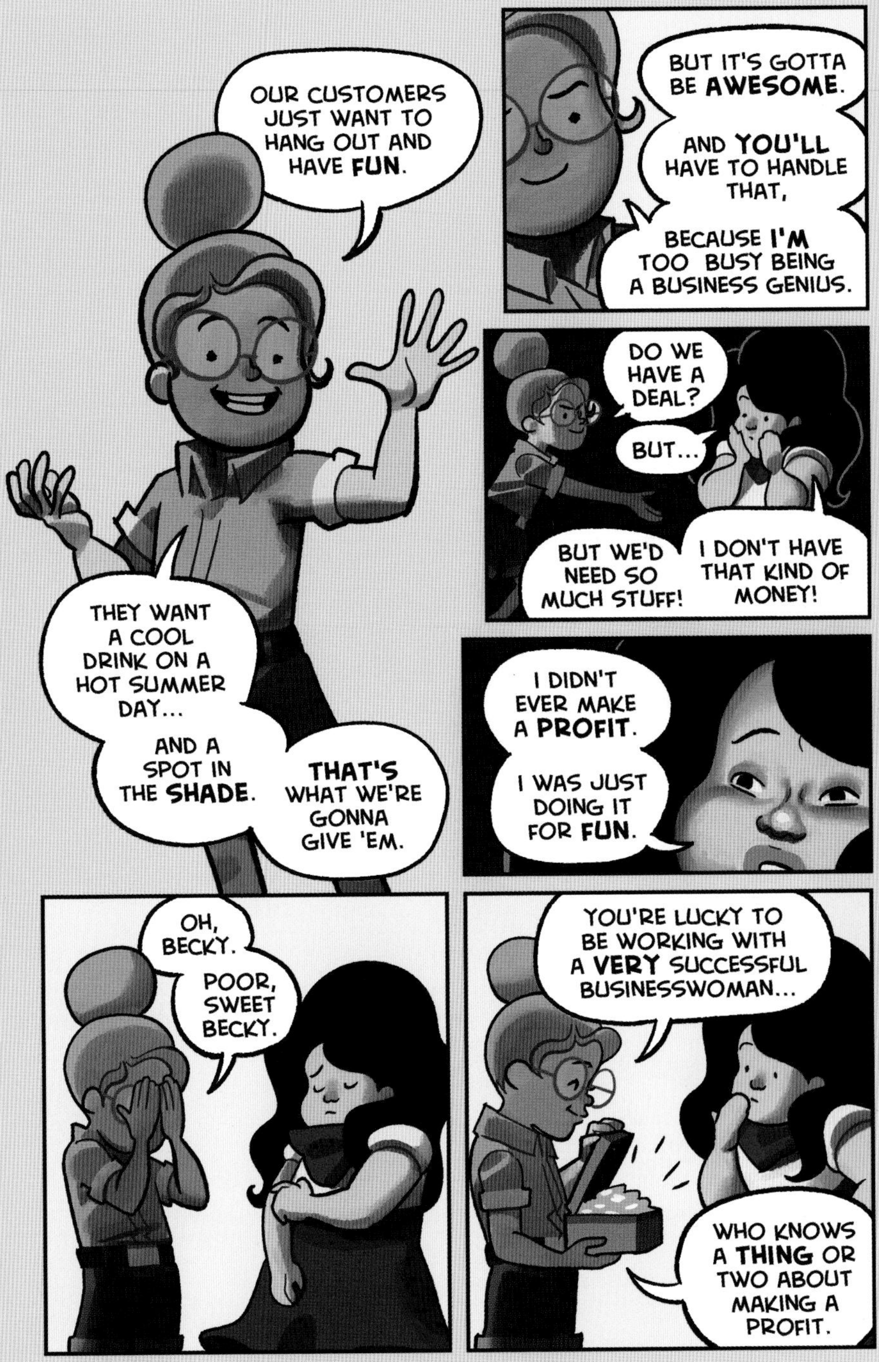
OUR CUSTOMERS JUST WANT TO HANG OUT AND HAVE FUN.
THEY WANT A COOL DRINK ON A HOT SUMMER DAY...
AND A SPOT IN THE SHADE.
THAT'S WHAT WE'RE GONNA GIVE 'EM.
BUT IT'S GOTTA BE AWESOME.
AND YOU'LL HAVE TO HANDLE THAT,
BECAUSE I'M TOO BUSY BEING A BUSINESS GENIUS.
DO WE HAVE A DEAL?
BUT...
BUT WE'D NEED SO MUCH STUFF!
I DON'T HAVE THAT KIND OF MONEY!
I DIDN'T EVER MAKE A PROFIT.
I WAS JUST DOING IT FOR FUN.
OH, BECKY.
POOR, SWEET BECKY.
YOU'RE LUCKY TO BE WORKING WITH A VERY SUCCESSFUL BUSINESSWOMAN...
WHO KNOWS A THING OR TWO ABOUT MAKING A PROFIT.

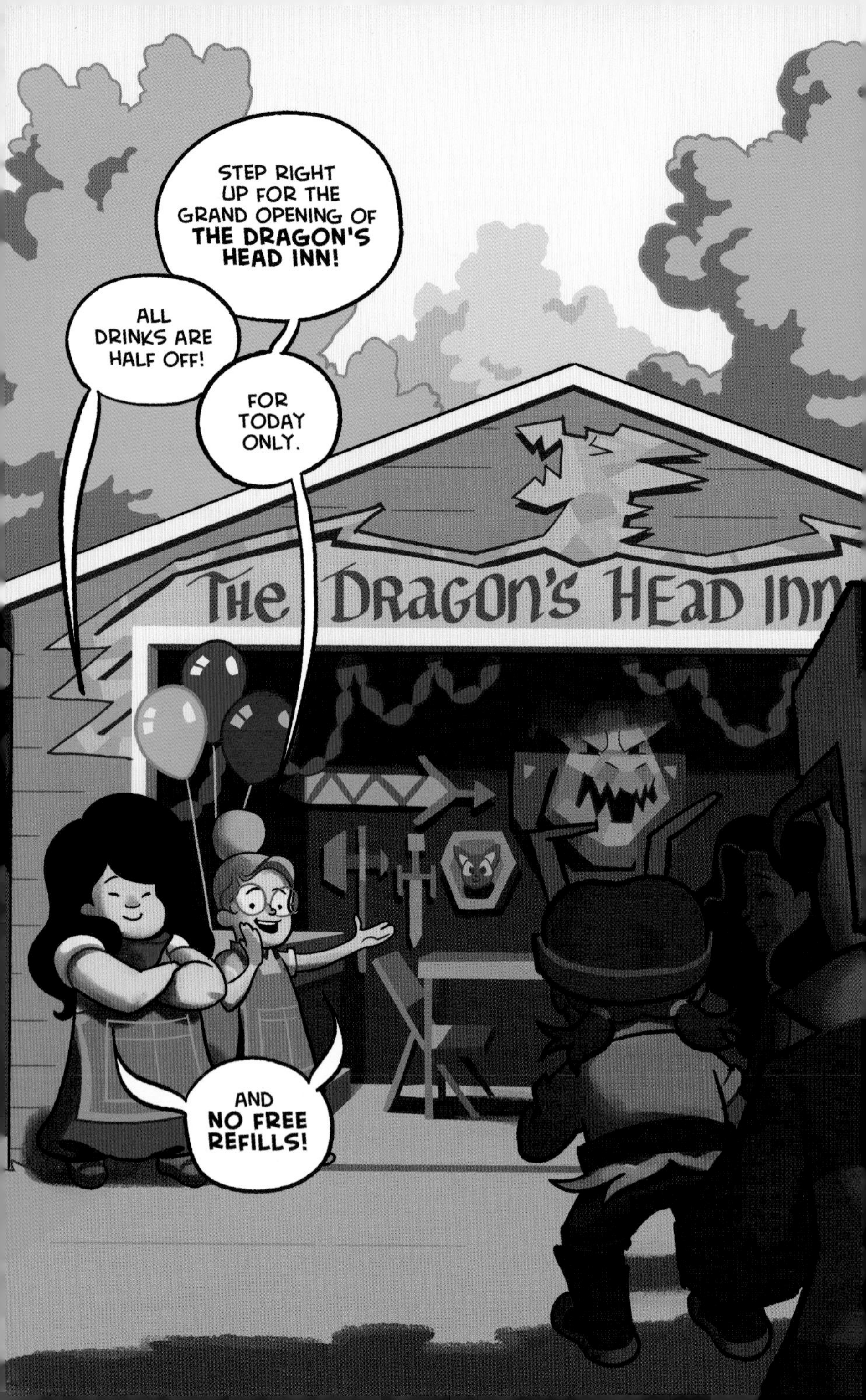
STEP RIGHT UP FOR THE GRAND OPENING OF **THE DRAGON'S HEAD INN!**
ALL DRINKS ARE HALF OFF!
FOR TODAY ONLY.
The Dragon's Head Inn
AND **NO FREE REFILLS!**

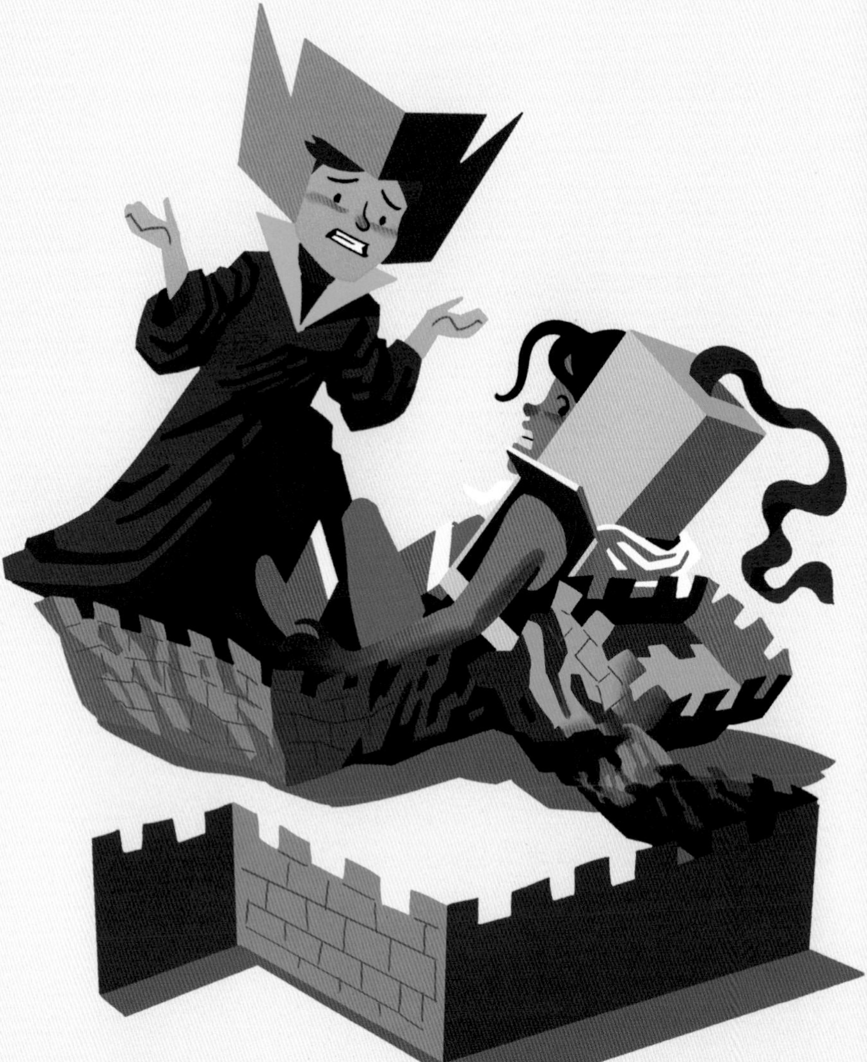

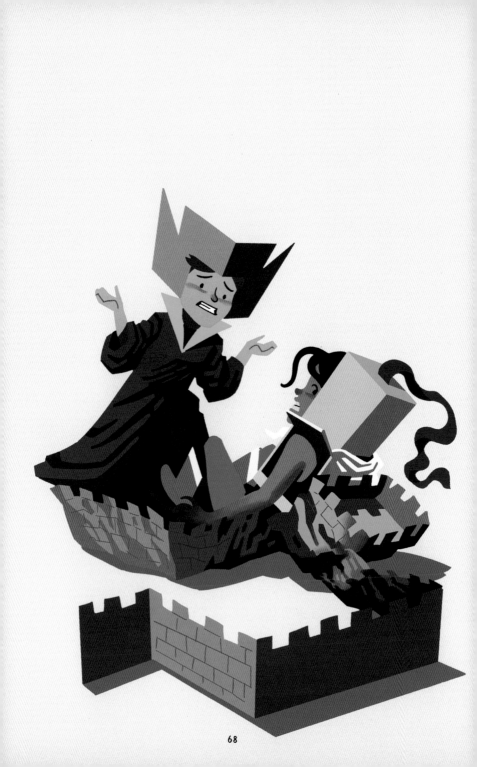

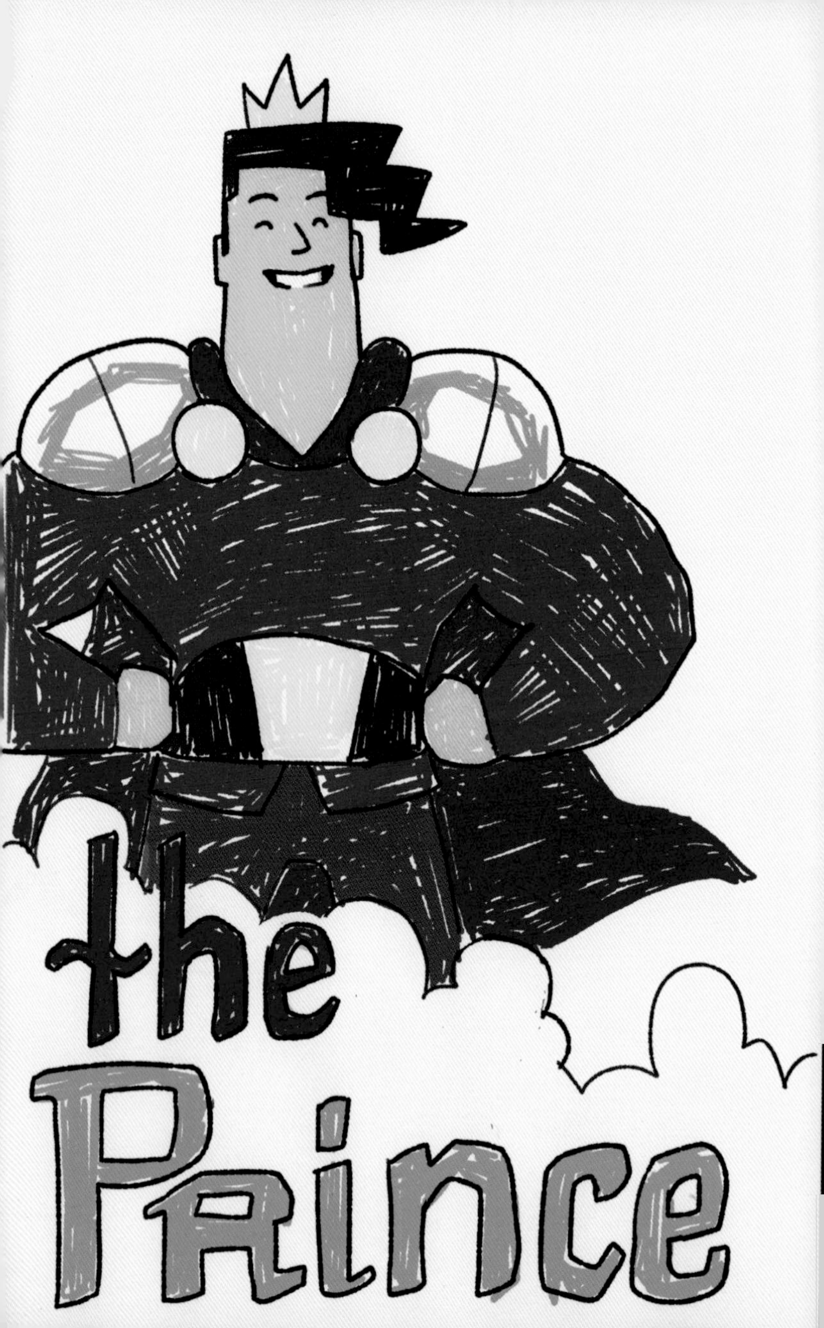
the
Prince

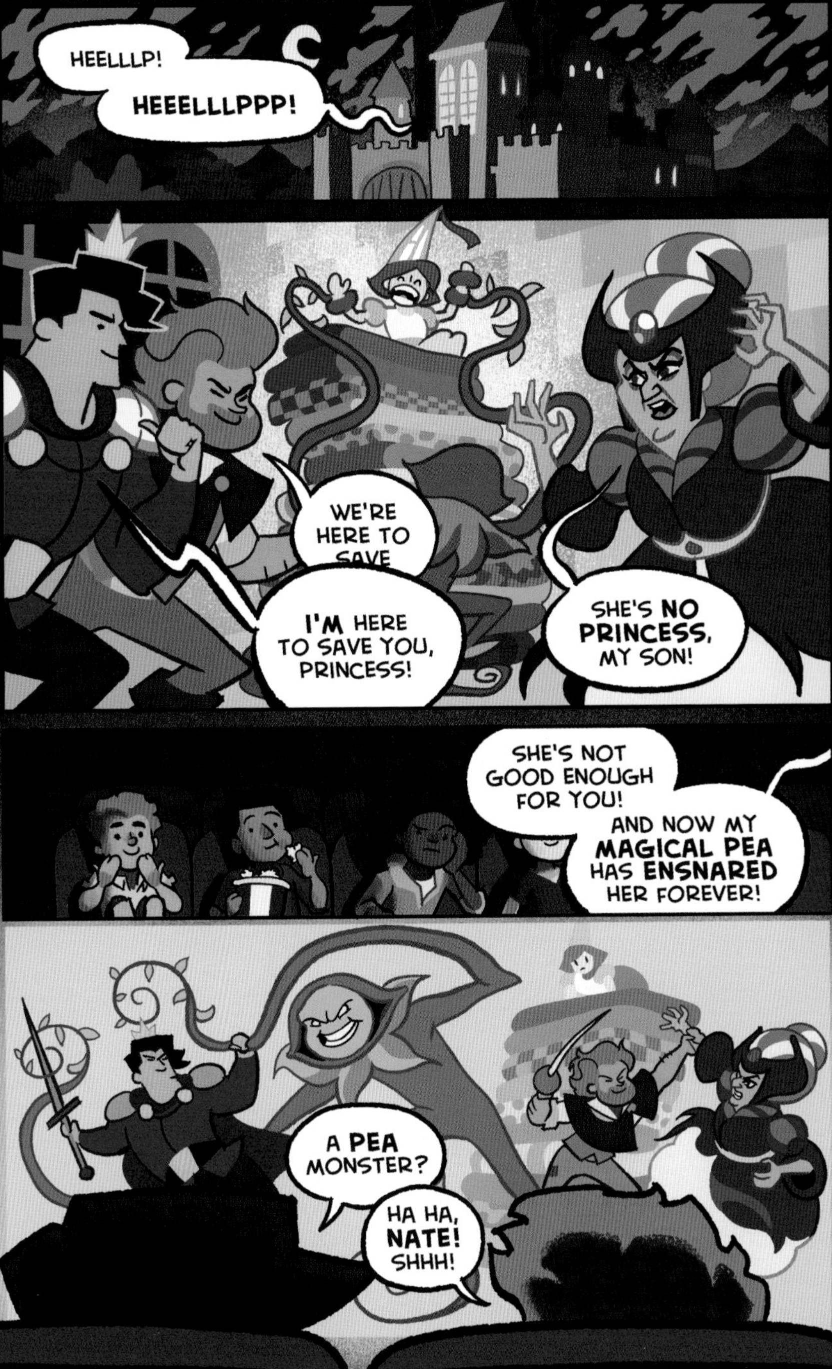

HEELLLP!
HEEELLLPPP!
WE'RE HERE TO SAVE
I'M HERE TO SAVE YOU, PRINCESS!
SHE'S NO PRINCESS, MY SON!
SHE'S NOT GOOD ENOUGH FOR YOU!
AND NOW MY MAGICAL PEA HAS ENSNARED HER FOREVER!
A PEA MONSTER?
HA HA, NATE! SHHH!

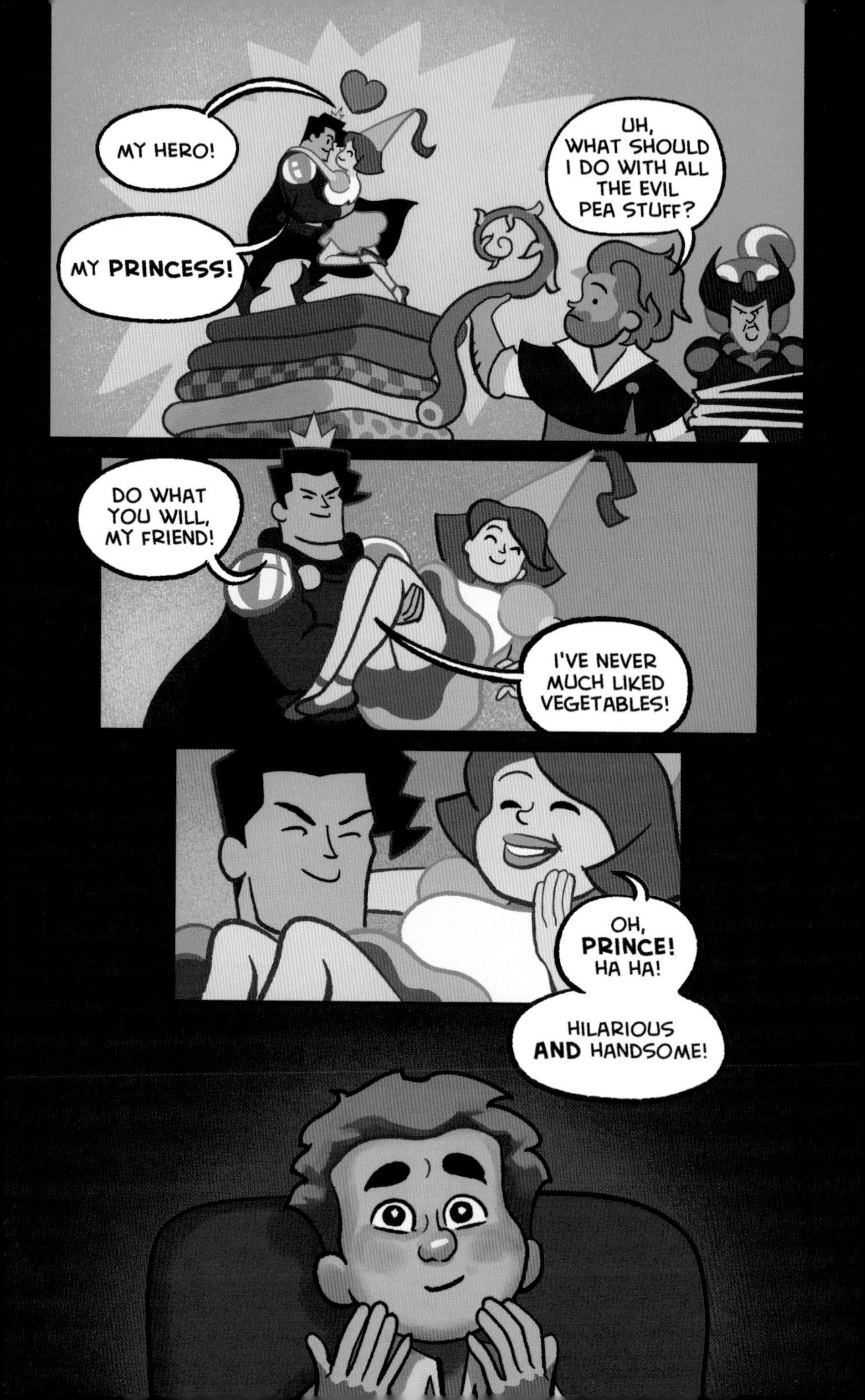
MY HERO!
MY PRINCESS!
UH, WHAT SHOULD I DO WITH ALL THE EVIL PEA STUFF?
DO WHAT YOU WILL, MY FRIEND!
I'VE NEVER MUCH LIKED VEGETABLES!
OH, PRINCE! HA HA!
HILARIOUS AND HANDSOME!

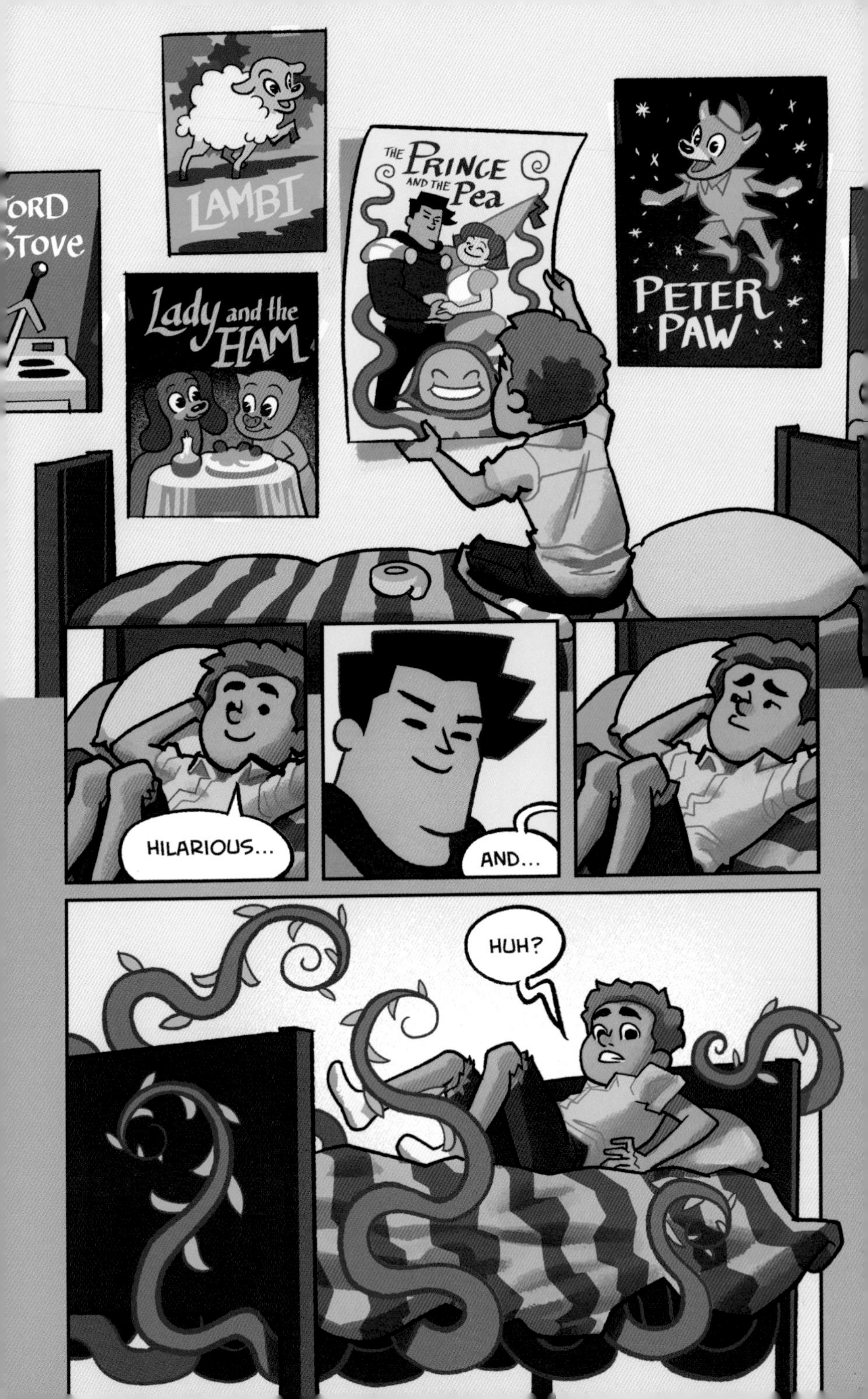
LAMBI
Lady and the HAM
THE PRINCE AND THE Pea
PETER PAW
HILARIOUS...
AND...
HUH?

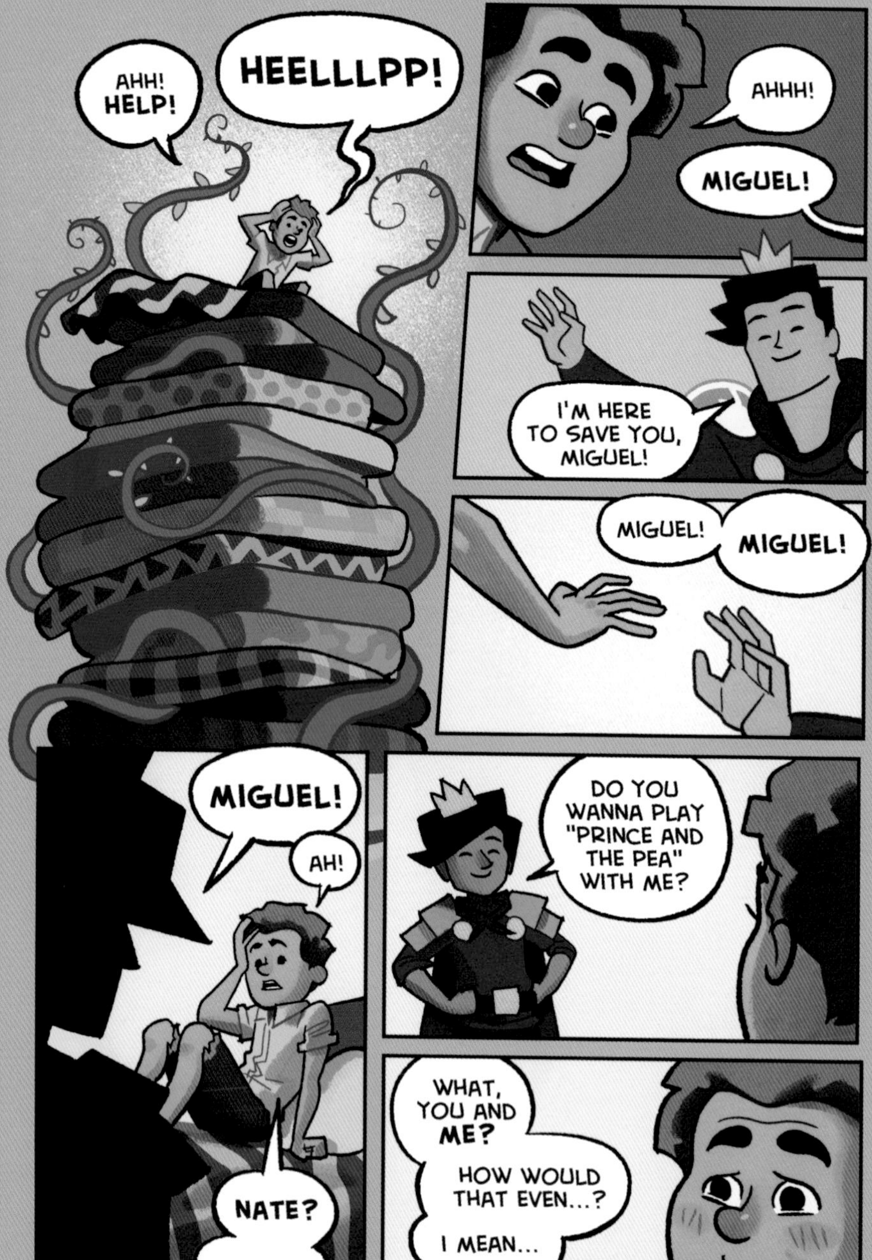

AHH! HELP!
HEELLLPP!
AHHH!
MIGUEL!
I'M HERE TO SAVE YOU, MIGUEL!
MIGUEL!
MIGUEL!
MIGUEL!
AH!
NATE?
WHAT...?
DO YOU WANNA PLAY "PRINCE AND THE PEA" WITH ME?
WHAT, YOU AND ME?
HOW WOULD THAT EVEN...?
I MEAN...
OKAY?

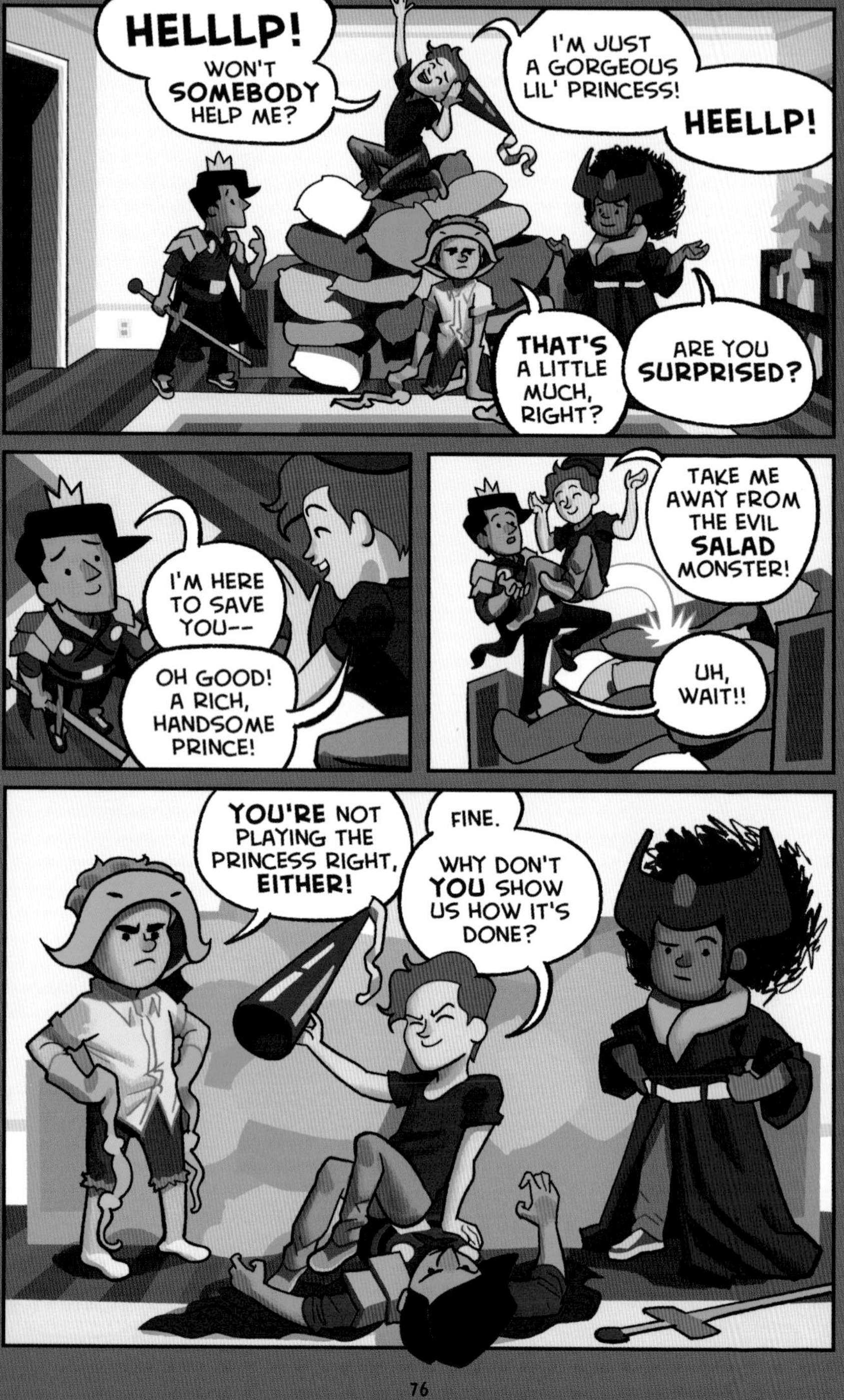
HELLLP! WON'T SOMEBODY HELP ME?
I'M JUST A GORGEOUS LIL' PRINCESS! HEELLP!
THAT'S A LITTLE MUCH, RIGHT?
ARE YOU SURPRISED?
I'M HERE TO SAVE YOU--
OH GOOD! A RICH, HANDSOME PRINCE!
TAKE ME AWAY FROM THE EVIL SALAD MONSTER!
UH, WAIT!!
YOU'RE NOT PLAYING THE PRINCESS RIGHT, EITHER!
FINE.
WHY DON'T YOU SHOW US HOW IT'S DONE?

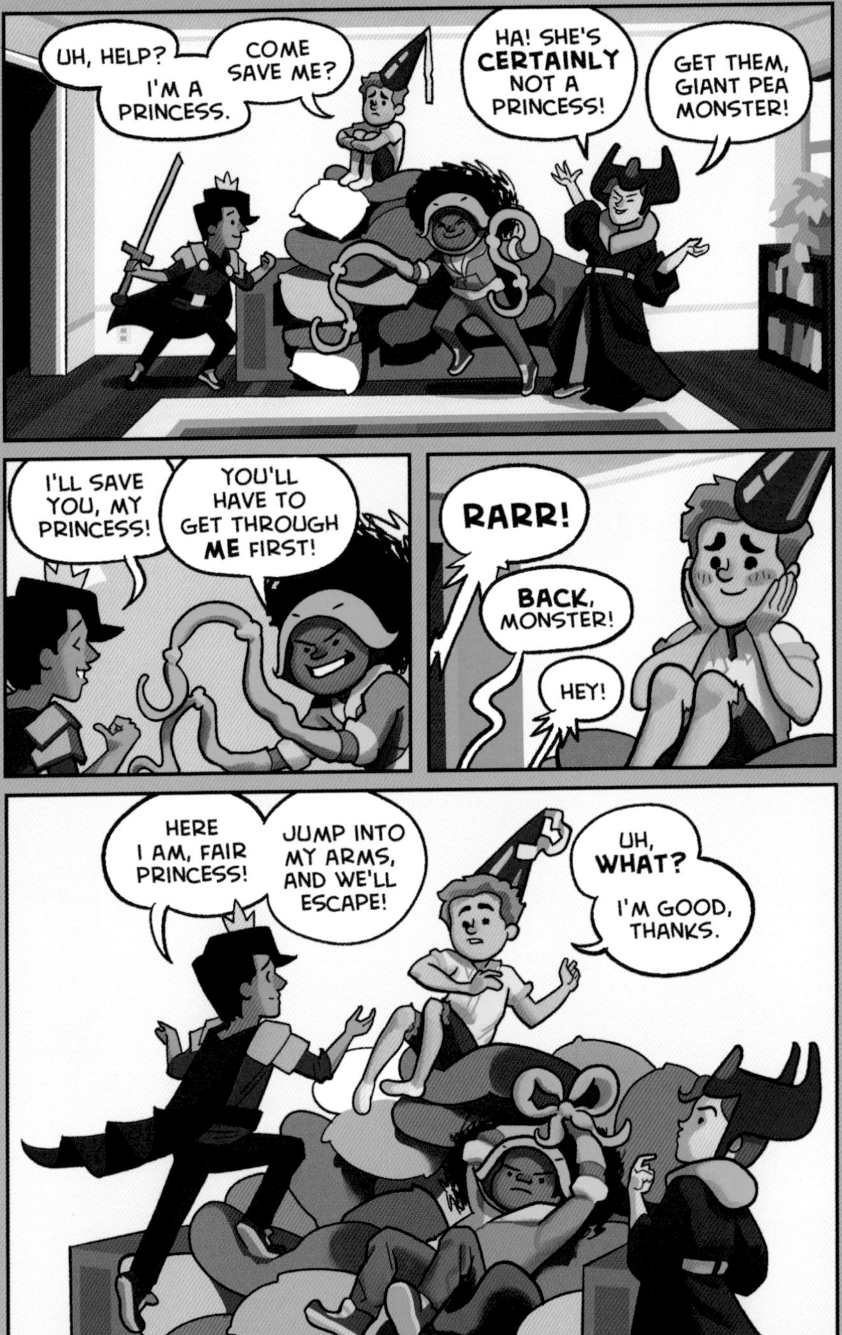
UH, HELP?
I'M A PRINCESS.
COME SAVE ME?
HA! SHE'S **CERTAINLY** NOT A PRINCESS!
GET THEM, GIANT PEA MONSTER!
I'LL SAVE YOU, MY PRINCESS!
YOU'LL HAVE TO GET THROUGH **ME** FIRST!
RARR!
BACK, MONSTER!
HEY!
HERE I AM, FAIR PRINCESS!
JUMP INTO MY ARMS, AND WE'LL ESCAPE!
UH, **WHAT?**
I'M GOOD, THANKS.

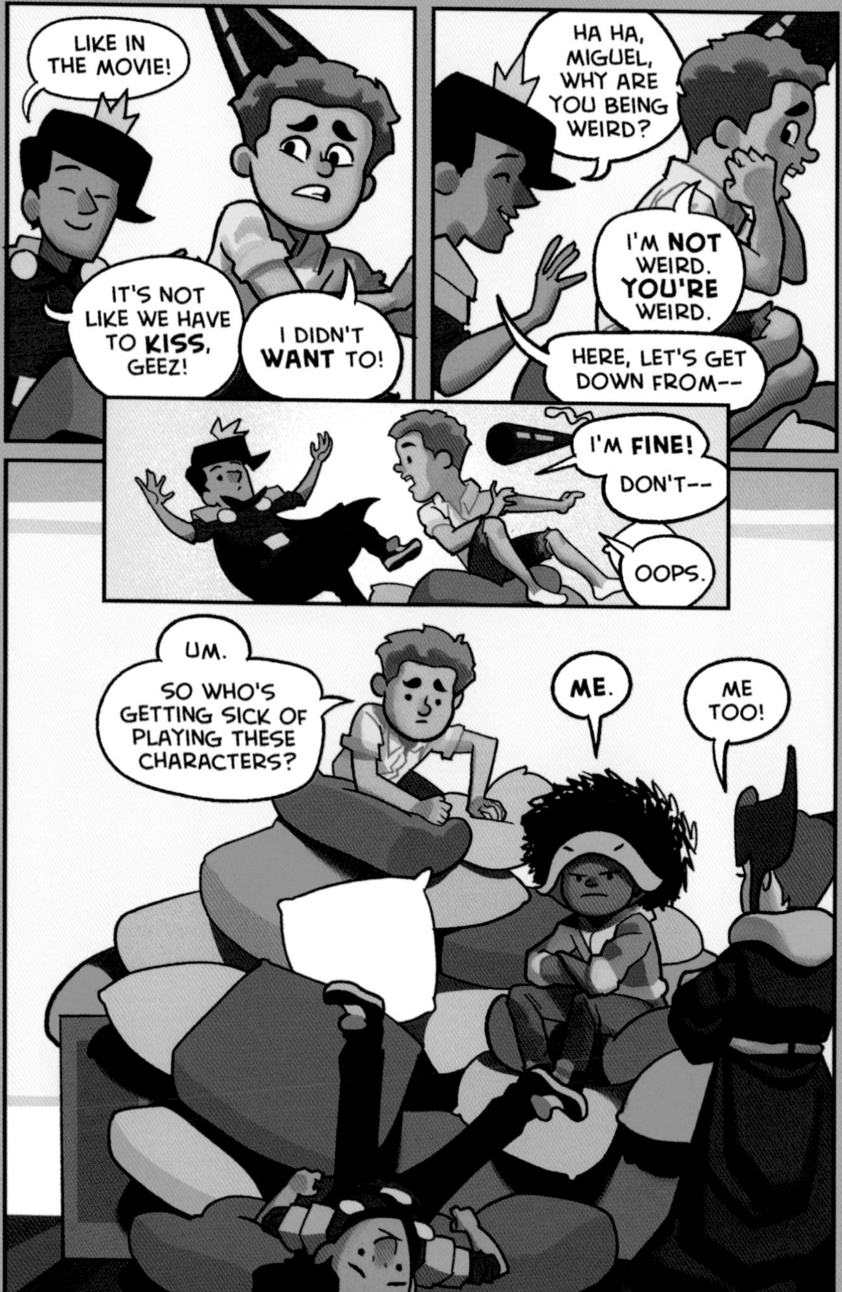
LIKE IN THE MOVIE!
IT'S NOT LIKE WE HAVE TO **KISS**, GEEZ!
I DIDN'T **WANT** TO!
HA HA, MIGUEL, WHY ARE YOU BEING WEIRD?
I'M **NOT** WEIRD. **YOU'RE** WEIRD.
HERE, LET'S GET DOWN FROM--
I'M **FINE!**
DON'T--
OOPS.
UM.
SO WHO'S GETTING SICK OF PLAYING THESE CHARACTERS?
ME.
ME TOO!

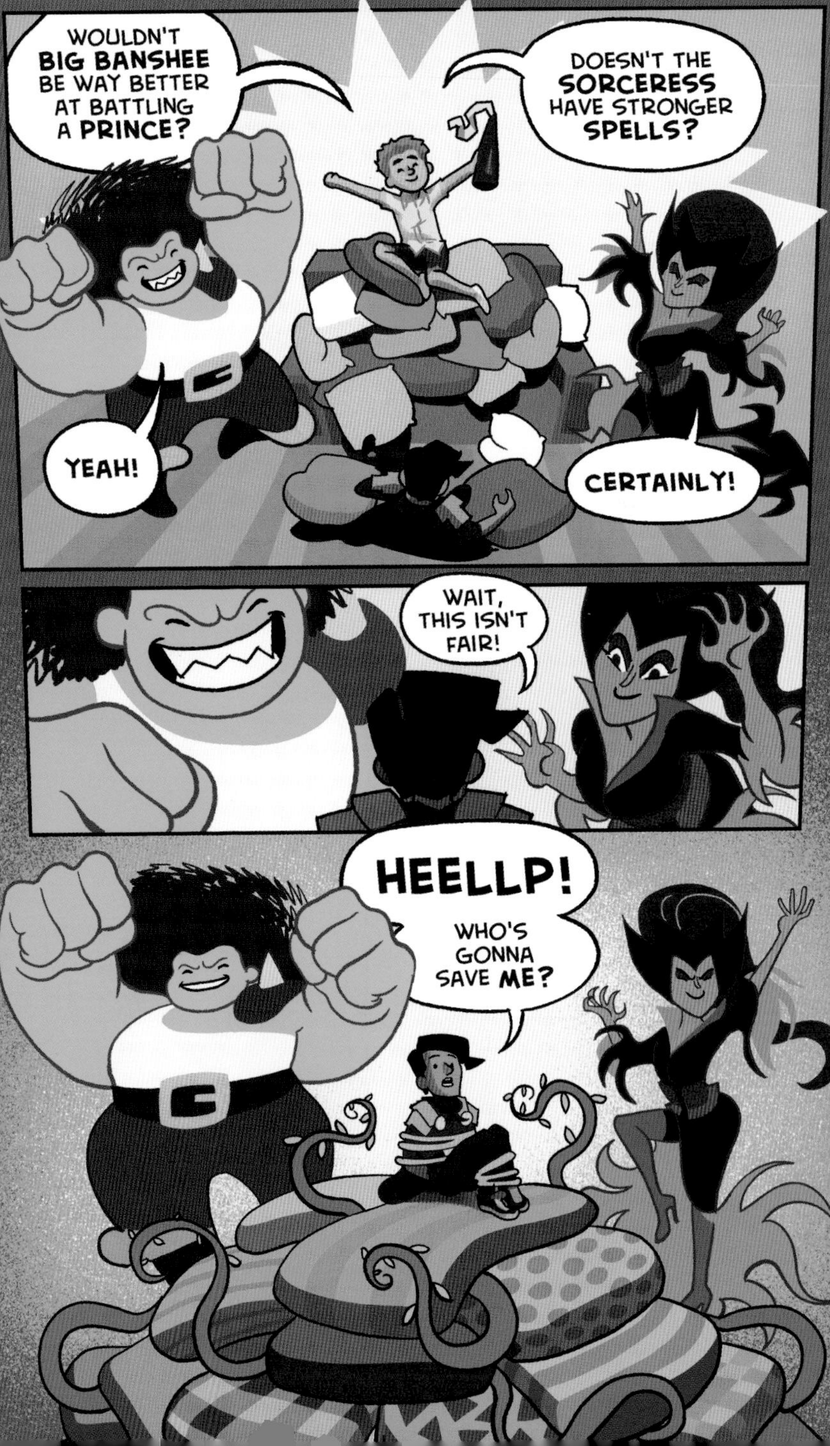
WOULDN'T BIG BANSHEE BE WAY BETTER AT BATTLING A PRINCE?
DOESN'T THE SORCERESS HAVE STRONGER SPELLS?
YEAH!
CERTAINLY!
WAIT, THIS ISN'T FAIR!
HEELLP!
WHO'S GONNA SAVE ME?

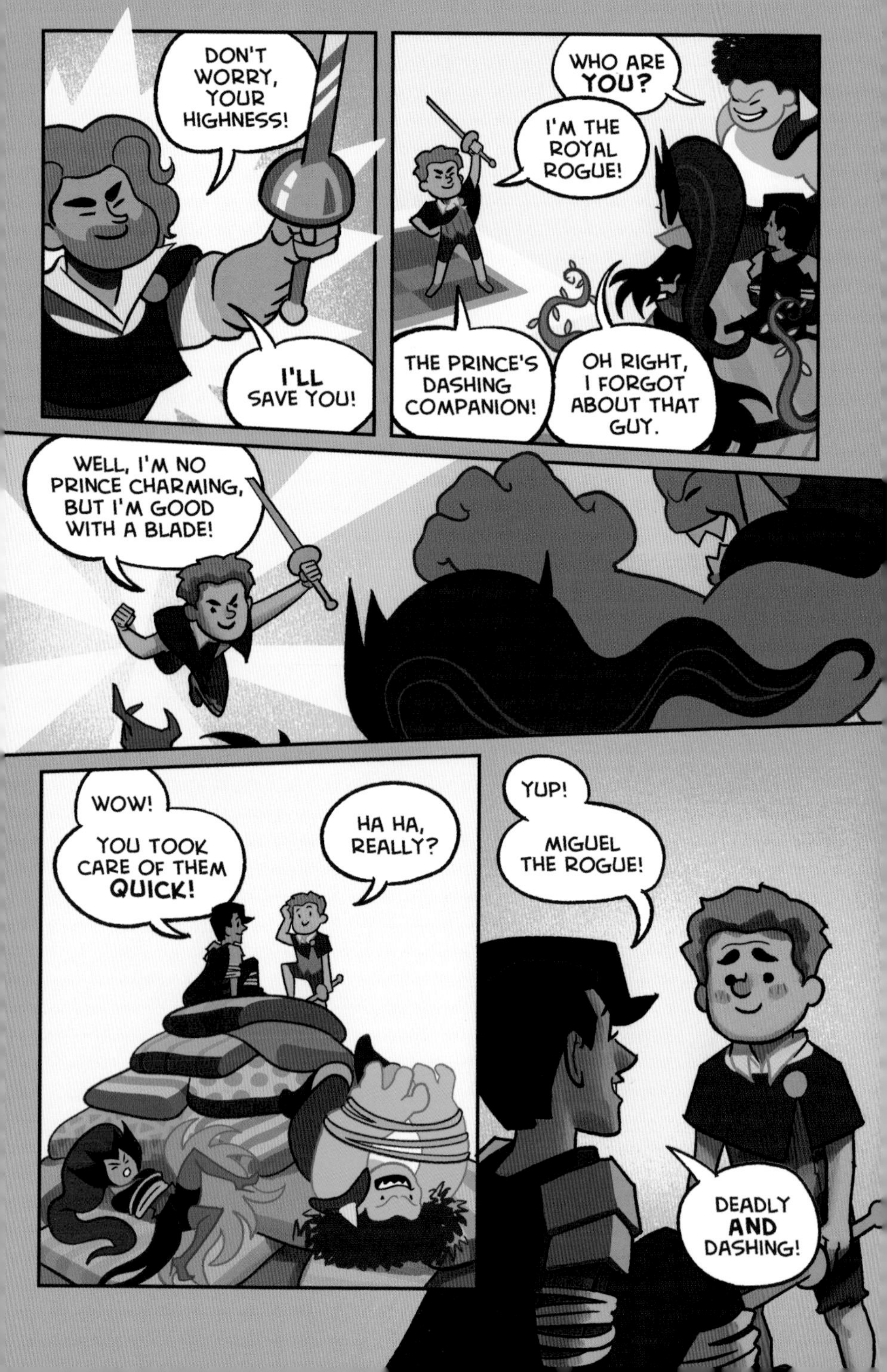
DON'T WORRY, YOUR HIGHNESS!
I'LL SAVE YOU!
WHO ARE YOU?
I'M THE ROYAL ROGUE!
THE PRINCE'S DASHING COMPANION!
OH RIGHT, I FORGOT ABOUT THAT GUY.
WELL, I'M NO PRINCE CHARMING, BUT I'M GOOD WITH A BLADE!
WOW!
YOU TOOK CARE OF THEM QUICK!
HA HA, REALLY?
YUP!
MIGUEL THE ROGUE!
DEADLY AND DASHING!

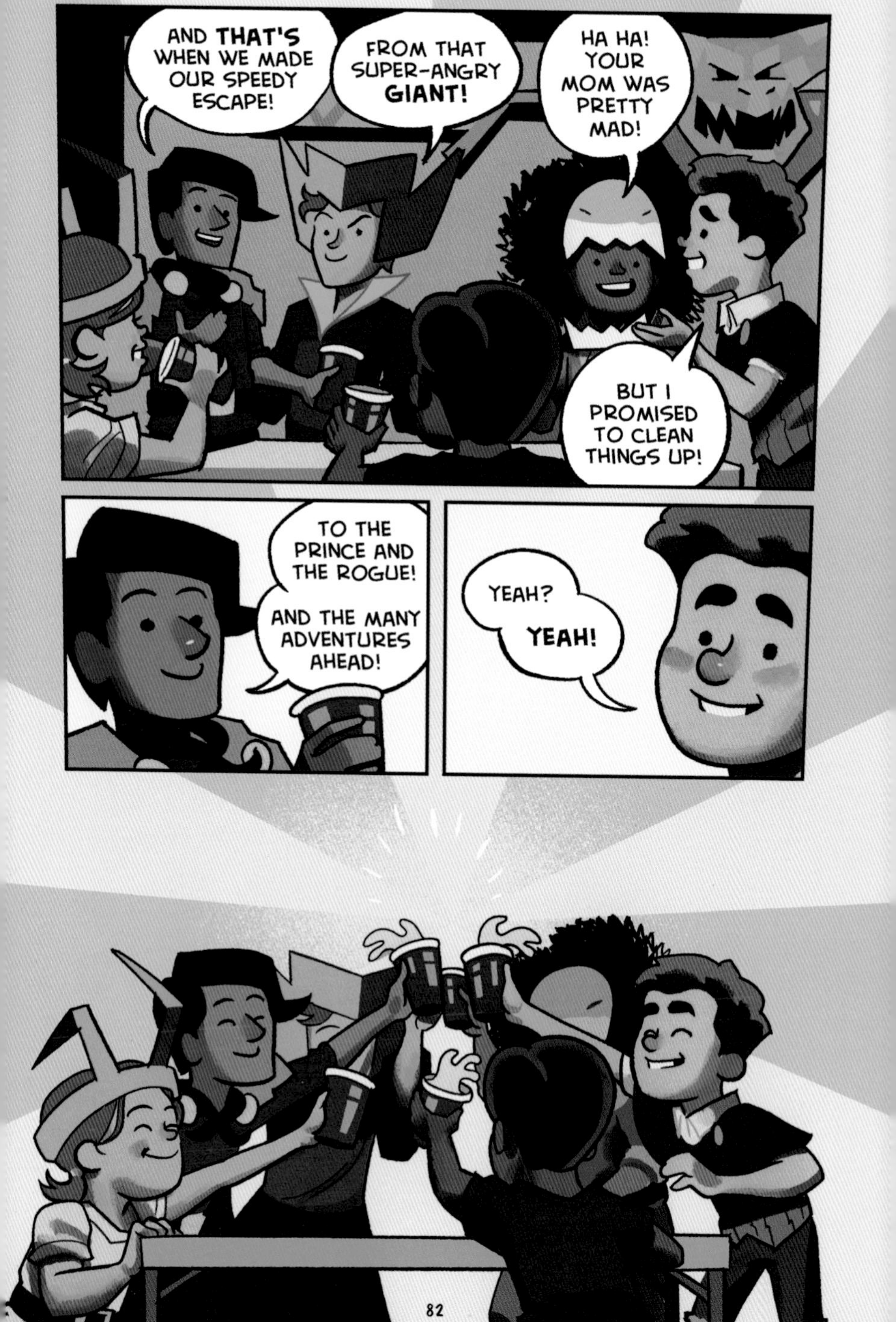
AND THAT'S WHEN WE MADE OUR SPEEDY ESCAPE!
FROM THAT SUPER-ANGRY GIANT!
HA HA! YOUR MOM WAS PRETTY MAD!
BUT I PROMISED TO CLEAN THINGS UP!
TO THE PRINCE AND THE ROGUE!
AND THE MANY ADVENTURES AHEAD!
YEAH?
YEAH!

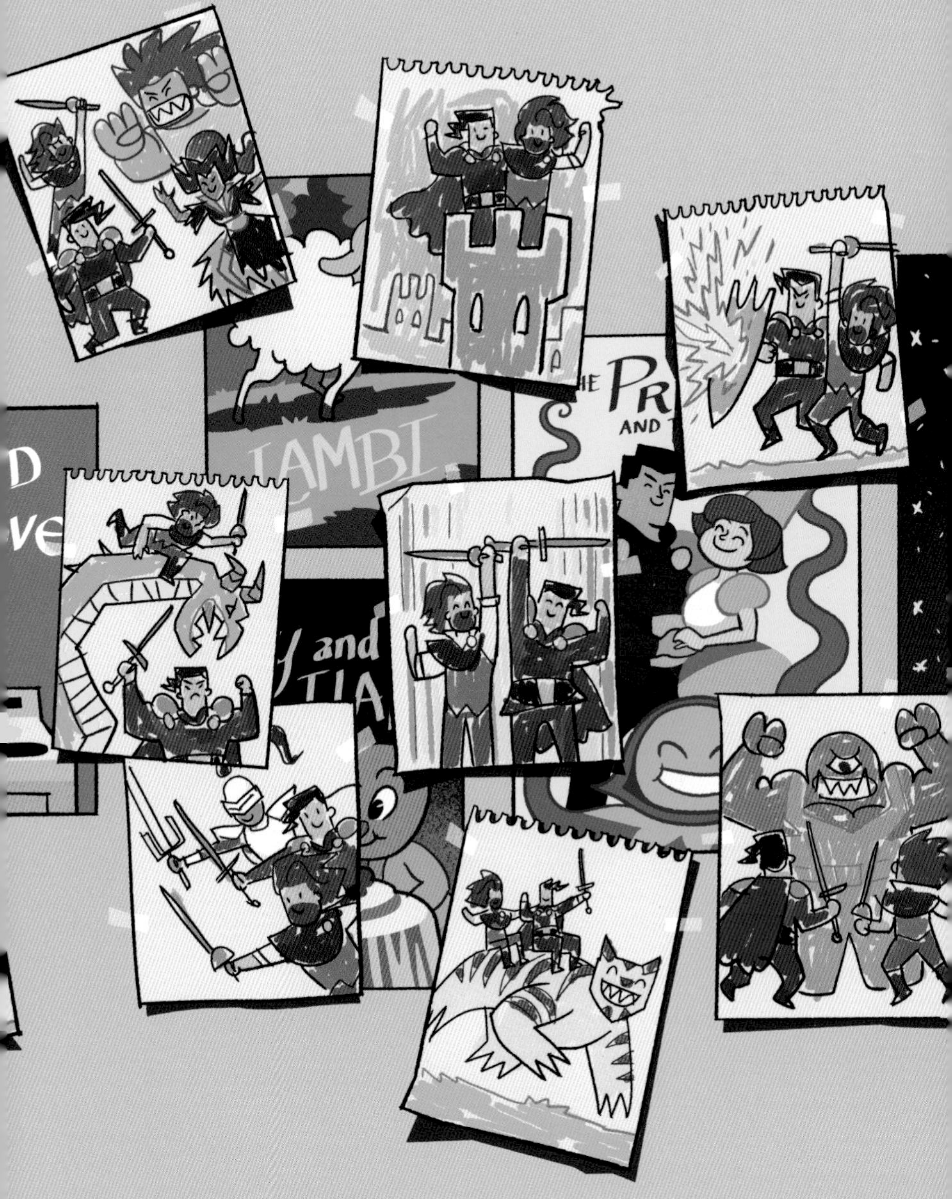
LAMBI
AND
and

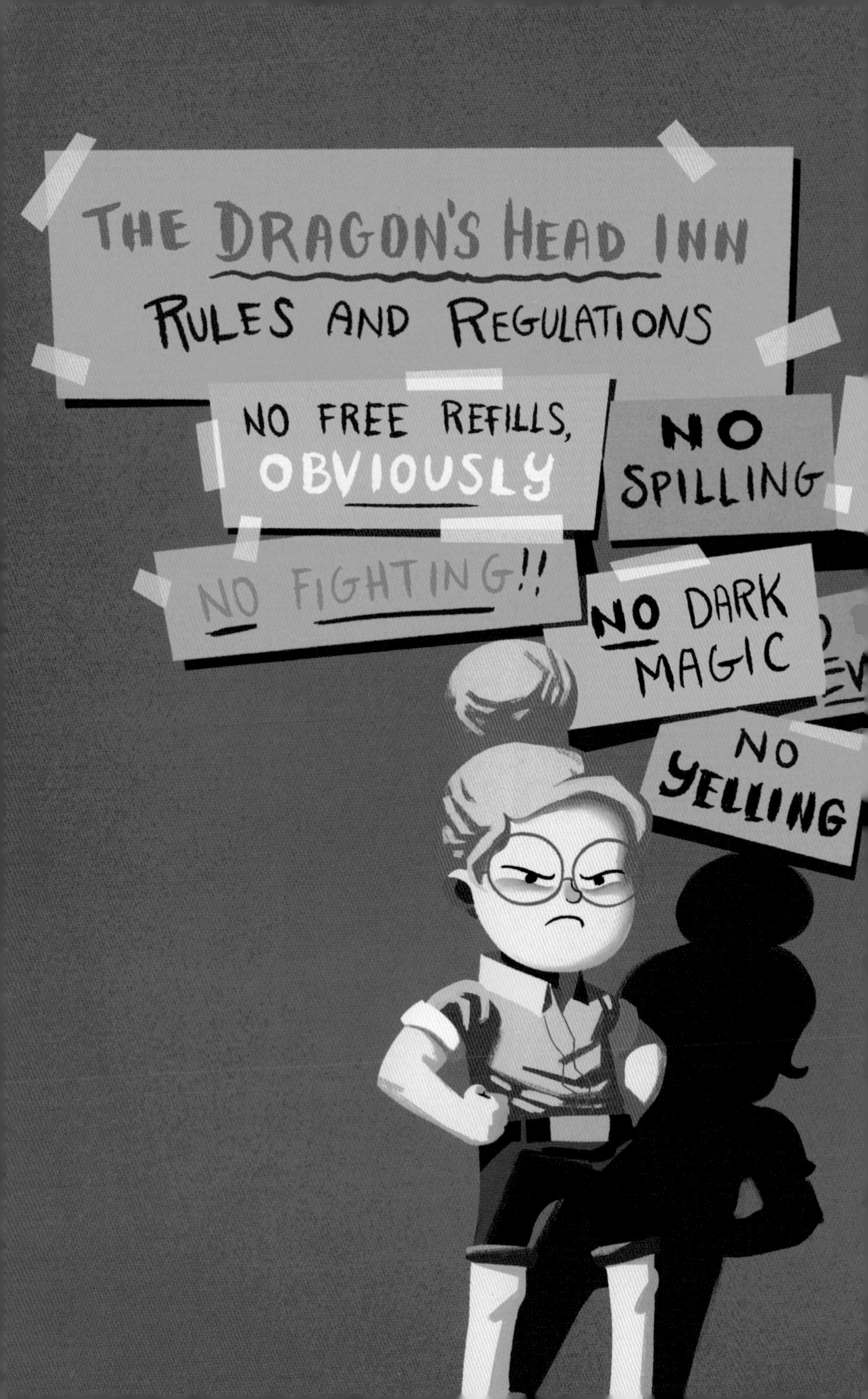
THE DRAGON'S HEAD INN
RULES AND REGULATIONS
NO FREE REFILLS, OBVIOUSLY
NO SPILLING
NO FIGHTING!!
NO DARK MAGIC
NO YELLING

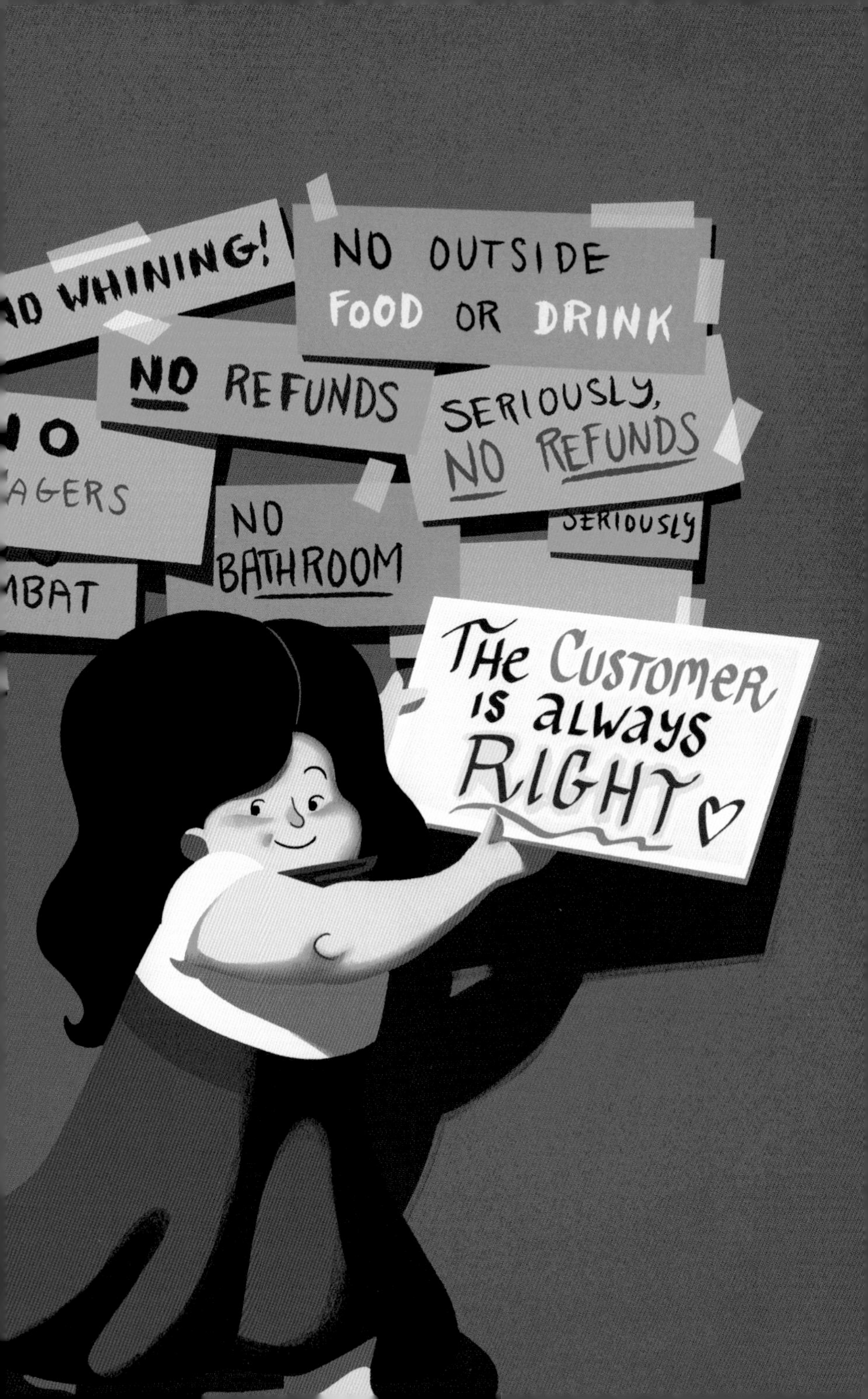
NO WHINING!
NO OUTSIDE FOOD OR DRINK
NO REFUNDS
SERIOUSLY, NO REFUNDS
AGERS
NO BATHROOM
SERIOUSLY
BAT
The Customer is always RIGHT

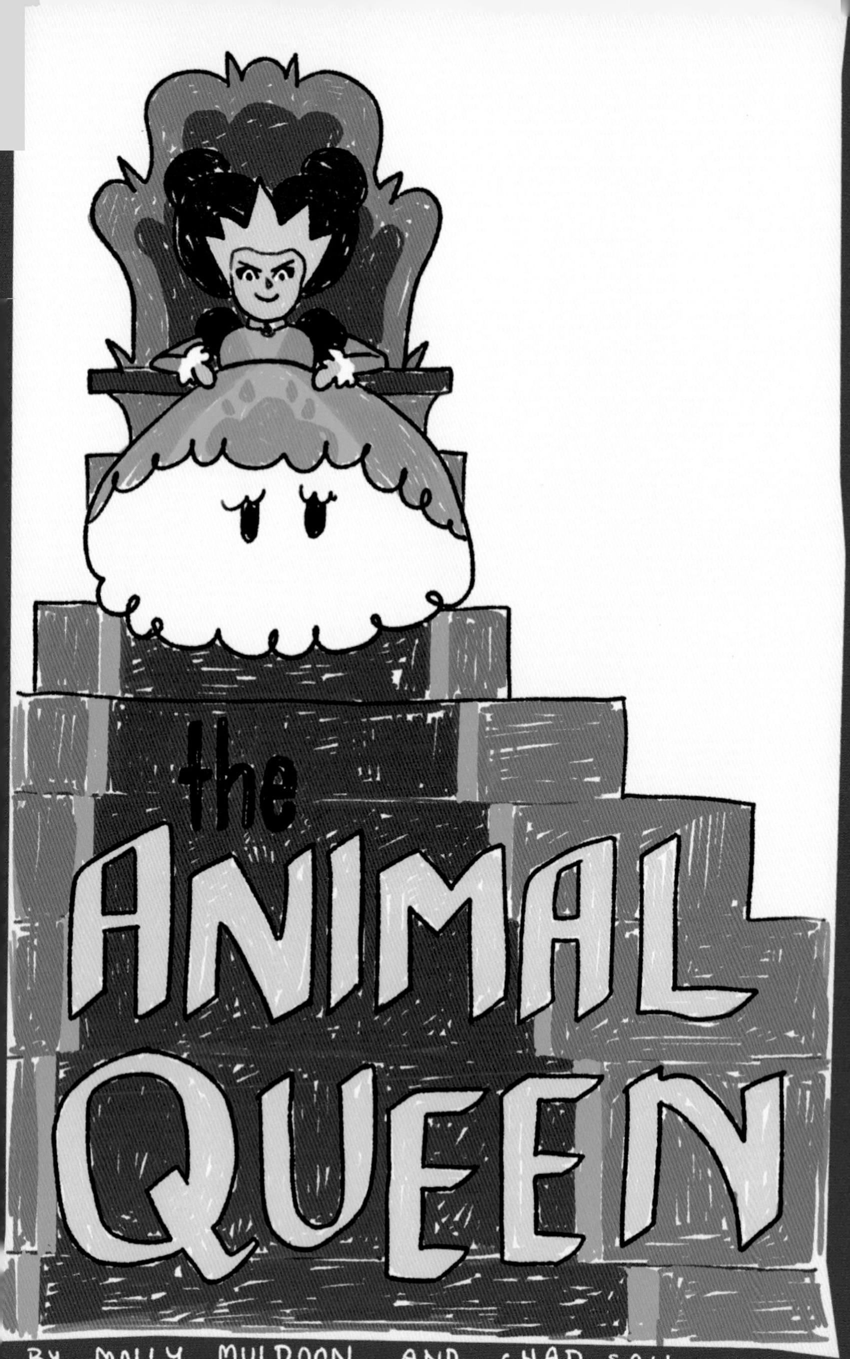
the ANIMAL QUEEN
BY MOLLY MULDOON AND CHAD SELL

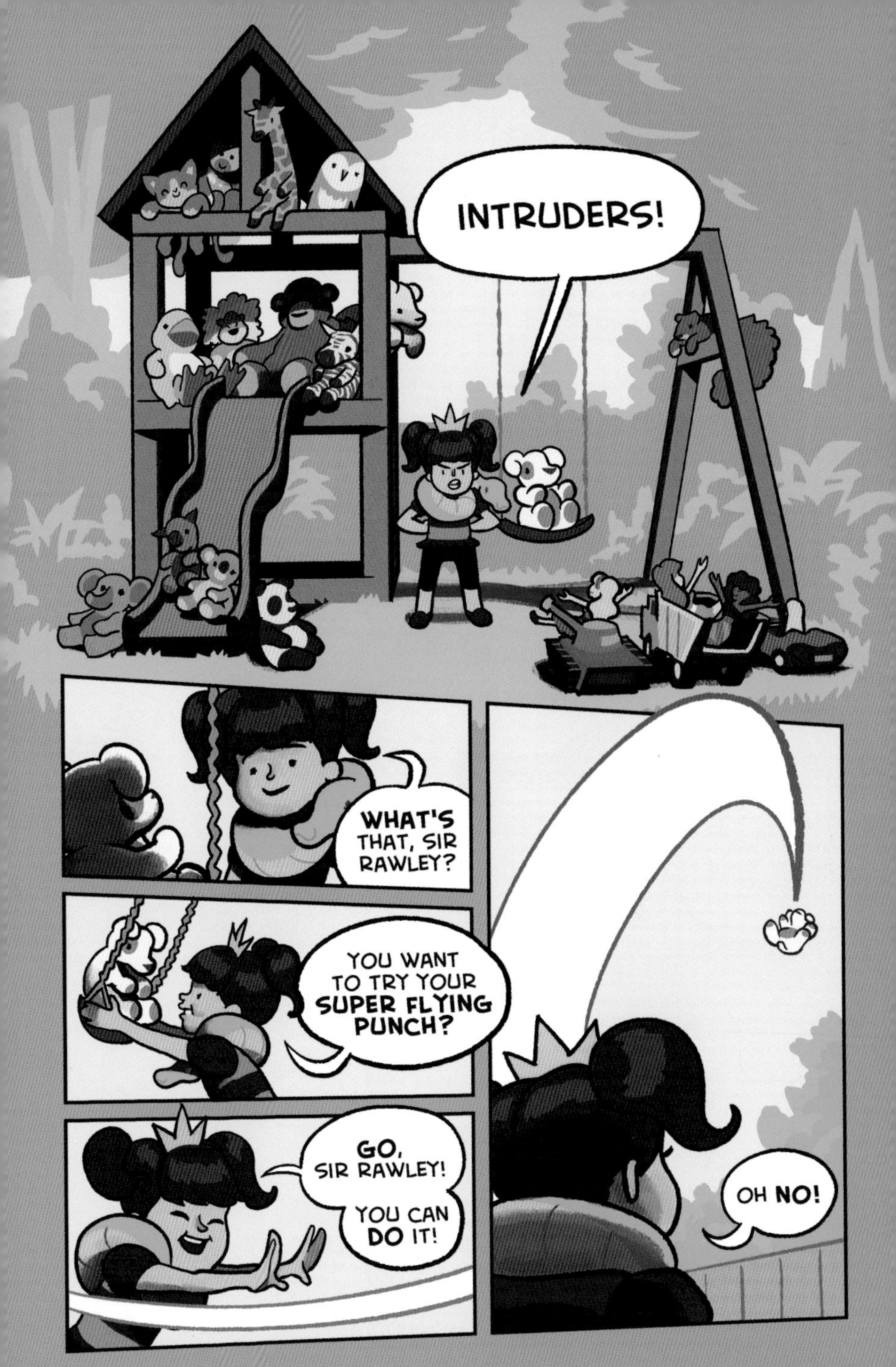
INTRUDERS!
WHAT'S THAT, SIR RAWLEY?
YOU WANT TO TRY YOUR SUPER FLYING PUNCH?
GO, SIR RAWLEY!
YOU CAN DO IT!
OH NO!

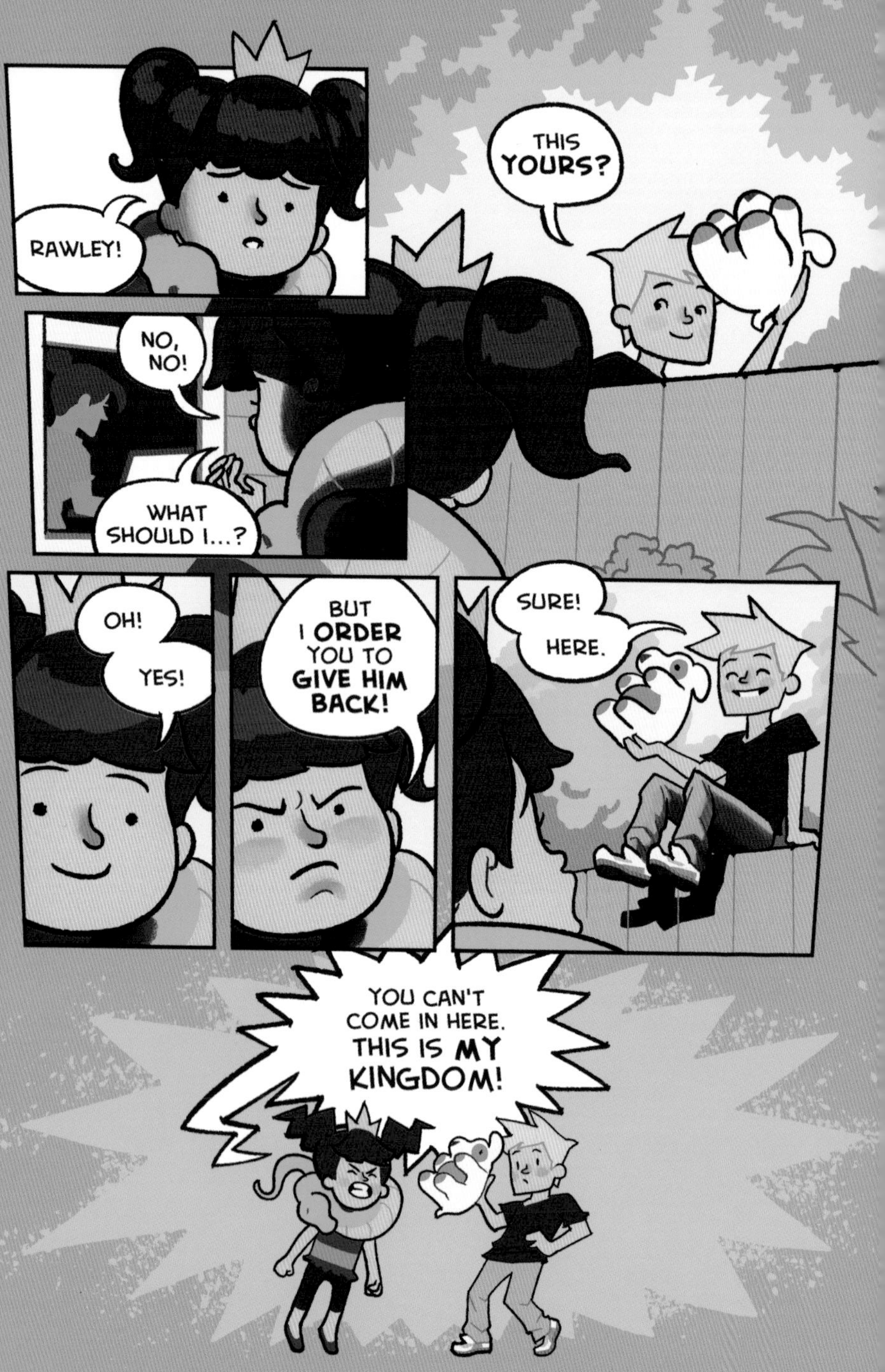
RAWLEY!
THIS YOURS?
NO, NO!
WHAT SHOULD I...?
OH!
YES!
BUT I ORDER YOU TO GIVE HIM BACK!
SURE!
HERE.
YOU CAN'T COME IN HERE. THIS IS MY KINGDOM!

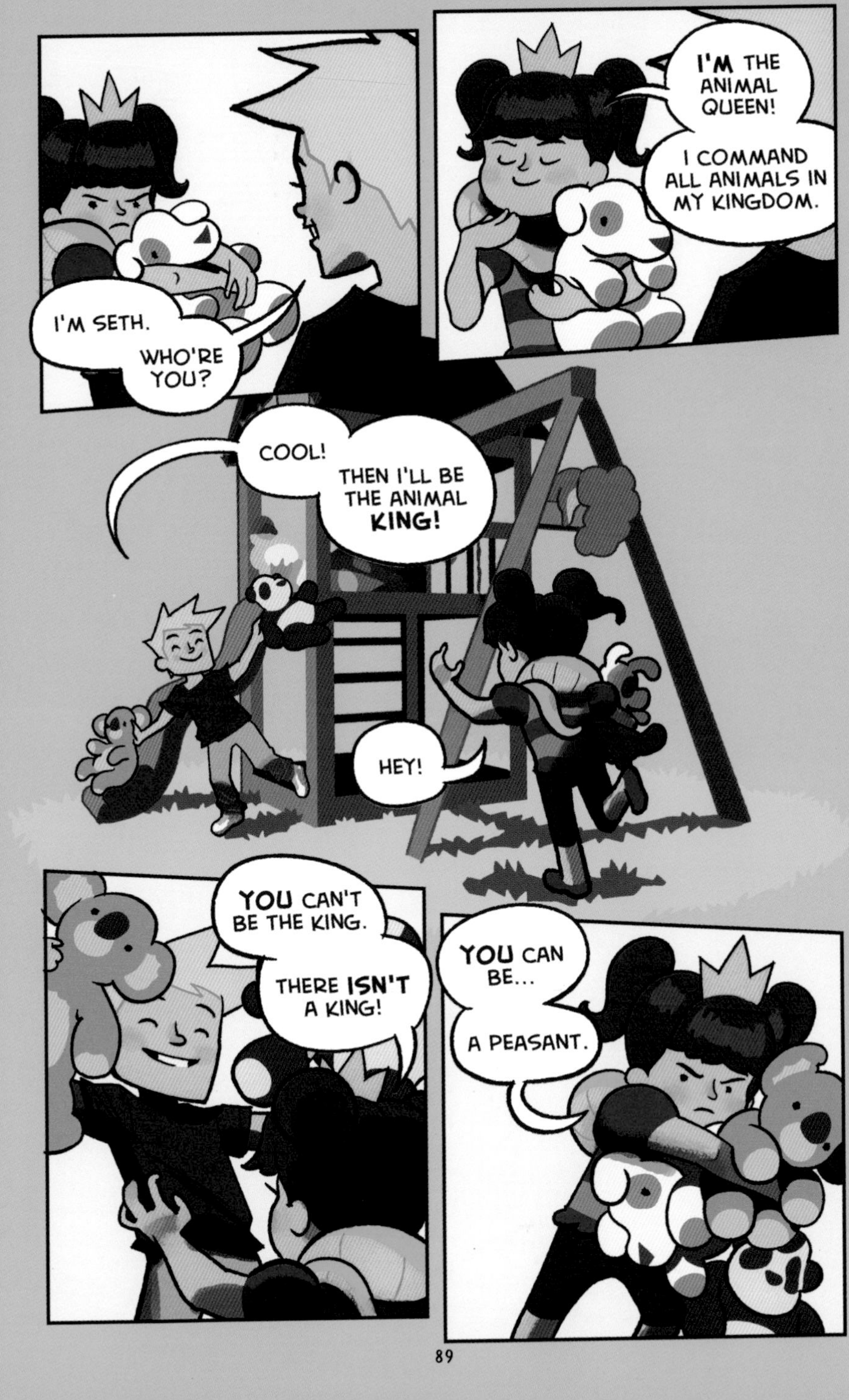
I'M SETH.
WHO'RE YOU?
I'M THE ANIMAL QUEEN!
I COMMAND ALL ANIMALS IN MY KINGDOM.
COOL!
THEN I'LL BE THE ANIMAL KING!
HEY!
YOU CAN'T BE THE KING.
THERE ISN'T A KING!
YOU CAN BE...
A PEASANT.

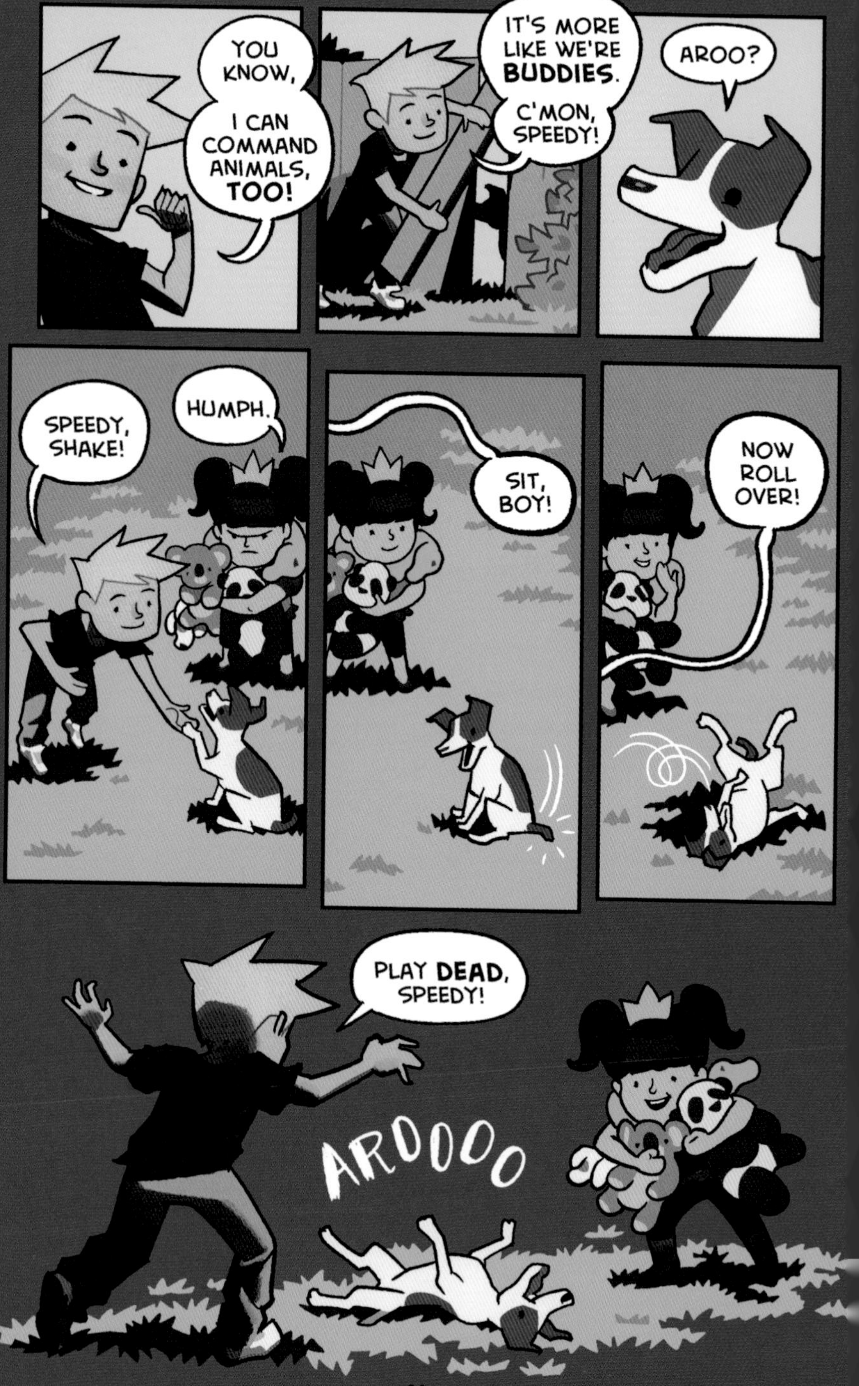
YOU KNOW,
I CAN COMMAND ANIMALS, TOO!
IT'S MORE LIKE WE'RE BUDDIES.
C'MON, SPEEDY!
AROO?
SPEEDY, SHAKE!
HUMPH.
SIT, BOY!
NOW ROLL OVER!
PLAY DEAD, SPEEDY!
ARDOOO

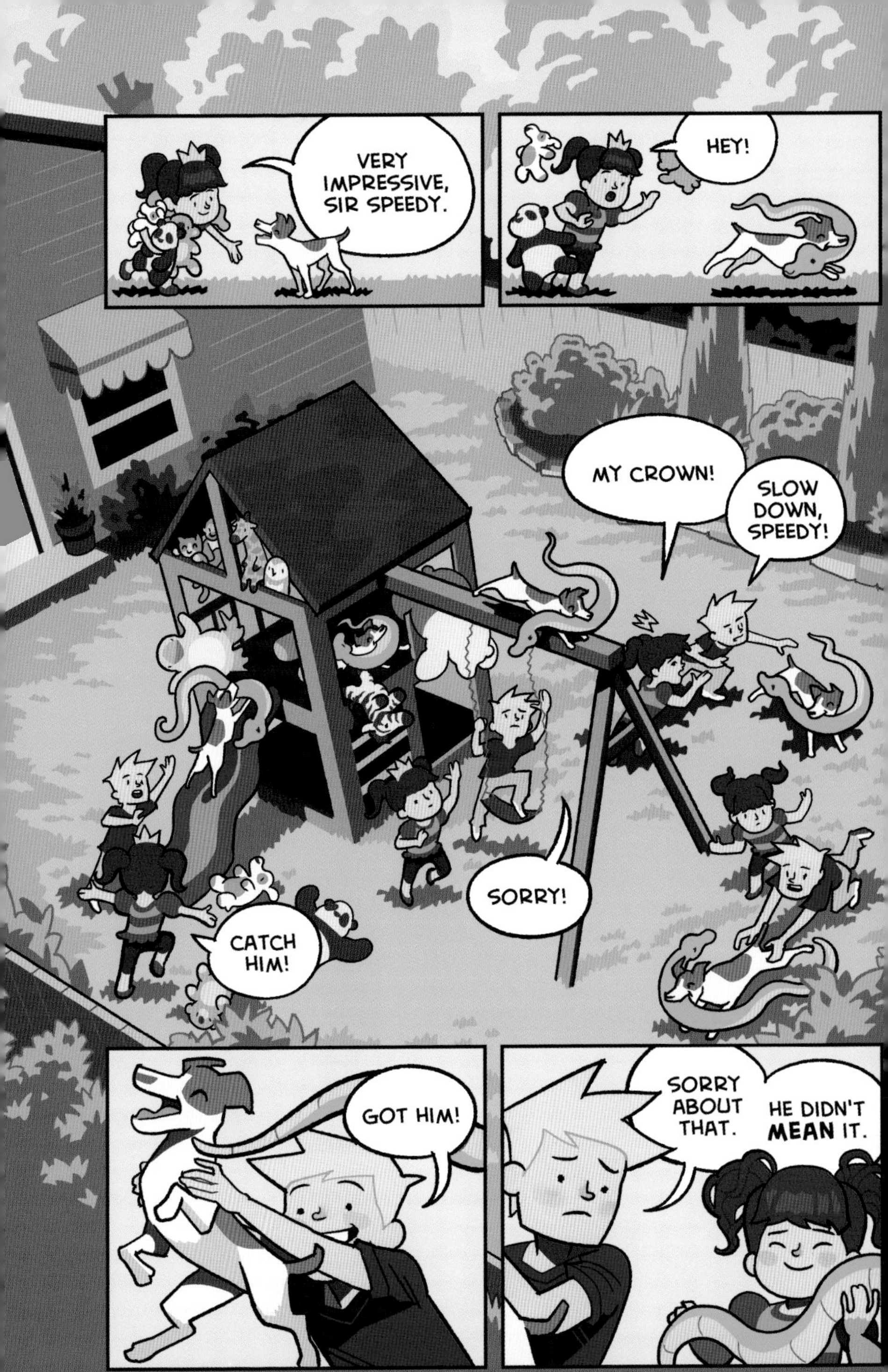
VERY IMPRESSIVE, SIR SPEEDY.
HEY!
MY CROWN!
SLOW DOWN, SPEEDY!
SORRY!
CATCH HIM!
GOT HIM!
SORRY ABOUT THAT.
HE DIDN'T **MEAN** IT.

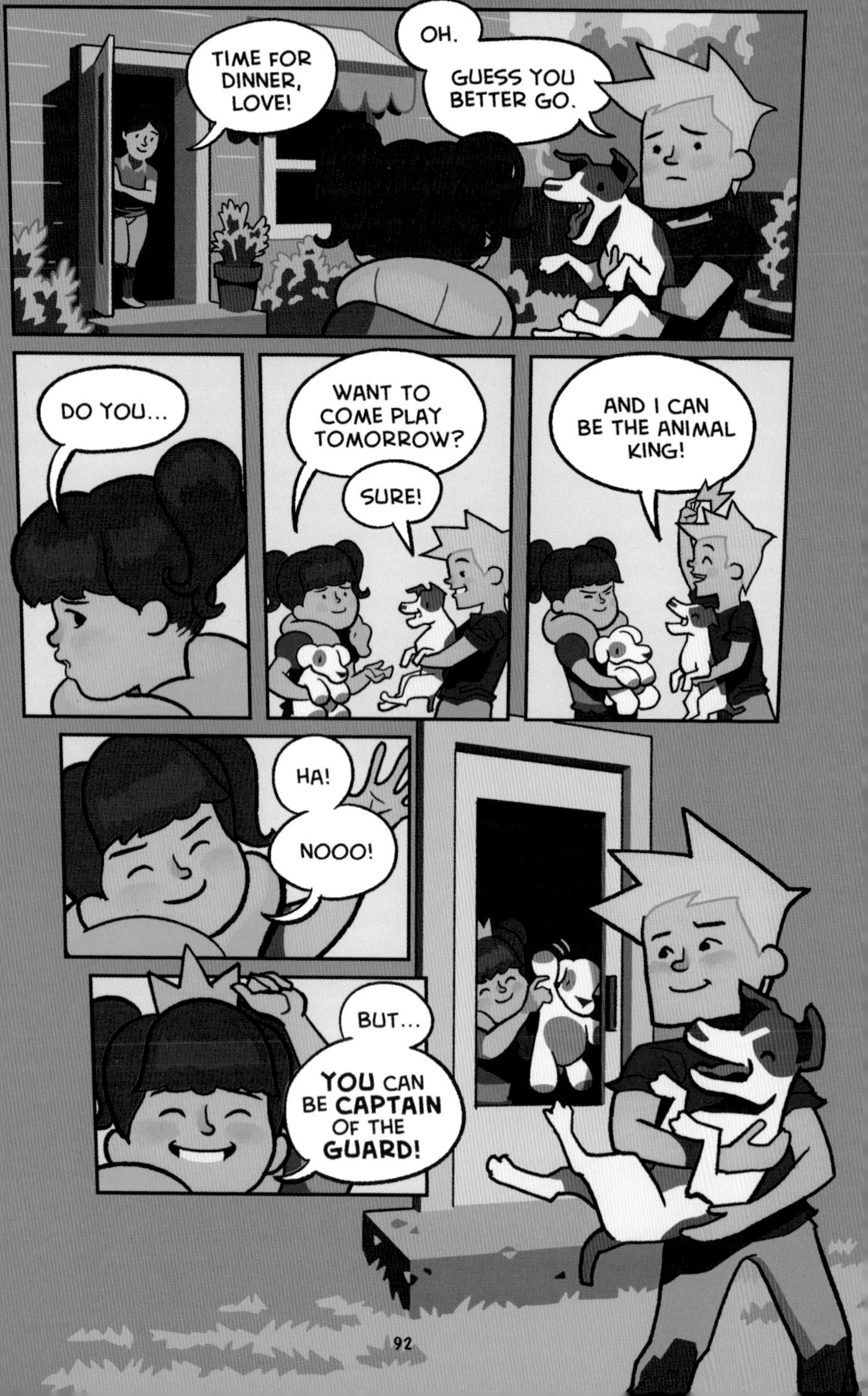
TIME FOR DINNER, LOVE!
OH.
GUESS YOU BETTER GO.
DO YOU...
WANT TO COME PLAY TOMORROW?
SURE!
AND I CAN BE THE ANIMAL KING!
HA!
NOOO!
BUT...
YOU CAN BE **CAPTAIN** OF THE **GUARD!**

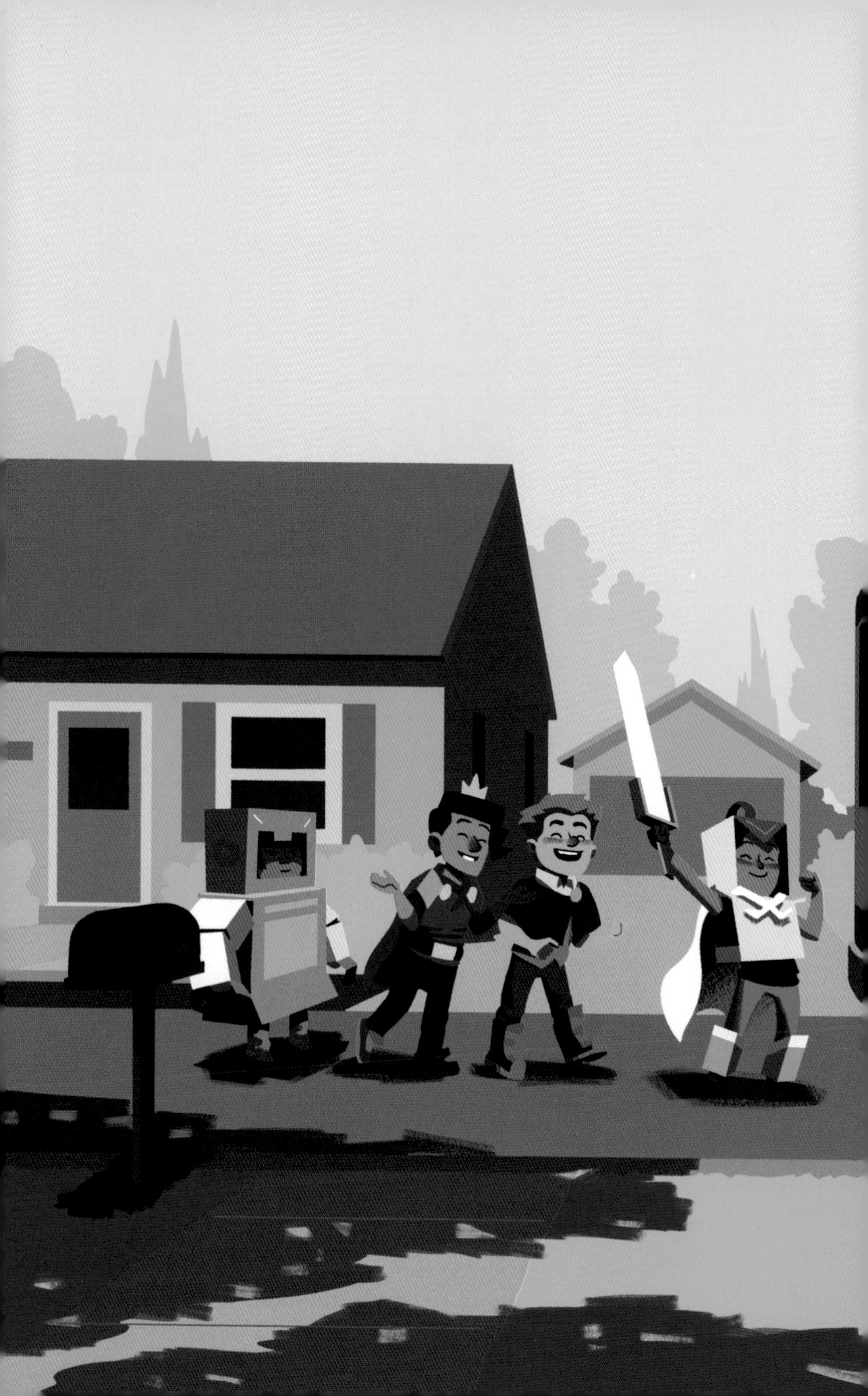

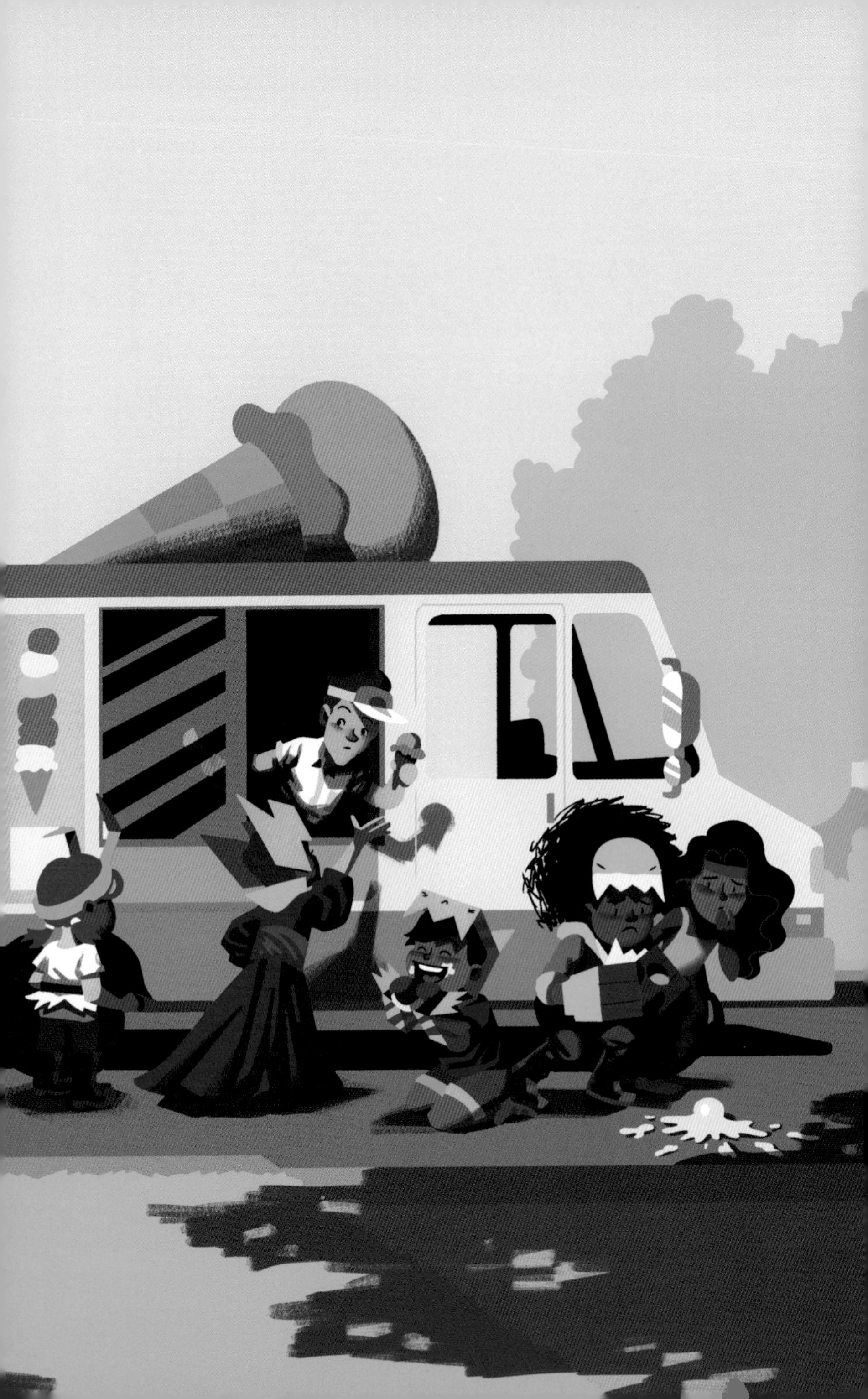

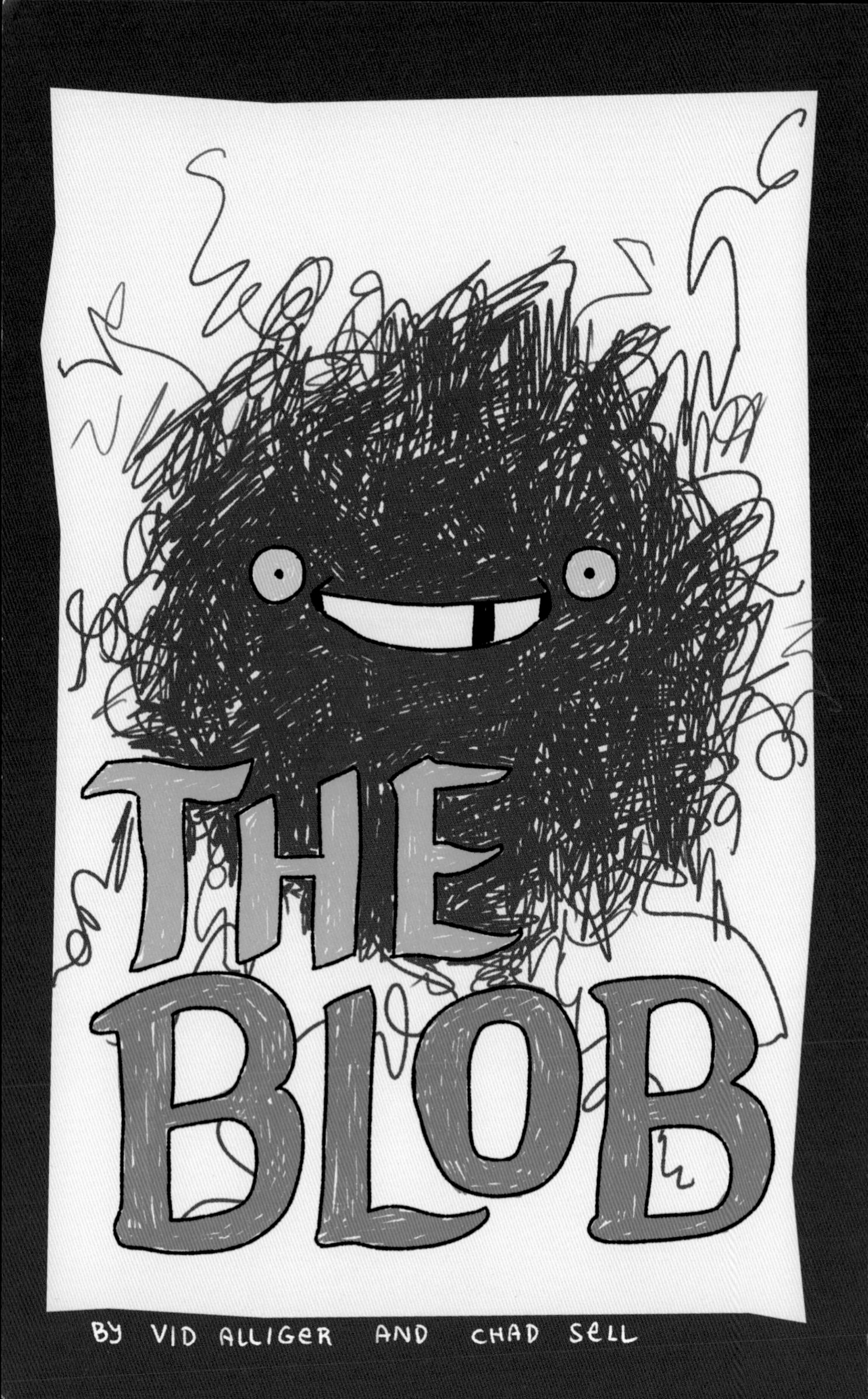
THE
BLOB
BY VID ALLIGER AND CHAD SELL

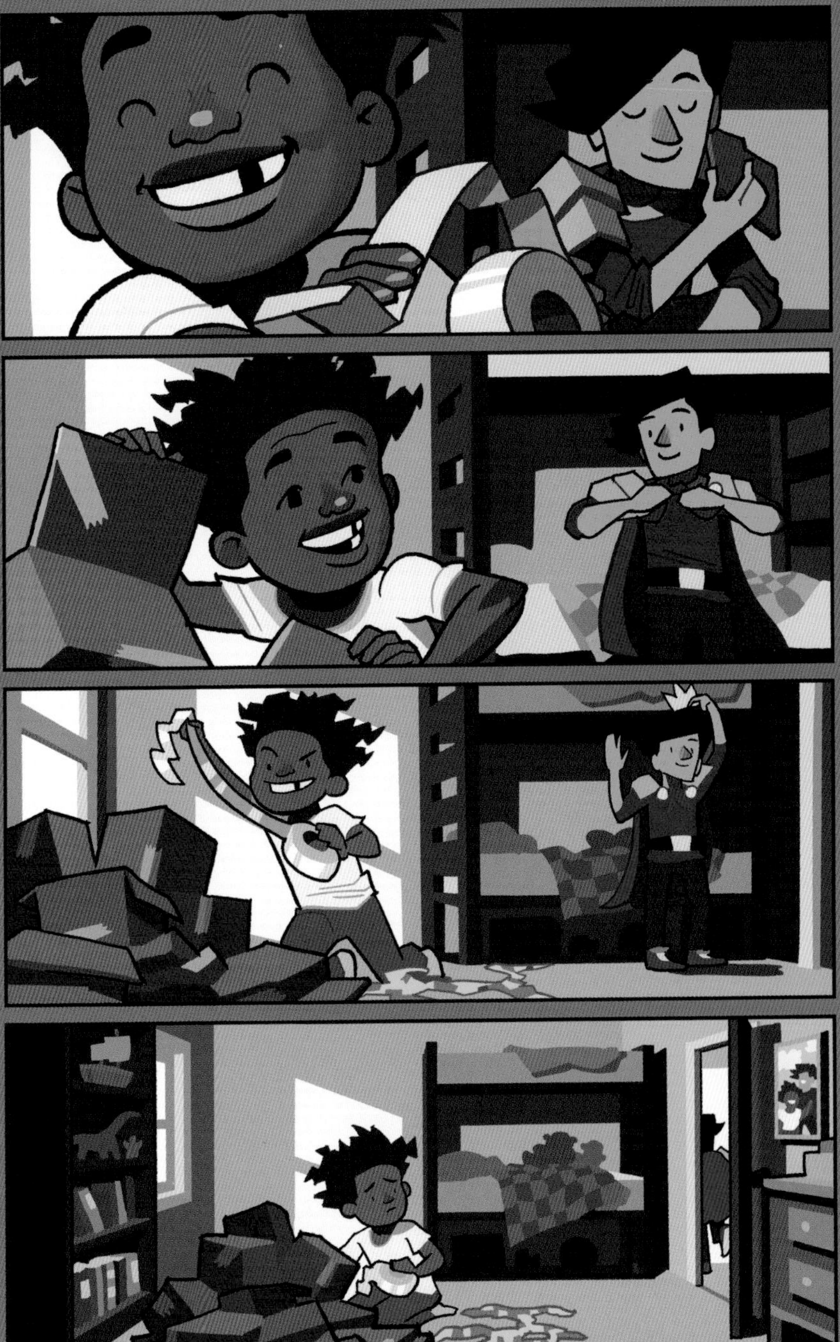

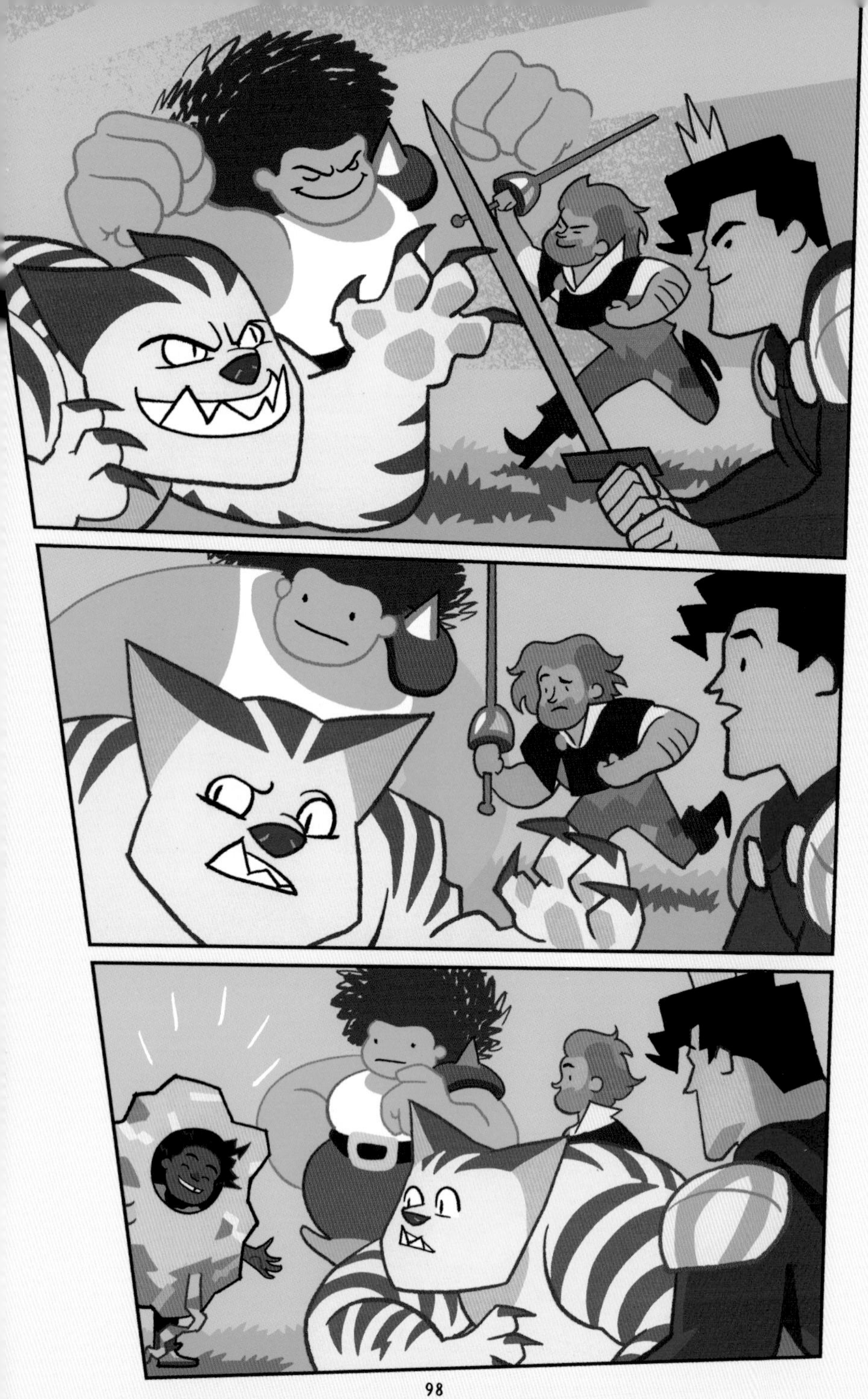

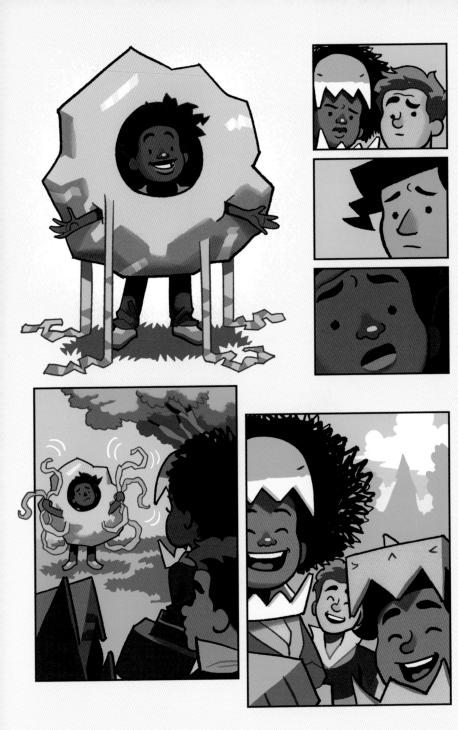

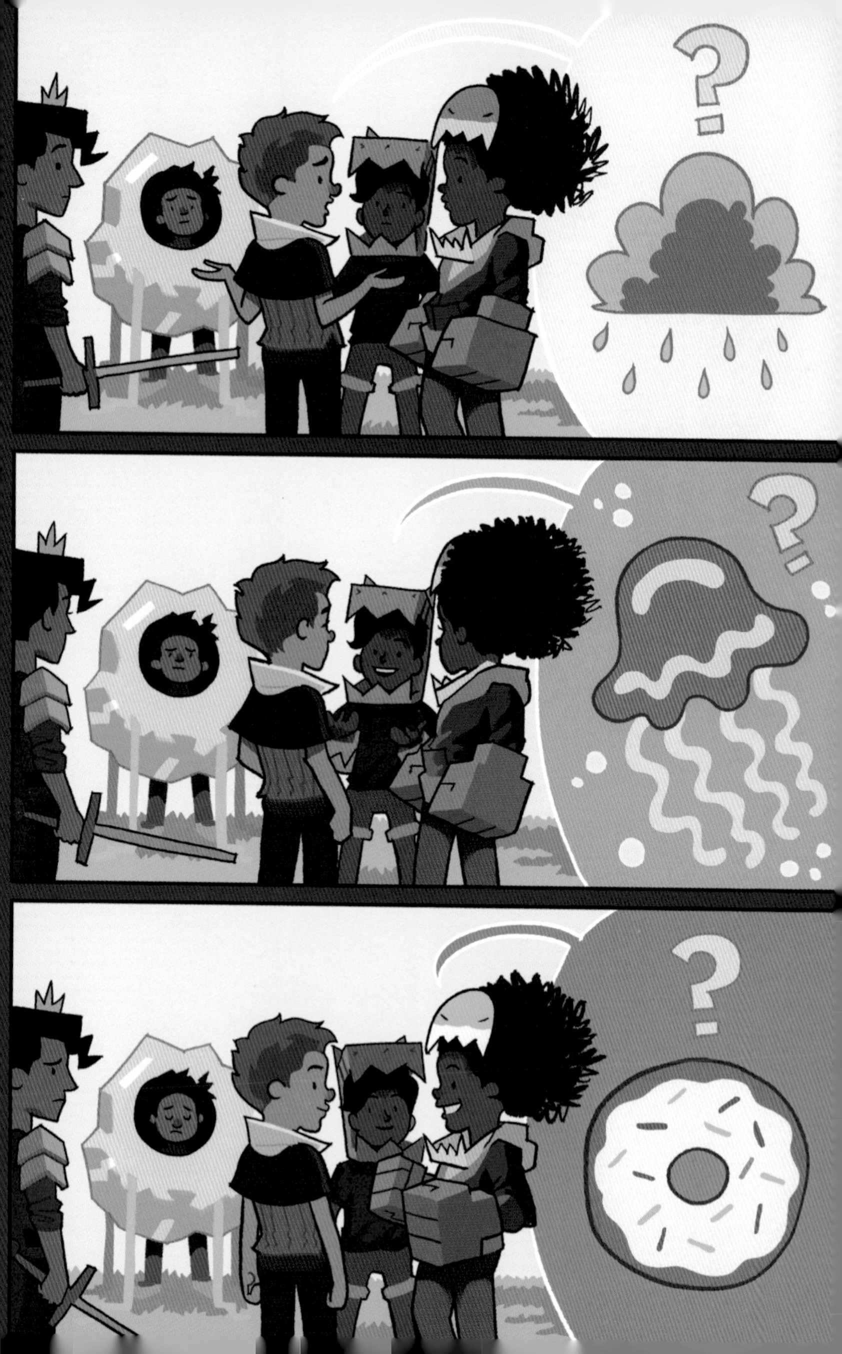

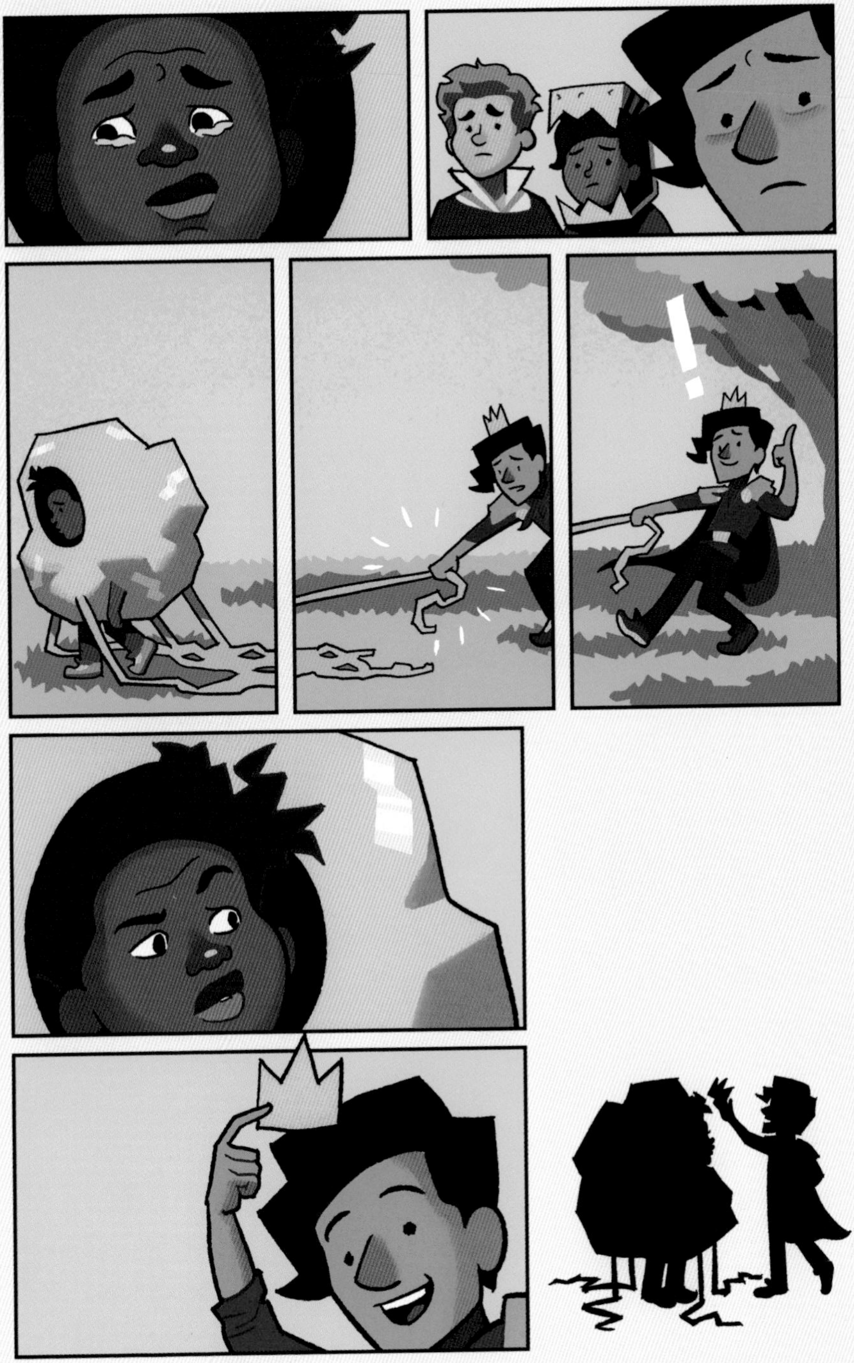
!!

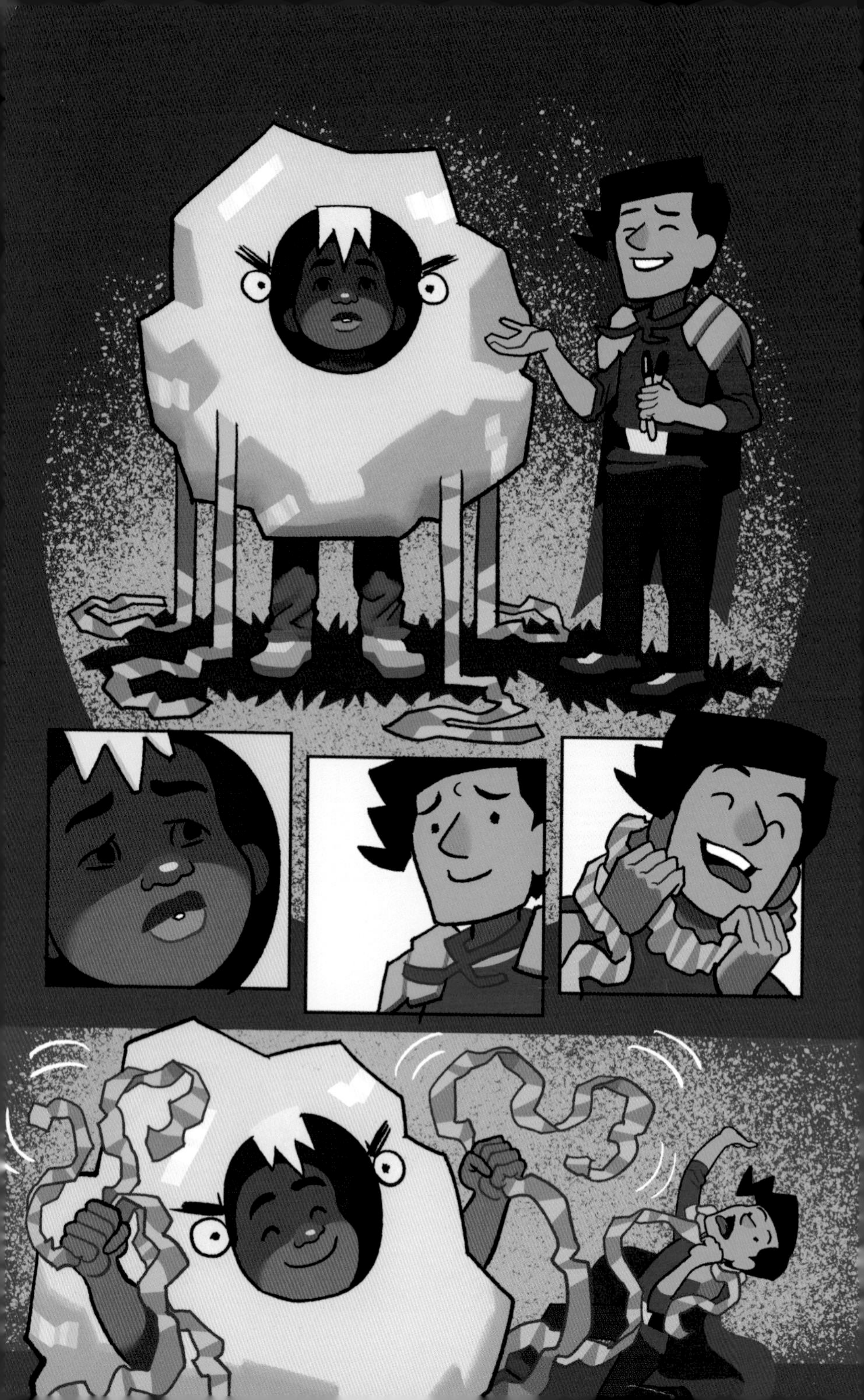

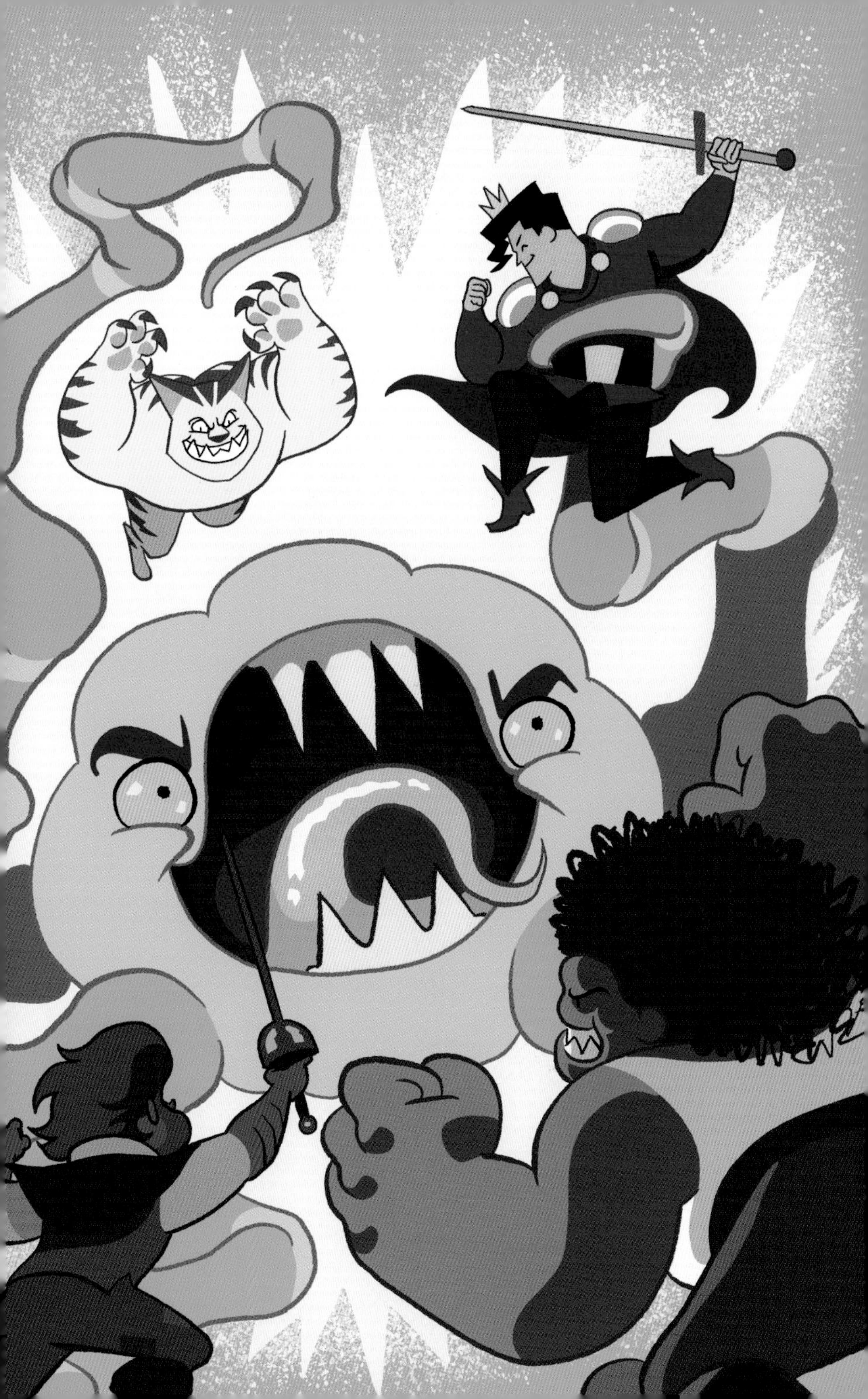

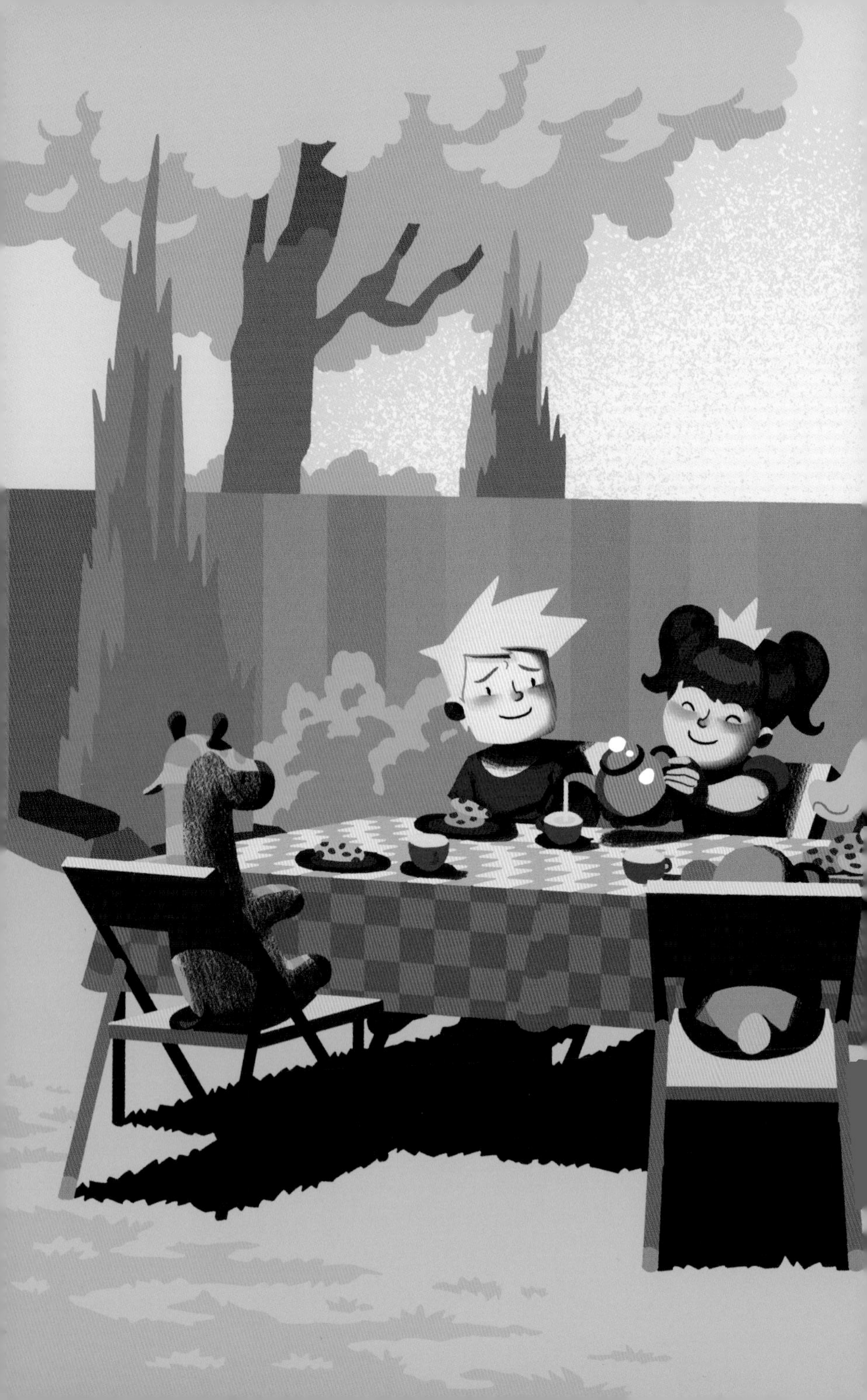

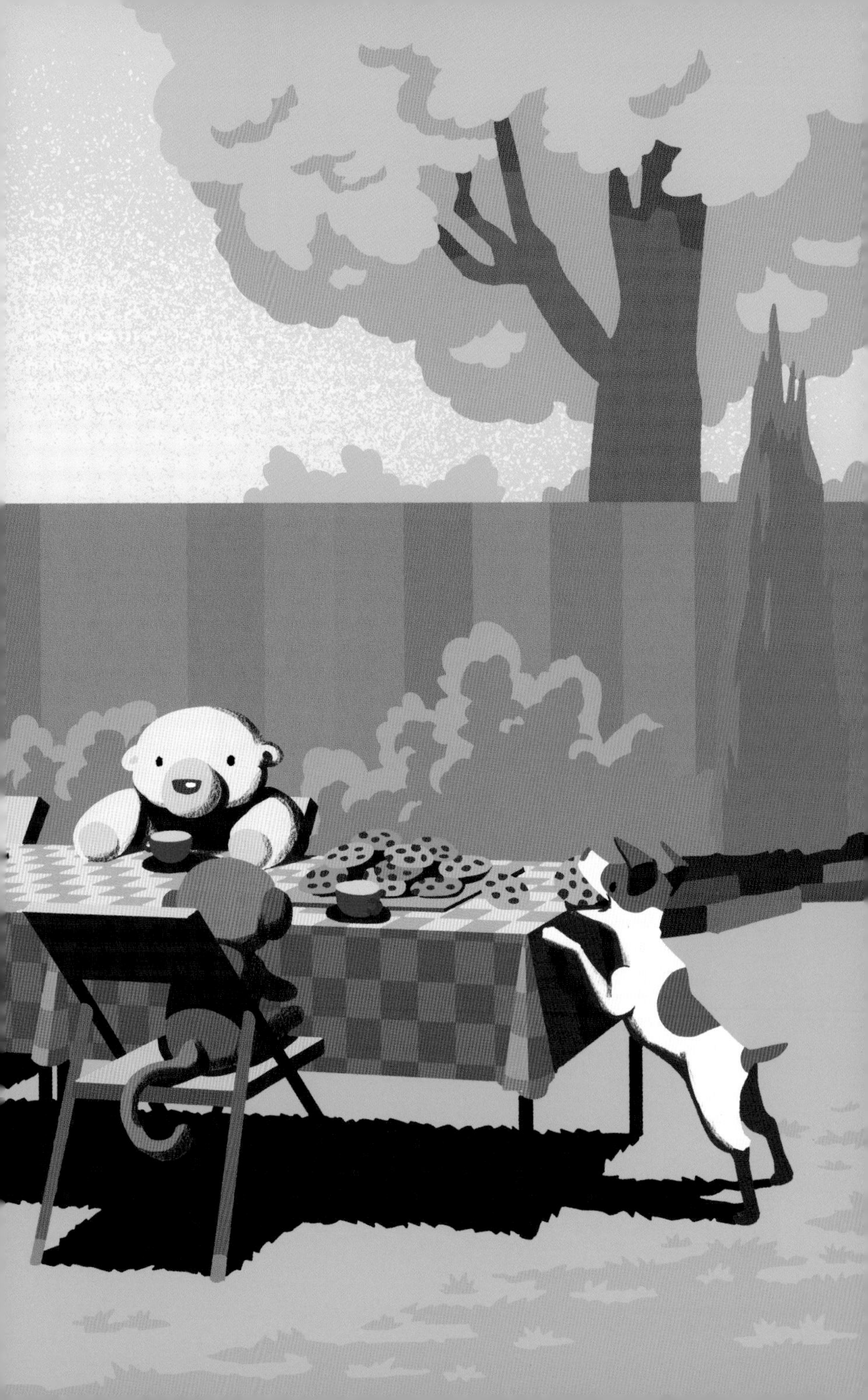

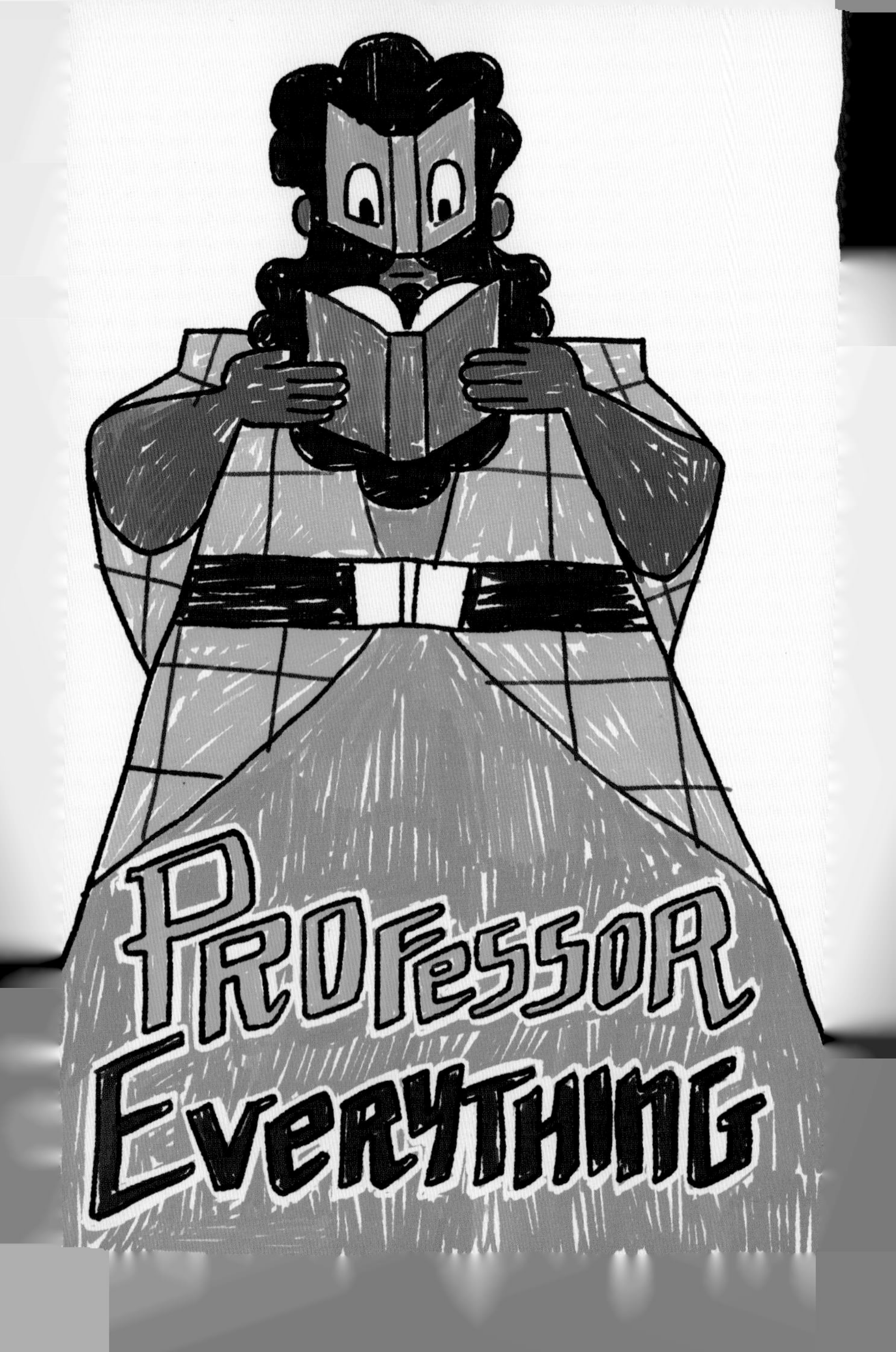
PROFESSOR
EVERYTHING

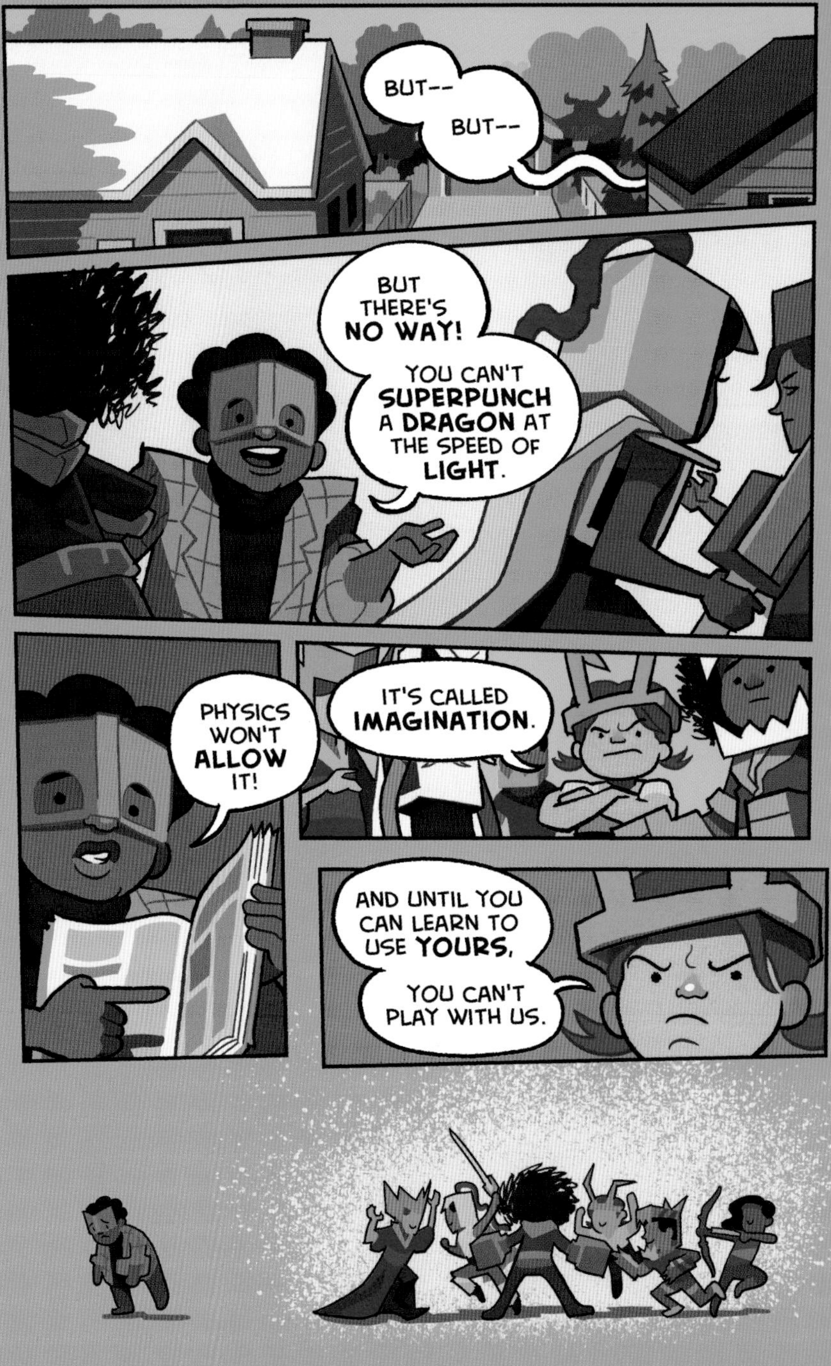
BUT--
BUT--
BUT THERE'S NO WAY!
YOU CAN'T SUPERPUNCH A DRAGON AT THE SPEED OF LIGHT.
PHYSICS WON'T ALLOW IT!
IT'S CALLED IMAGINATION.
AND UNTIL YOU CAN LEARN TO USE YOURS,
YOU CAN'T PLAY WITH US.

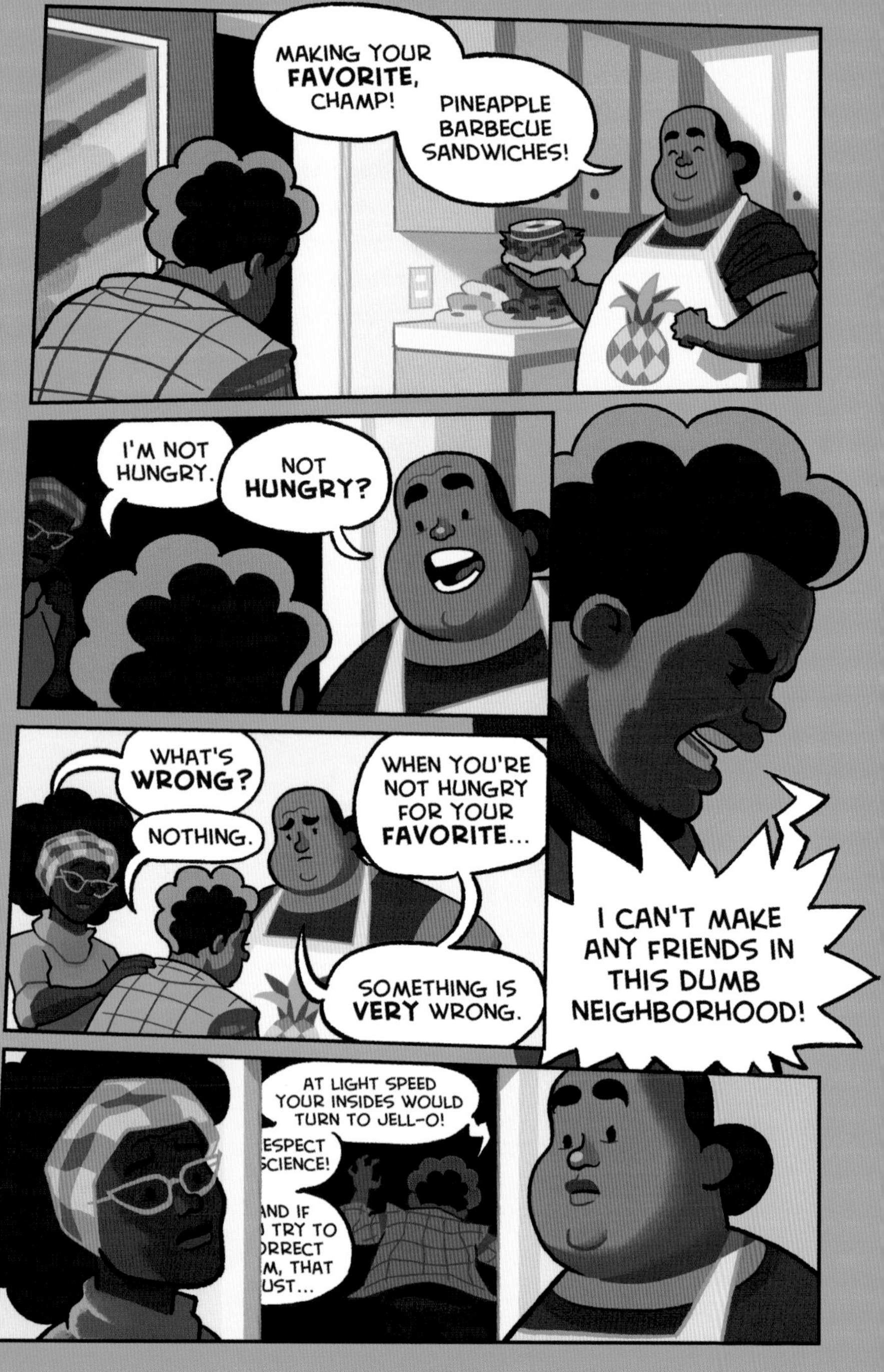
MAKING YOUR **FAVORITE**, CHAMP!
PINEAPPLE BARBECUE SANDWICHES!
I'M NOT HUNGRY.
NOT **HUNGRY?**
WHAT'S **WRONG?**
NOTHING.
WHEN YOU'RE NOT HUNGRY FOR YOUR **FAVORITE**...
SOMETHING IS **VERY** WRONG.
I CAN'T MAKE ANY FRIENDS IN THIS DUMB NEIGHBORHOOD!
AT LIGHT SPEED YOUR INSIDES WOULD TURN TO JELL-O!
ESPECT SCIENCE!
AND IF TRY TO ORRECT M, THAT UST...

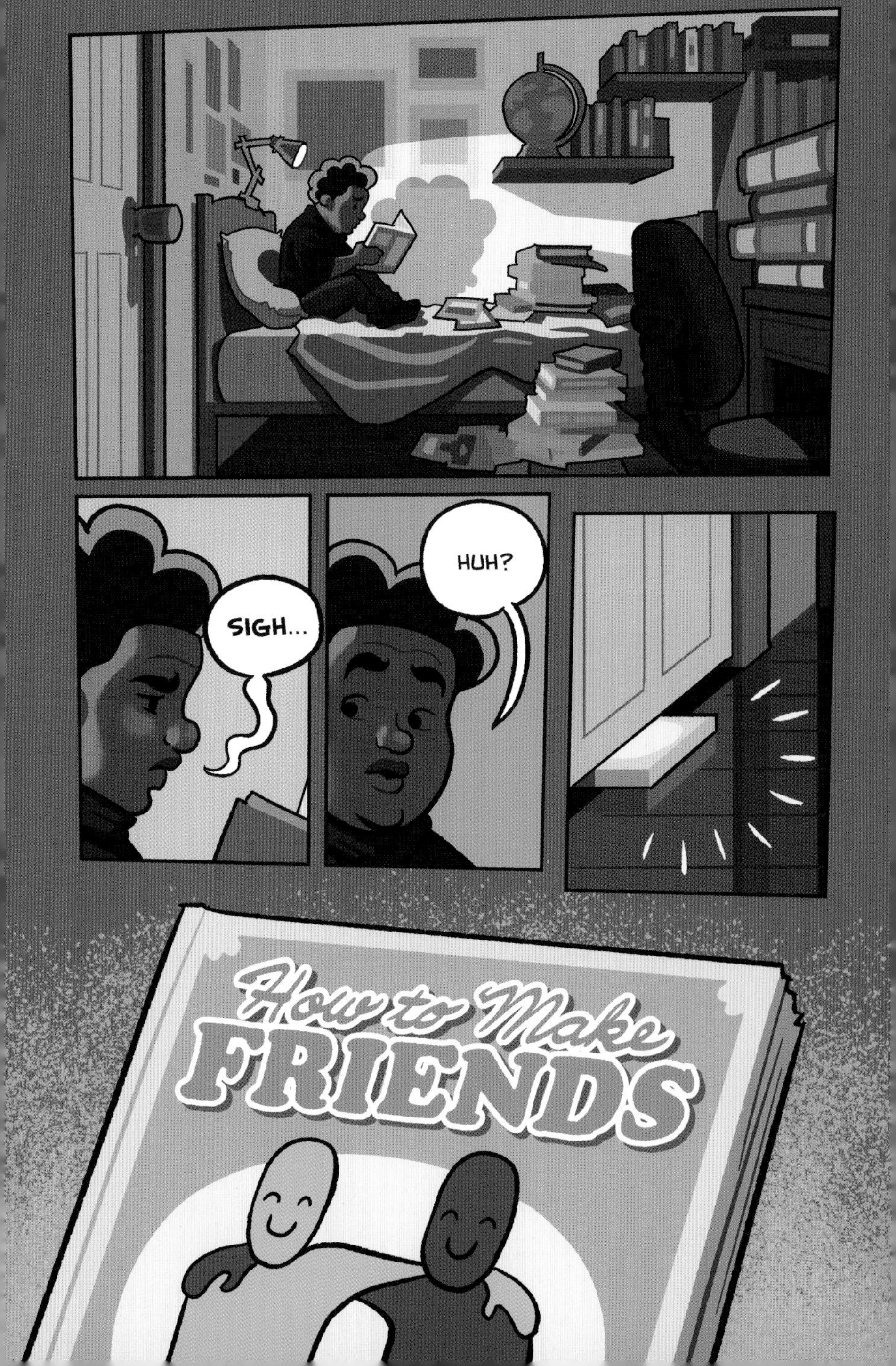
SIGH...
HUH?
How to Make
FRIENDS

TIP #1: SMILE!

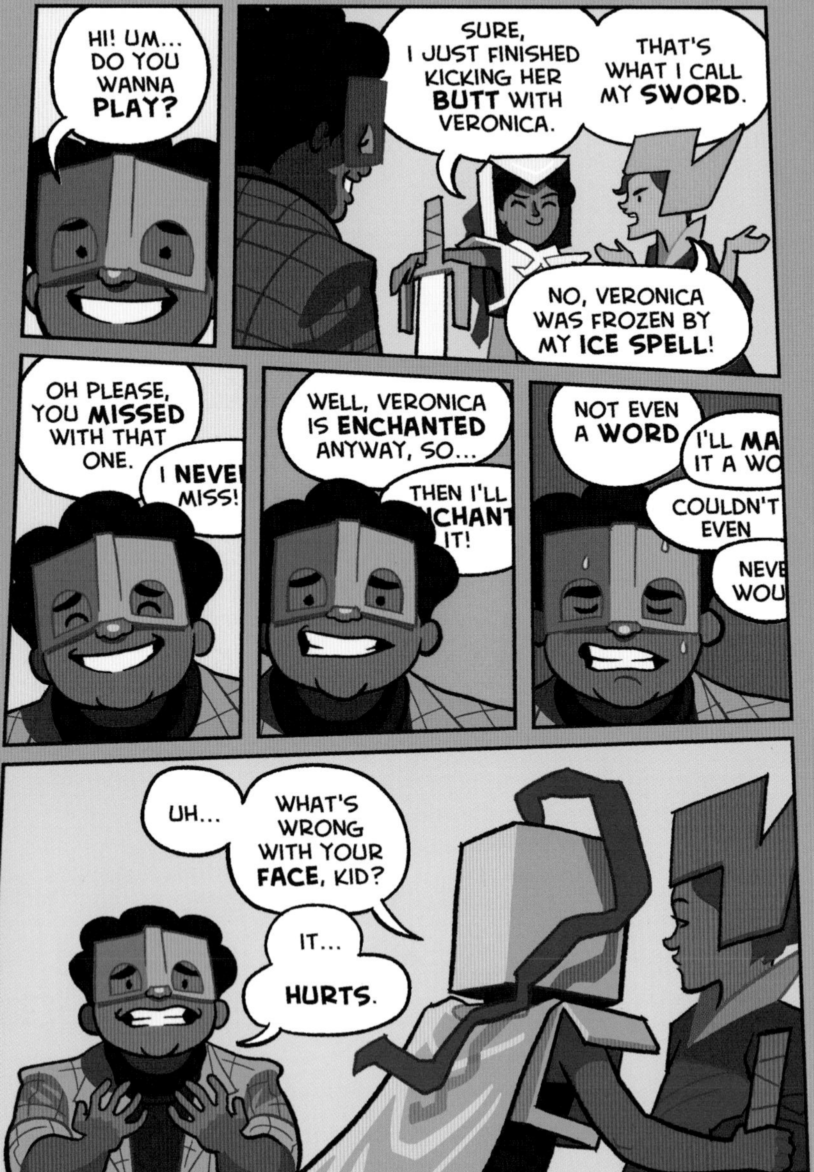
HI! UM... DO YOU WANNA PLAY?
SURE, I JUST FINISHED KICKING HER BUTT WITH VERONICA.
THAT'S WHAT I CALL MY SWORD.
NO, VERONICA WAS FROZEN BY MY ICE SPELL!
OH PLEASE, YOU MISSED WITH THAT ONE.
I NEVE MISS!
WELL, VERONICA IS ENCHANTED ANYWAY, SO...
THEN I'LL CHANT IT!
NOT EVEN A WORD
I'LL MA IT A WO
COULDN'T EVEN
NEVE WOU
UH...
WHAT'S WRONG WITH YOUR FACE, KID?
IT... HURTS.

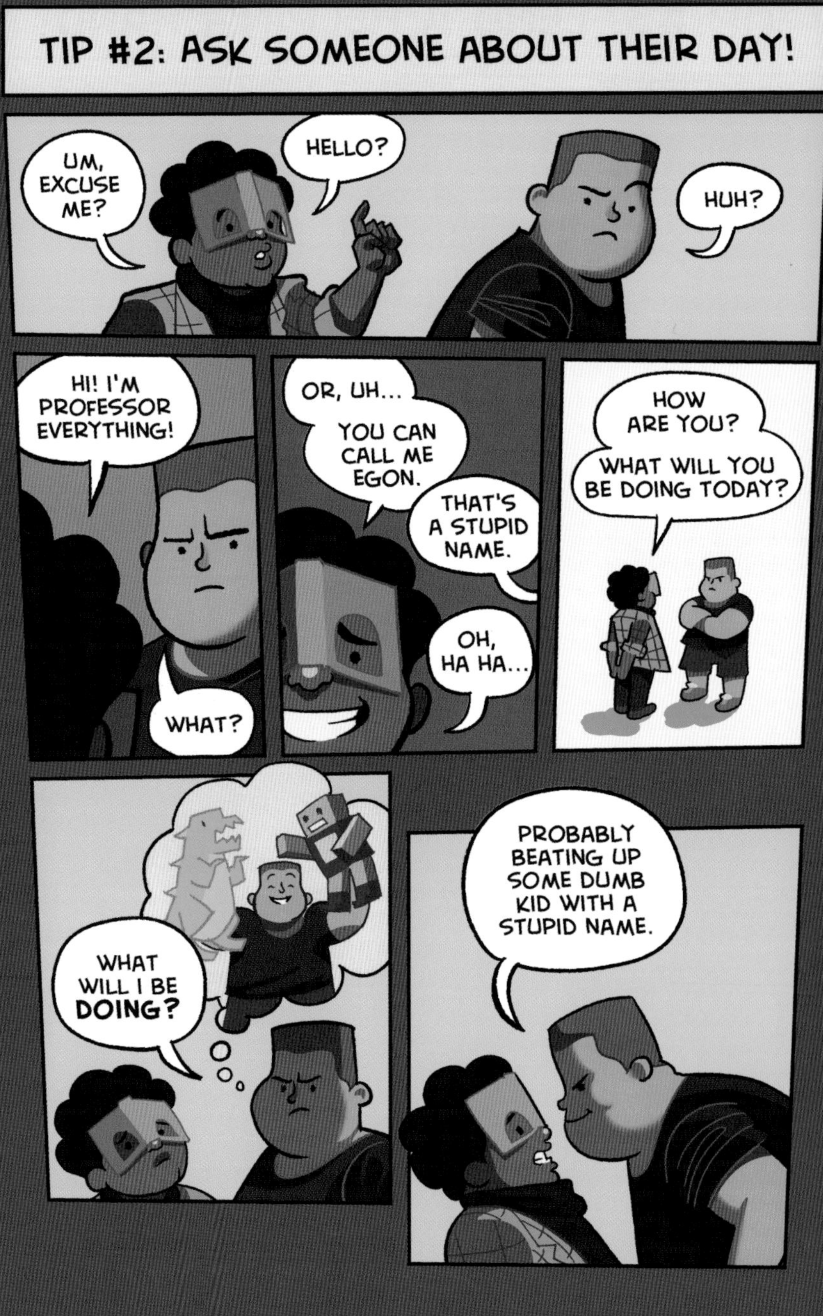
TIP #2: ASK SOMEONE ABOUT THEIR DAY!
UM, EXCUSE ME?
HELLO?
HUH?
HI! I'M PROFESSOR EVERYTHING!
WHAT?
OR, UH...
YOU CAN CALL ME EGON.
THAT'S A STUPID NAME.
OH, HA HA...
HOW ARE YOU?
WHAT WILL YOU BE DOING TODAY?
WHAT WILL I BE DOING?
PROBABLY BEATING UP SOME DUMB KID WITH A STUPID NAME.

TIP #3: LEND A HELPING HAND!

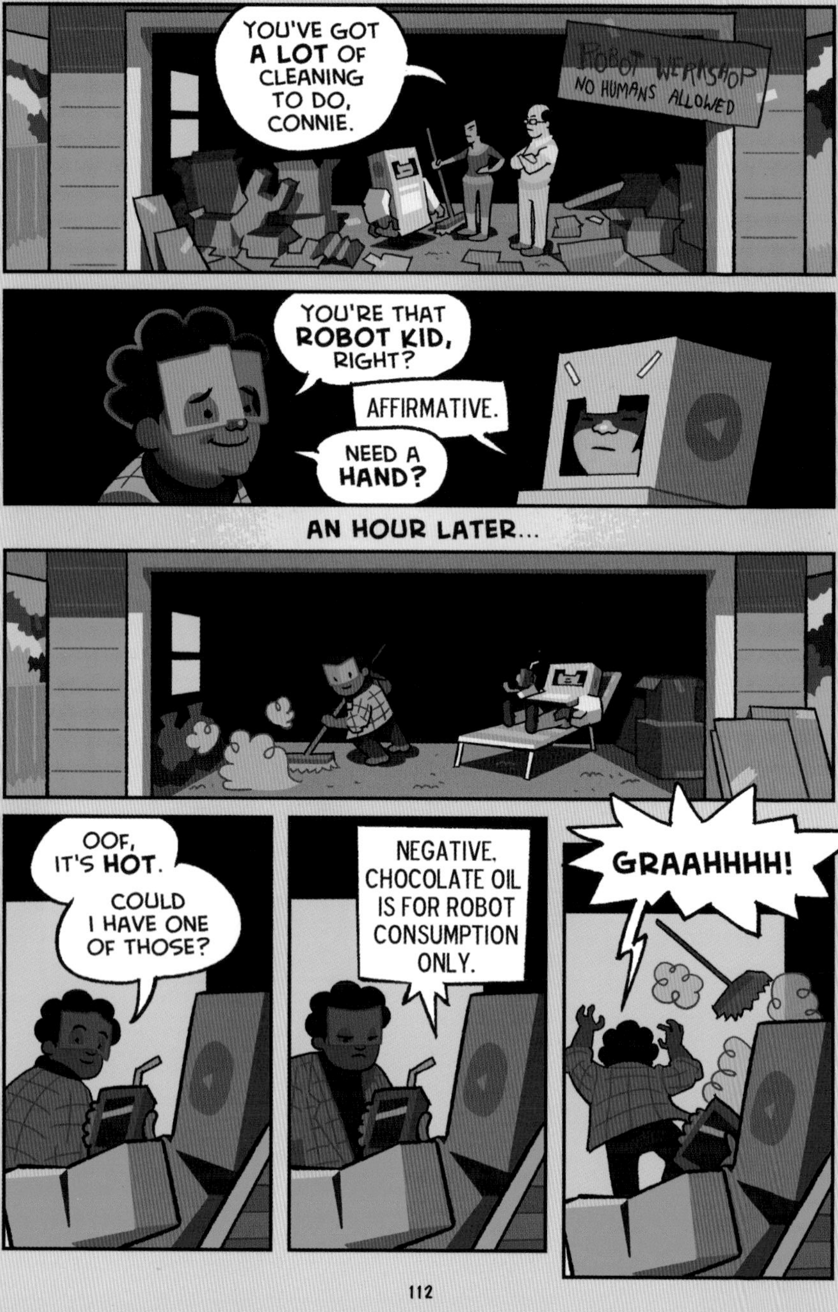
YOU'VE GOT **A LOT** OF CLEANING TO DO, CONNIE.
ROBOT WERKSHOP
NO HUMANS ALLOWED
YOU'RE THAT **ROBOT KID,** RIGHT?
AFFIRMATIVE.
NEED A **HAND?**
AN HOUR LATER...
OOF, IT'S **HOT**.
COULD I HAVE ONE OF THOSE?
NEGATIVE. CHOCOLATE OIL IS FOR ROBOT CONSUMPTION ONLY.
GRAAHHHH!

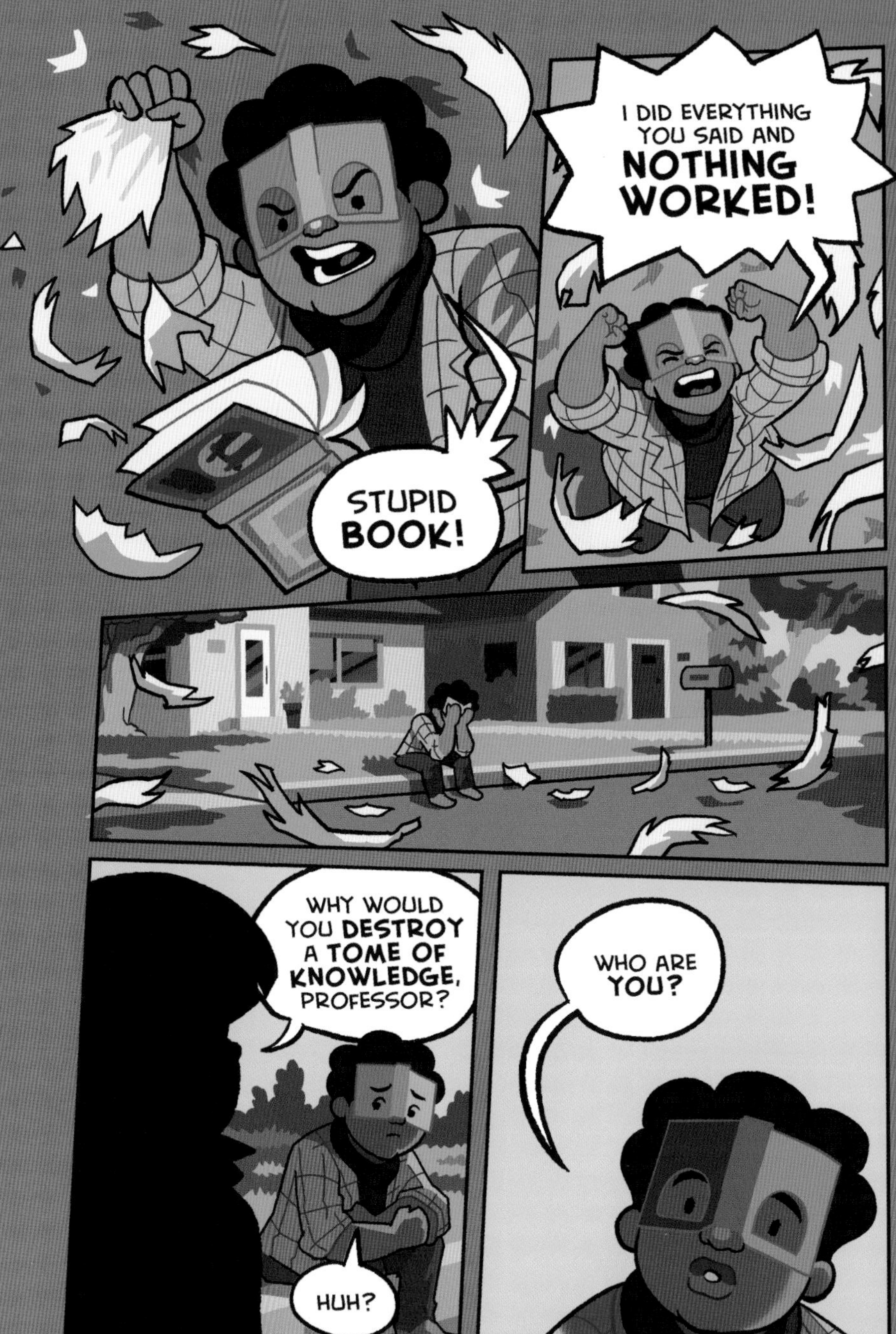
STUPID BOOK!
I DID EVERYTHING YOU SAID AND NOTHING WORKED!
WHY WOULD YOU DESTROY A TOME OF KNOWLEDGE, PROFESSOR?
HUH?
WHO ARE YOU?

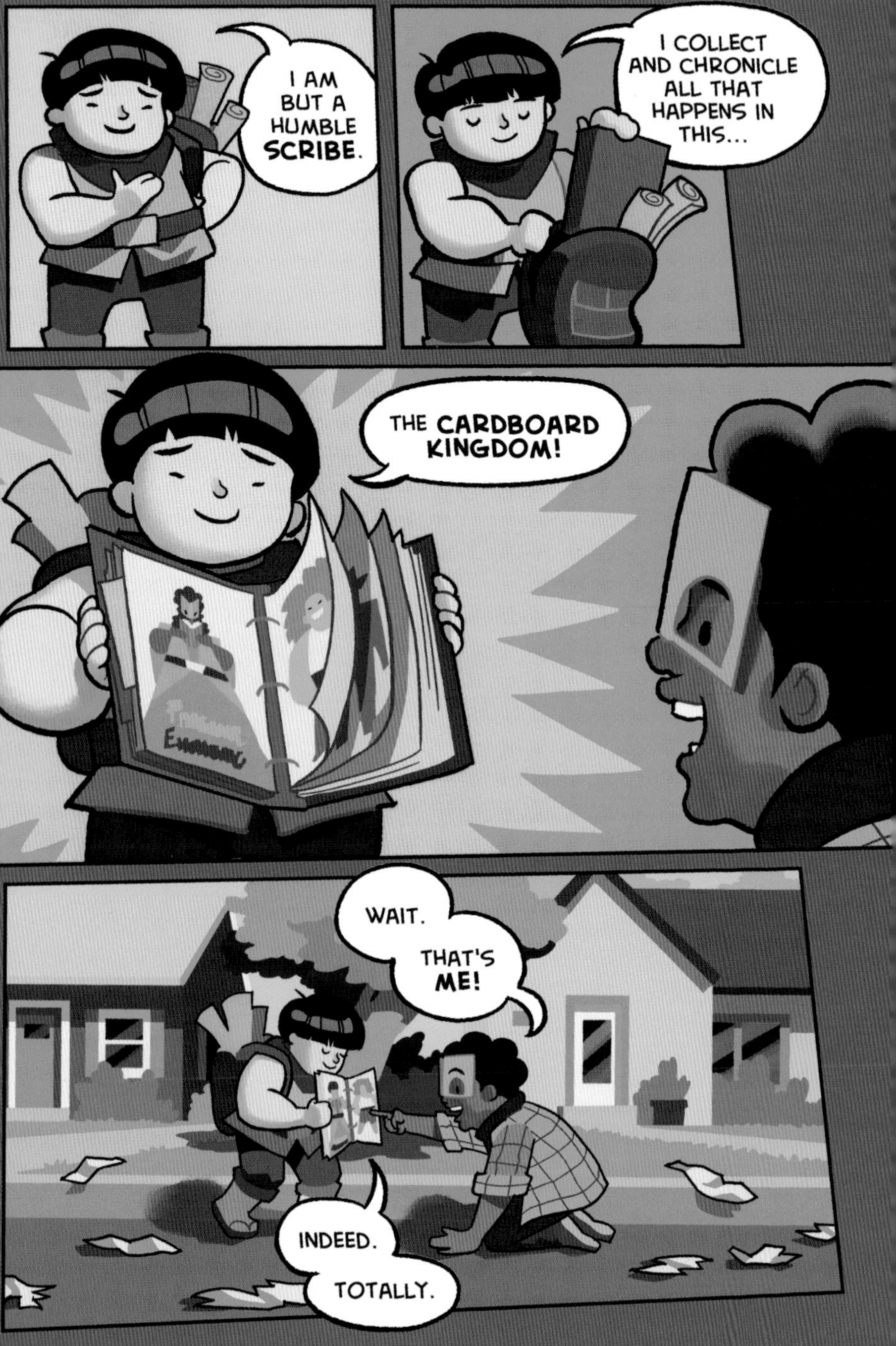
I AM BUT A HUMBLE **SCRIBE**.
I COLLECT AND CHRONICLE ALL THAT HAPPENS IN THIS...
THE **CARDBOARD KINGDOM!**
WAIT.
THAT'S **ME!**
INDEED.
TOTALLY.

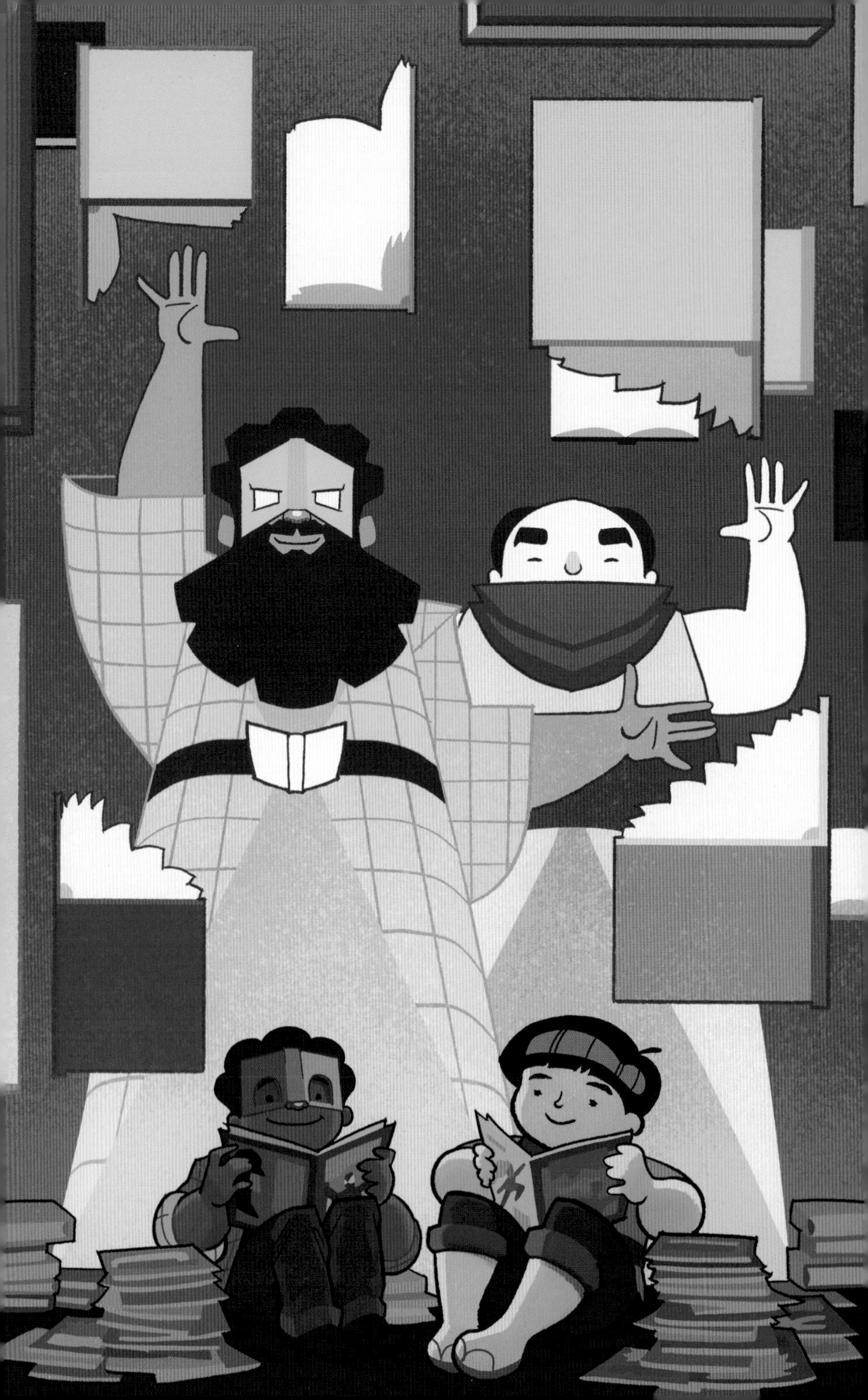

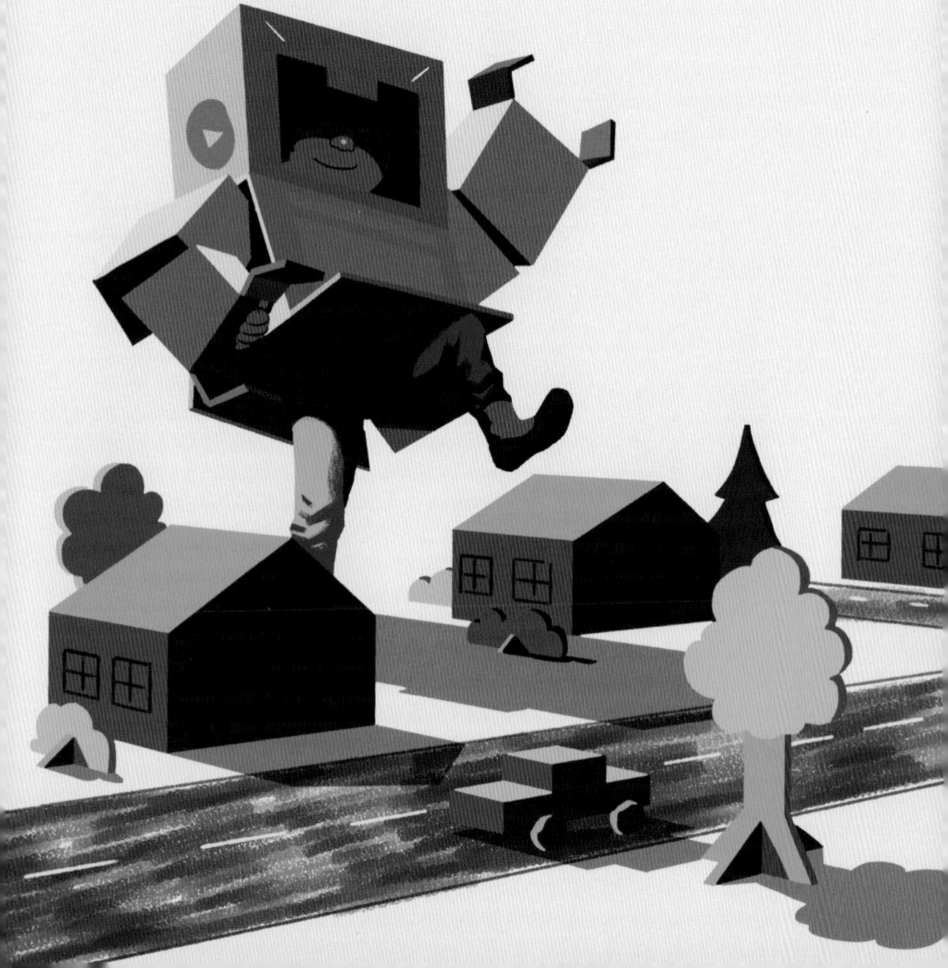

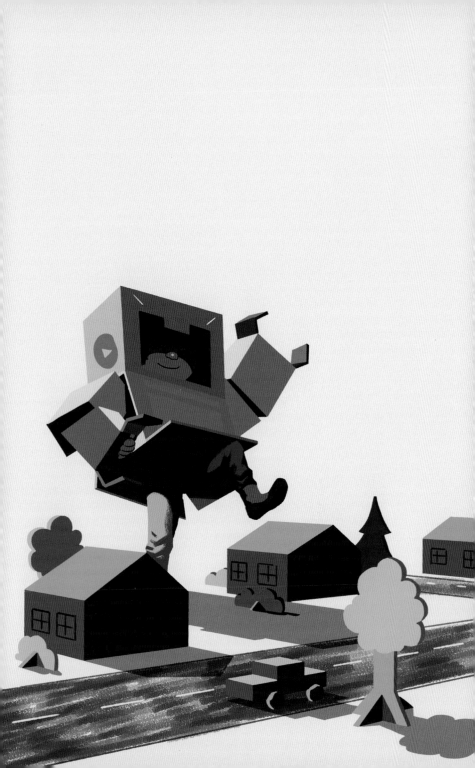

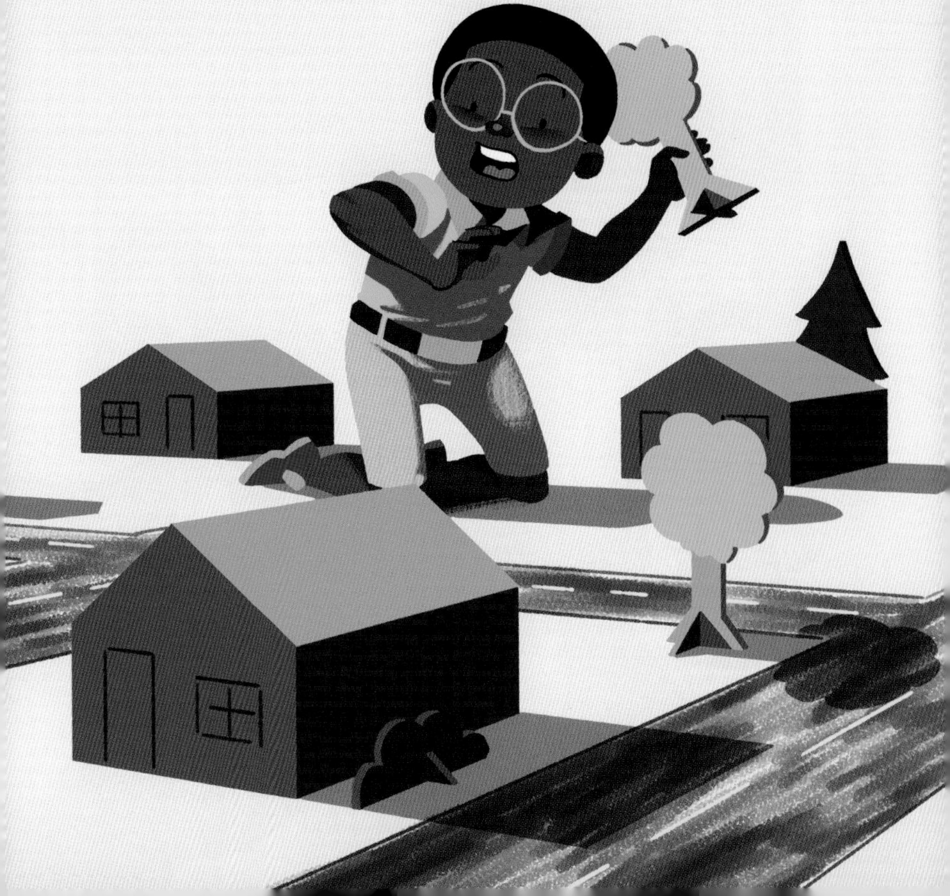

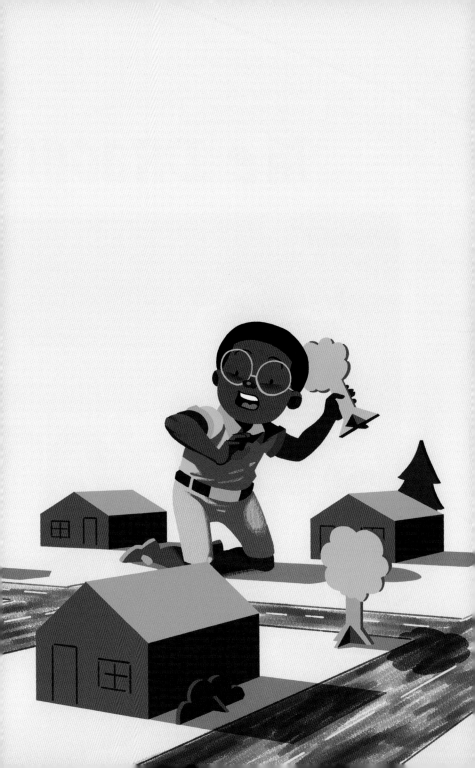

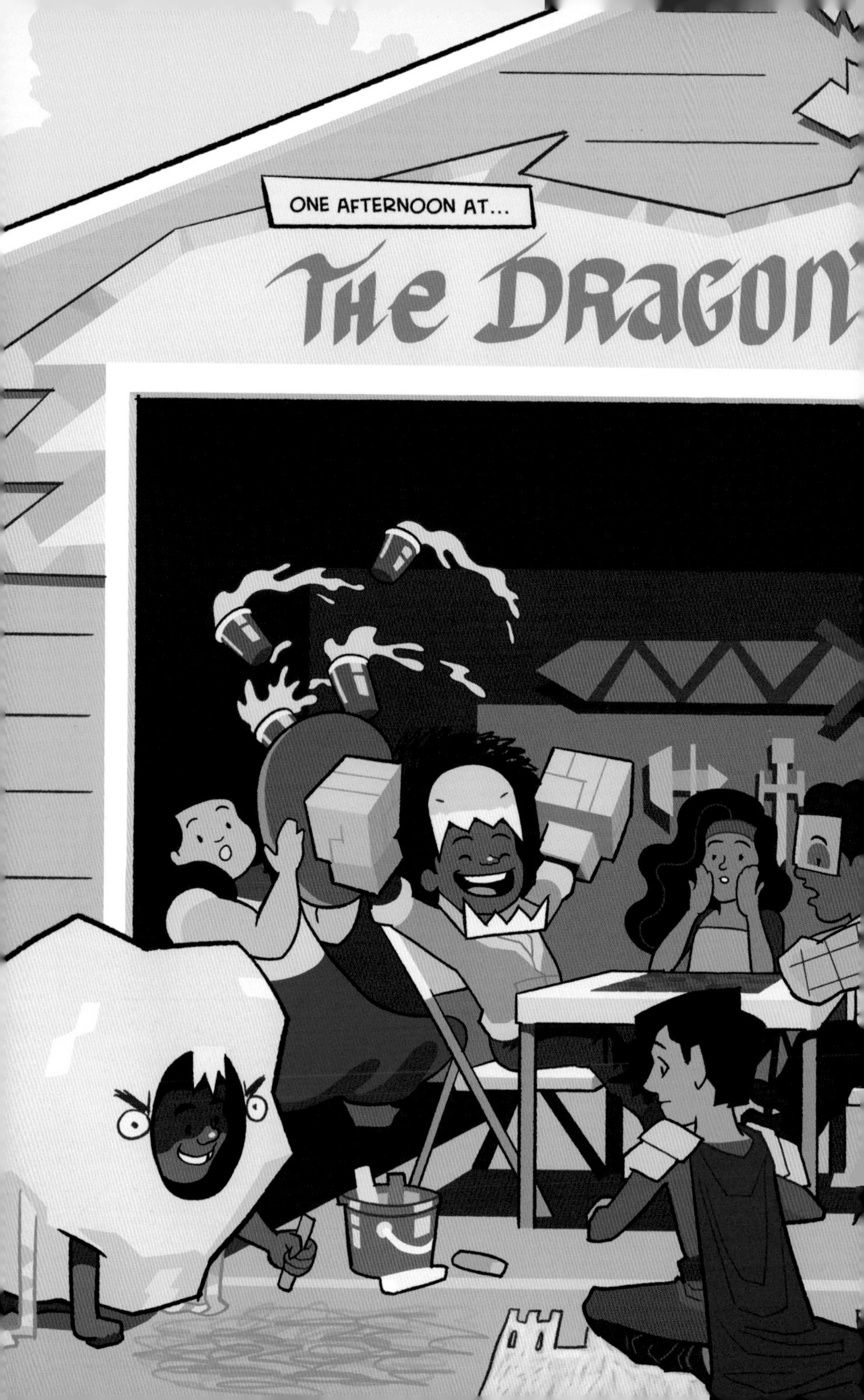
ONE AFTERNOON AT...
THE DRAGON

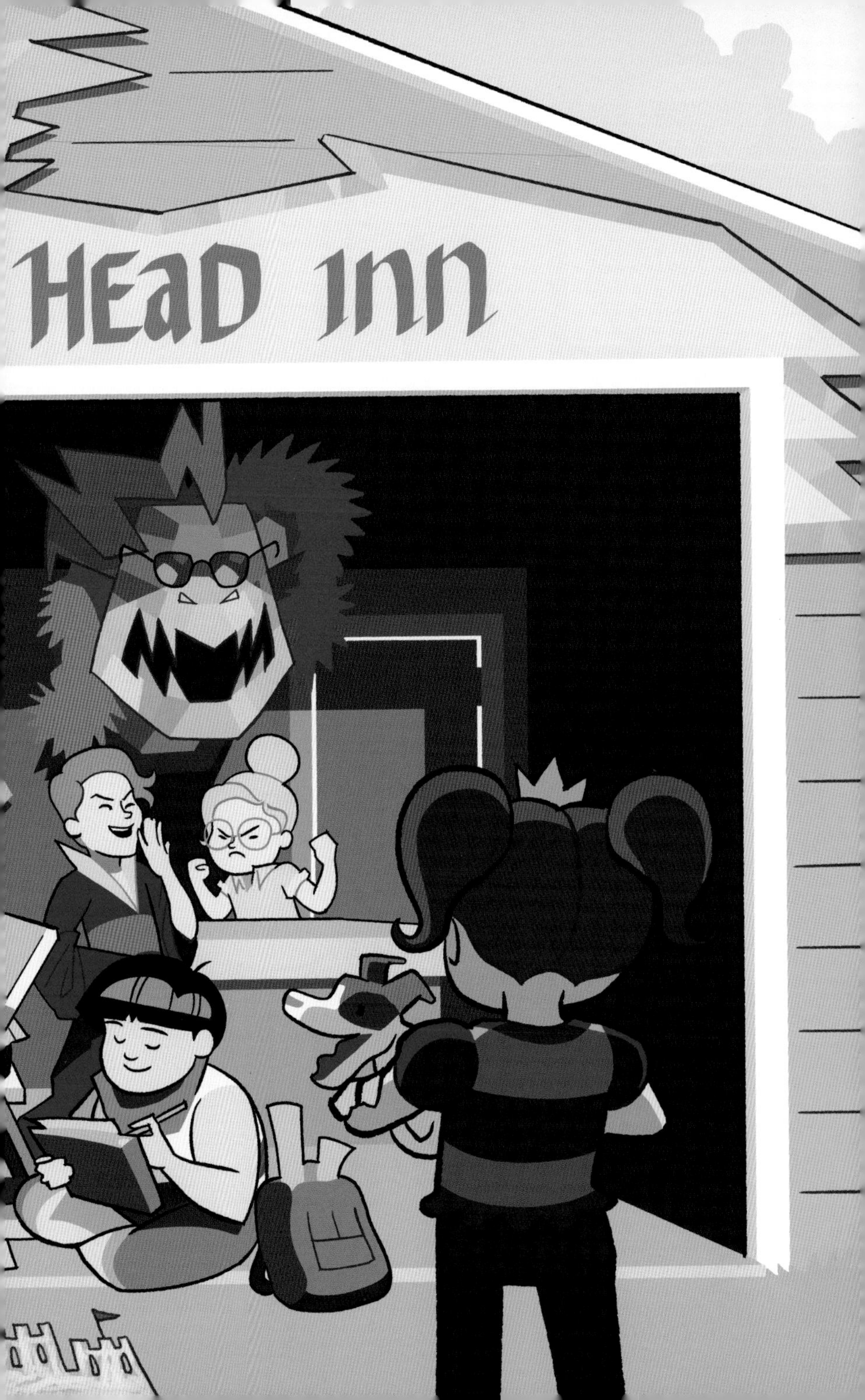
HEAD INN

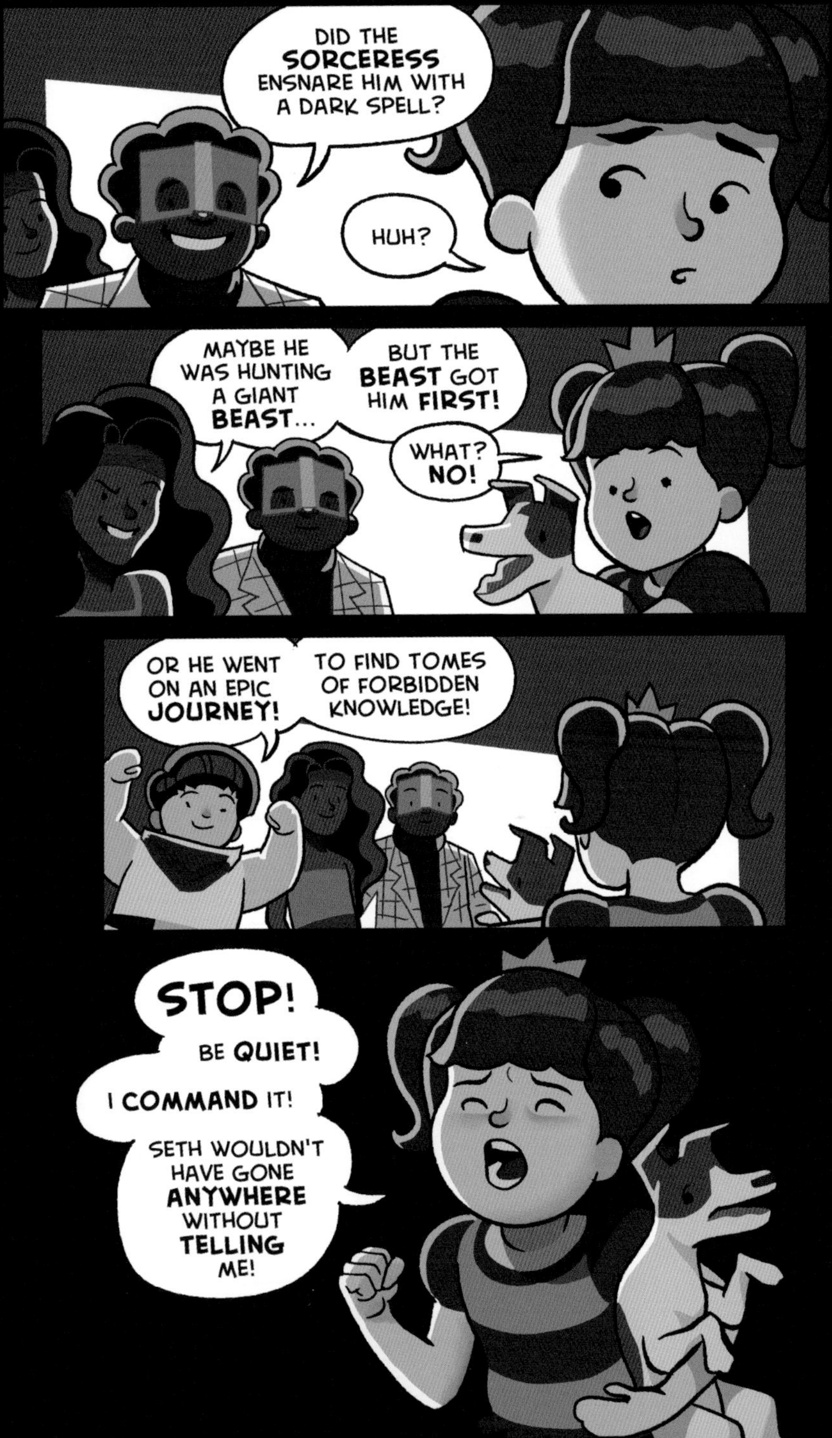
DID THE SORCERESS ENSNARE HIM WITH A DARK SPELL?
HUH?
MAYBE HE WAS HUNTING A GIANT BEAST...
BUT THE BEAST GOT HIM FIRST!
WHAT? NO!
OR HE WENT ON AN EPIC JOURNEY!
TO FIND TOMES OF FORBIDDEN KNOWLEDGE!
STOP!
BE QUIET!
I COMMAND IT!
SETH WOULDN'T HAVE GONE ANYWHERE WITHOUT TELLING ME!

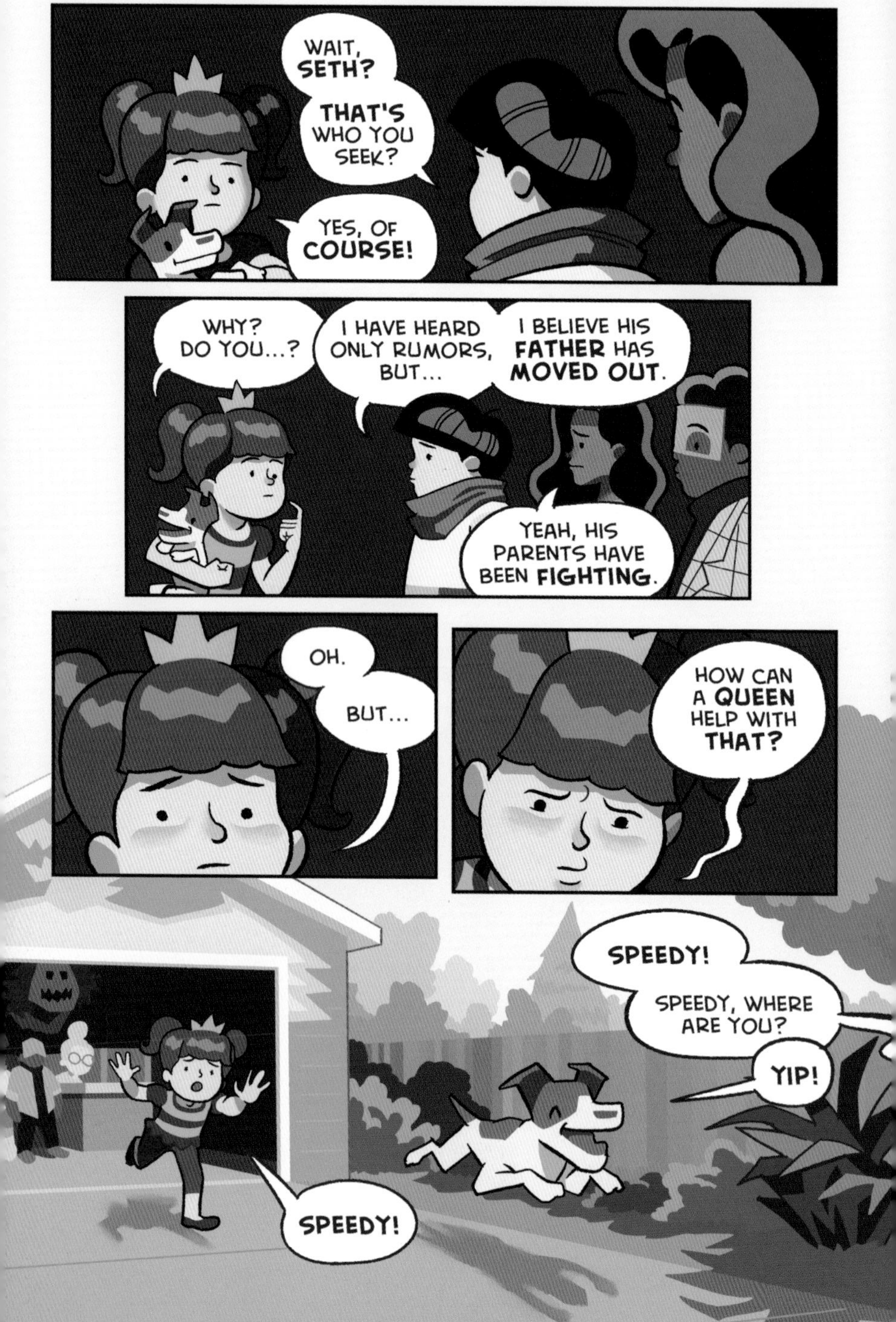
WAIT, SETH?
THAT'S WHO YOU SEEK?
YES, OF COURSE!
WHY? DO YOU...?
I HAVE HEARD ONLY RUMORS, BUT...
I BELIEVE HIS FATHER HAS MOVED OUT.
YEAH, HIS PARENTS HAVE BEEN FIGHTING.
OH.
BUT...
HOW CAN A QUEEN HELP WITH THAT?
SPEEDY!
SPEEDY, WHERE ARE YOU?
YIP!
SPEEDY!

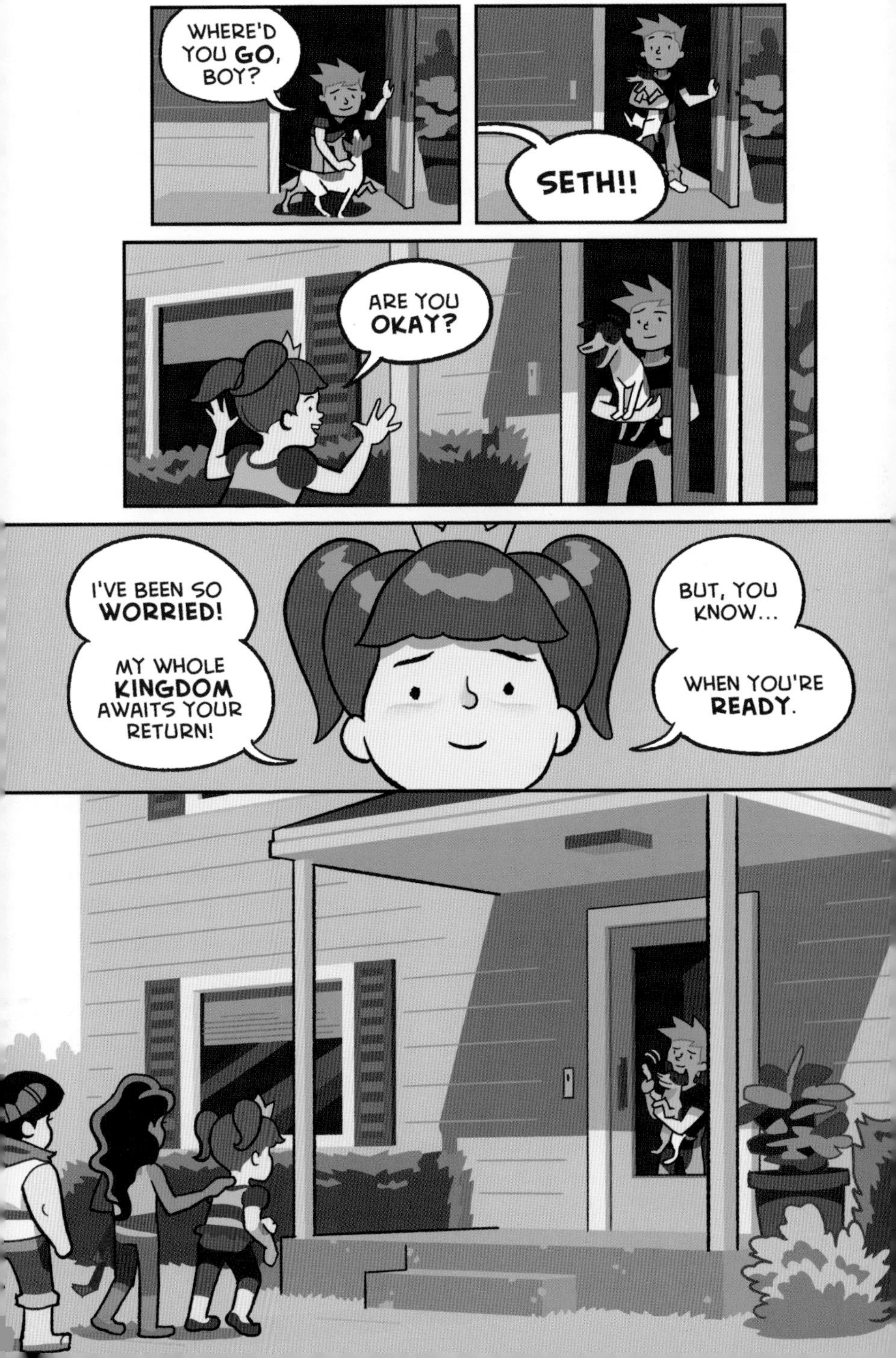
WHERE'D YOU GO, BOY?
SETH!!
ARE YOU OKAY?
I'VE BEEN SO WORRIED!
MY WHOLE KINGDOM AWAITS YOUR RETURN!
BUT, YOU KNOW...
WHEN YOU'RE READY.

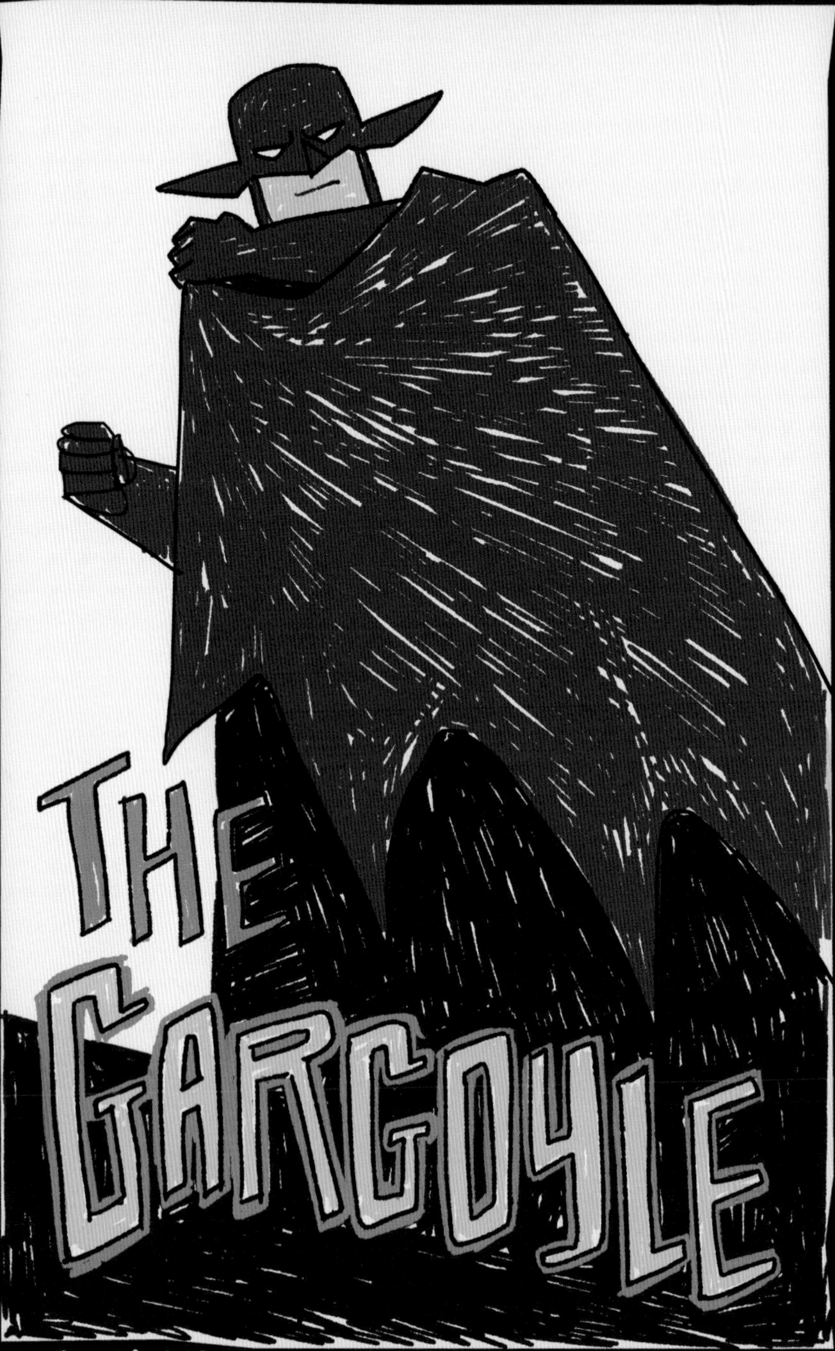
THE GARGOYLE

BY MICHAEL COLE AND CHAD SELL

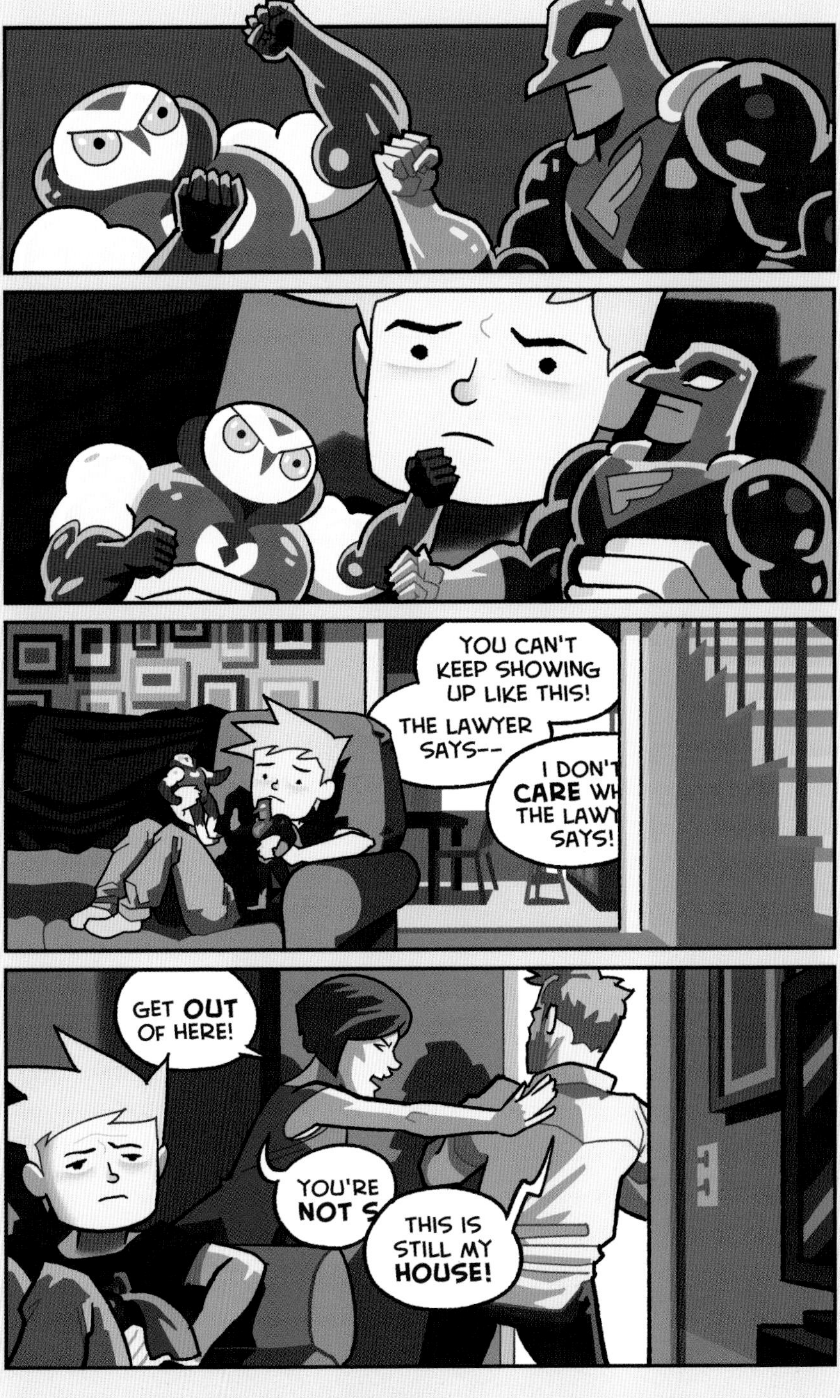
YOU CAN'T KEEP SHOWING UP LIKE THIS!
THE LAWYER SAYS--
I DON'T CARE WH THE LAWY SAYS!
GET OUT OF HERE!
YOU'RE NOT S
THIS IS STILL MY HOUSE!

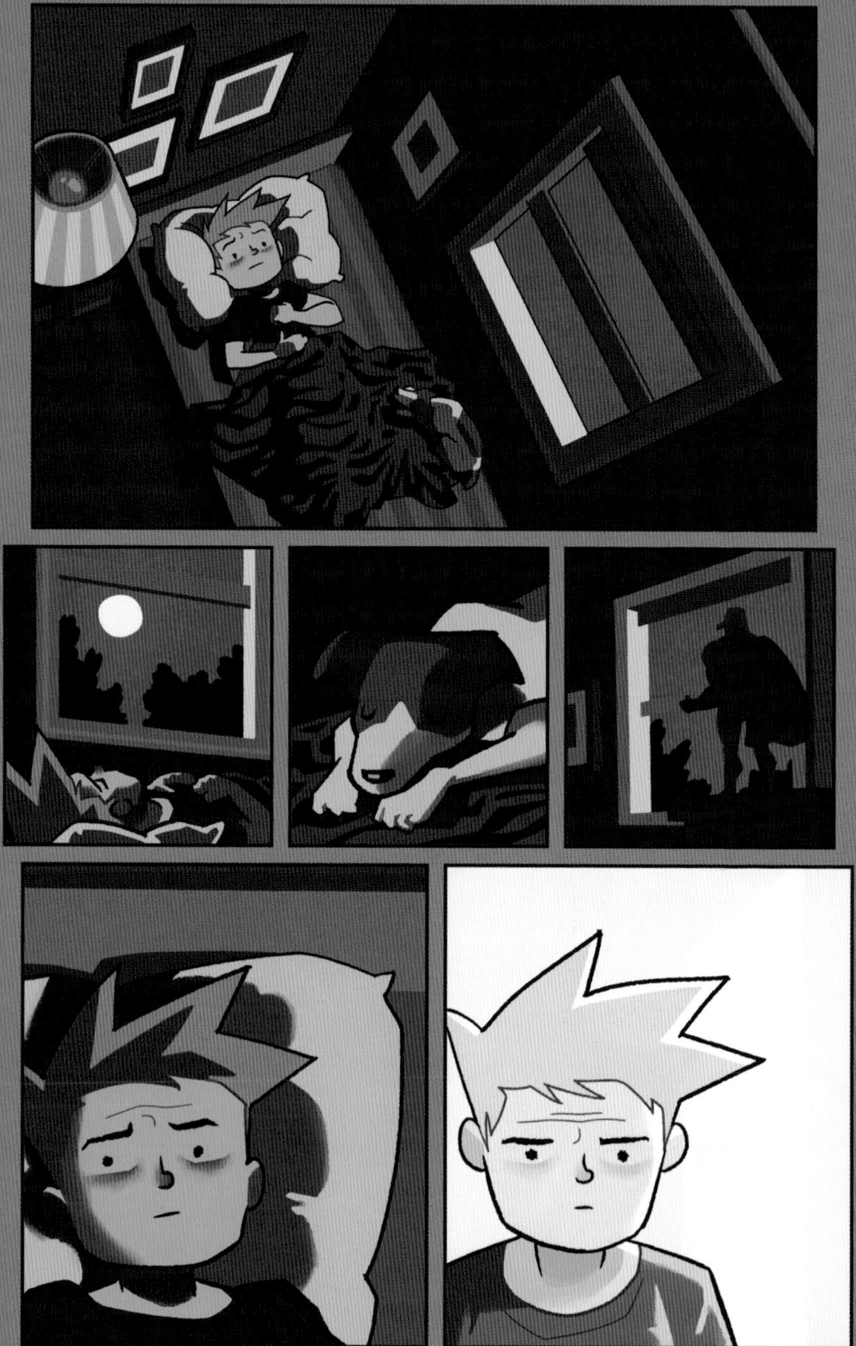

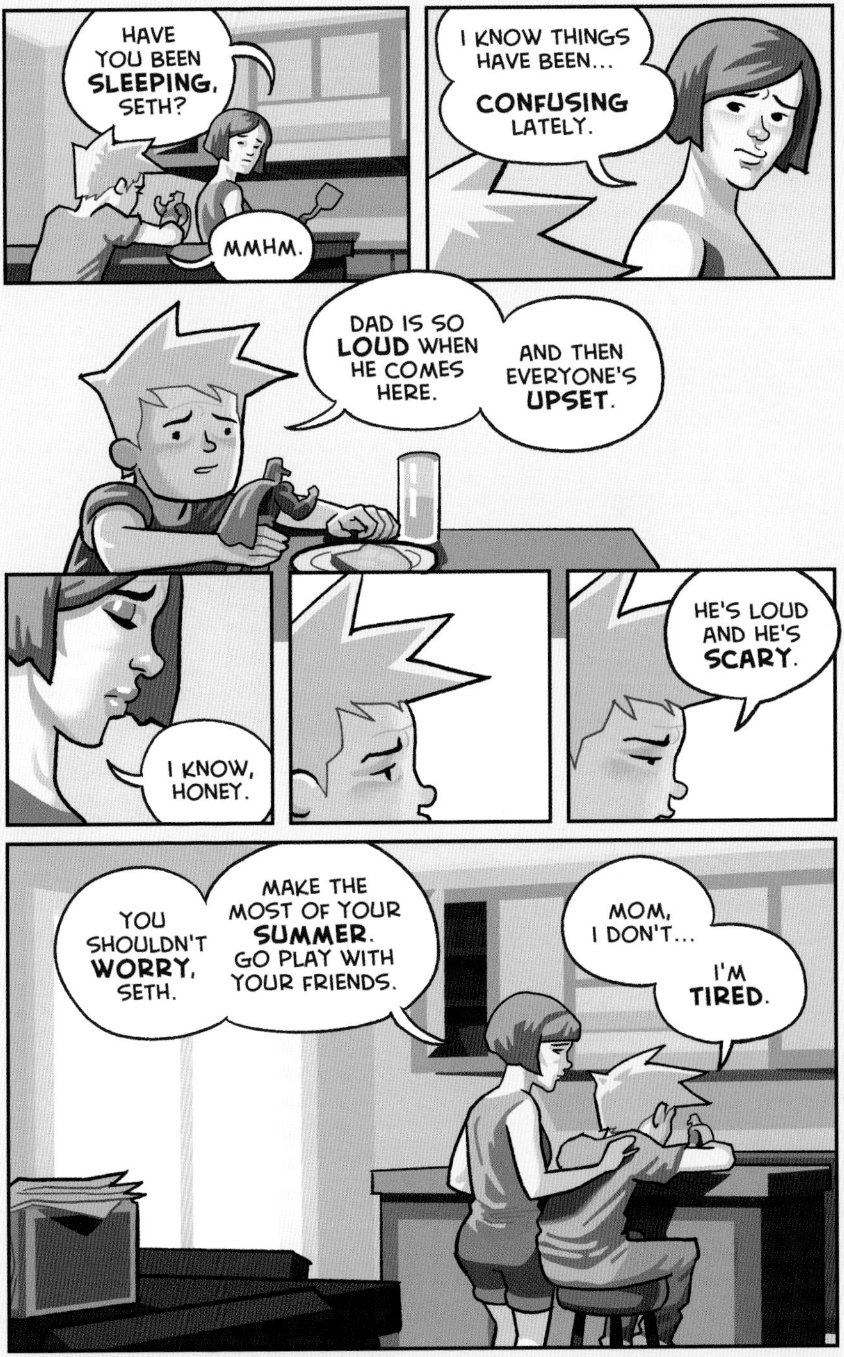
HAVE YOU BEEN SLEEPING, SETH?
MMHM.
I KNOW THINGS HAVE BEEN... CONFUSING LATELY.
DAD IS SO LOUD WHEN HE COMES HERE.
AND THEN EVERYONE'S UPSET.
I KNOW, HONEY.
HE'S LOUD AND HE'S SCARY.
YOU SHOULDN'T WORRY, SETH.
MAKE THE MOST OF YOUR SUMMER. GO PLAY WITH YOUR FRIENDS.
MOM, I DON'T...
I'M TIRED.

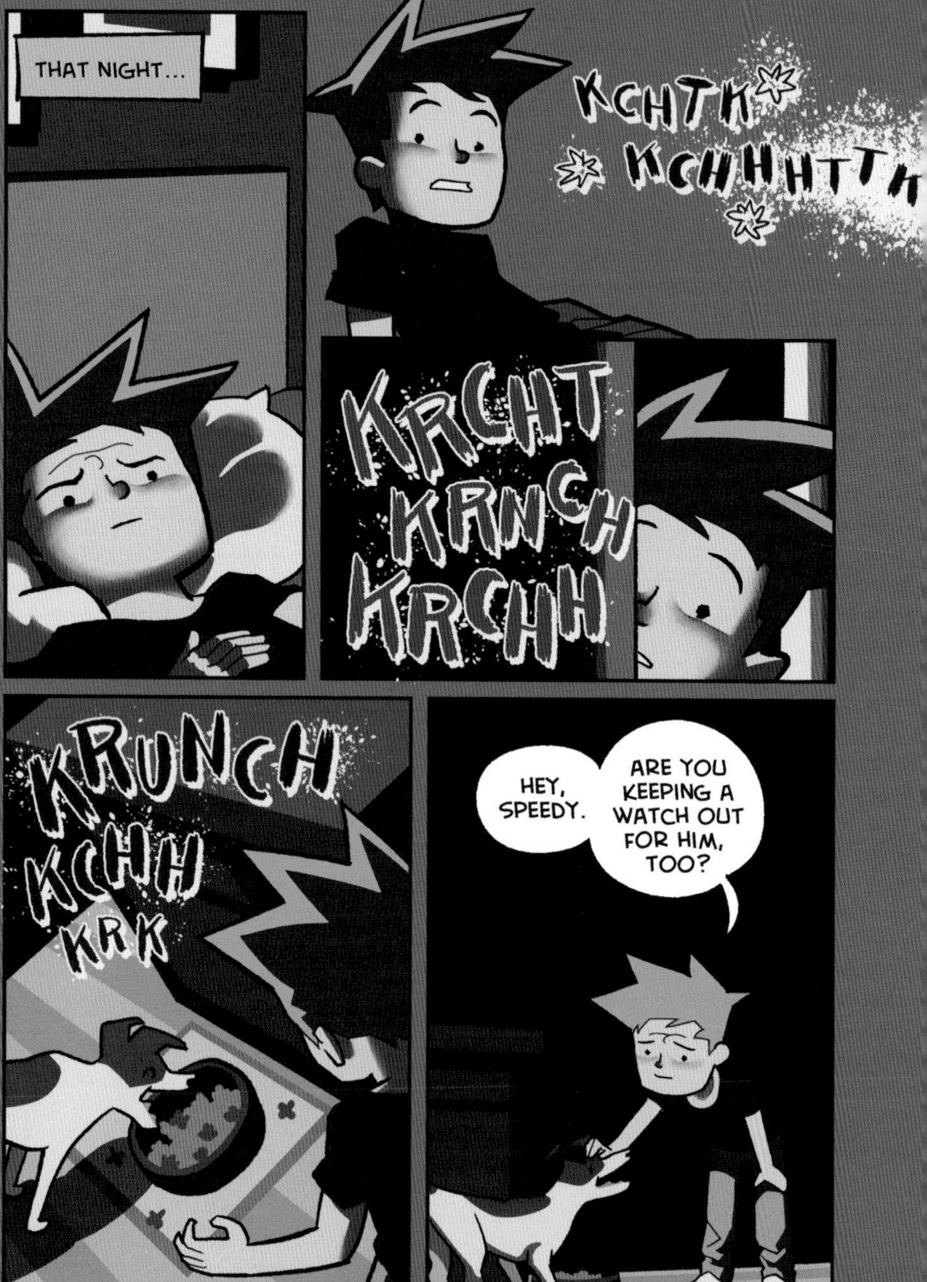
THAT NIGHT...
KCHTK
KCHHHTTK
KRCHT
KRNCH
KRCHH
KRUNCH
KCHH
KRK
HEY, SPEEDY.
ARE YOU KEEPING A WATCH OUT FOR HIM, TOO?

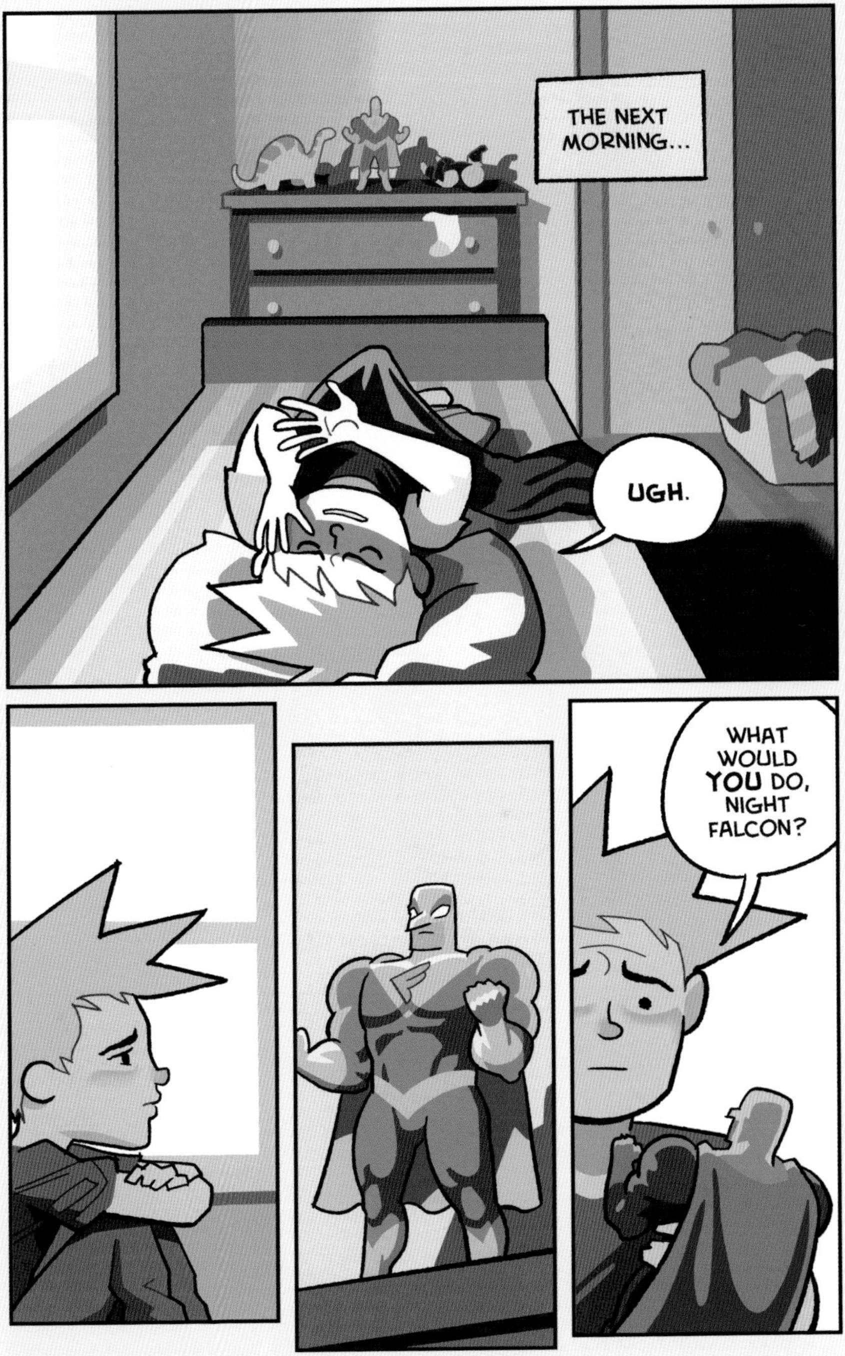
THE NEXT MORNING...
UGH.
WHAT WOULD YOU DO, NIGHT FALCON?

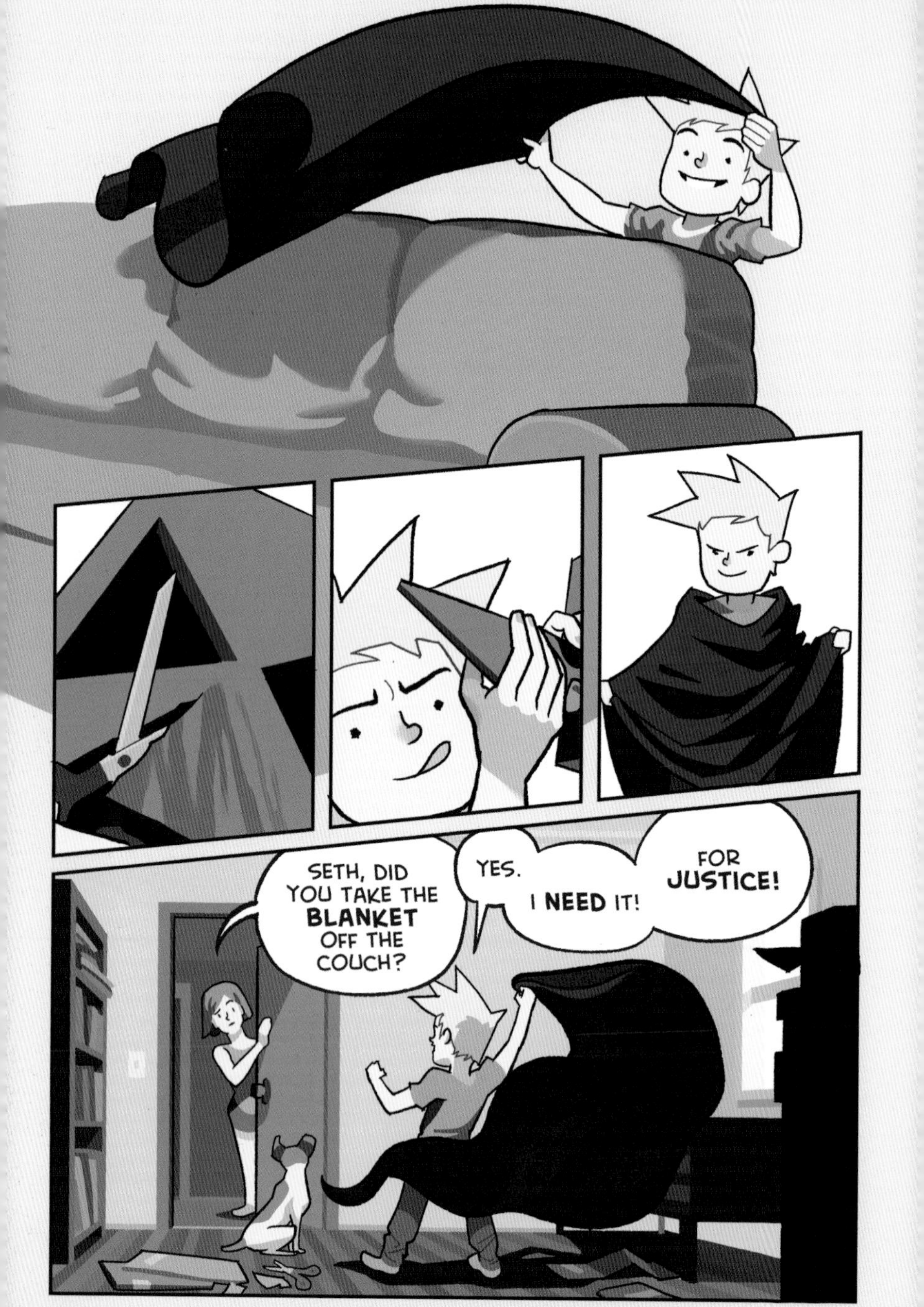
SETH, DID YOU TAKE THE BLANKET OFF THE COUCH?
YES.
I NEED IT!
FOR JUSTICE!

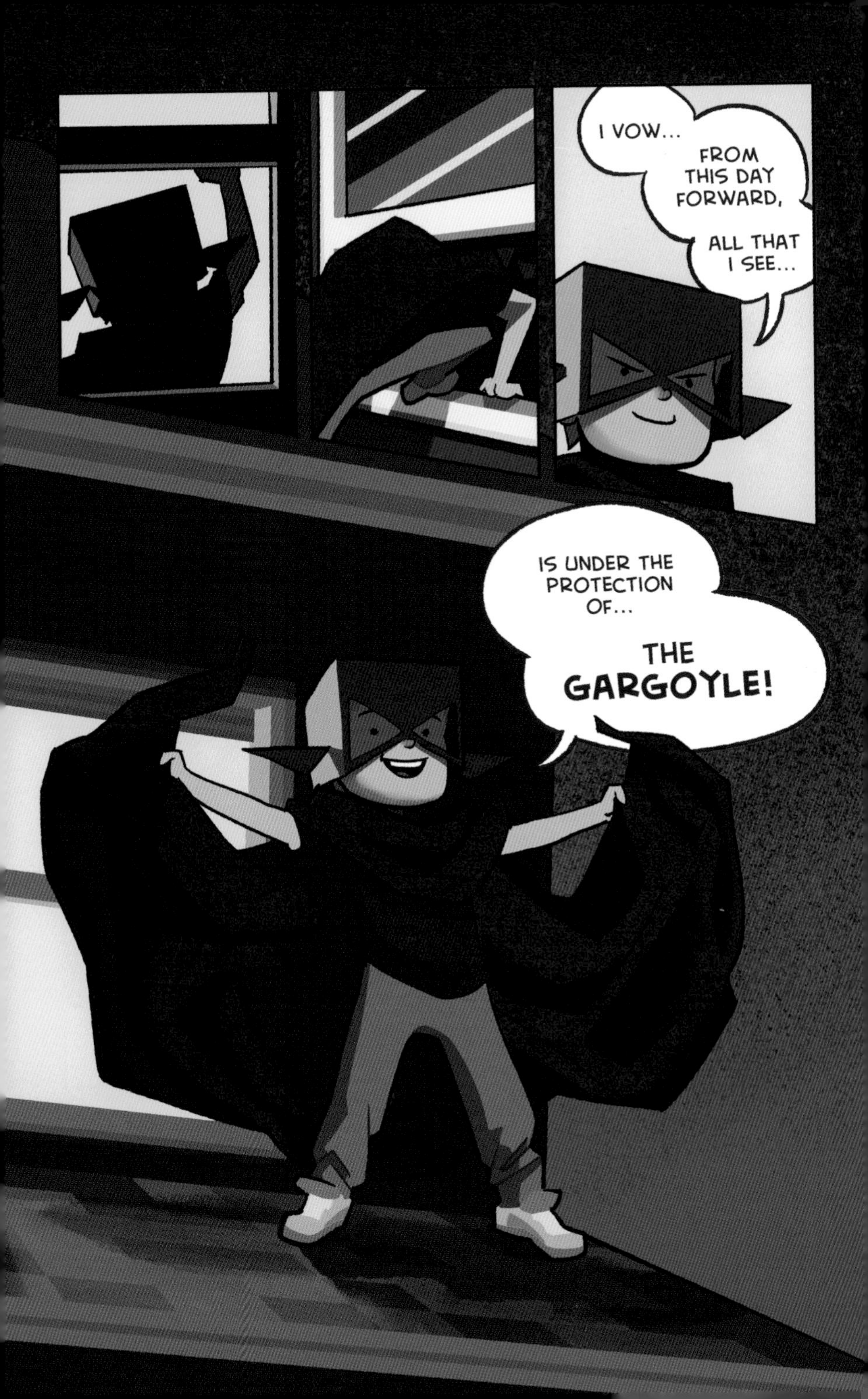
I VOW...
FROM THIS DAY FORWARD,
ALL THAT I SEE...
IS UNDER THE PROTECTION OF...
THE GARGOYLE!

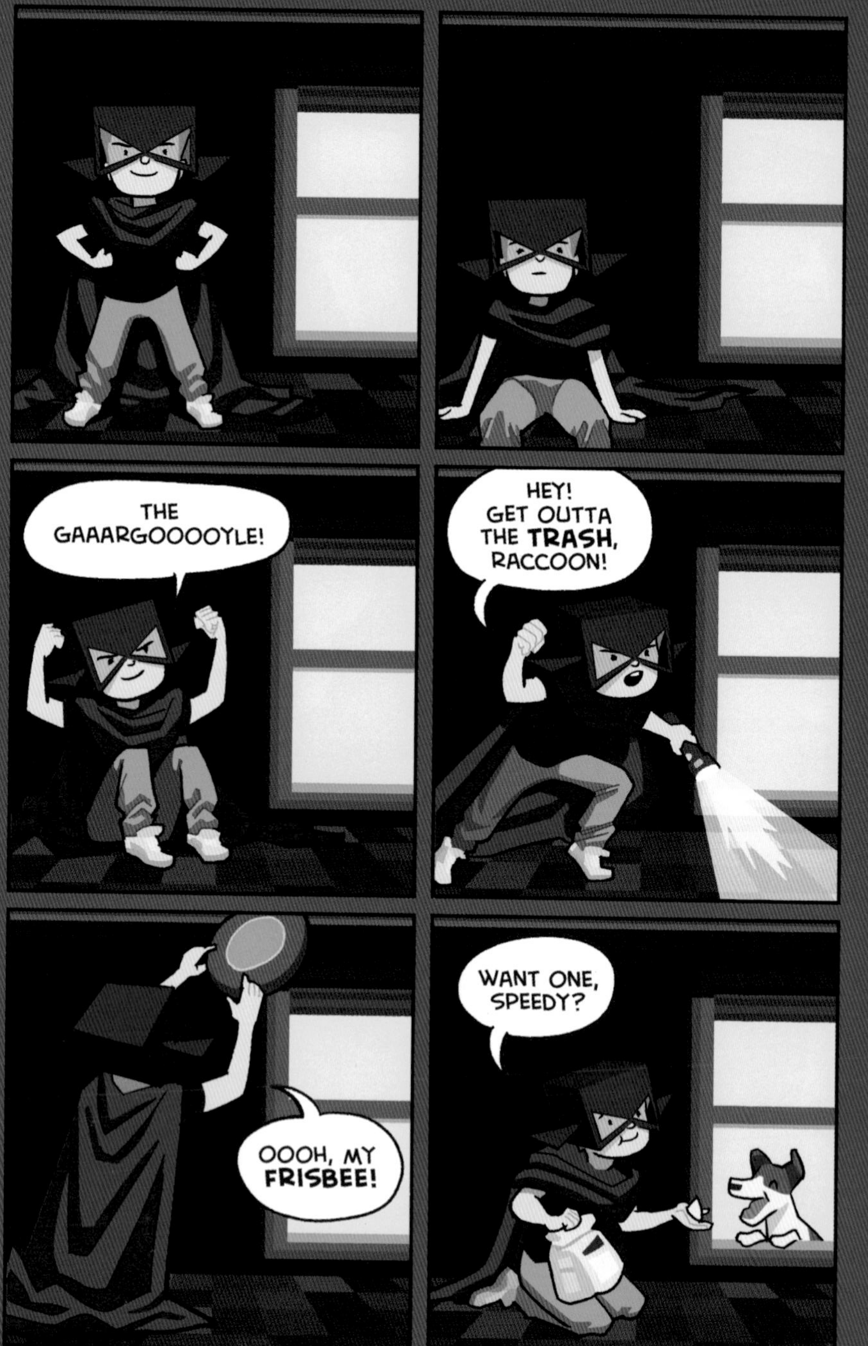
THE GAAARGOOOOOYLE!
HEY! GET OUTTA THE **TRASH**, RACCOON!
OOOH, MY **FRISBEE**!
WANT ONE, SPEEDY?

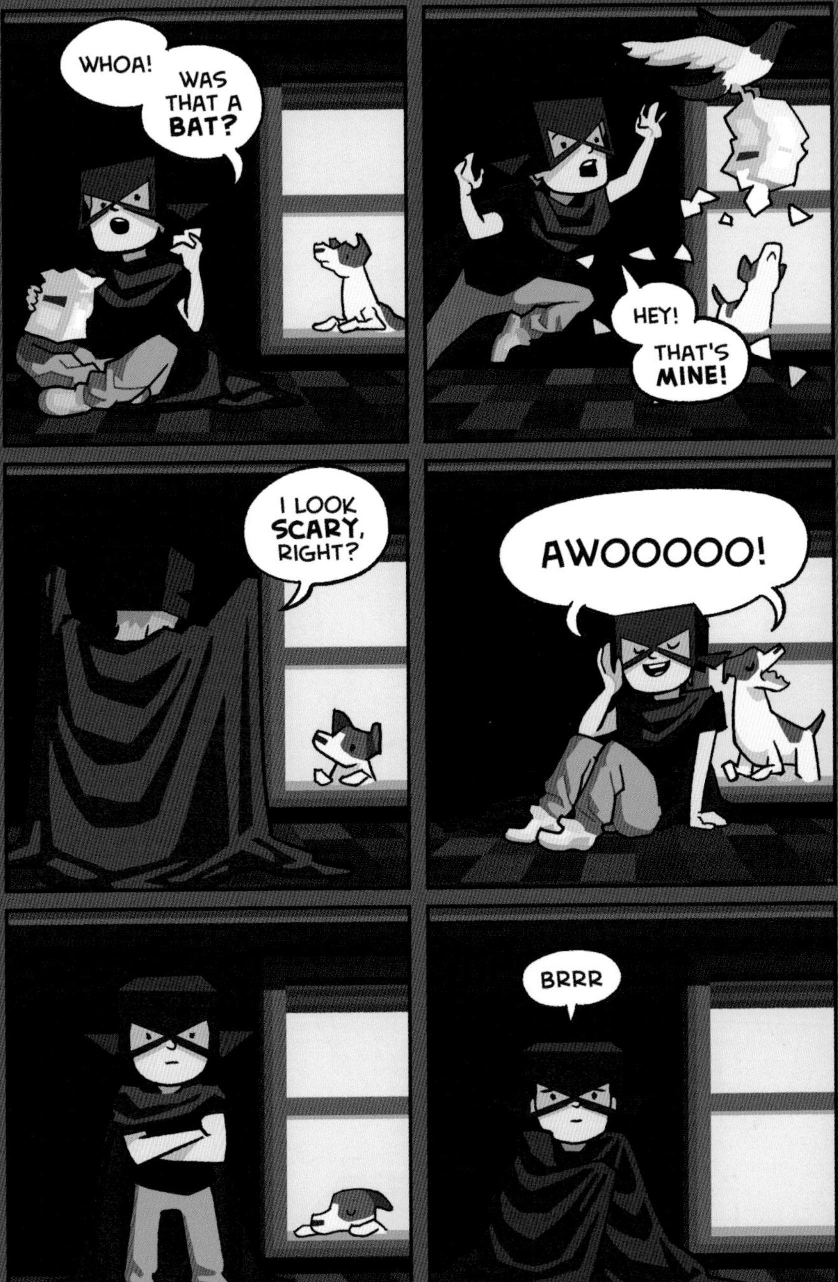

WHOA!
WAS THAT A BAT?
HEY! THAT'S MINE!
I LOOK SCARY, RIGHT?
AWOOOOO!
BRRR

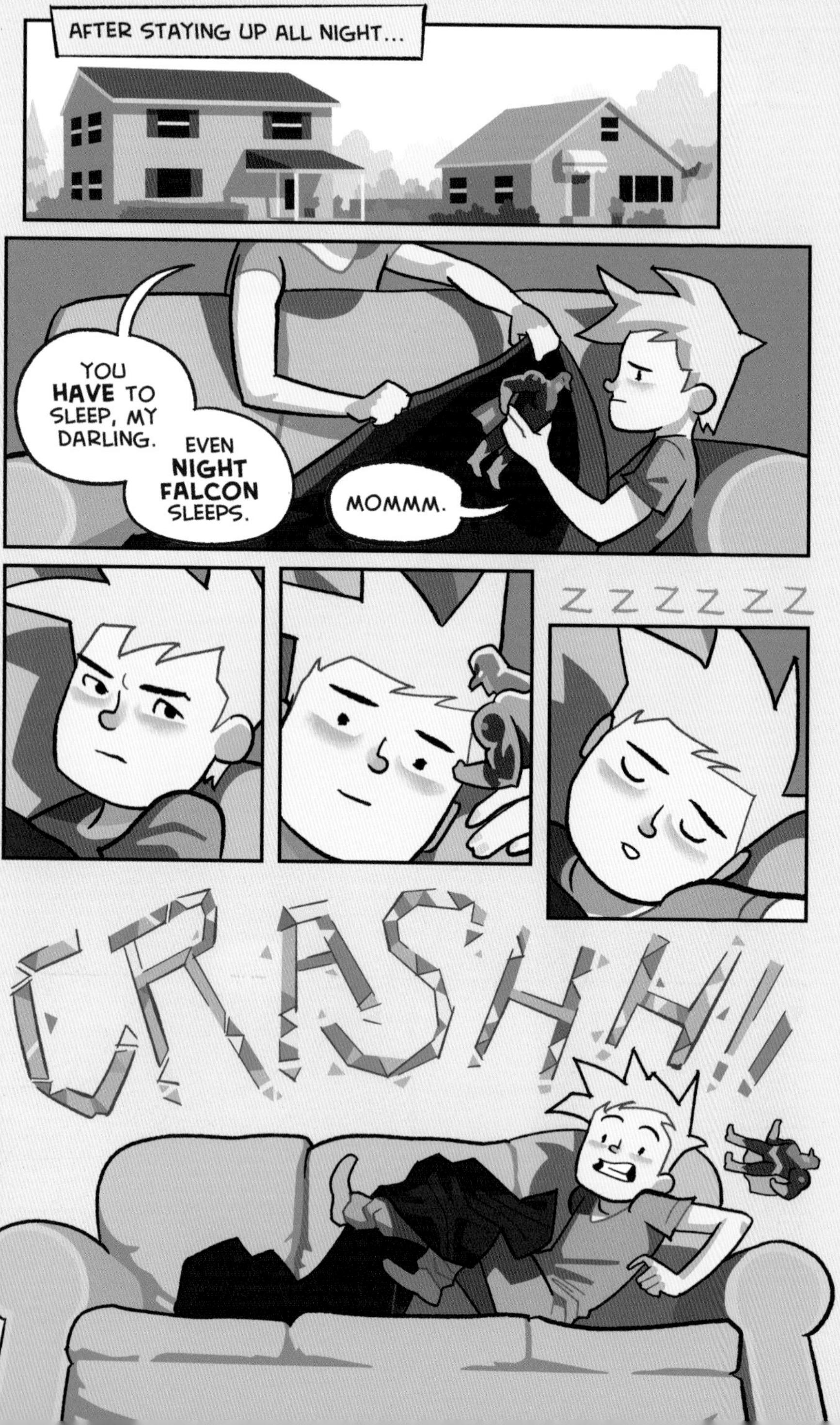
AFTER STAYING UP ALL NIGHT...
YOU **HAVE** TO SLEEP, MY DARLING.
EVEN **NIGHT FALCON** SLEEPS.
MOMMM.
ZZZZZZ
CRASH!!

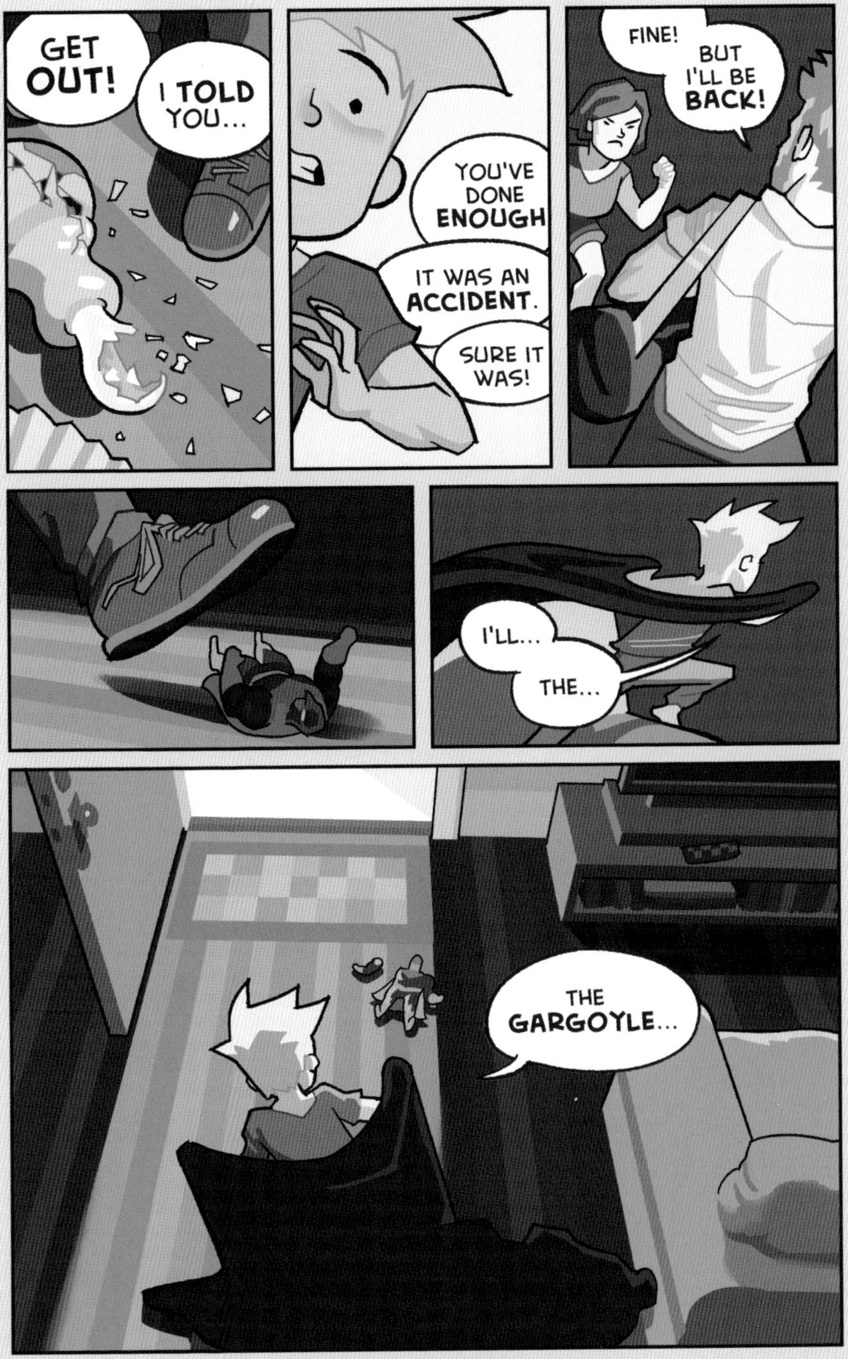
GET OUT!
I TOLD YOU...
YOU'VE DONE ENOUGH
IT WAS AN ACCIDENT.
SURE IT WAS!
FINE!
BUT I'LL BE BACK!
I'LL...
THE...
THE GARGOYLE...

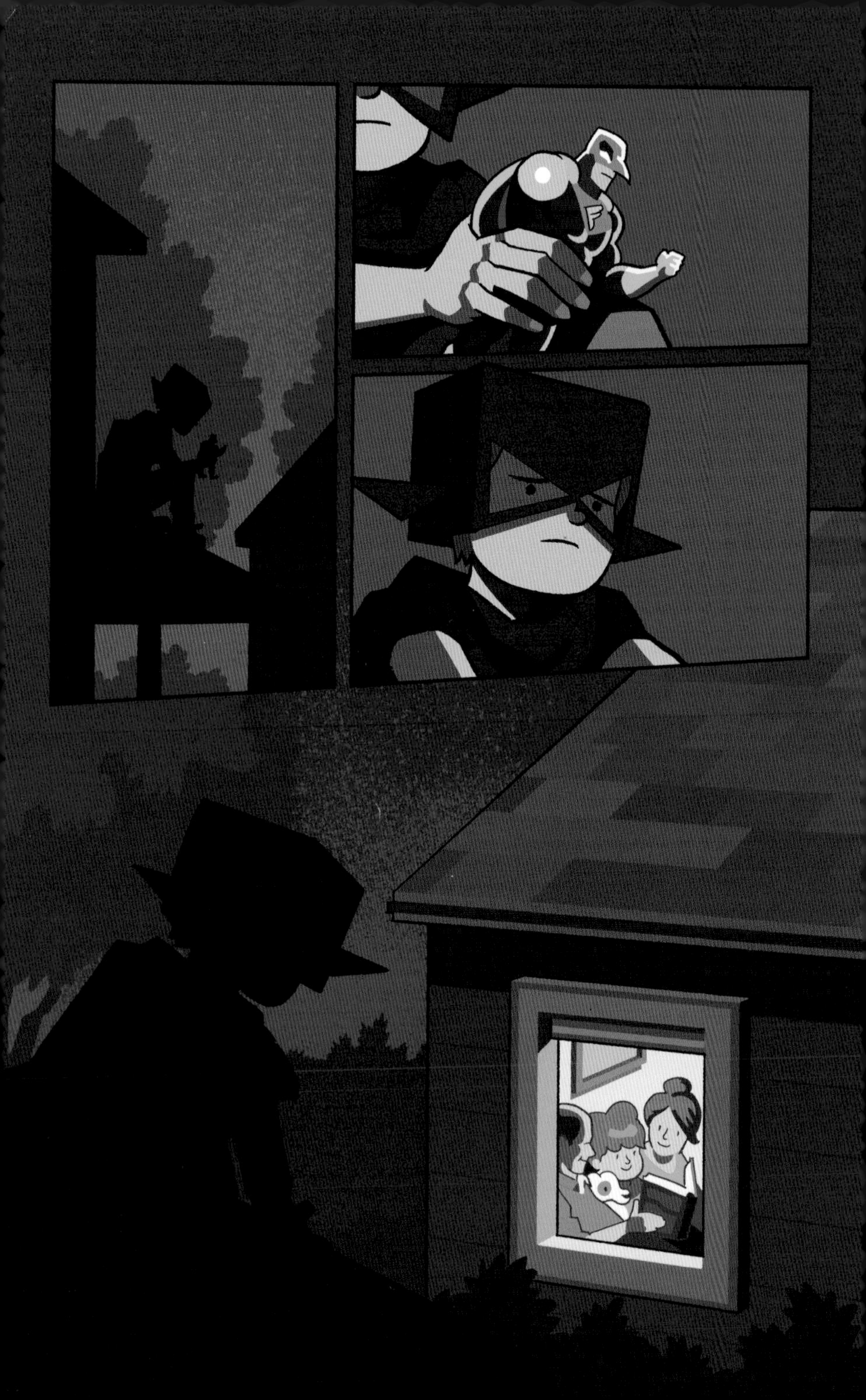

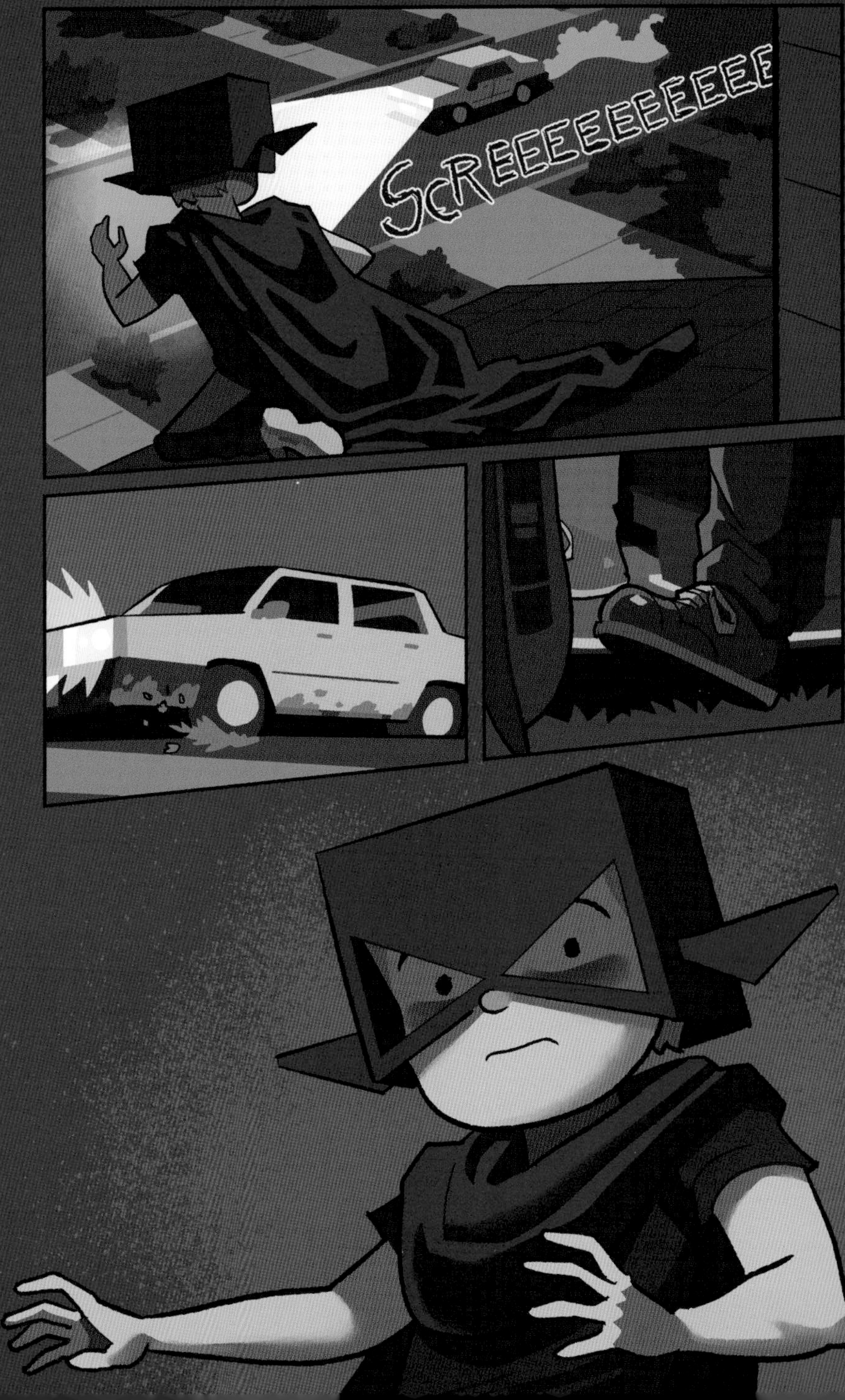
SCREEEEEEEEEEEE

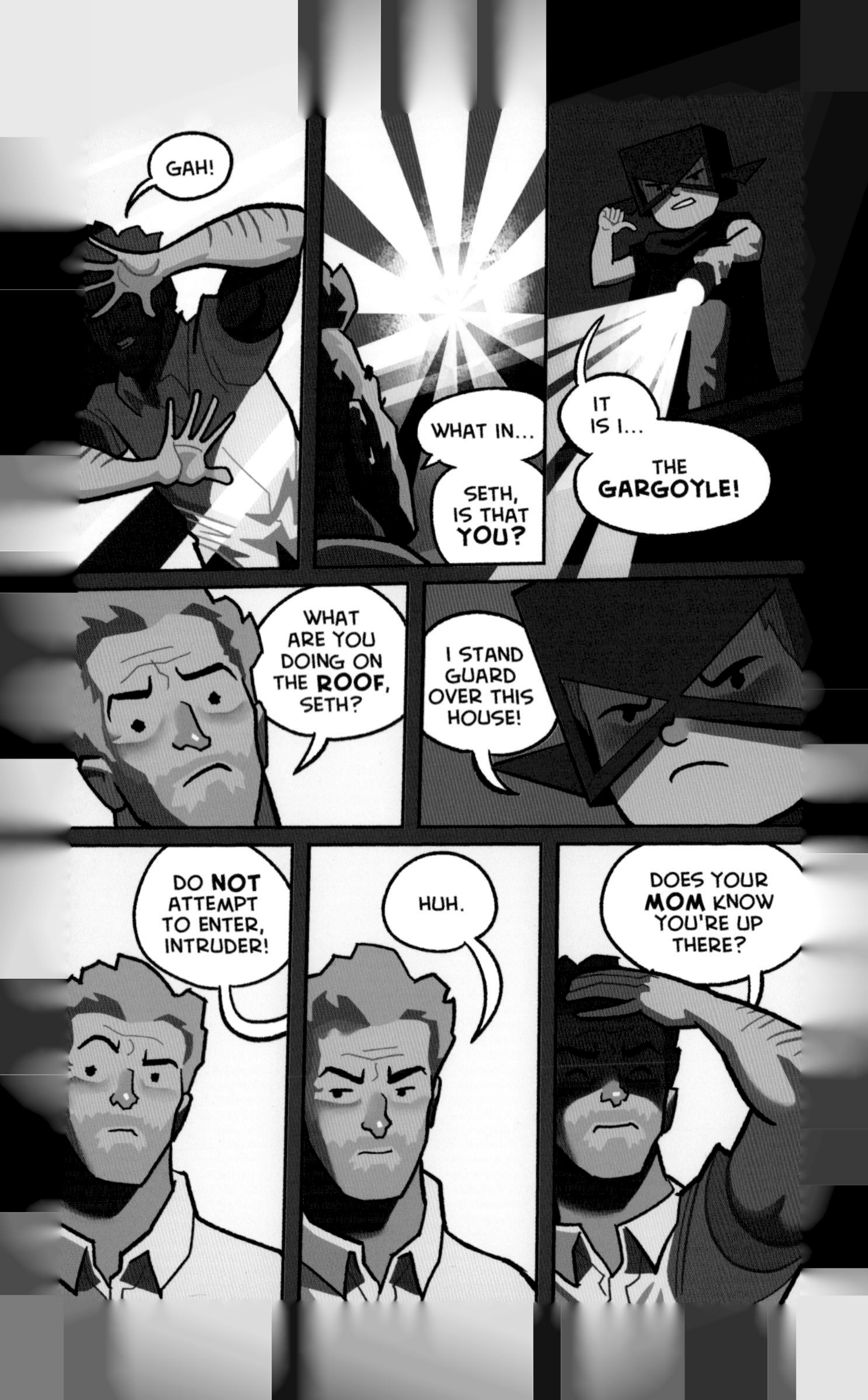
GAH!
WHAT IN...
SETH, IS THAT **YOU?**
IT IS I...
THE **GARGOYLE!**
WHAT ARE YOU DOING ON THE **ROOF,** SETH?
I STAND GUARD OVER THIS HOUSE!
DO **NOT** ATTEMPT TO ENTER, INTRUDER!
HUH.
DOES YOUR **MOM** KNOW YOU'RE UP THERE?

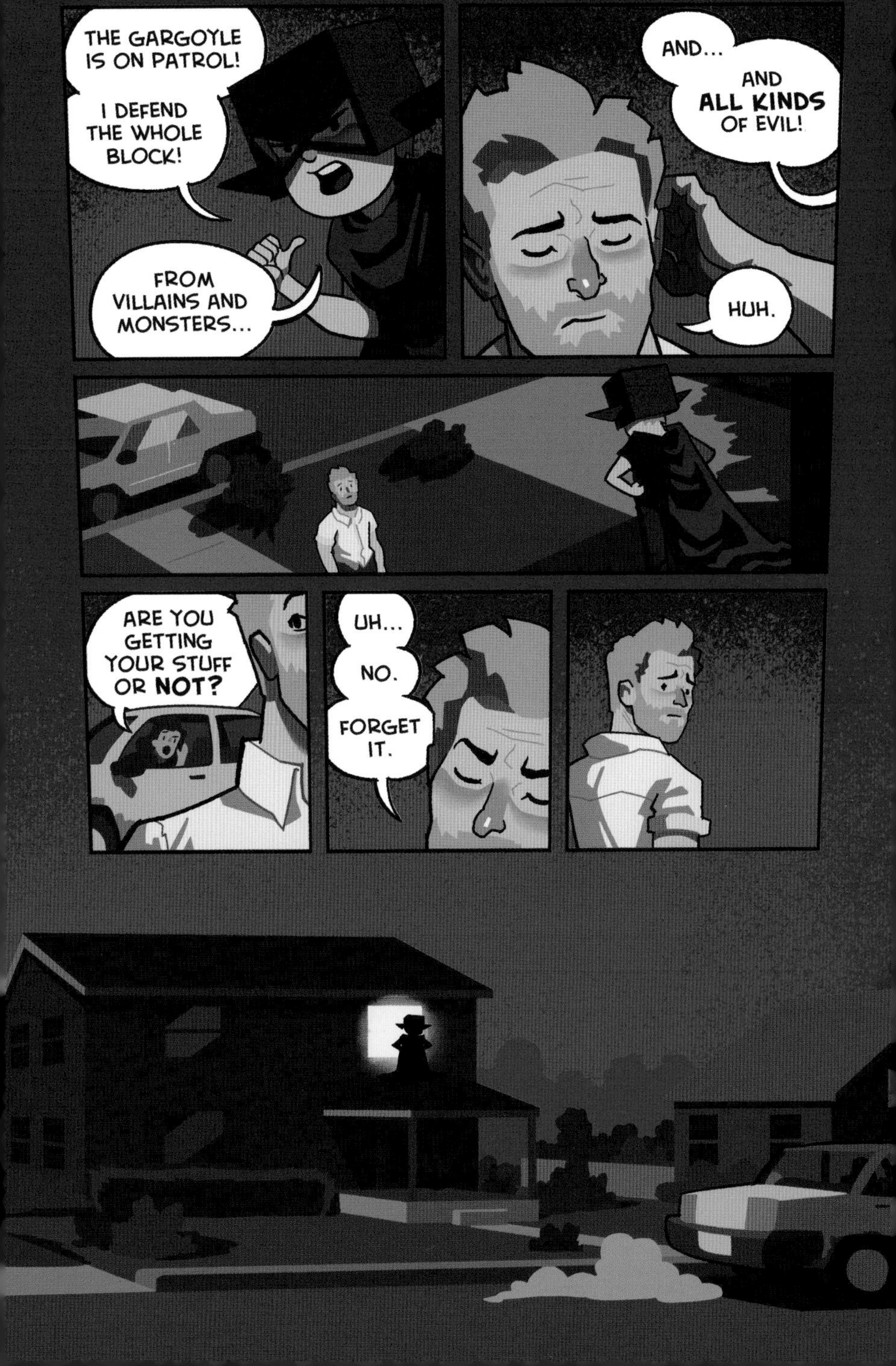
THE GARGOYLE IS ON PATROL!
I DEFEND THE WHOLE BLOCK!
FROM VILLAINS AND MONSTERS...
AND...
AND **ALL KINDS** OF EVIL!
HUH.
ARE YOU GETTING YOUR STUFF OR **NOT?**
UH...
NO.
FORGET IT.

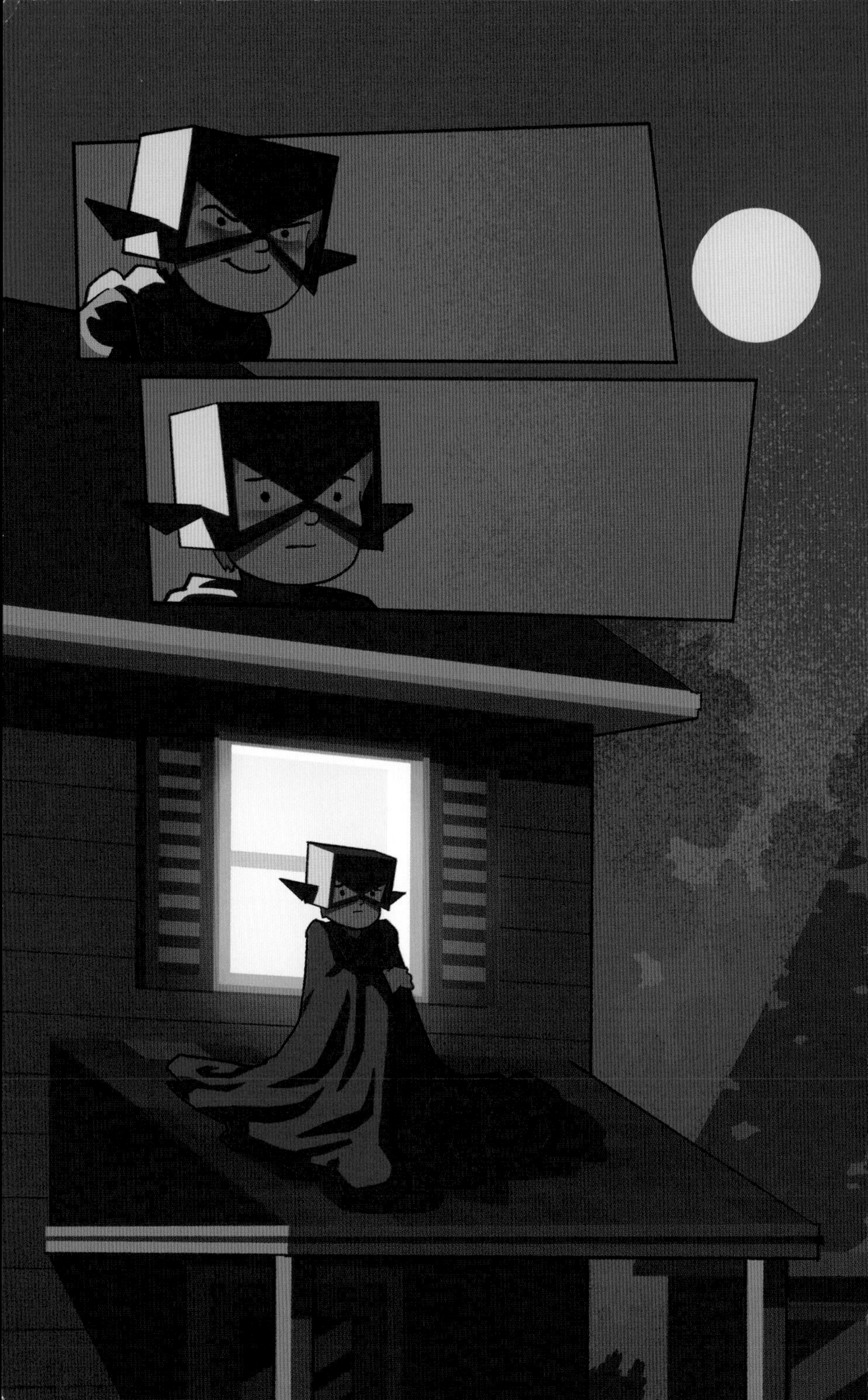

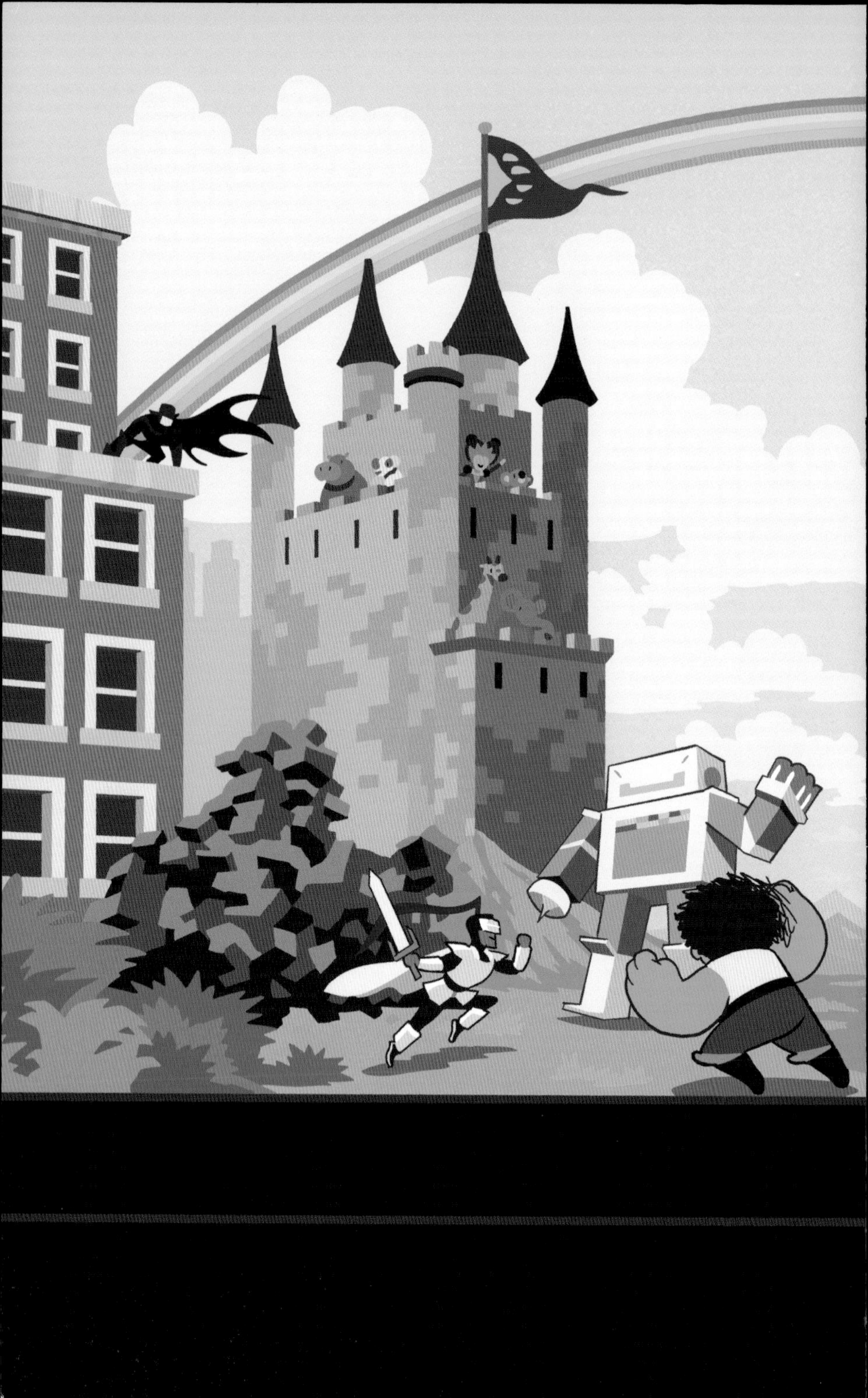

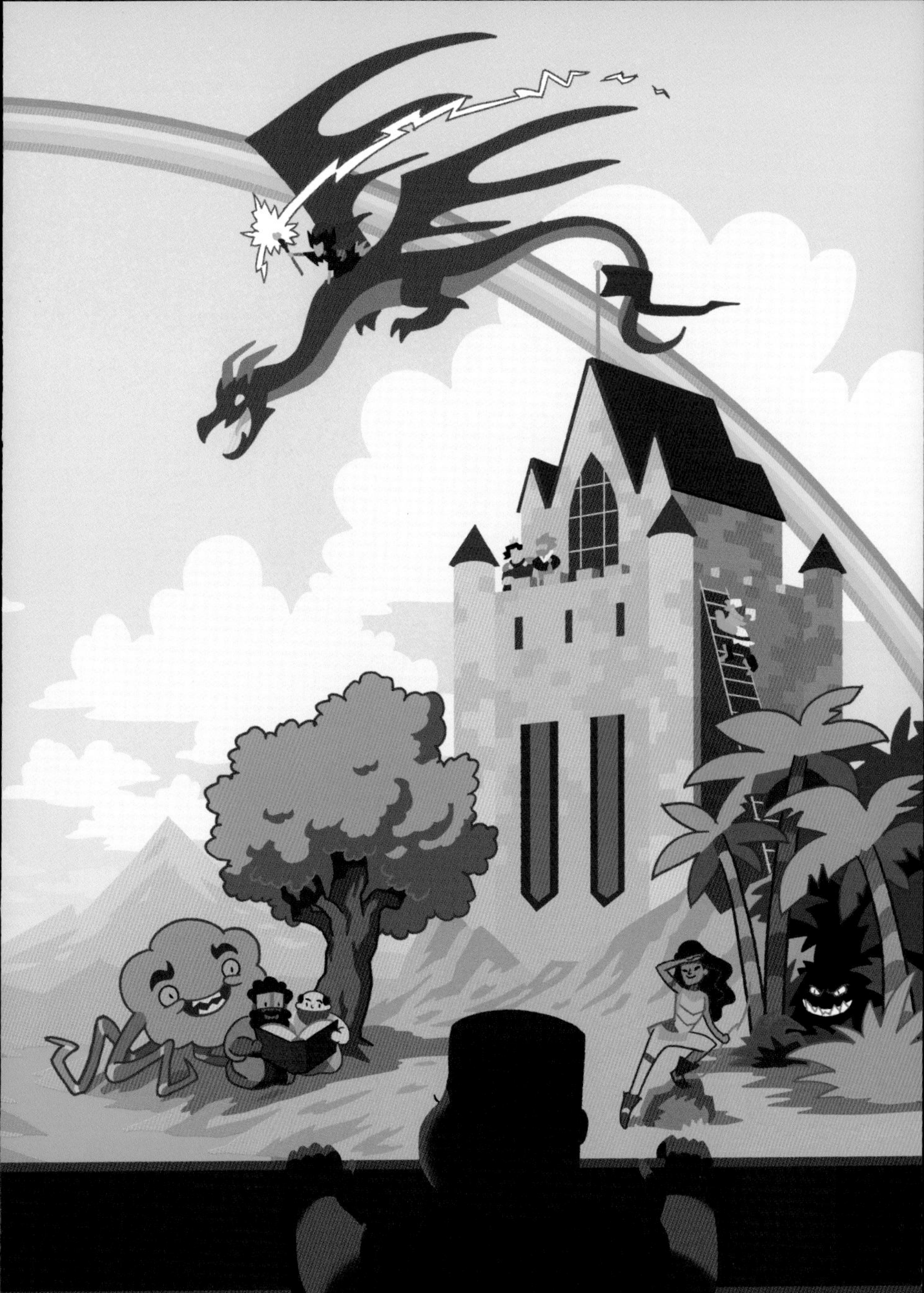

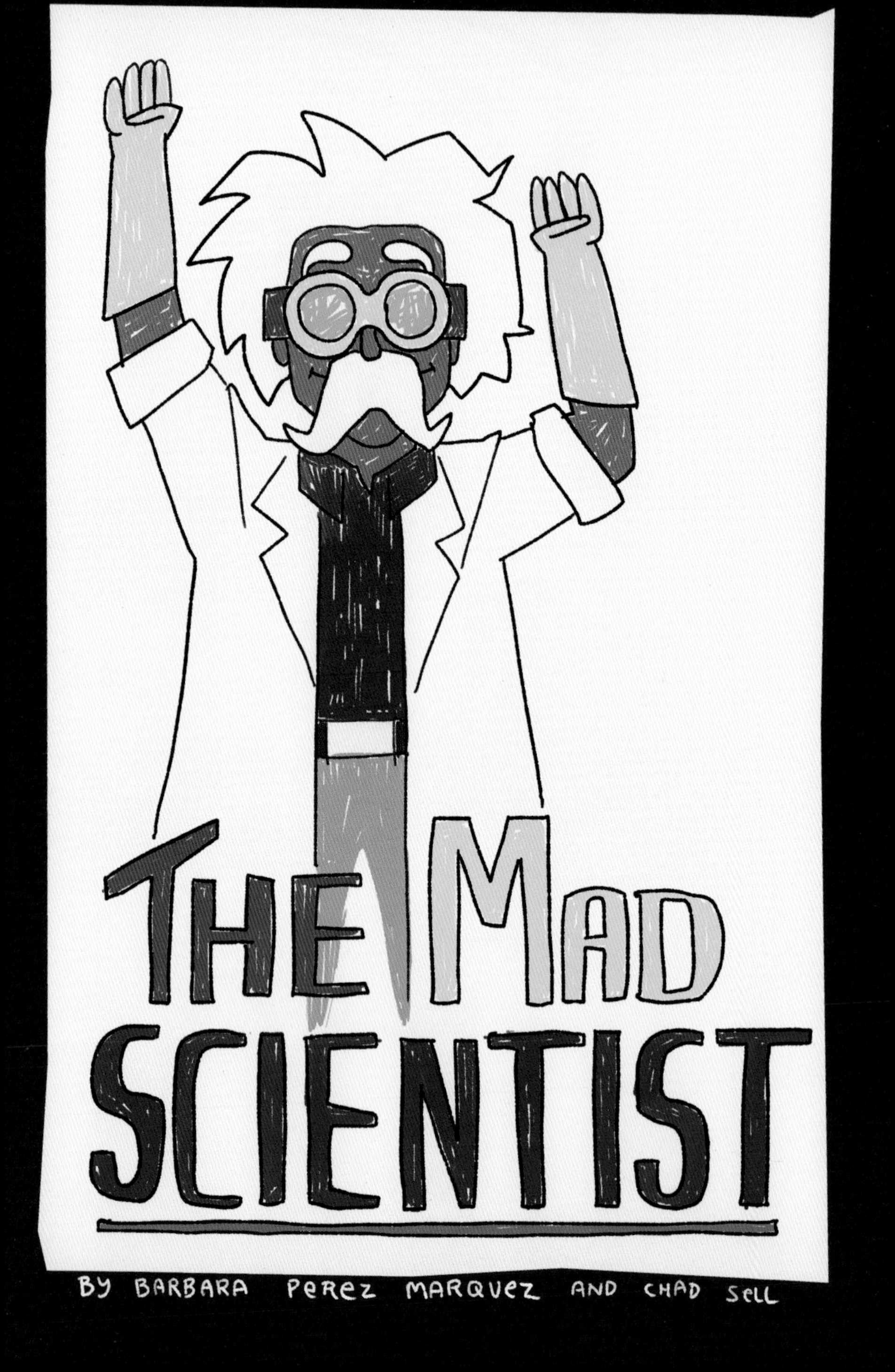
THE MAD
SCIENTIST

BY BARBARA PEREZ MARQUEZ AND CHAD SELL

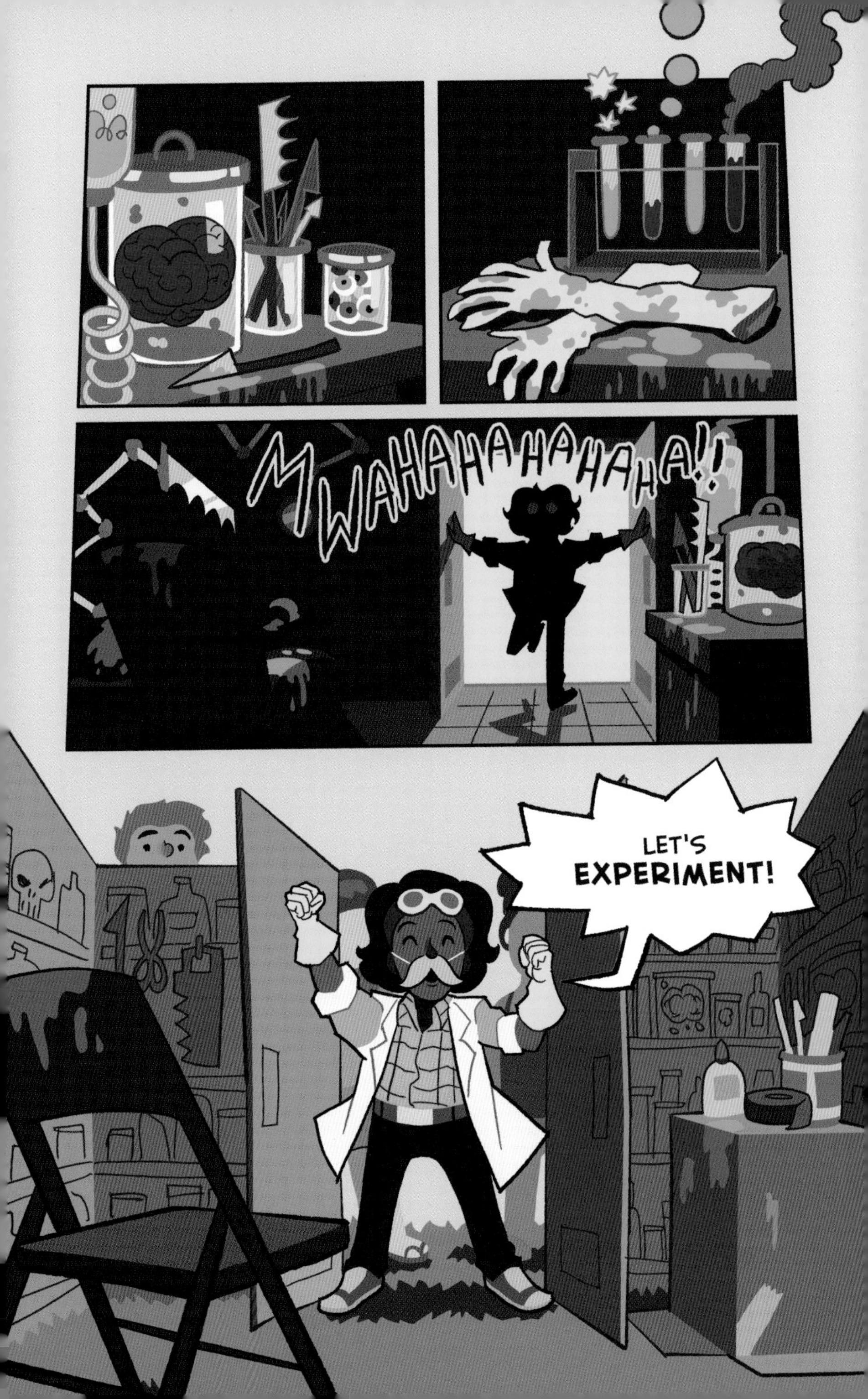
MWAHAHAHAHAHA!!
LET'S EXPERIMENT!

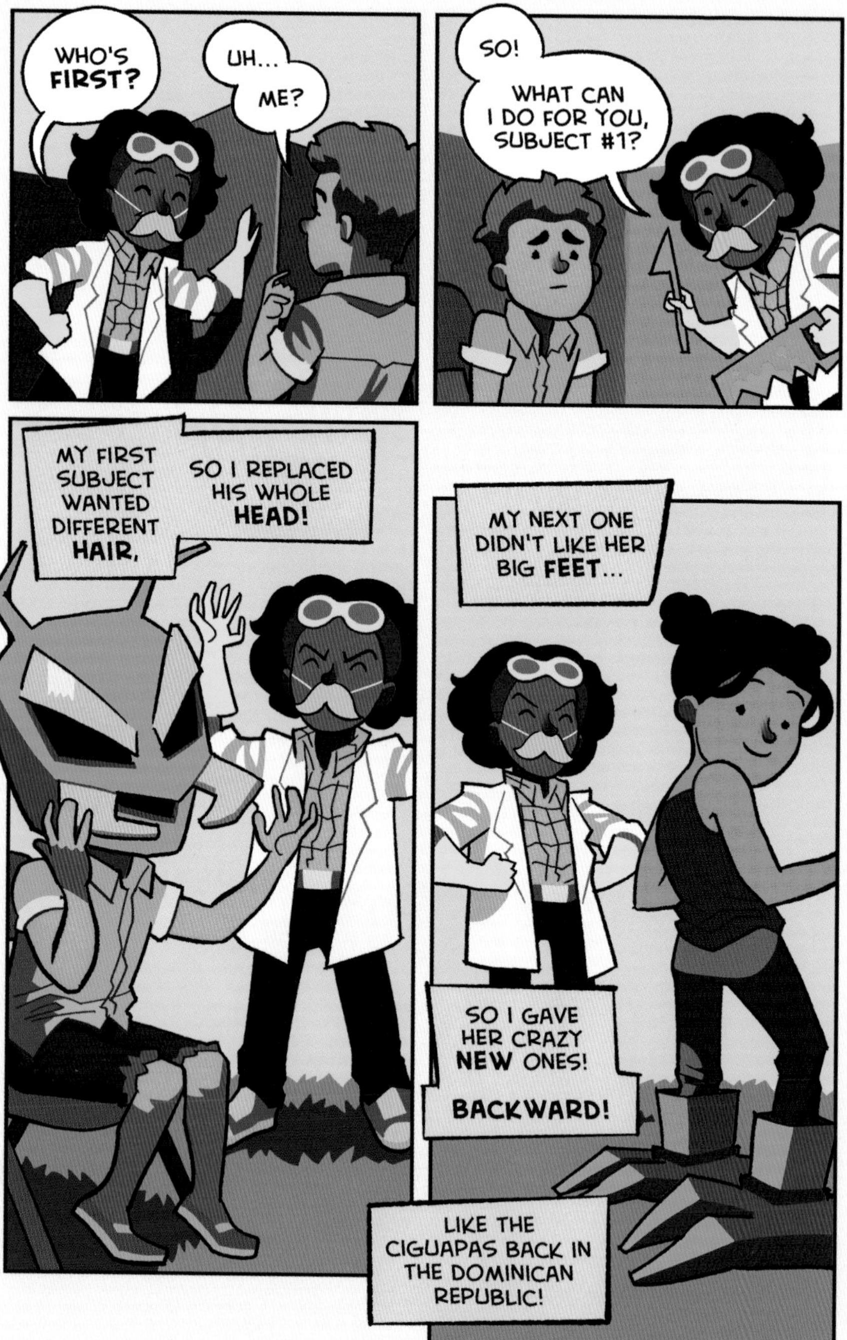
WHO'S FIRST?
UH... ME?
SO!
WHAT CAN I DO FOR YOU, SUBJECT #1?
MY FIRST SUBJECT WANTED DIFFERENT HAIR,
SO I REPLACED HIS WHOLE HEAD!
MY NEXT ONE DIDN'T LIKE HER BIG FEET...
SO I GAVE HER CRAZY NEW ONES!
BACKWARD!
LIKE THE CIGUAPAS BACK IN THE DOMINICAN REPUBLIC!

149

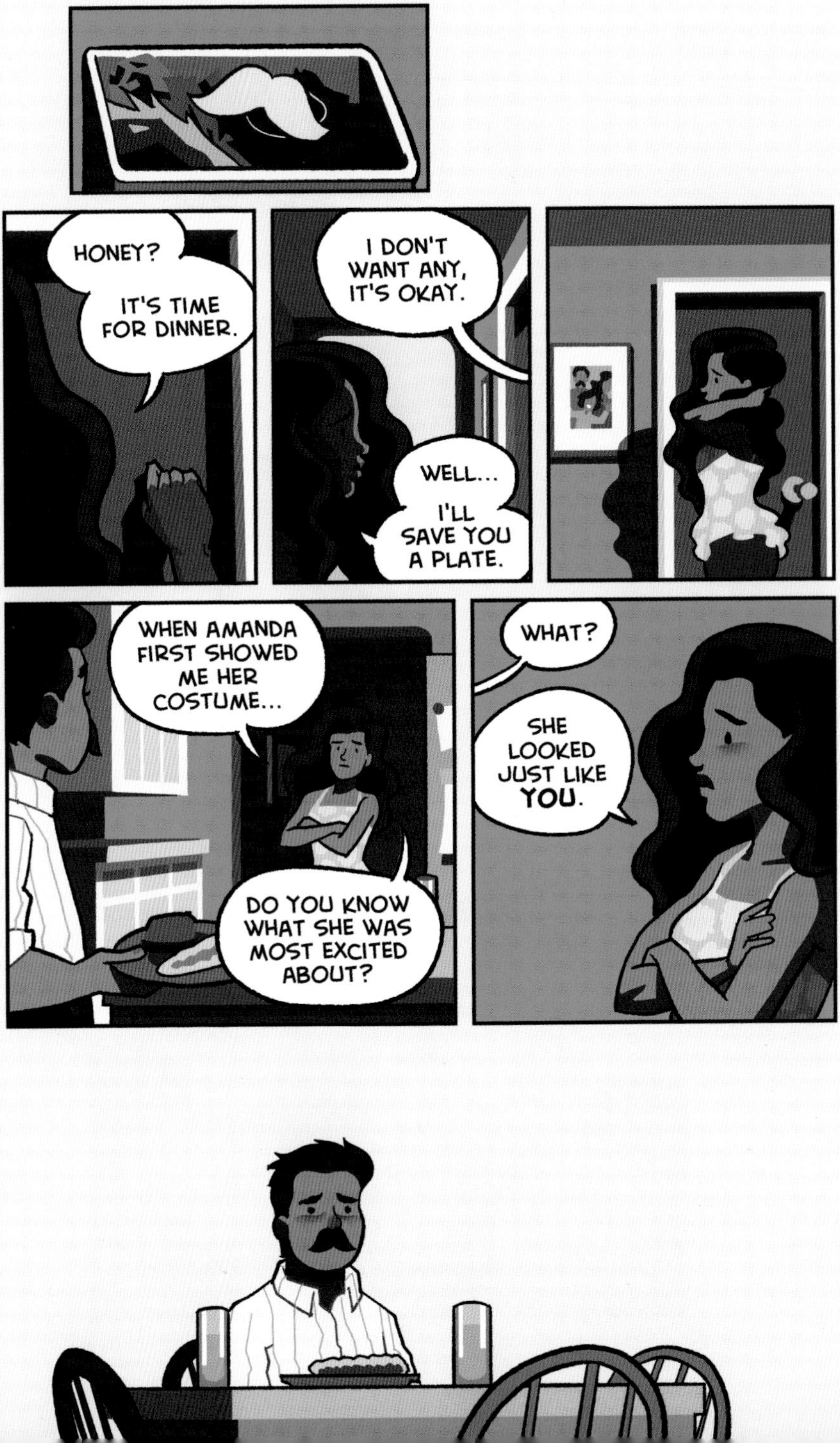
HONEY?
IT'S TIME FOR DINNER.
I DON'T WANT ANY, IT'S OKAY.
WELL...
I'LL SAVE YOU A PLATE.
WHEN AMANDA FIRST SHOWED ME HER COSTUME...
DO YOU KNOW WHAT SHE WAS MOST EXCITED ABOUT?
WHAT?
SHE LOOKED JUST LIKE **YOU**.

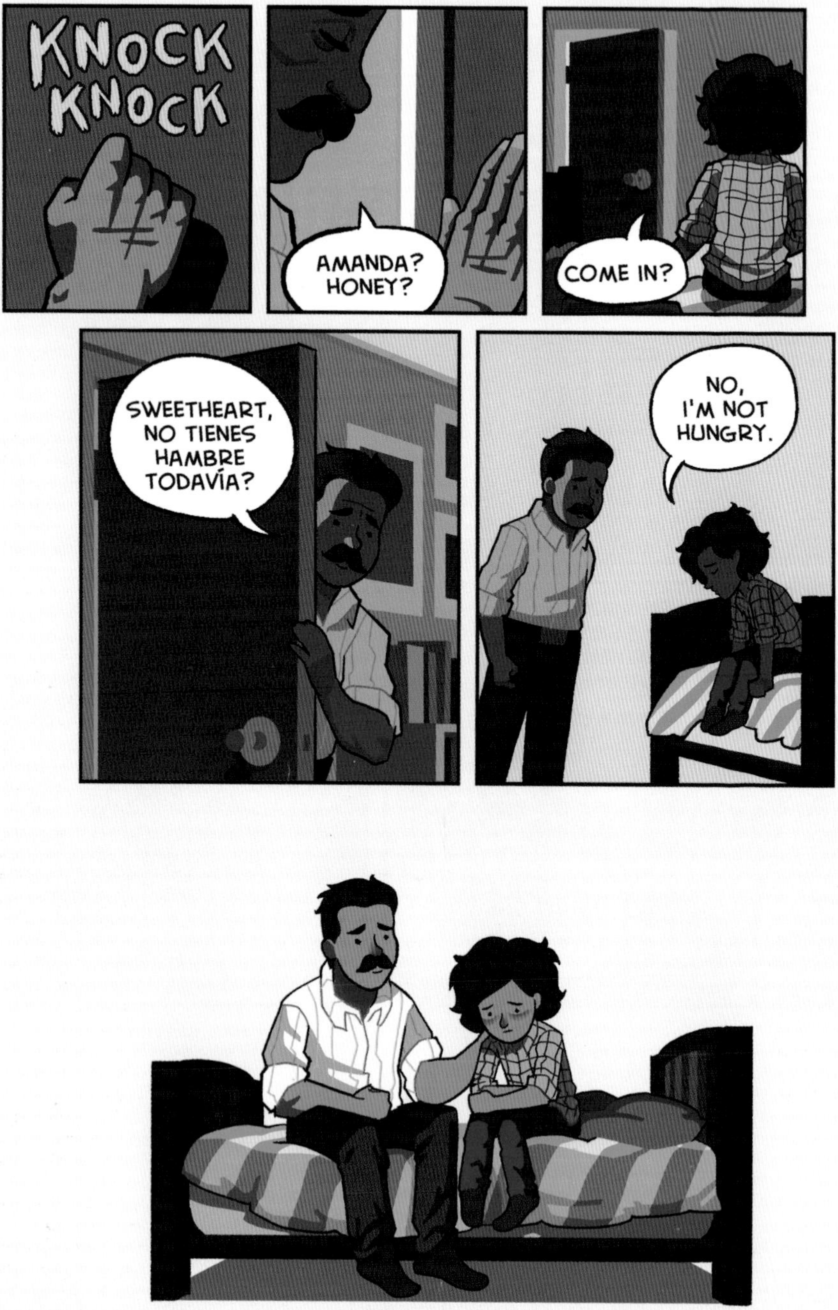
KNOCK
KNOCK
AMANDA? HONEY?
COME IN?
SWEETHEART, NO TIENES HAMBRE TODAVÍA?
NO, I'M NOT HUNGRY.

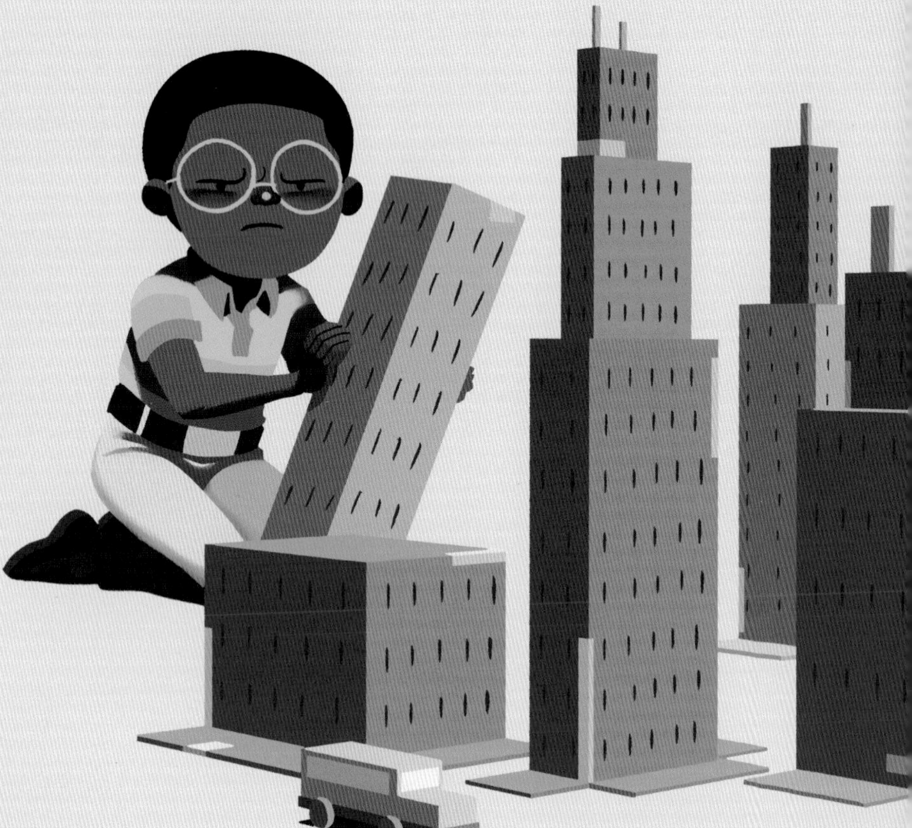

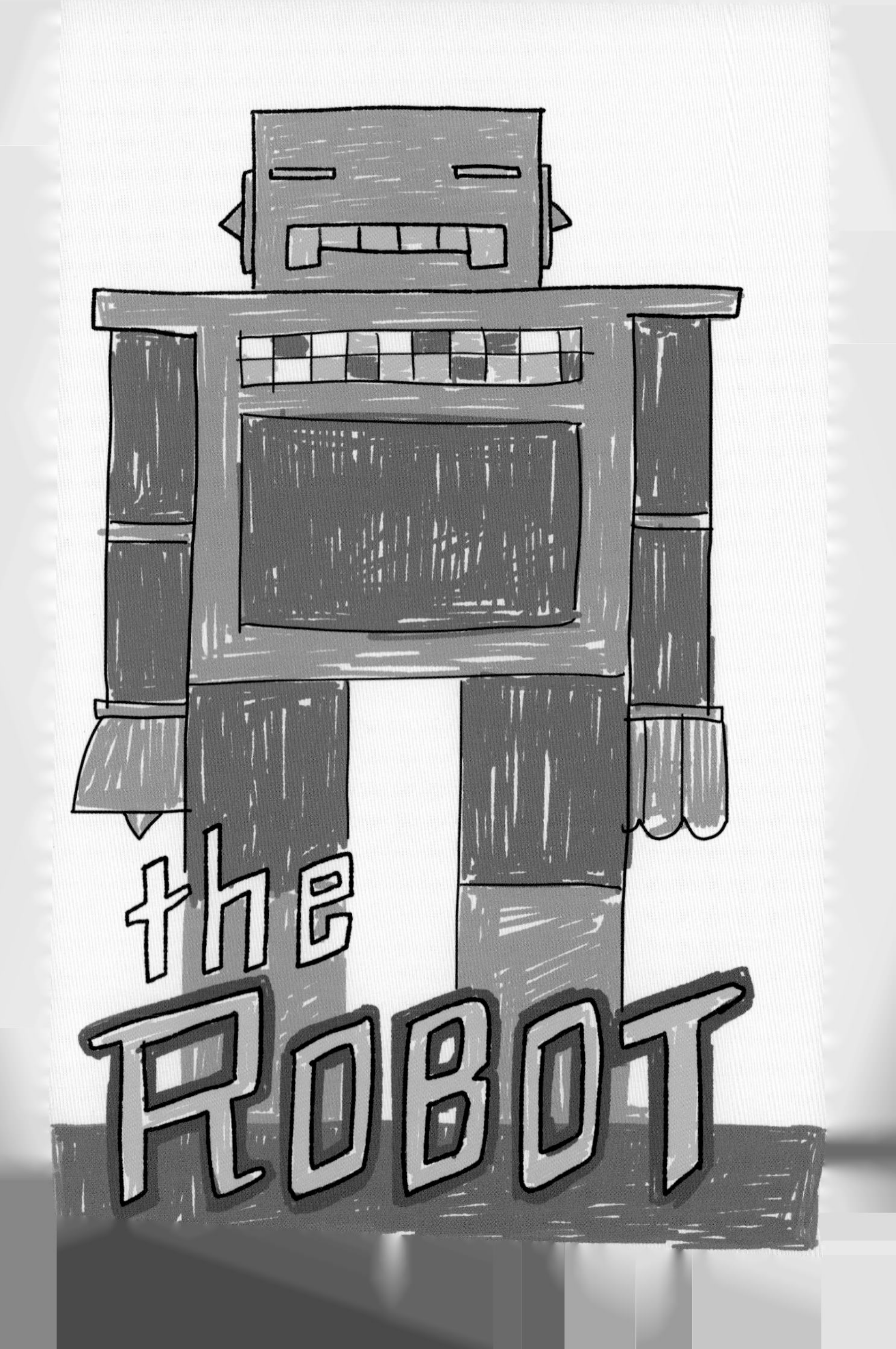
the
ROBOT

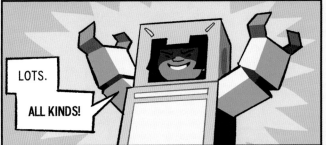

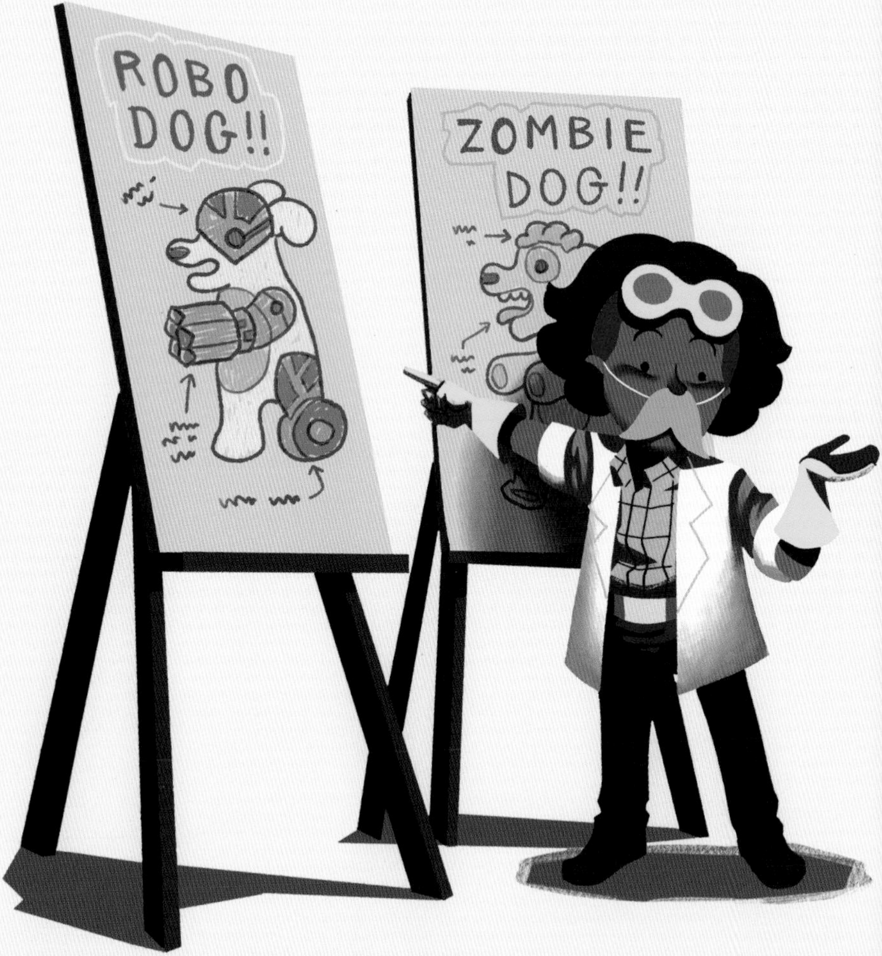
ROBO DOG!!
ZOMBIE DOG!!

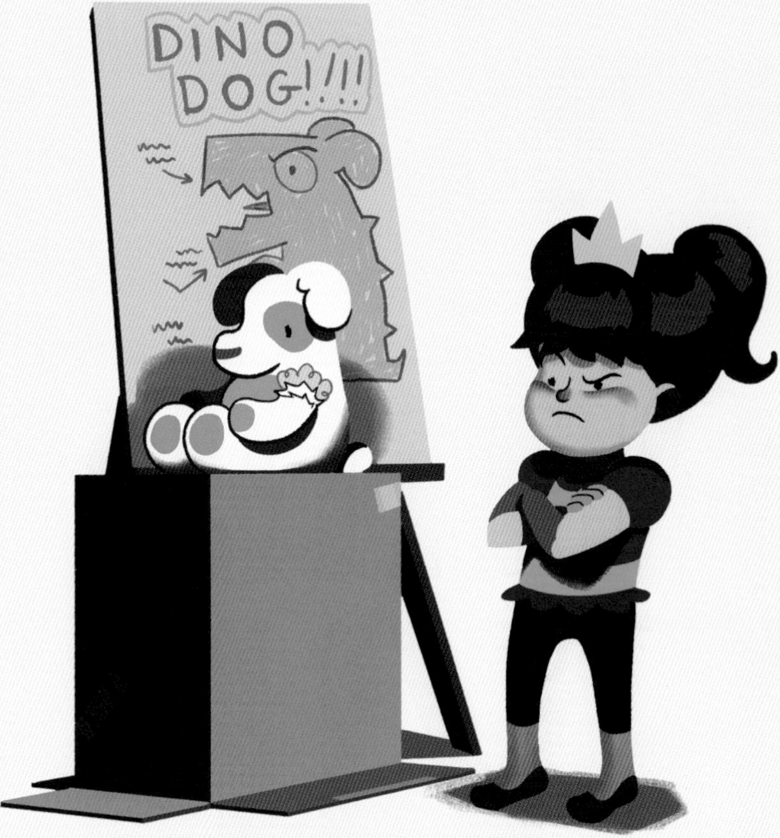
DINO DOG!!!!

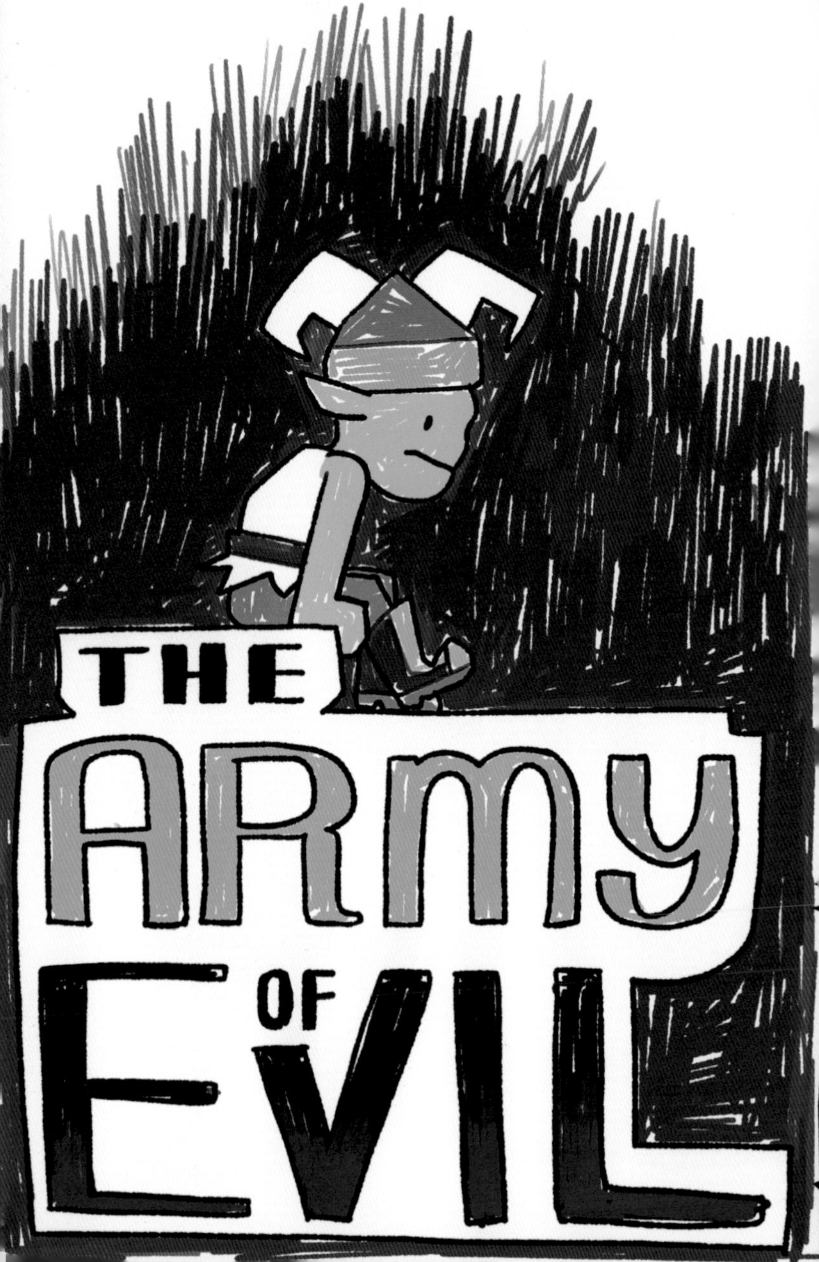
THE
ARMY
OF
EVIL

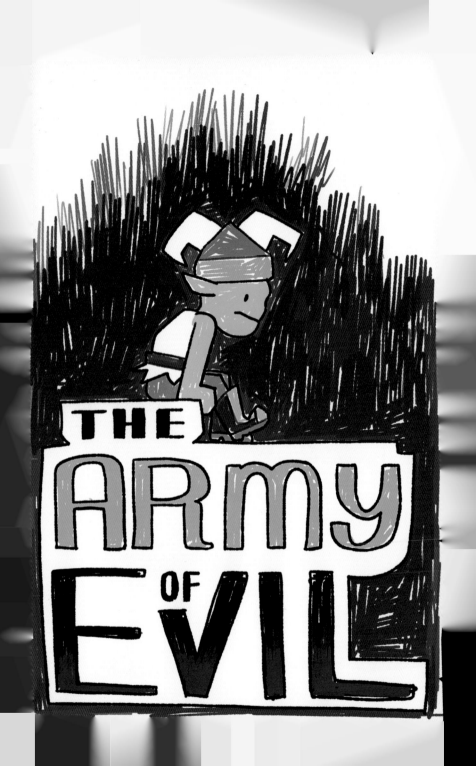

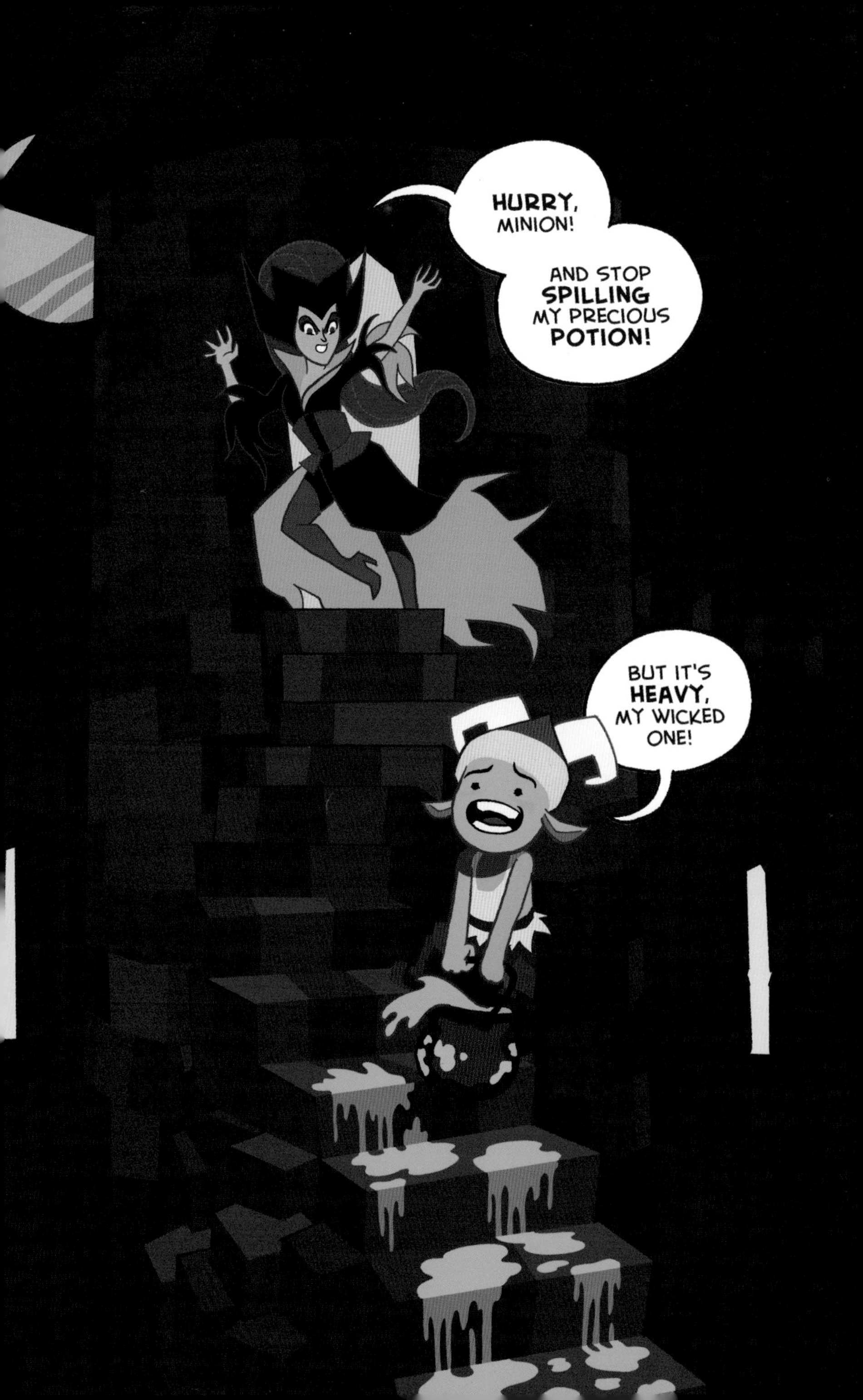
HURRY, MINION!
AND STOP SPILLING MY PRECIOUS POTION!
BUT IT'S HEAVY, MY WICKED ONE!

181

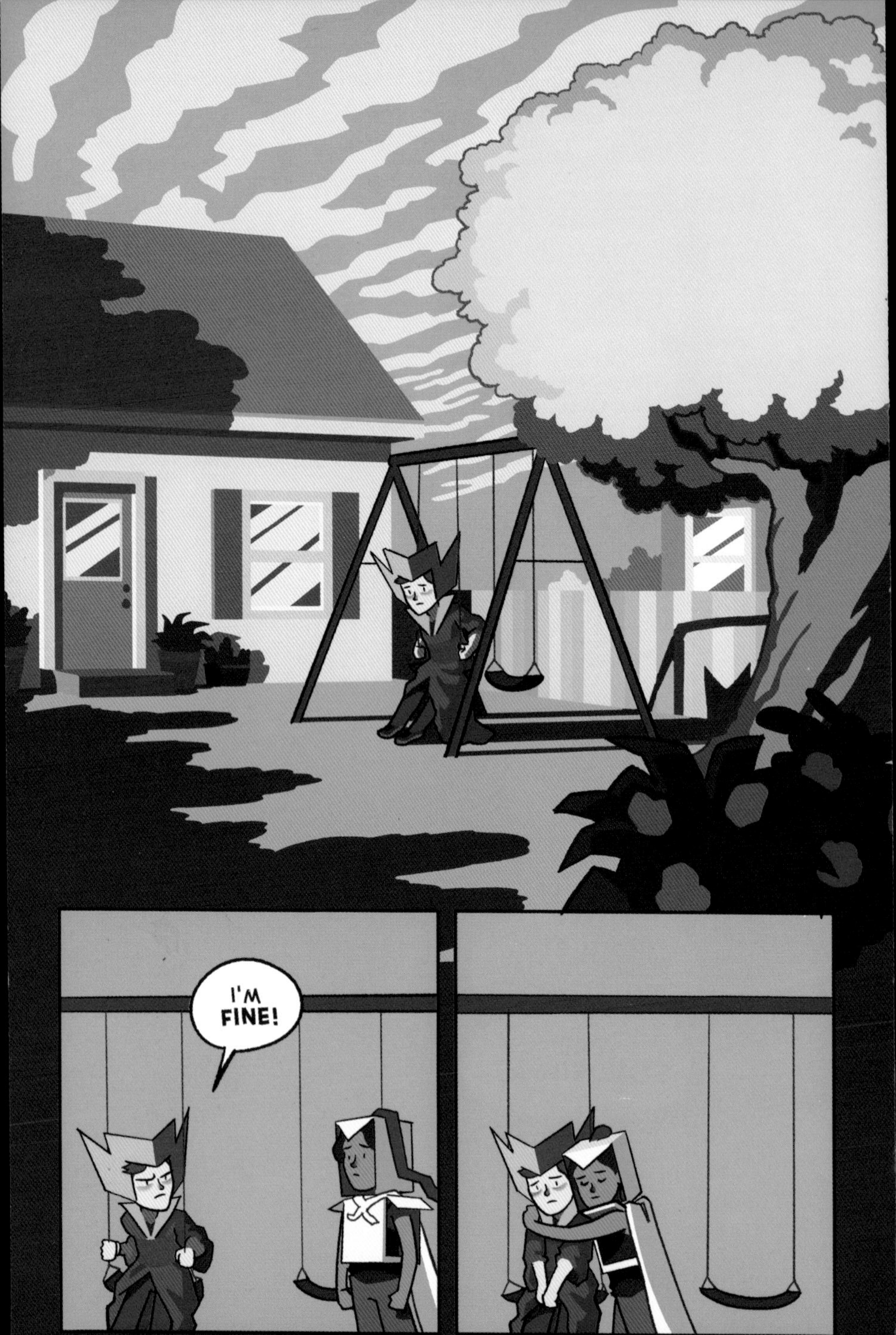
I'M FINE!

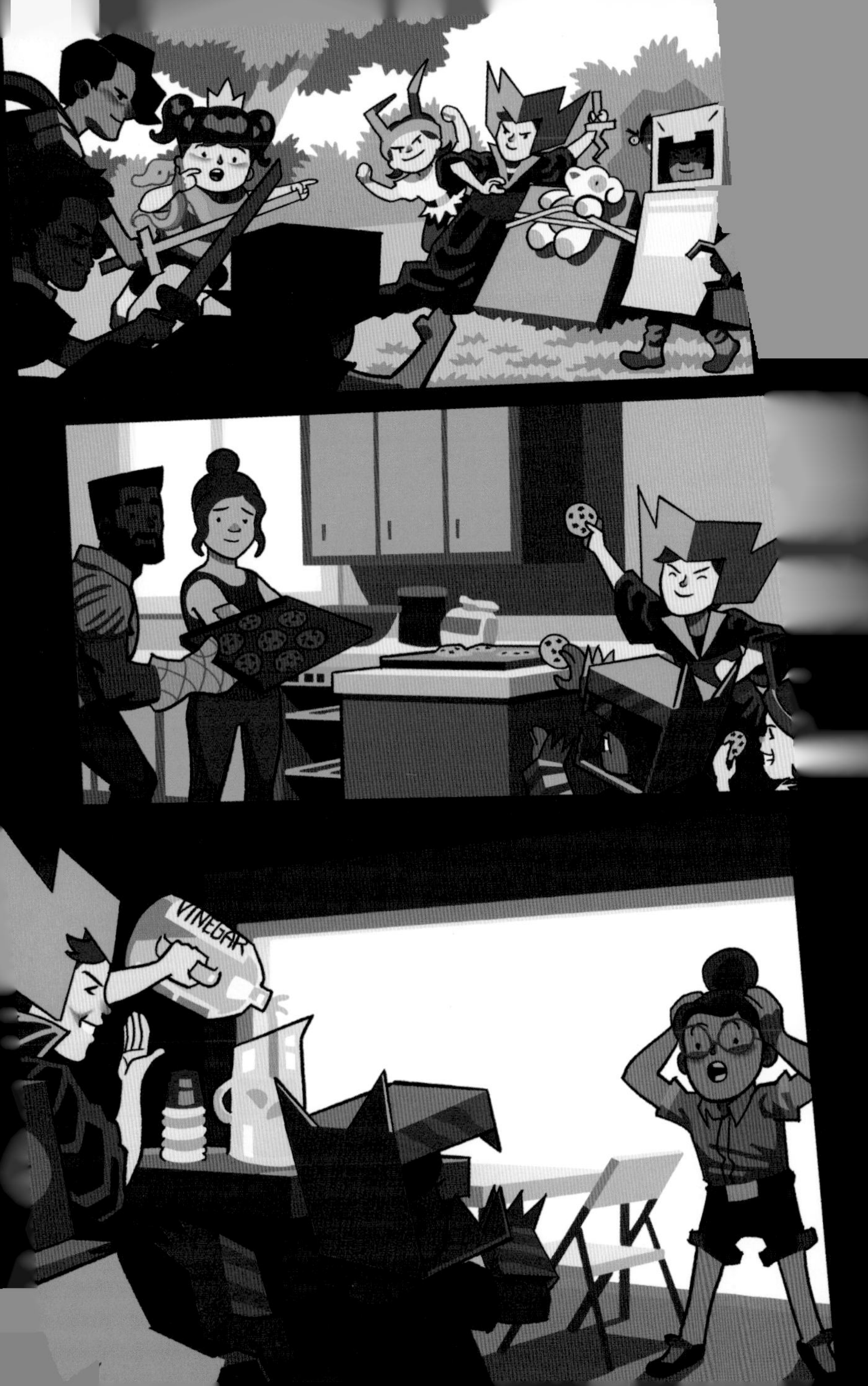
VINEGAR

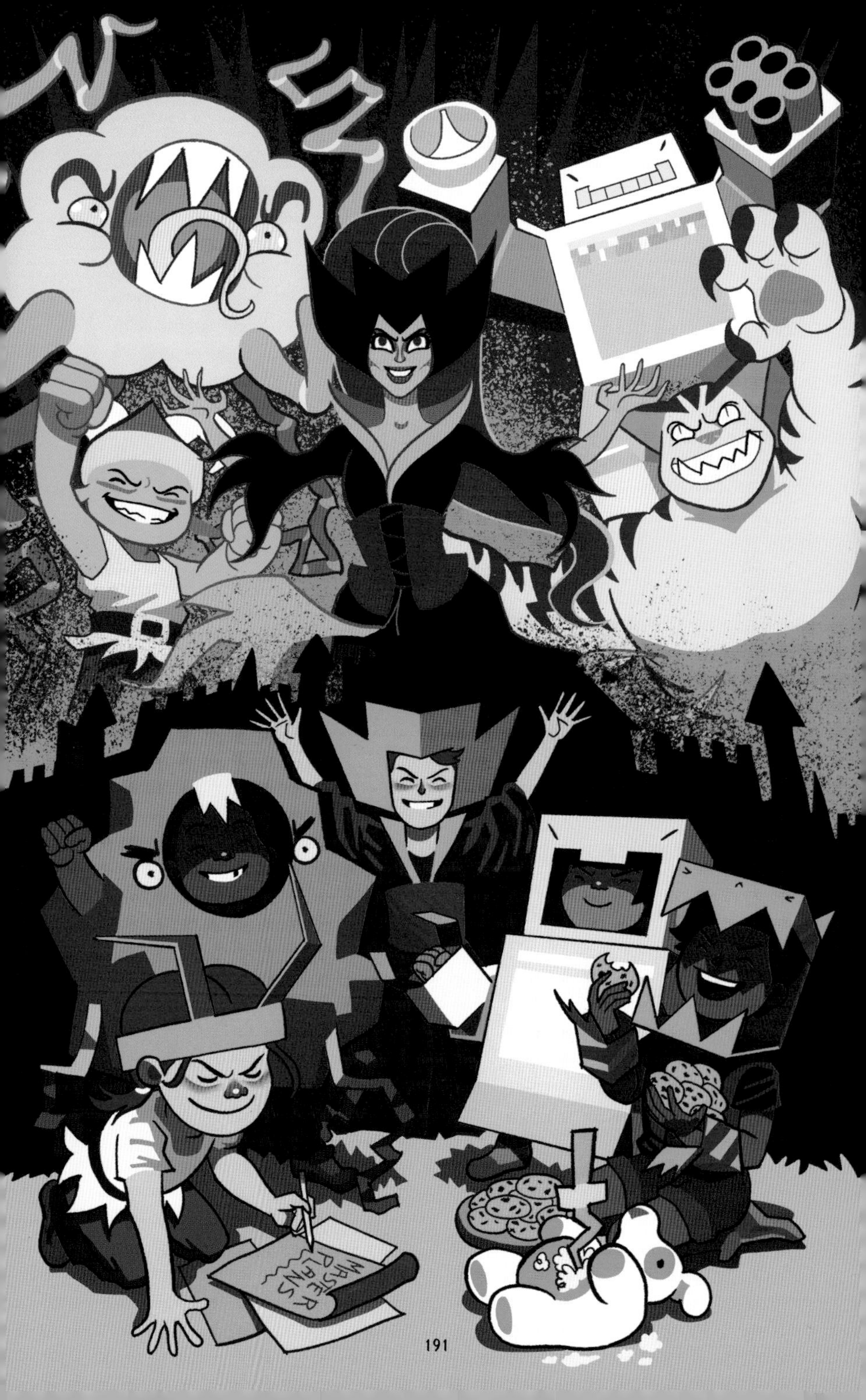
MASTER PLANS

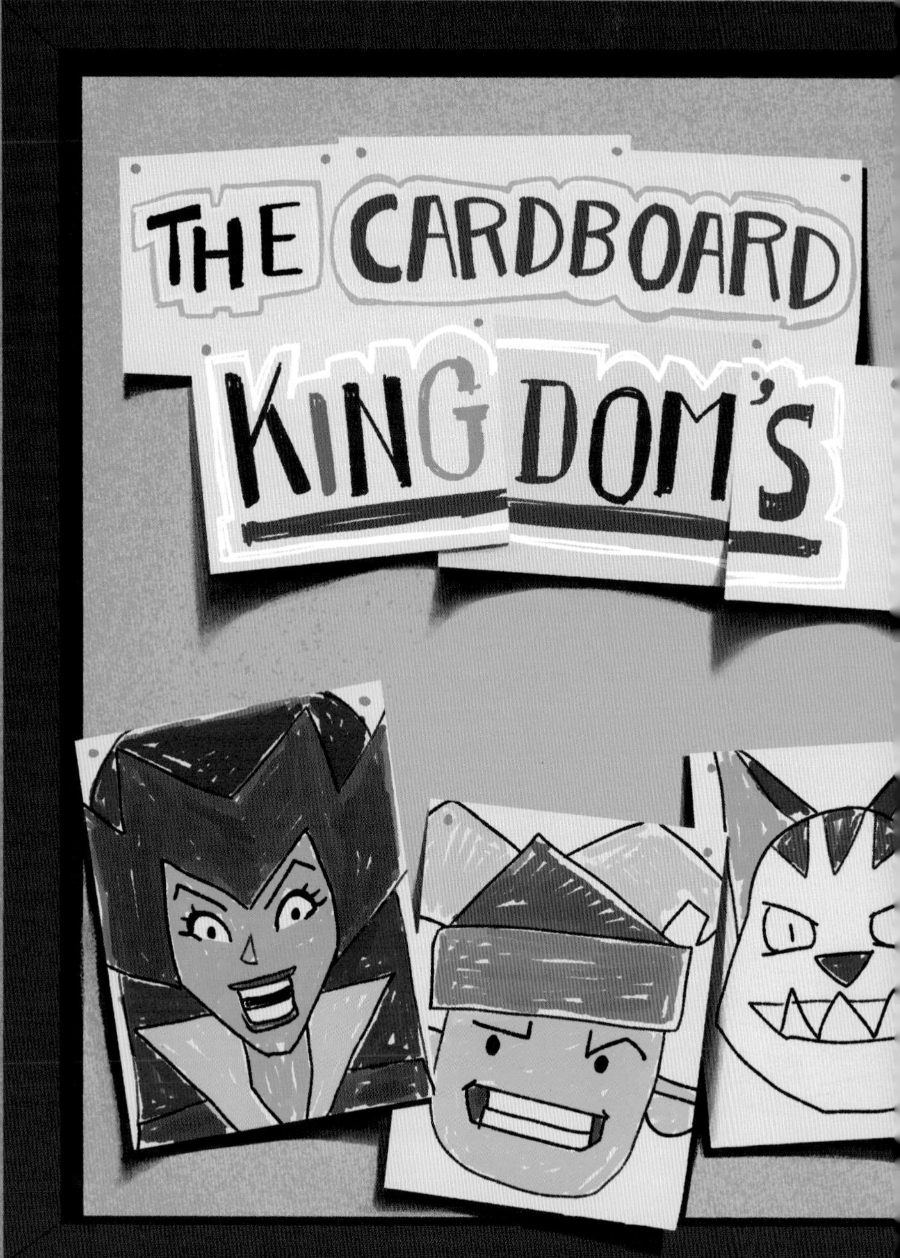
THE CARDBOARD
KINGDOM'S

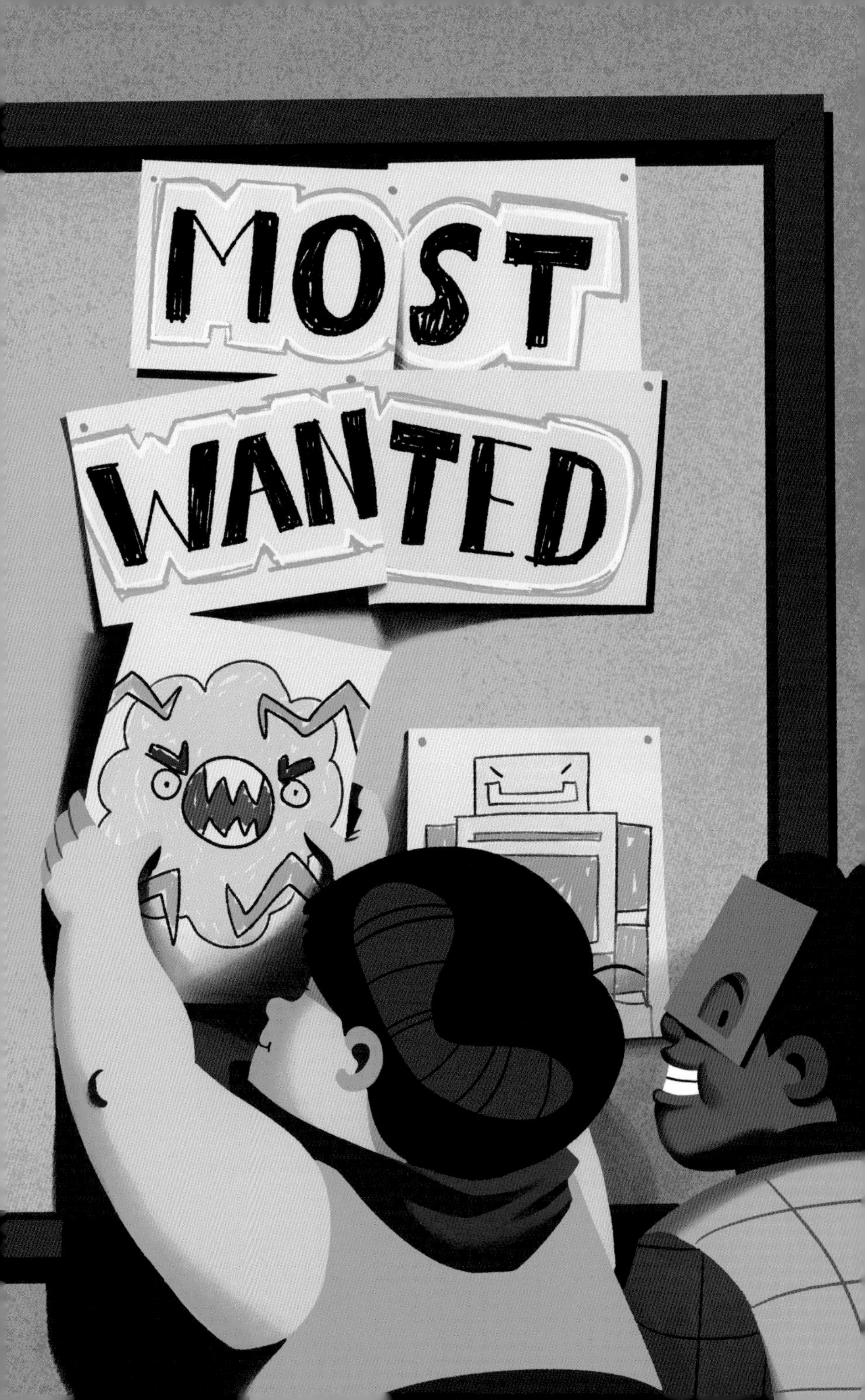
MOST
WANTED

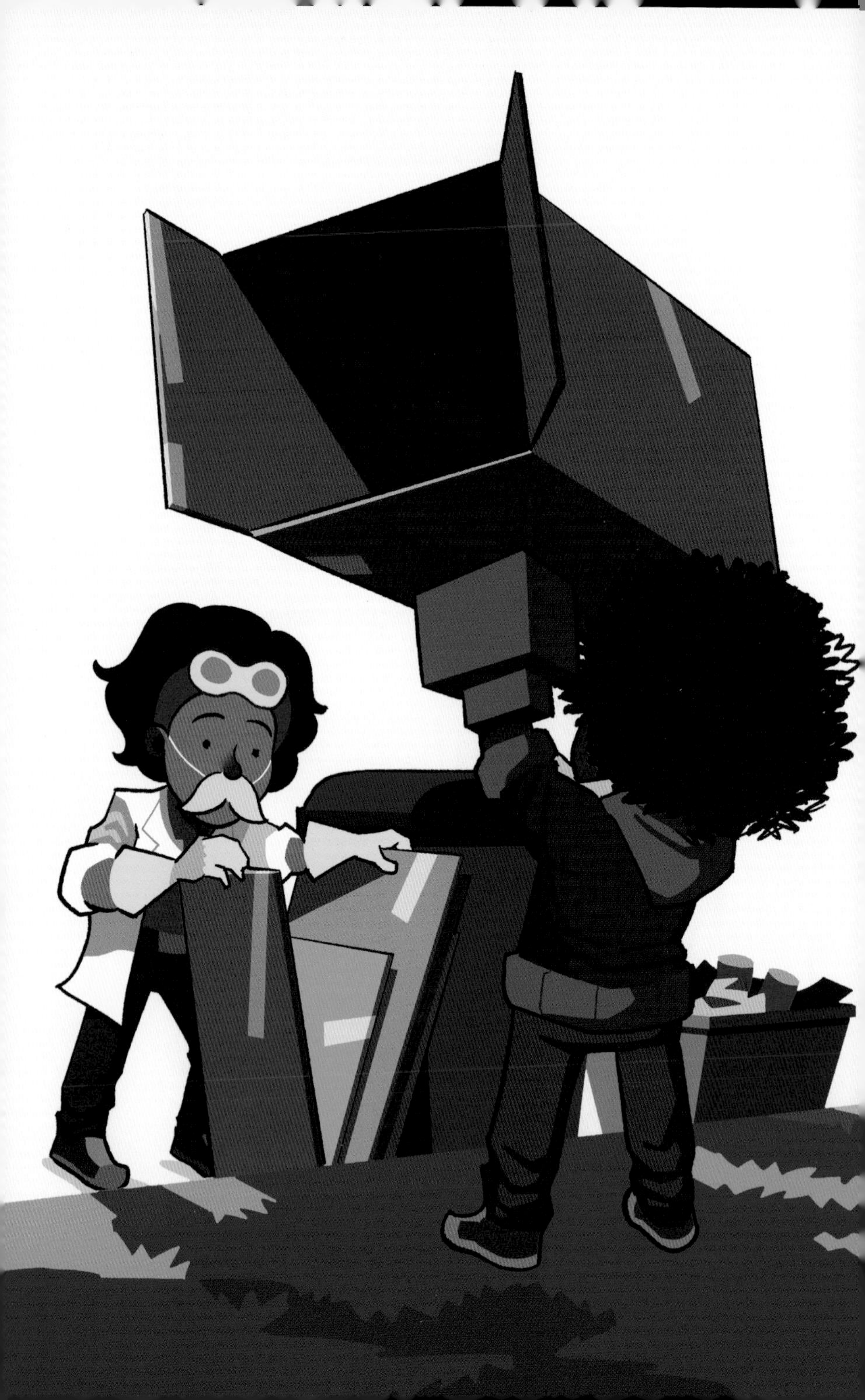

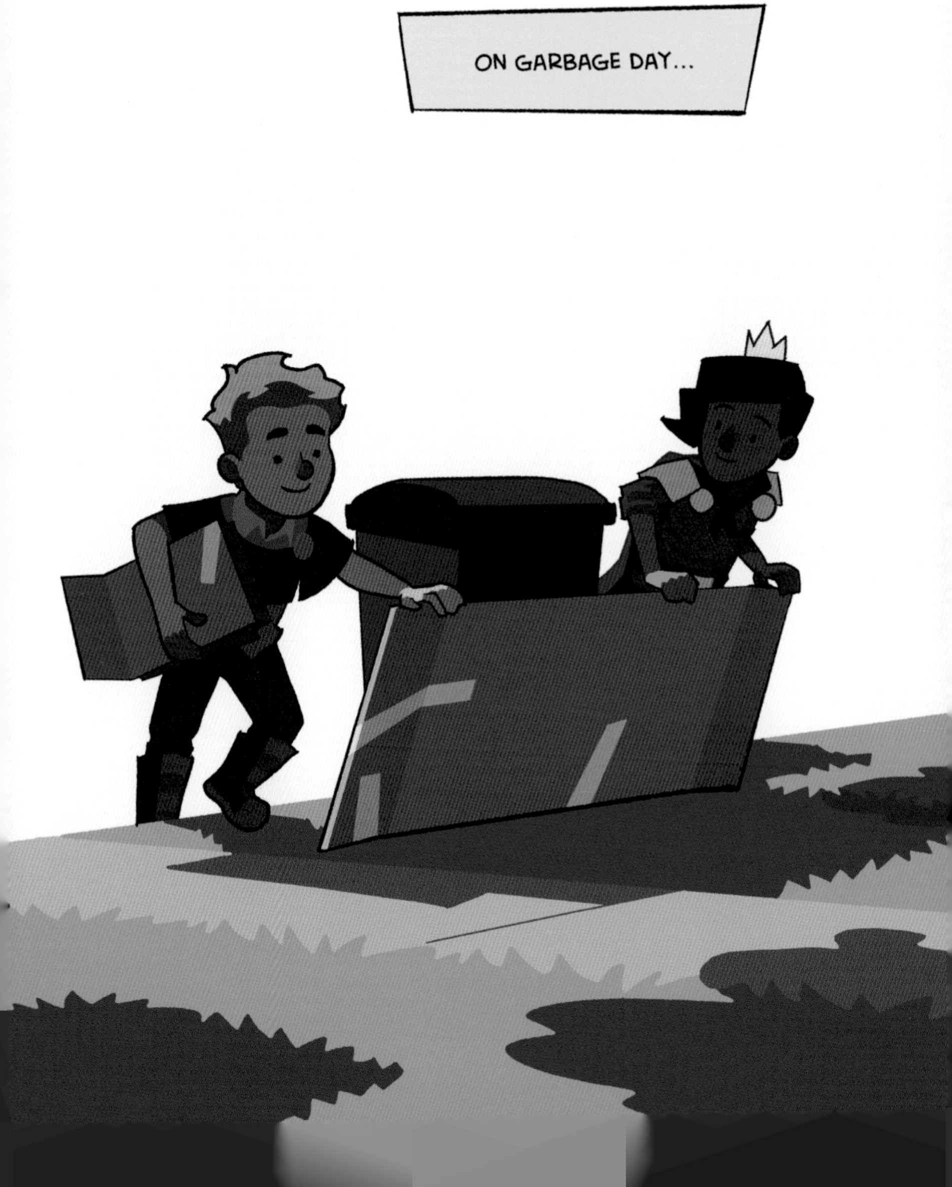
ON GARBAGE DAY...

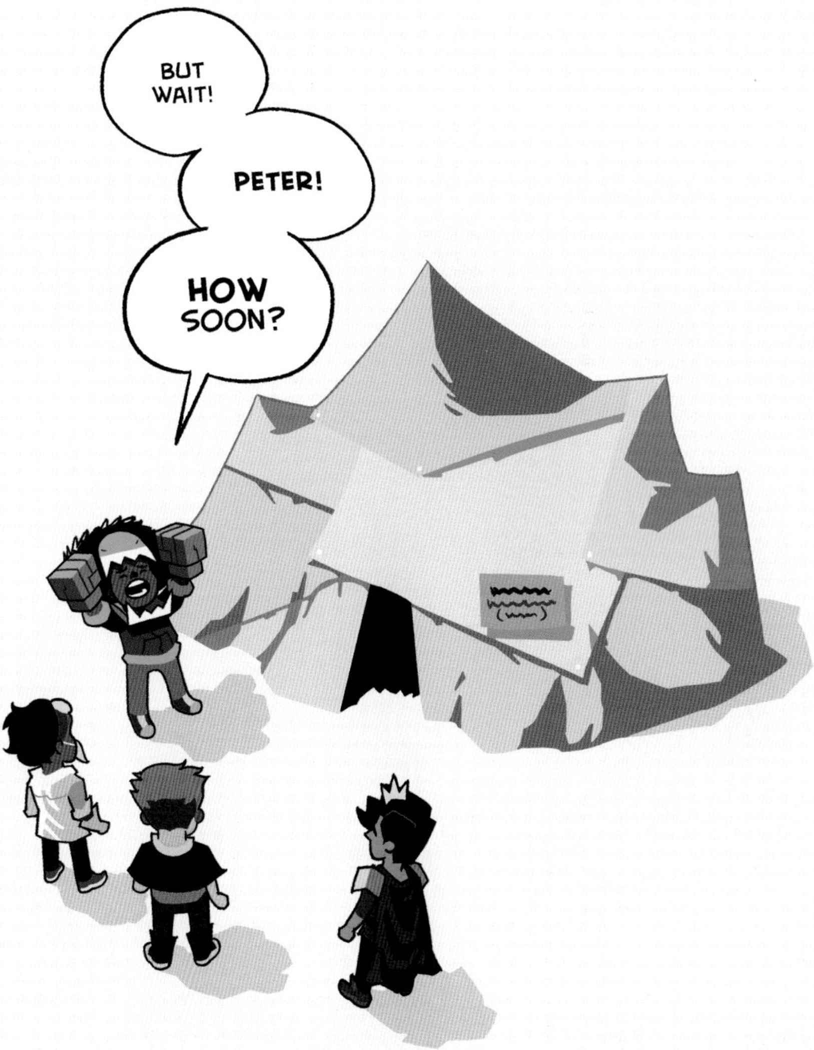
BUT WAIT!
PETER!
HOW SOON?

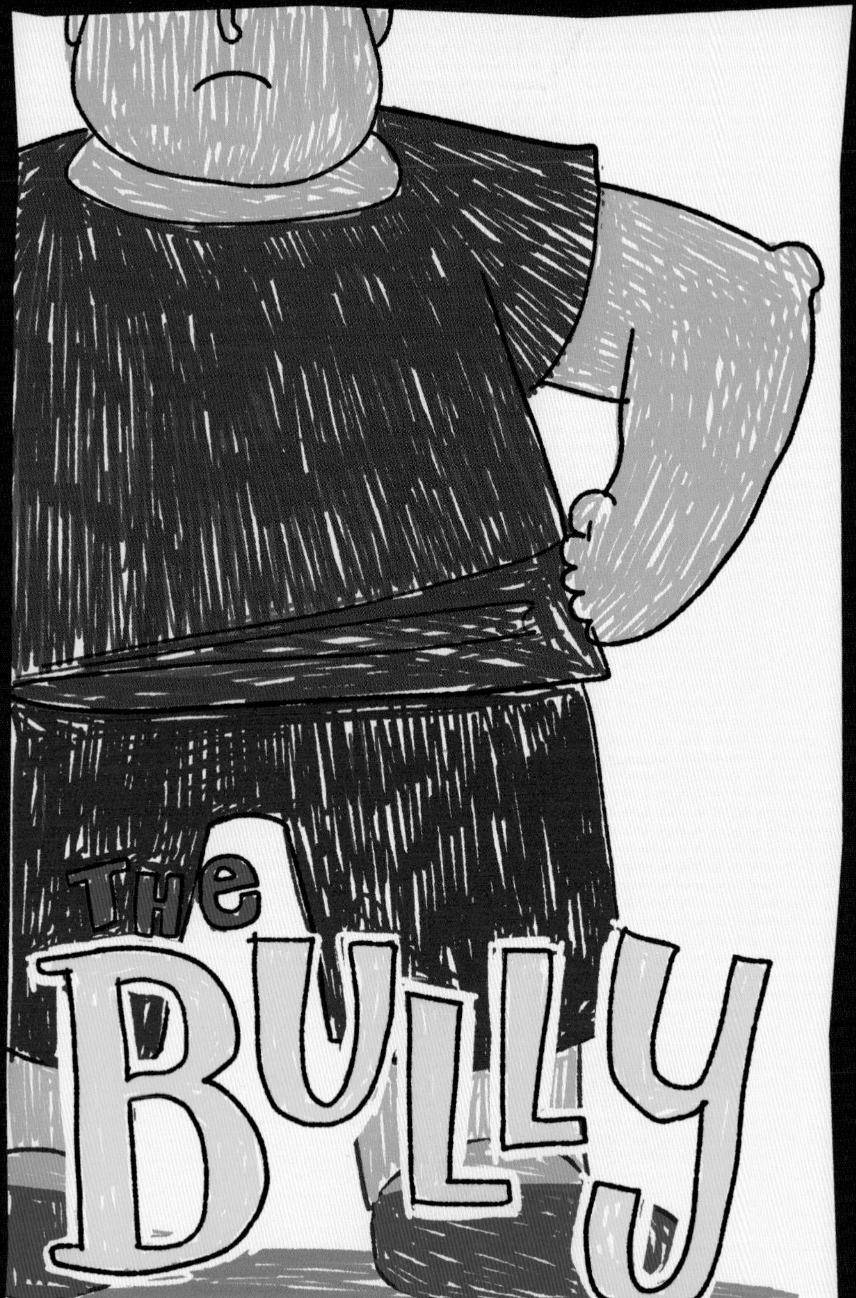
THE
BULLY

BY DAVID DEMEO AND CHAD SELL

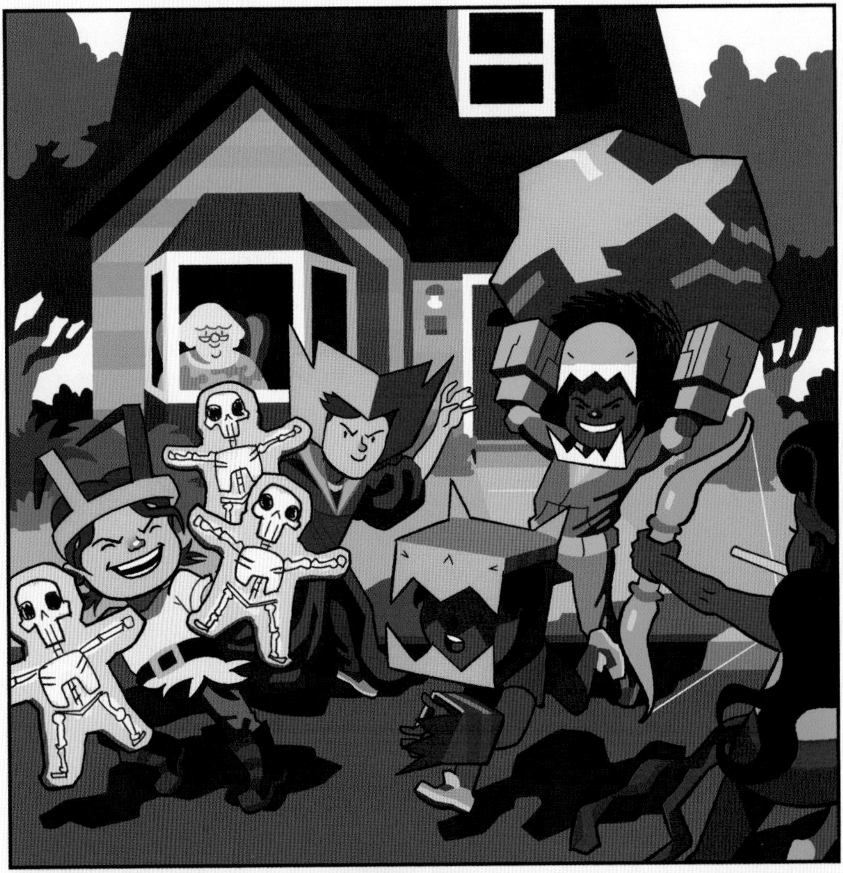

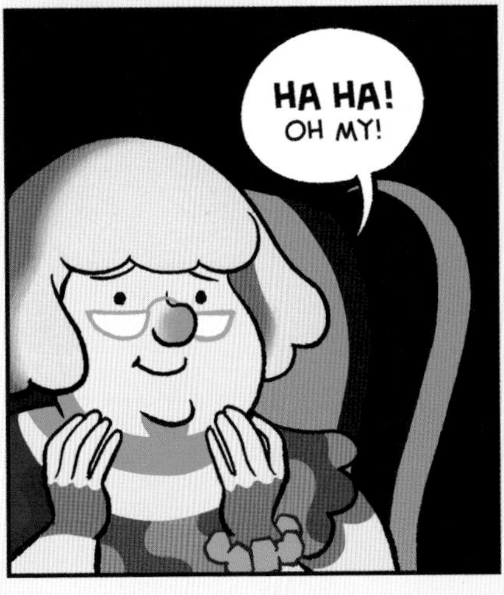
HA HA!
OH MY!

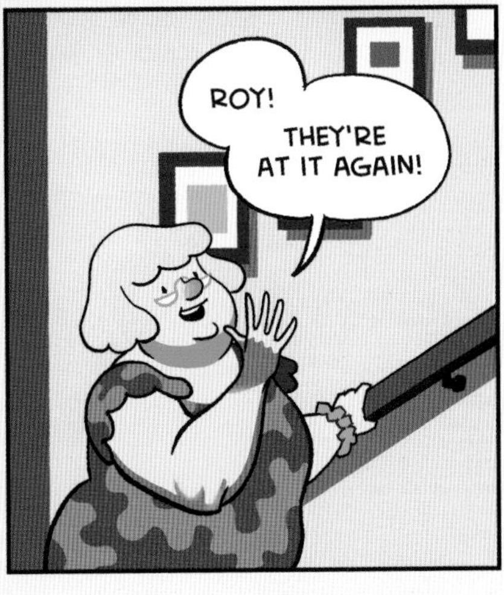
ROY!
THEY'RE
AT IT AGAIN!

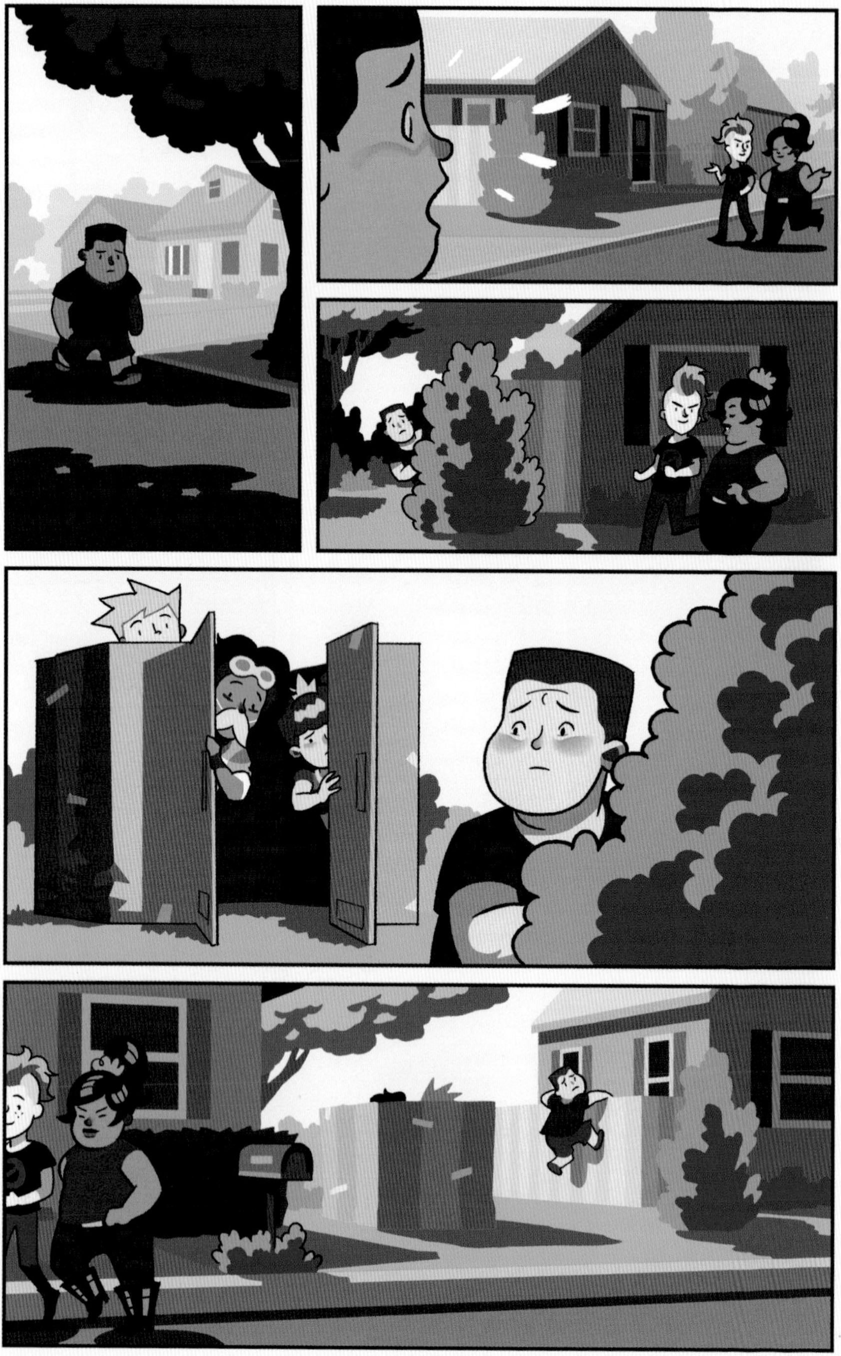

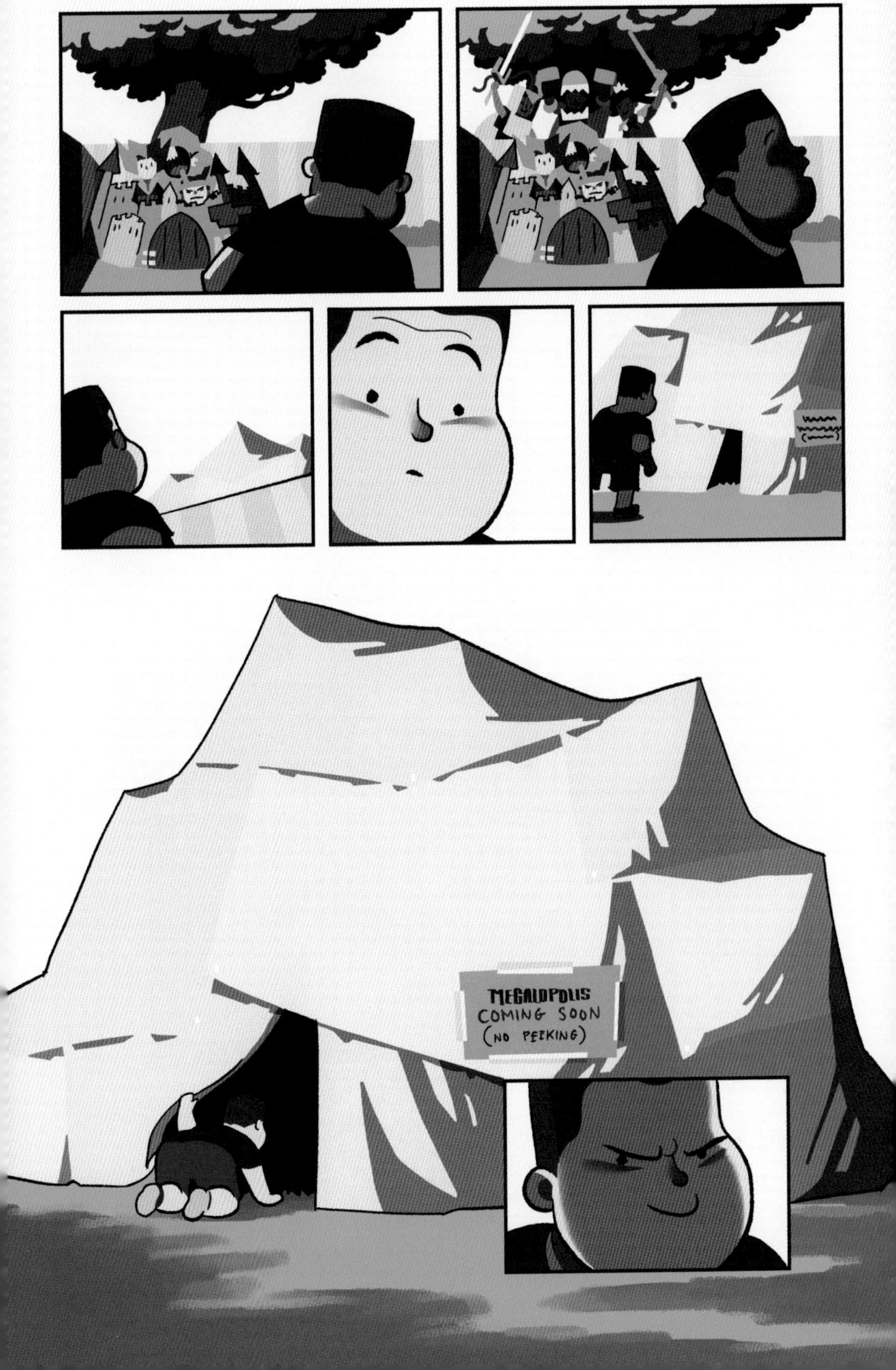
MEGALOPOLIS
COMING SOON
(NO PEEKING)

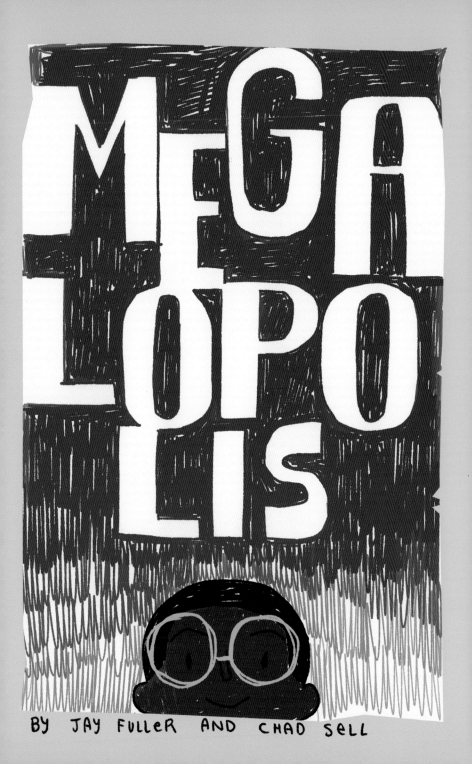

MEGALOPOLIS

BY JAY FULLER AND CHAD SELL

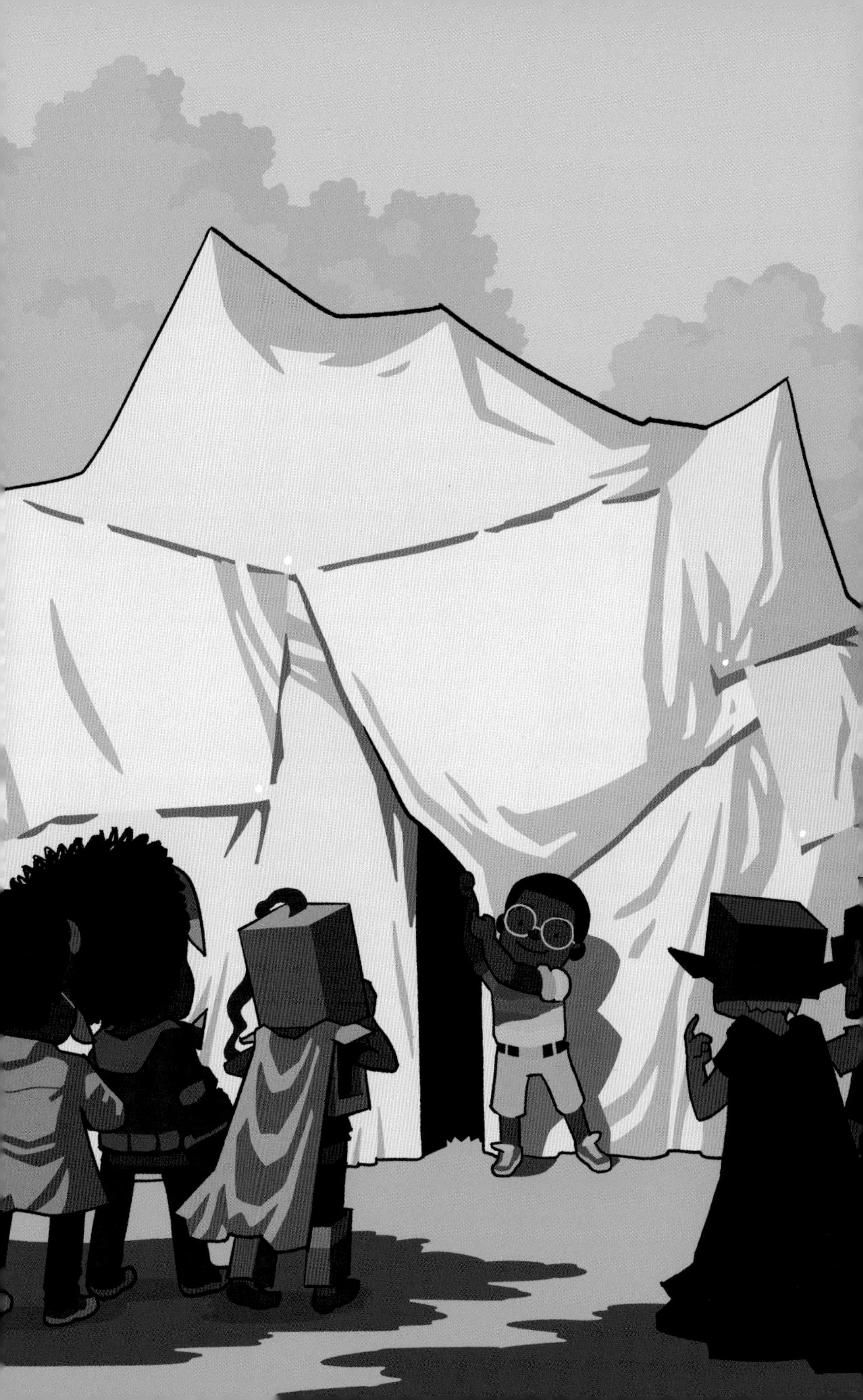

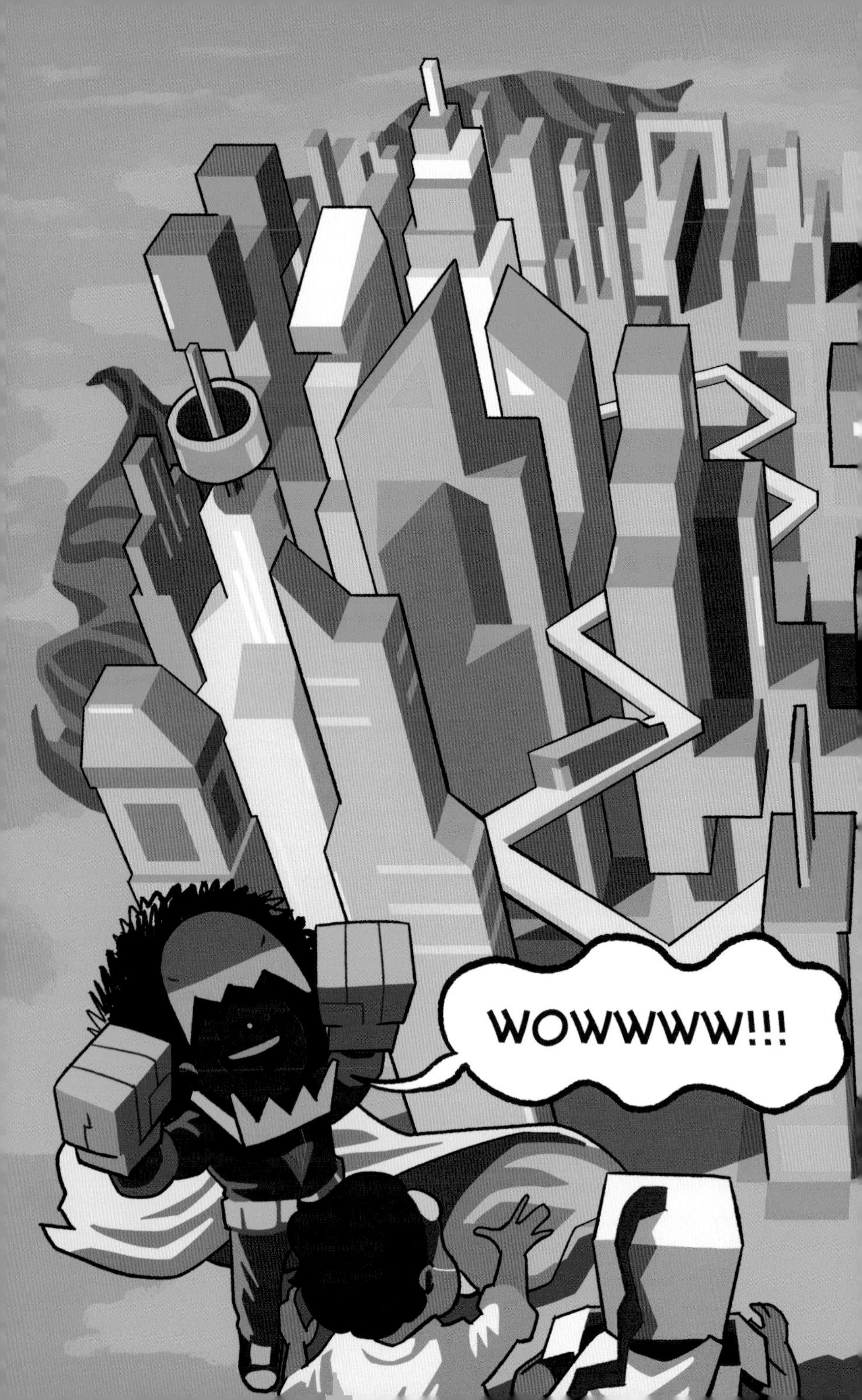
WOWWWW!!!

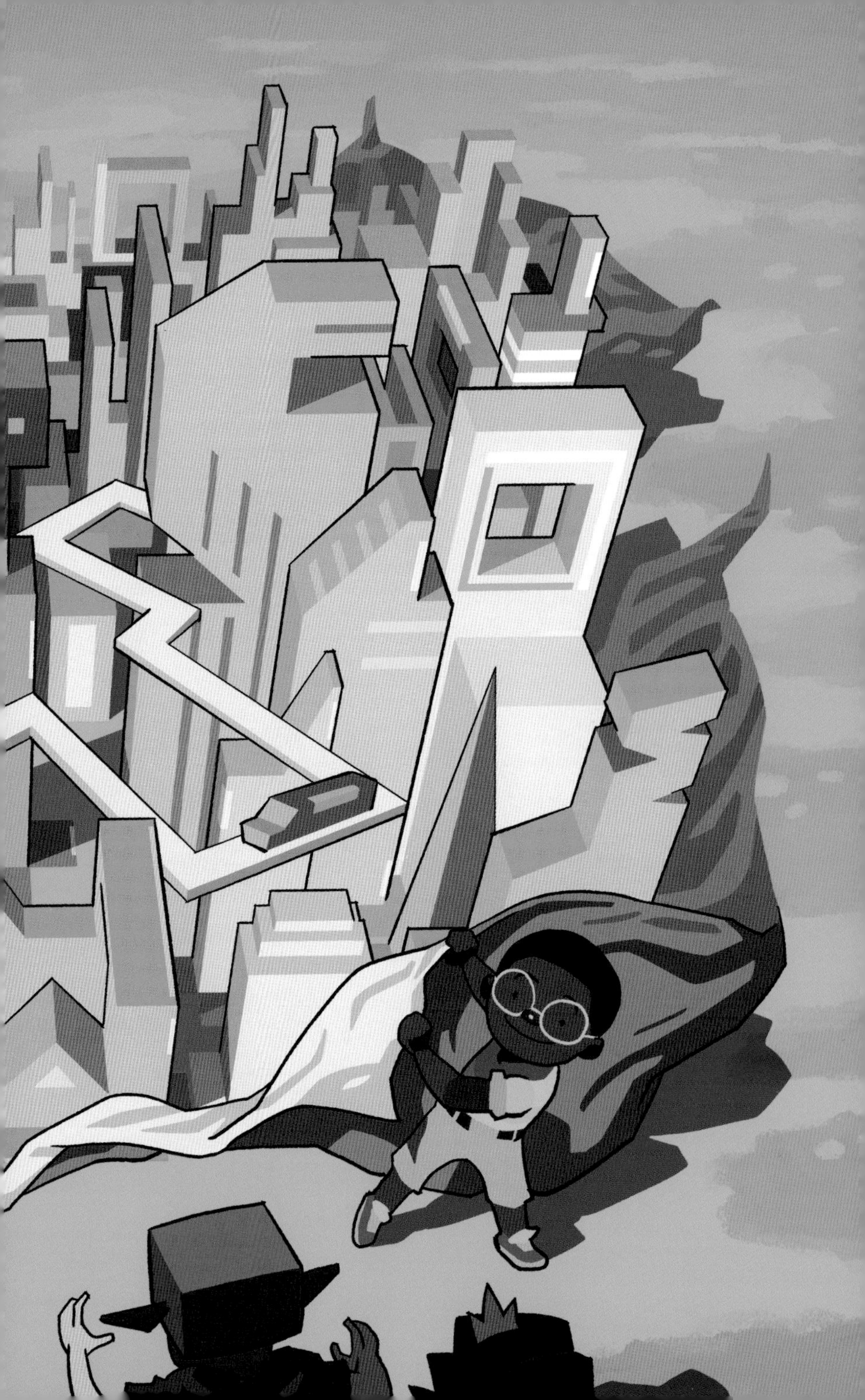

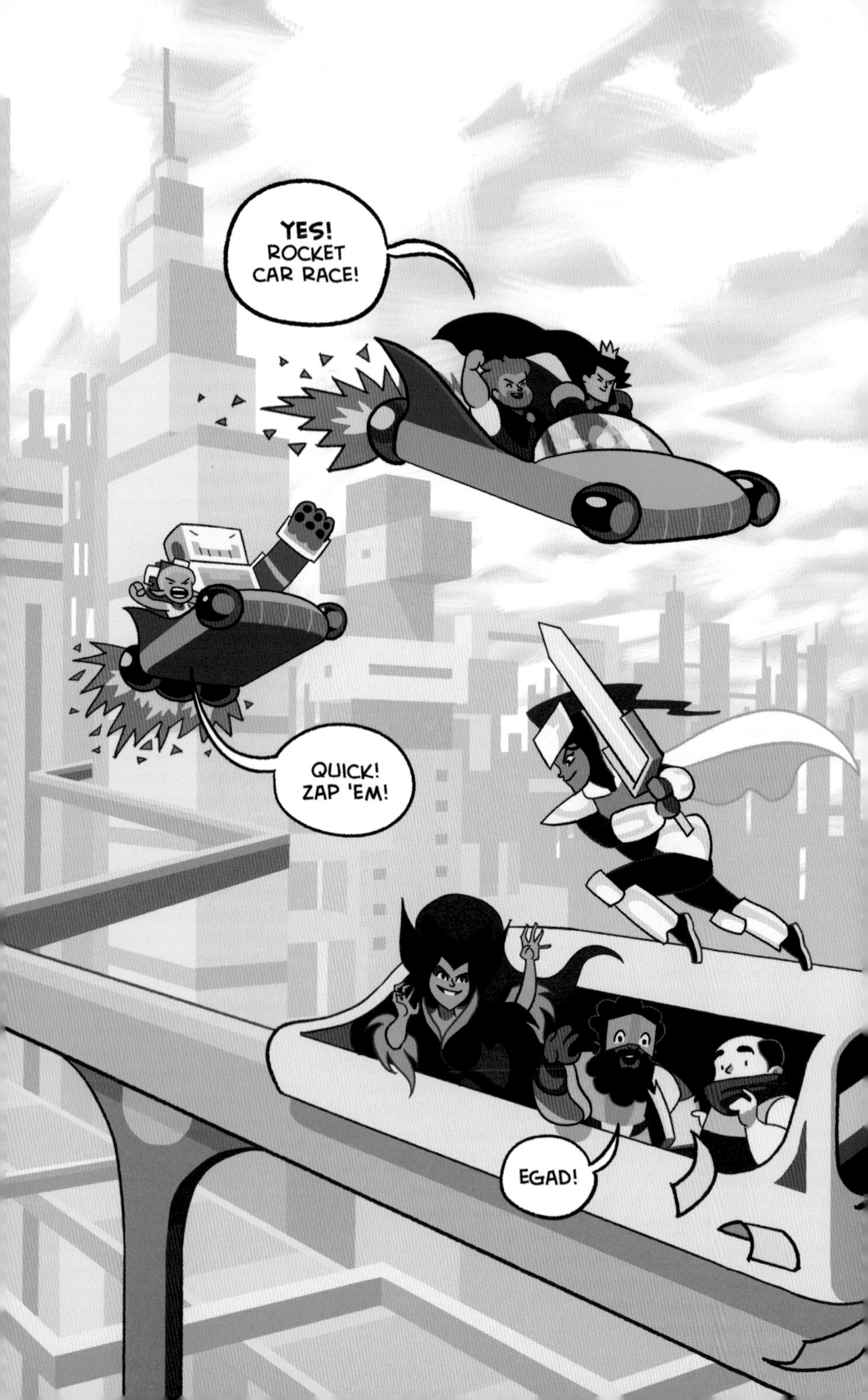
YES! ROCKET CAR RACE!
QUICK! ZAP 'EM!
EGAD!

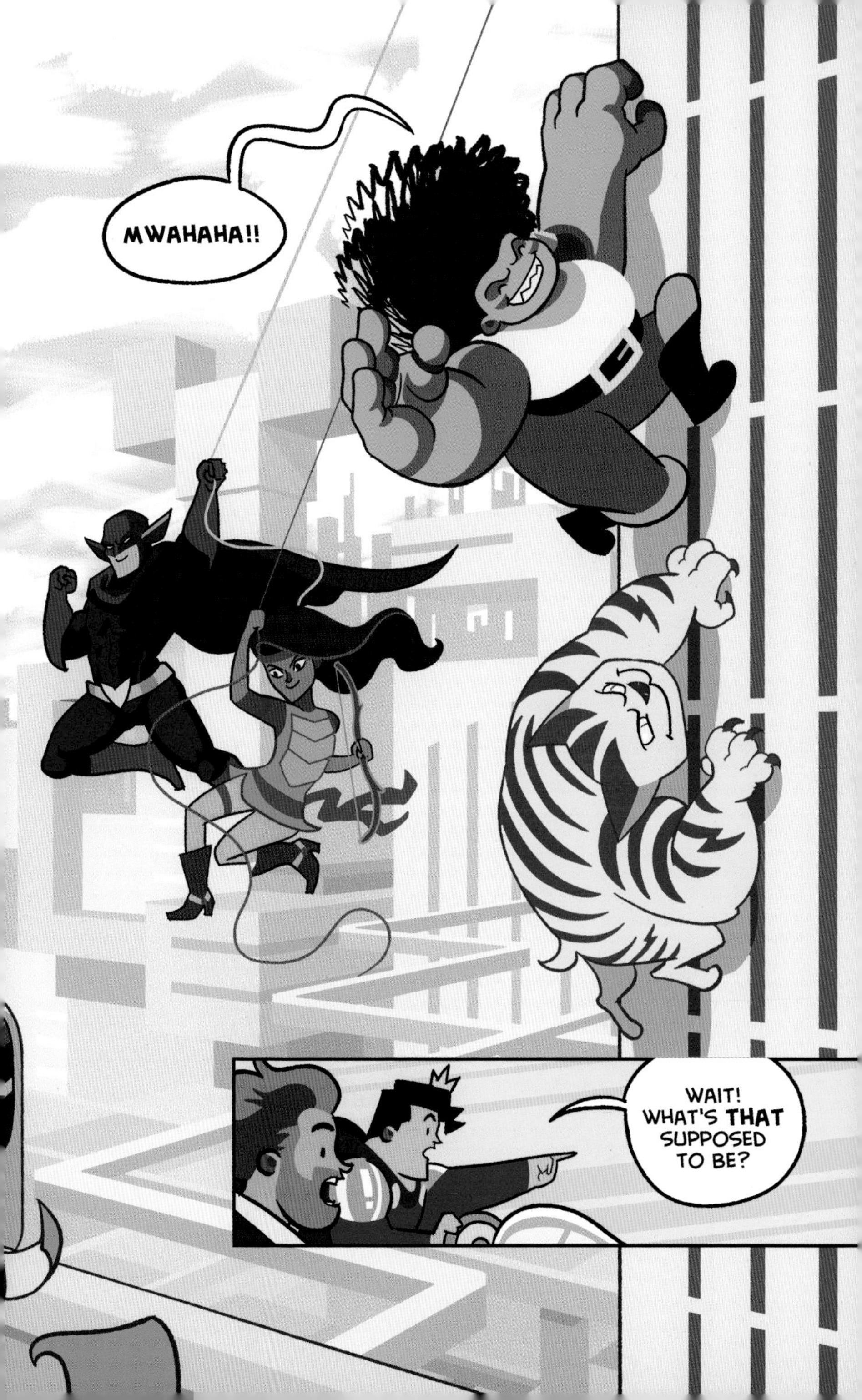
MWAHAHA!!
WAIT! WHAT'S **THAT** SUPPOSED TO BE?

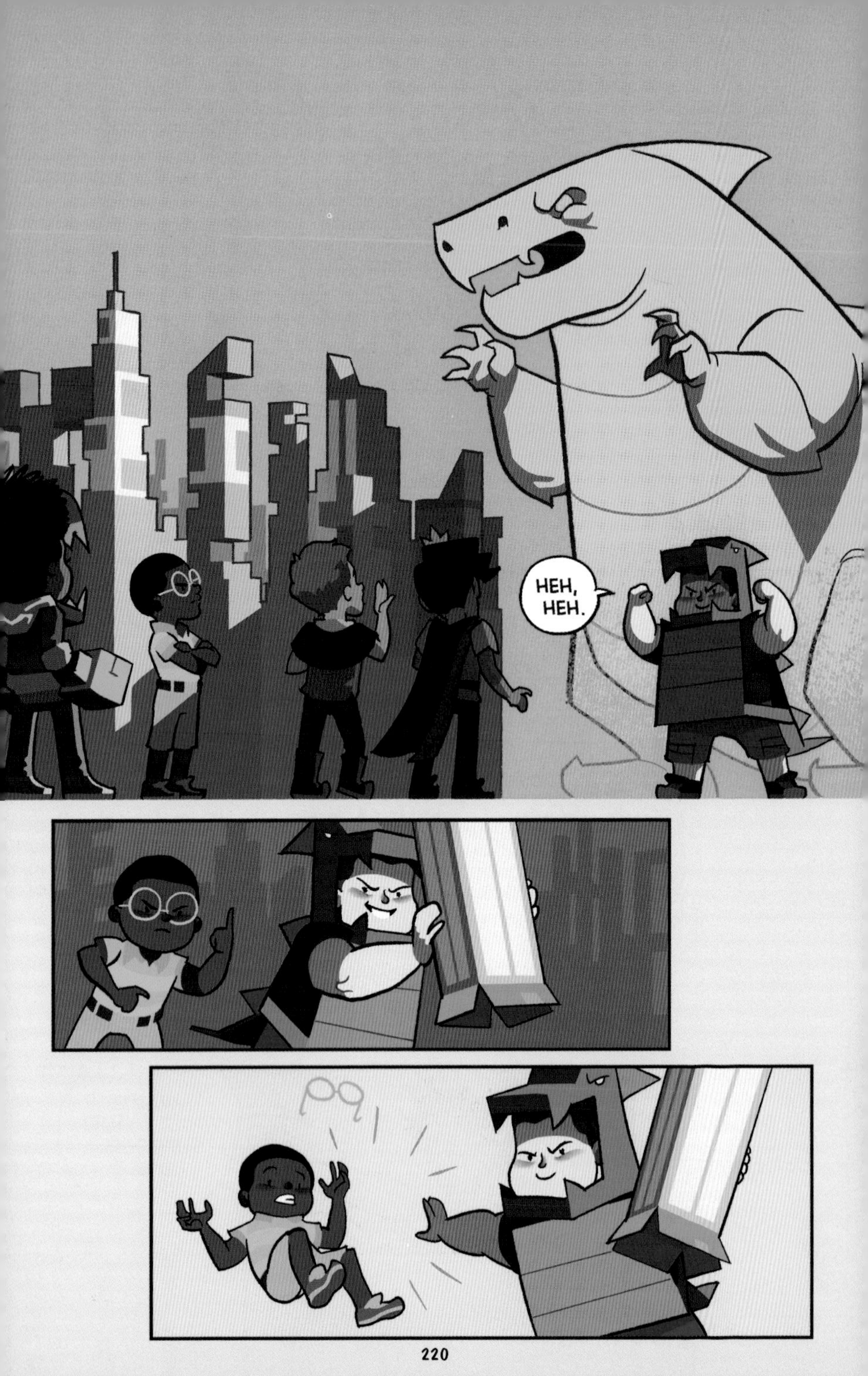
HEH,
HEH.

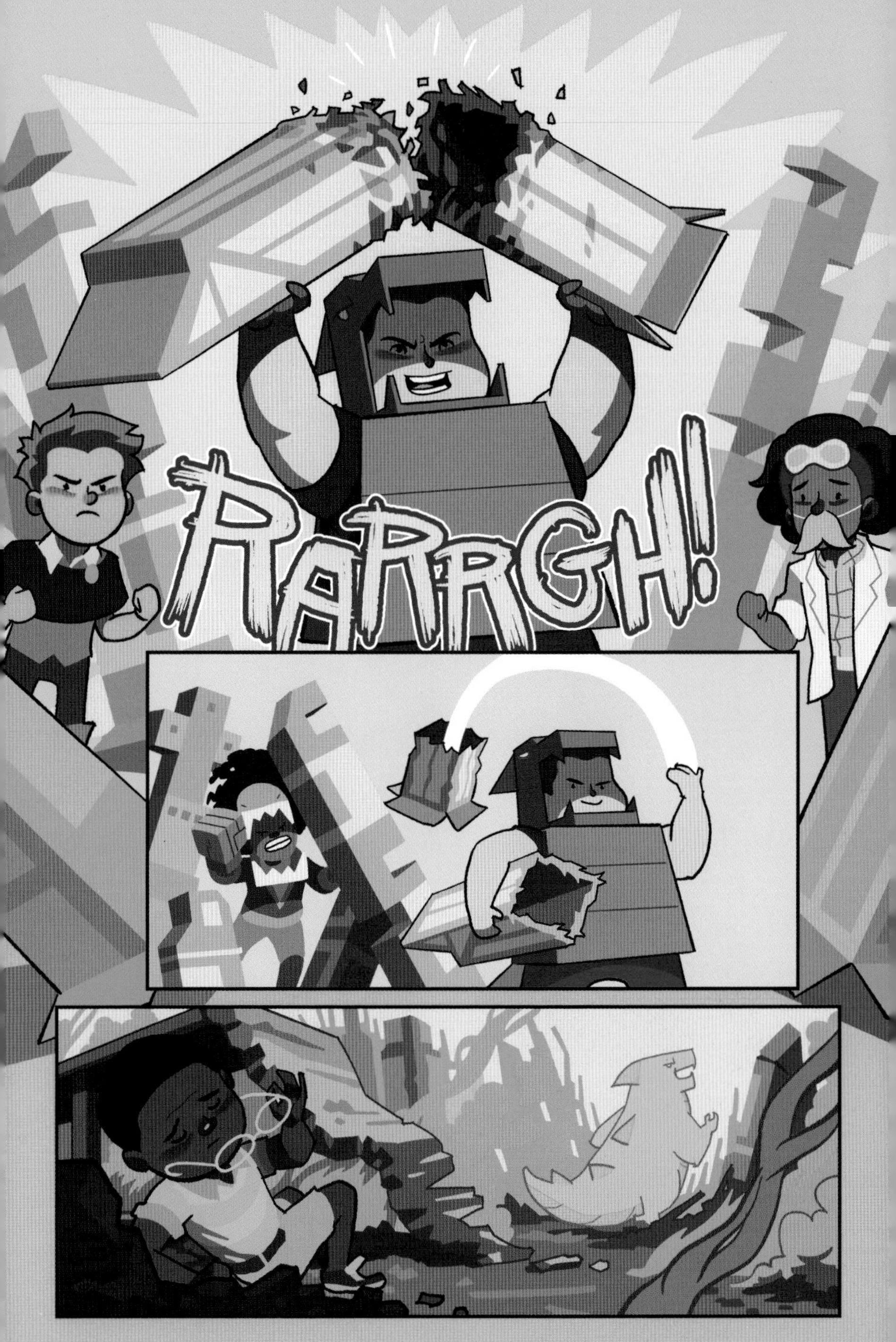
RARRGH!

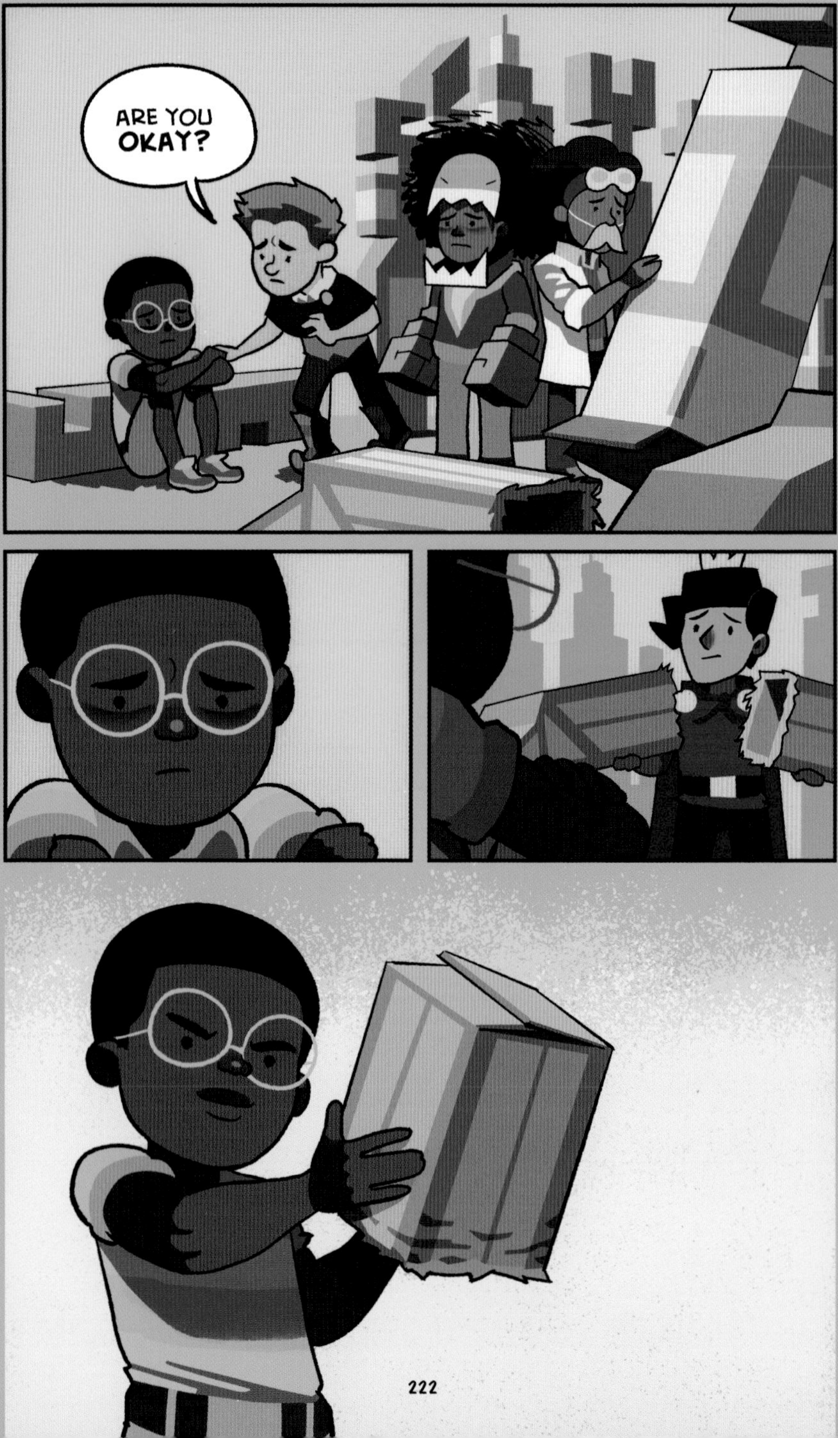
ARE YOU OKAY?

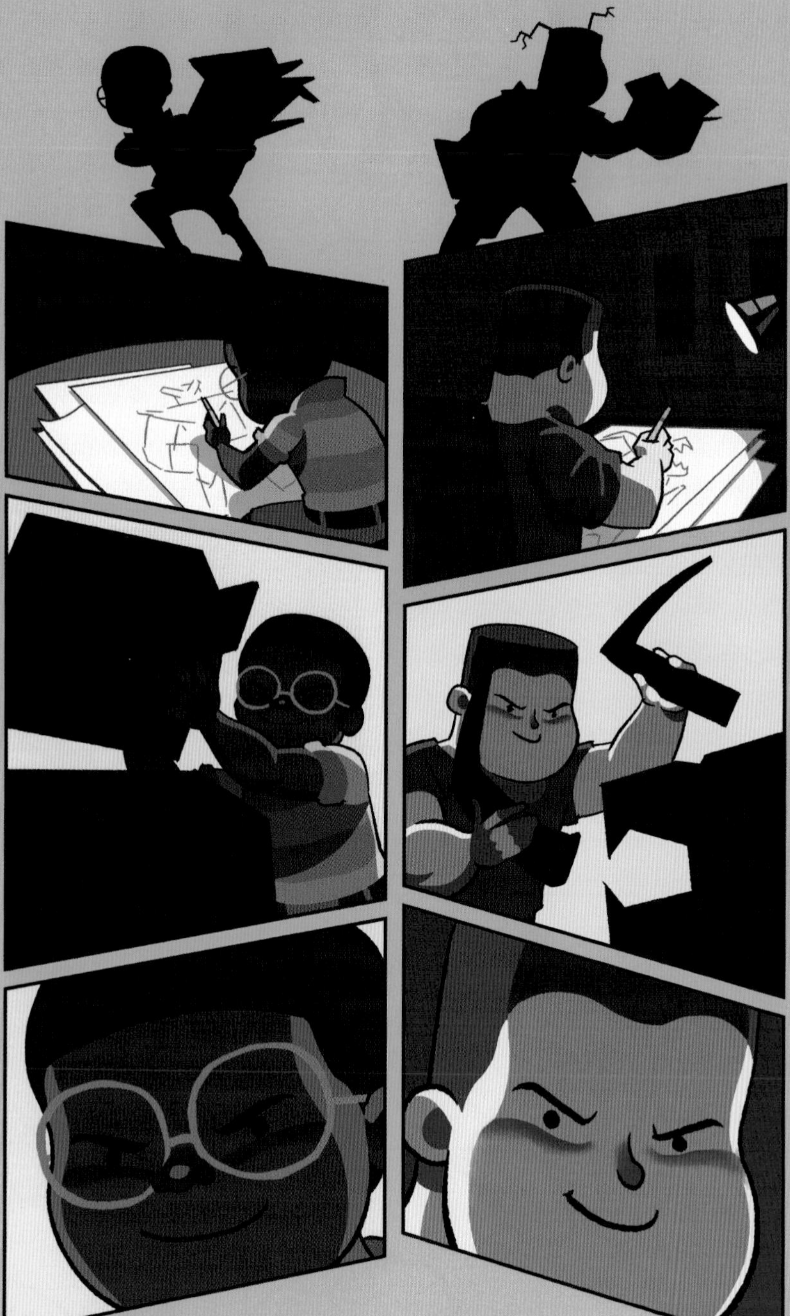

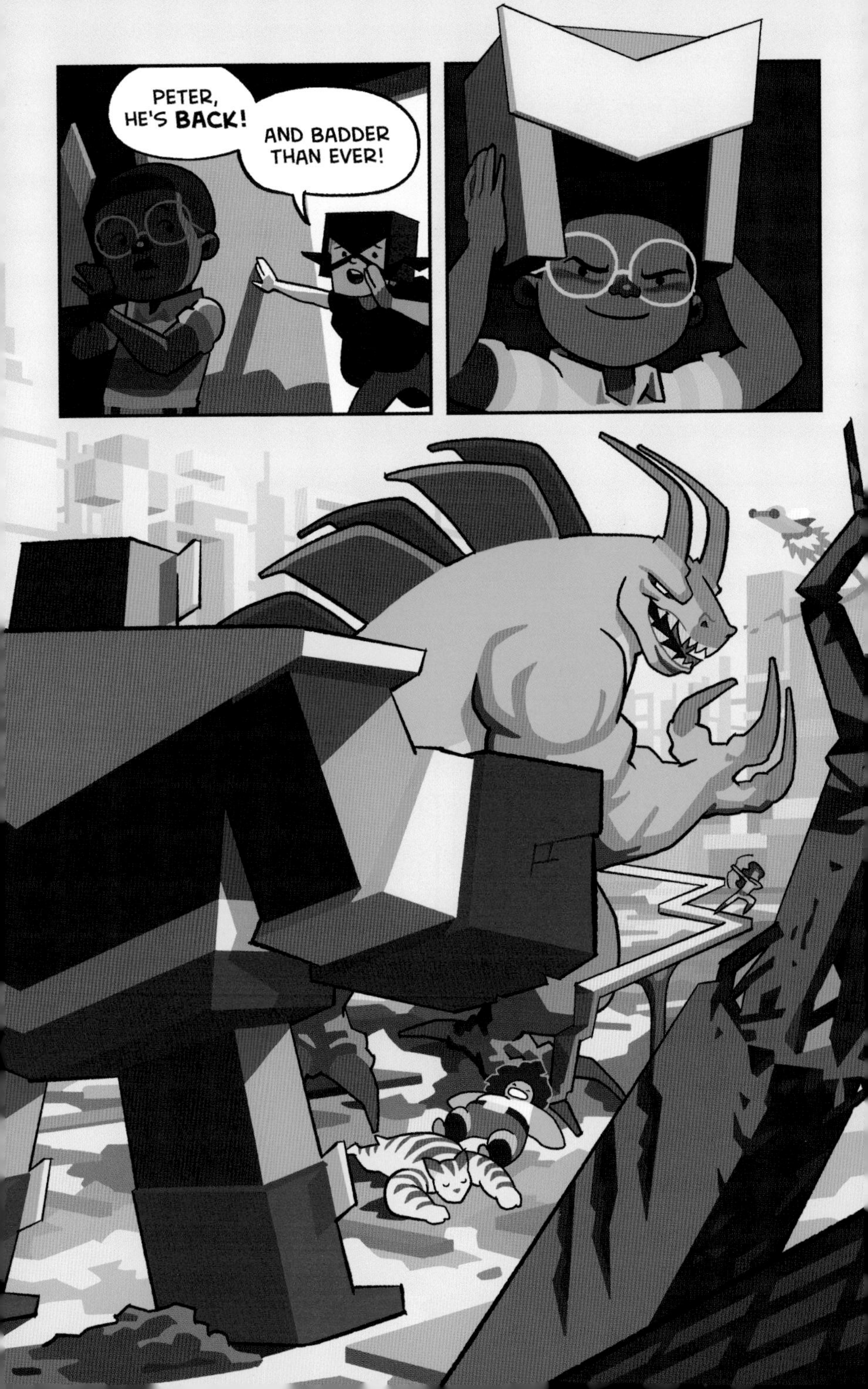
PETER, HE'S **BACK!**
AND BADDER THAN EVER!

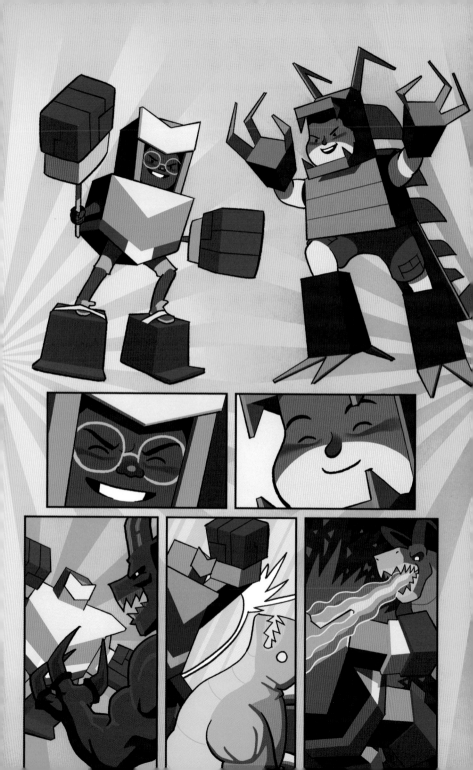

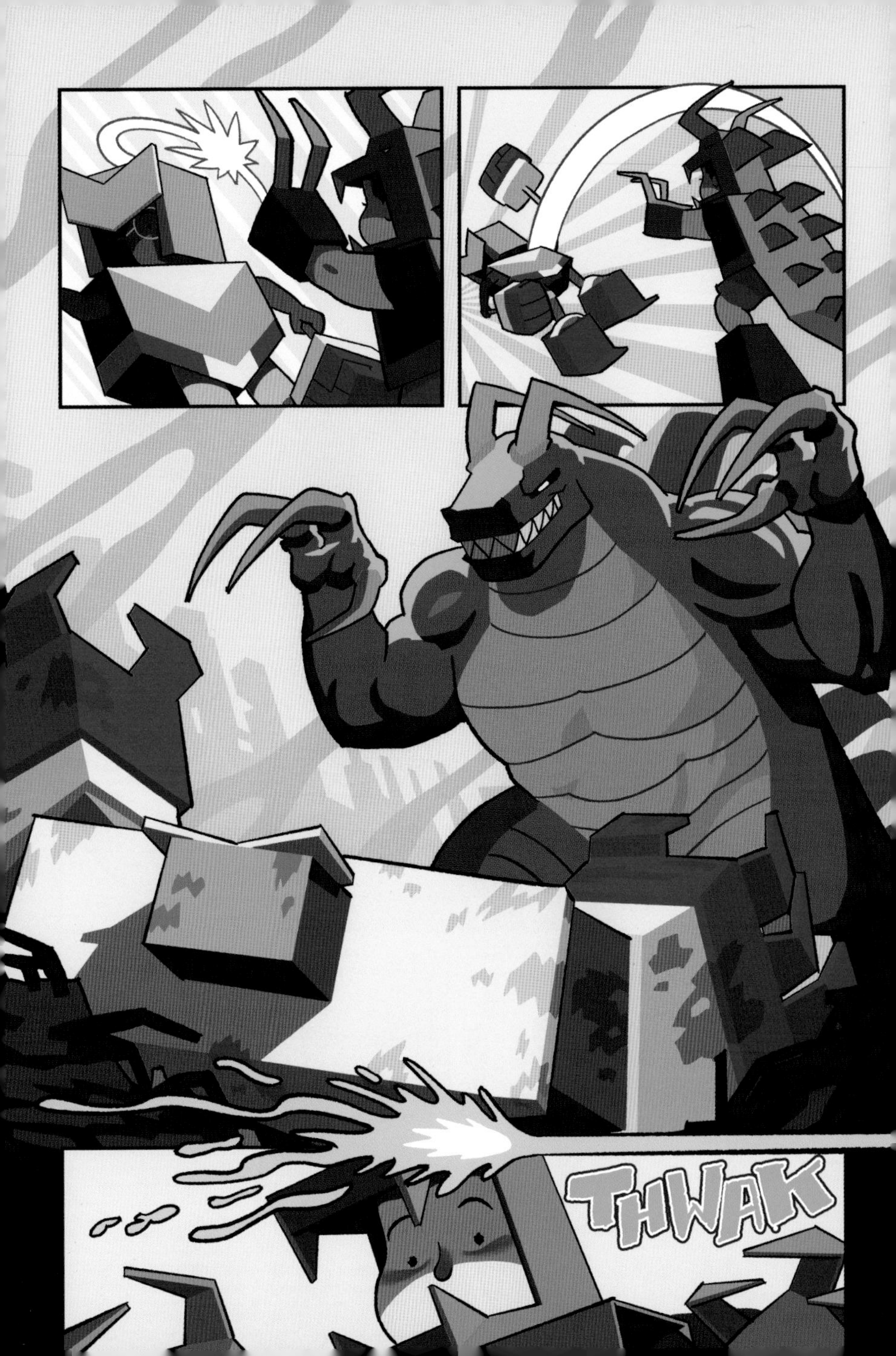
THWAK

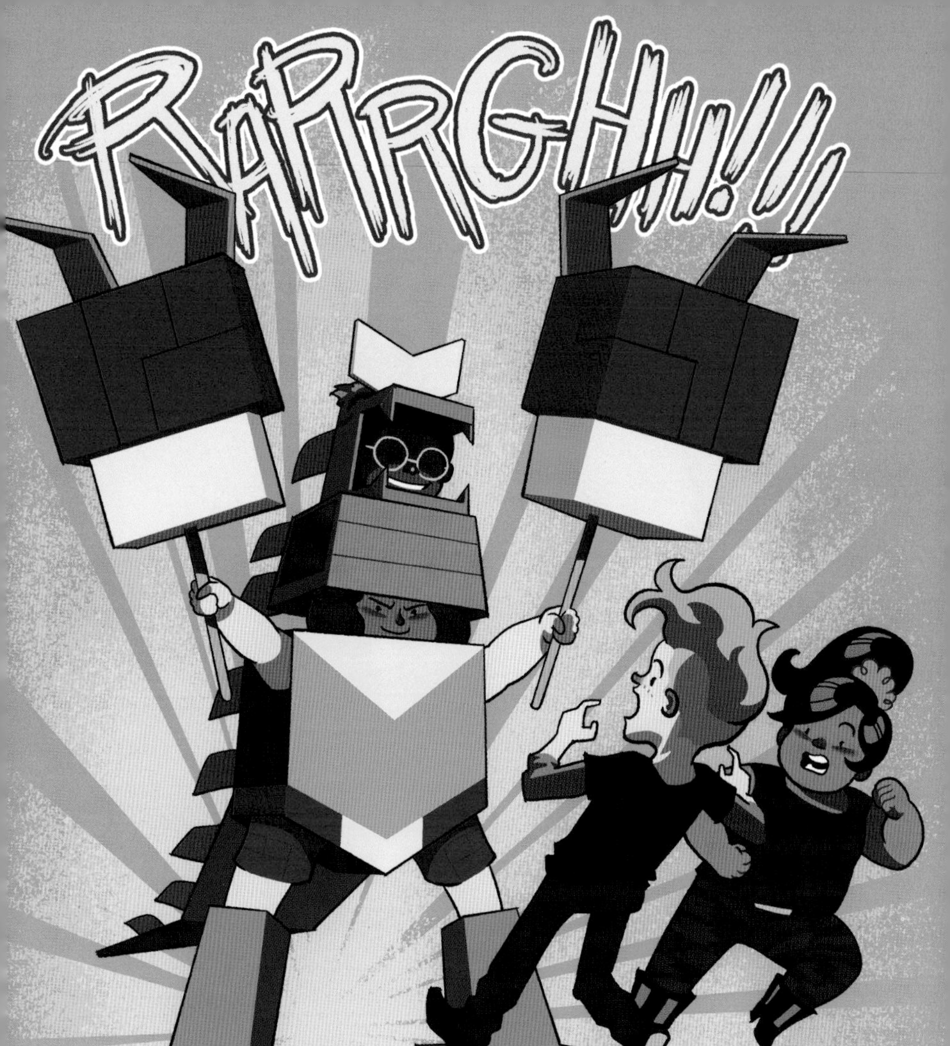
RARRGHH!!!

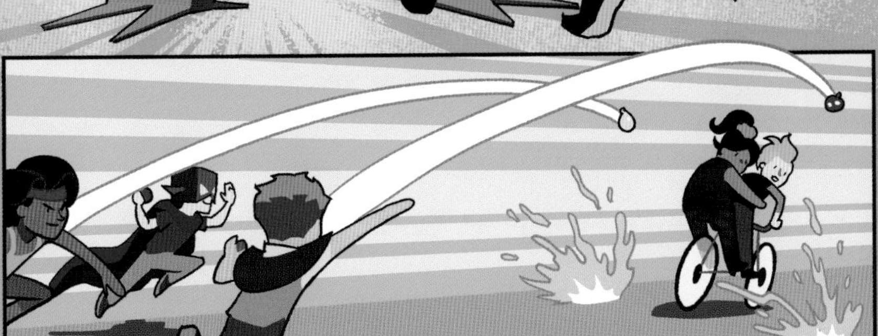

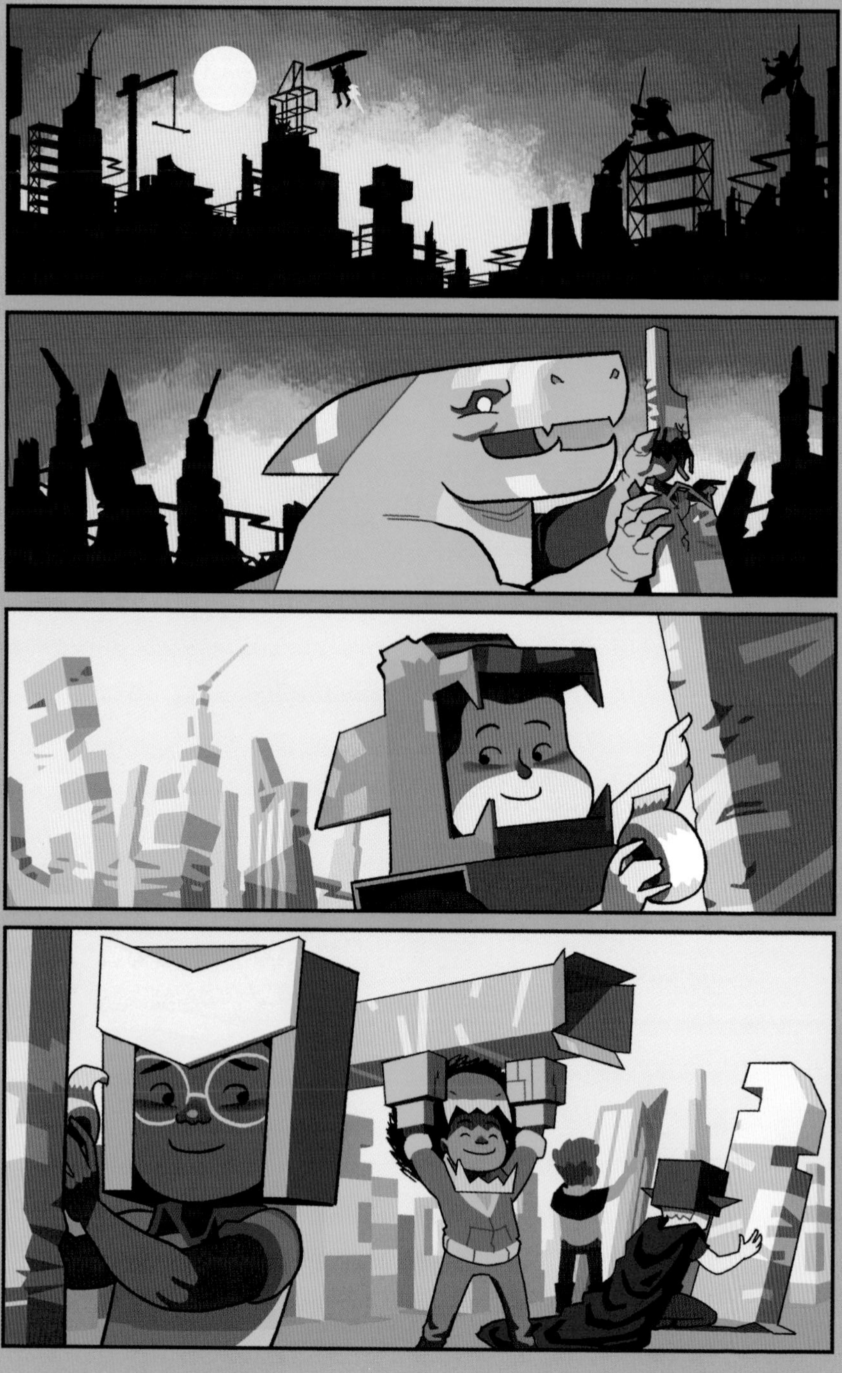

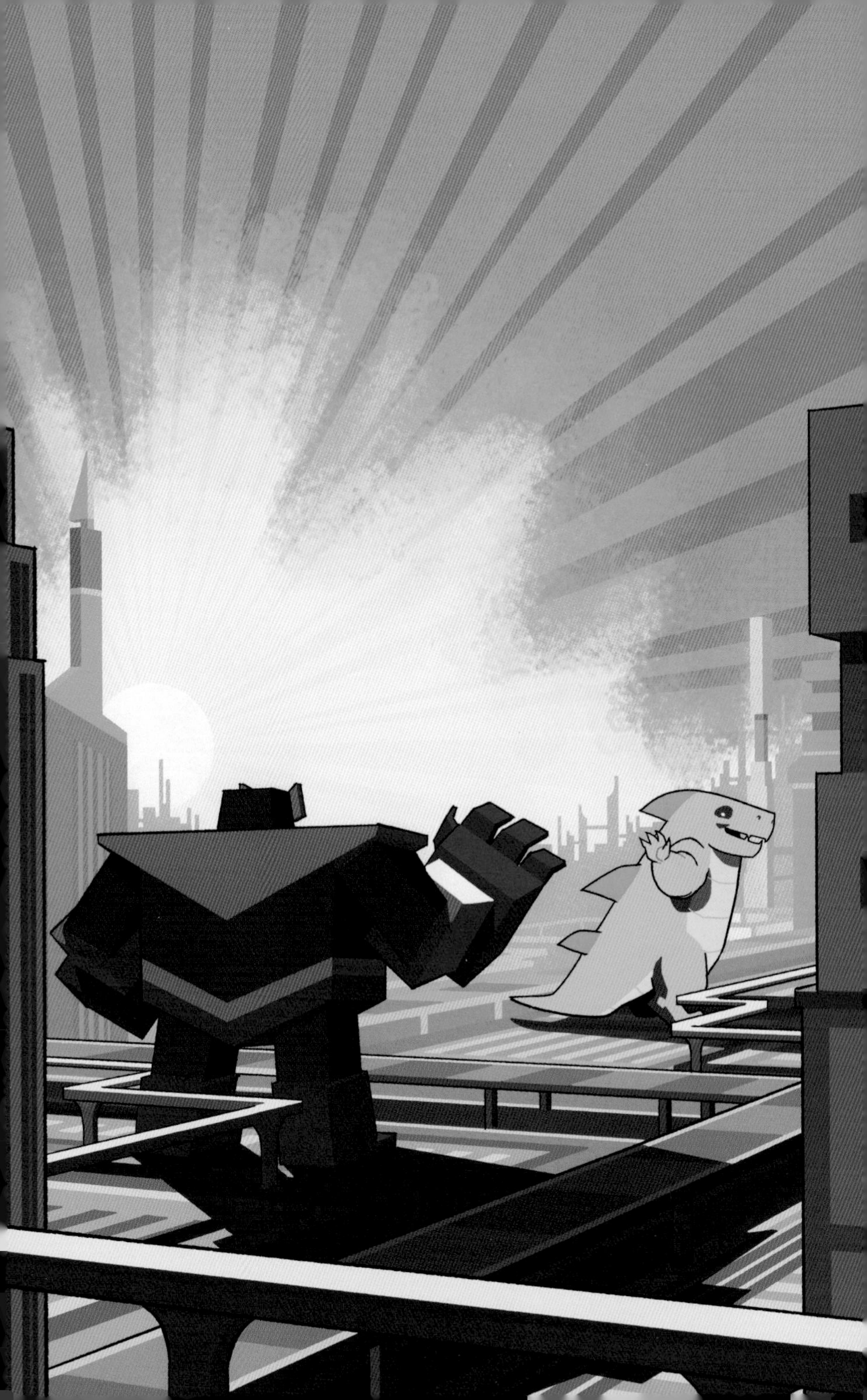

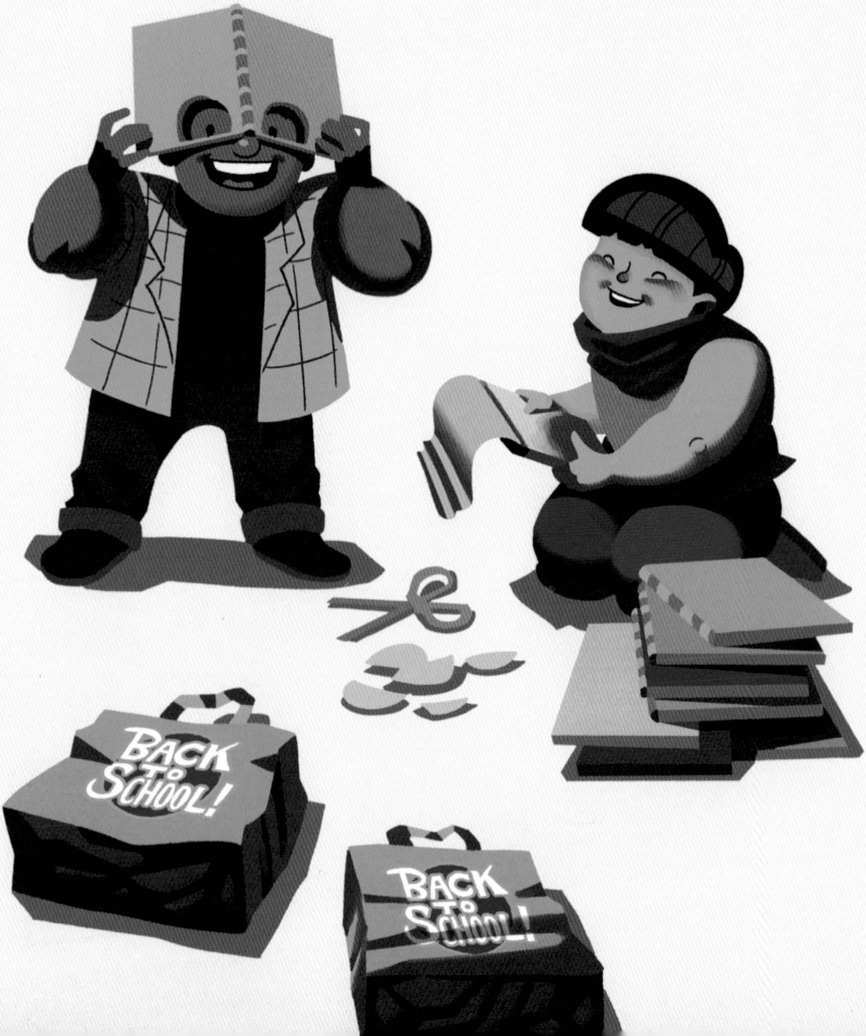
BACK TO SCHOOL!
BACK TO SCHOOL!

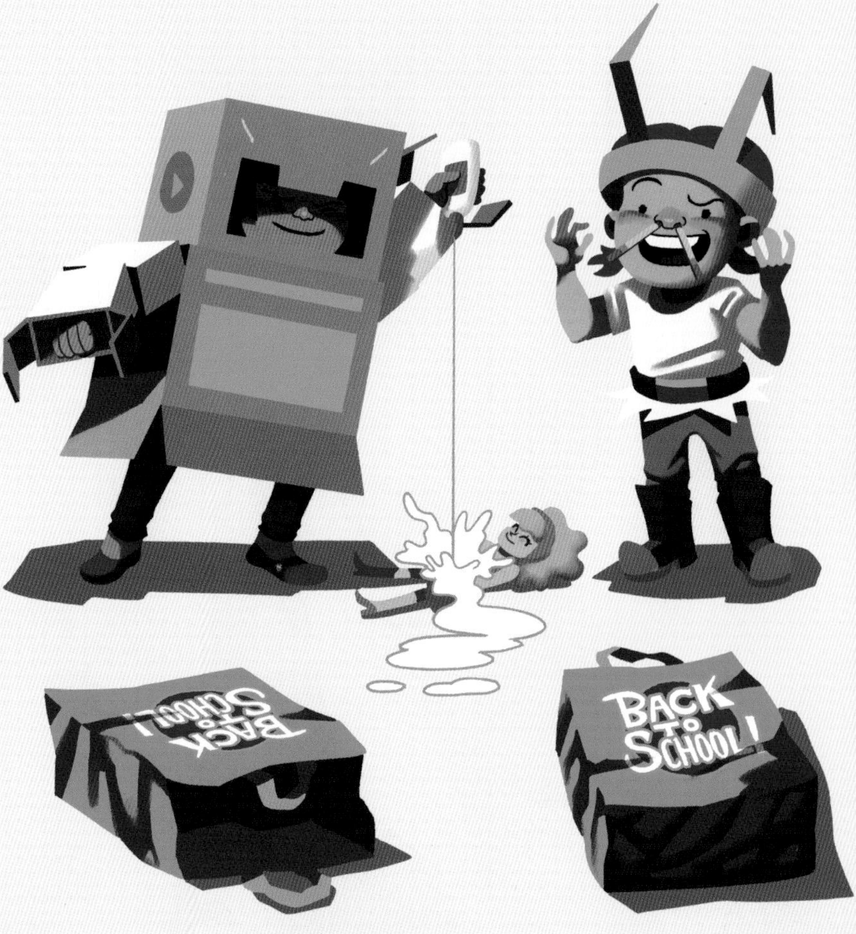
BACK To SCHOOL!
BACK To SCHOOL!

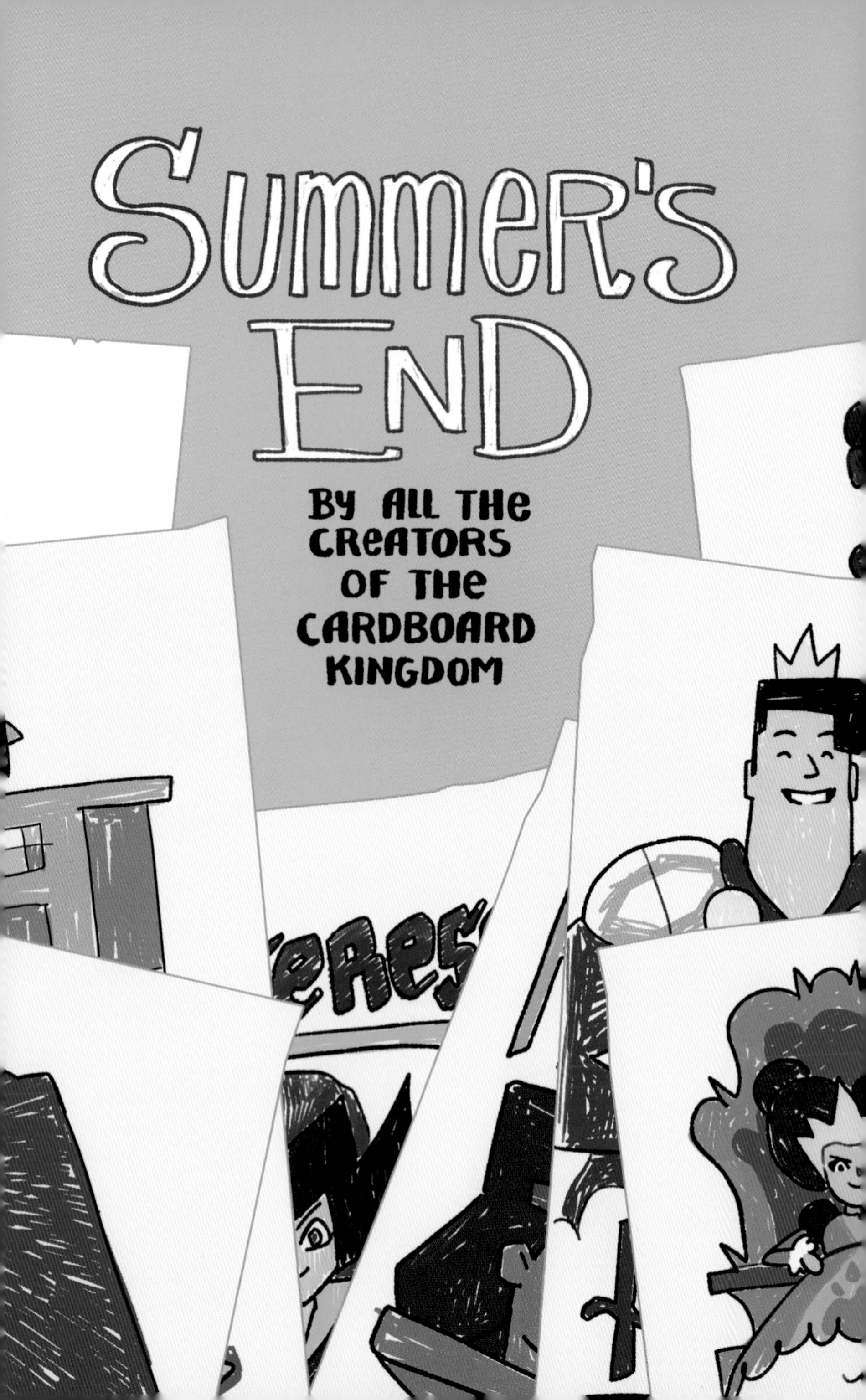
SUMMER'S END
BY ALL THE CREATORS OF THE CARDBOARD KINGDOM

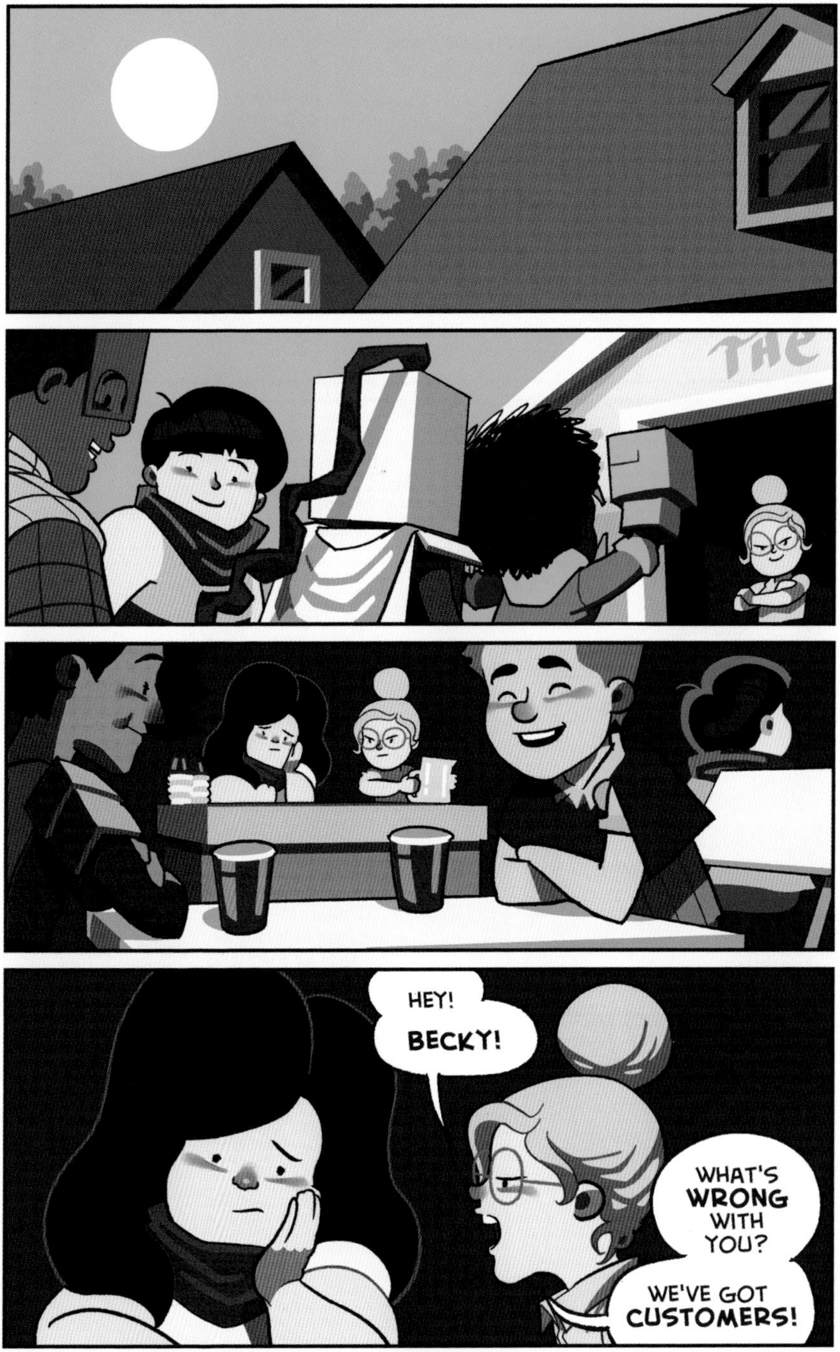
THE
HEY!
BECKY!
WHAT'S WRONG WITH YOU?
WE'VE GOT CUSTOMERS!

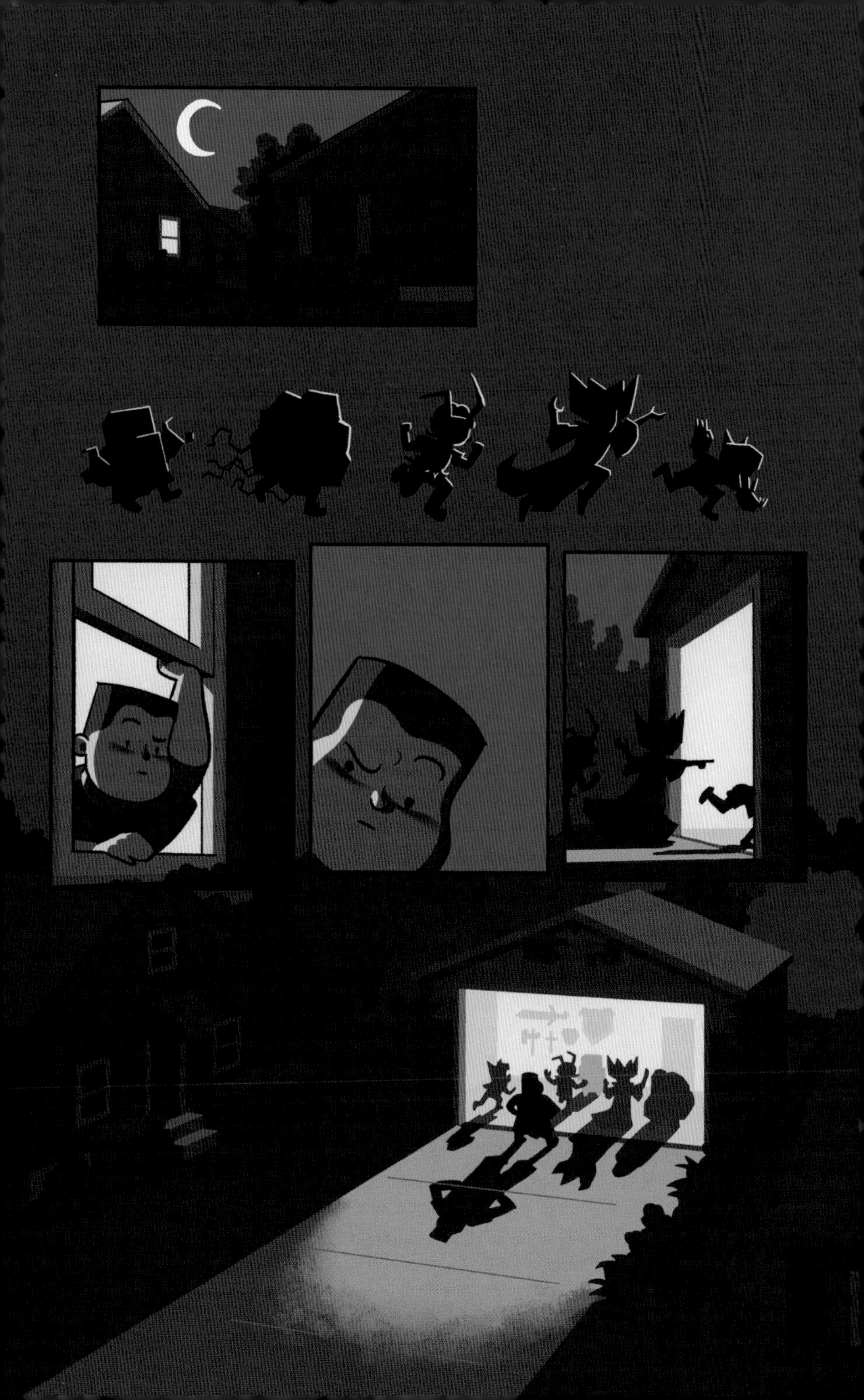

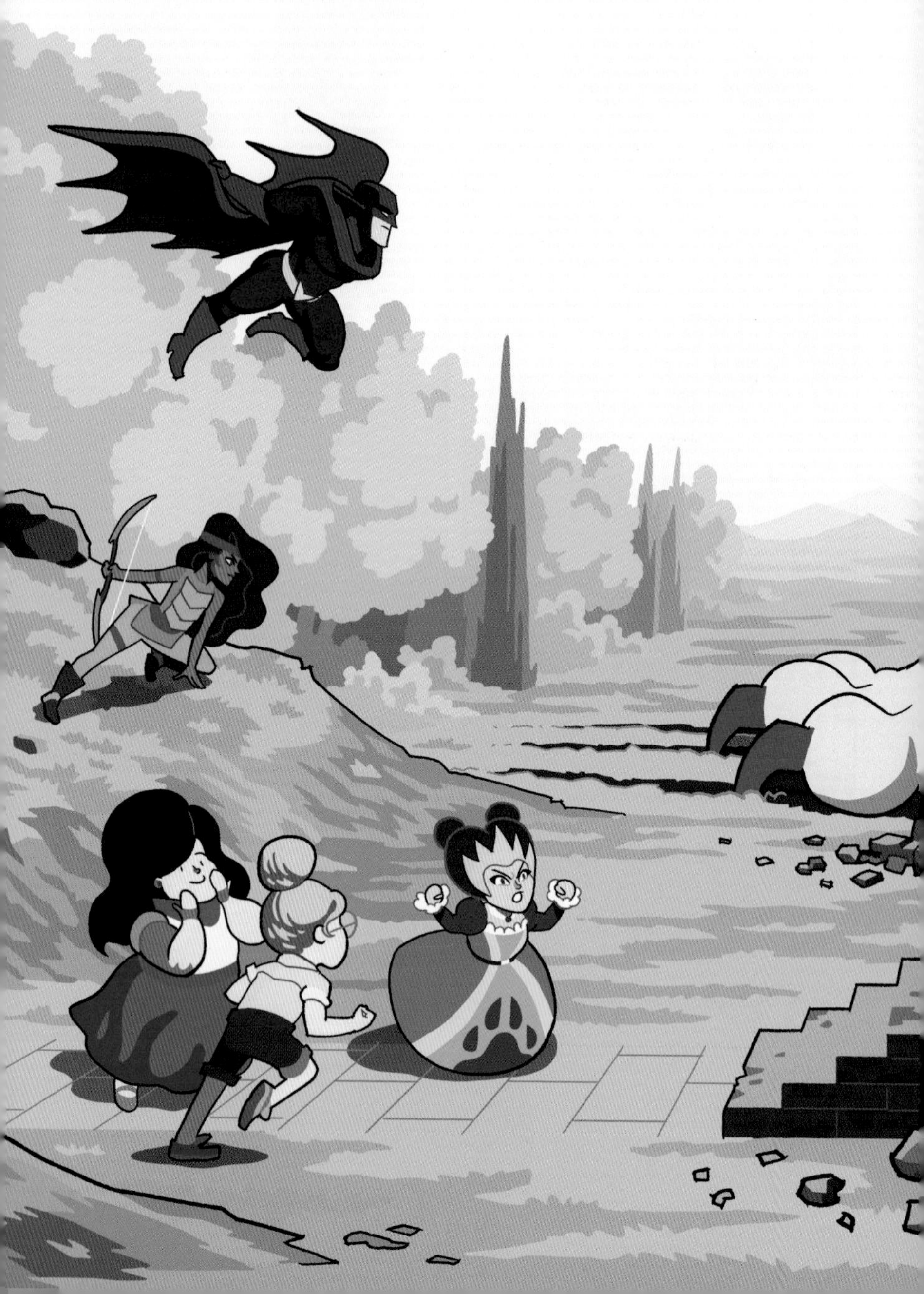

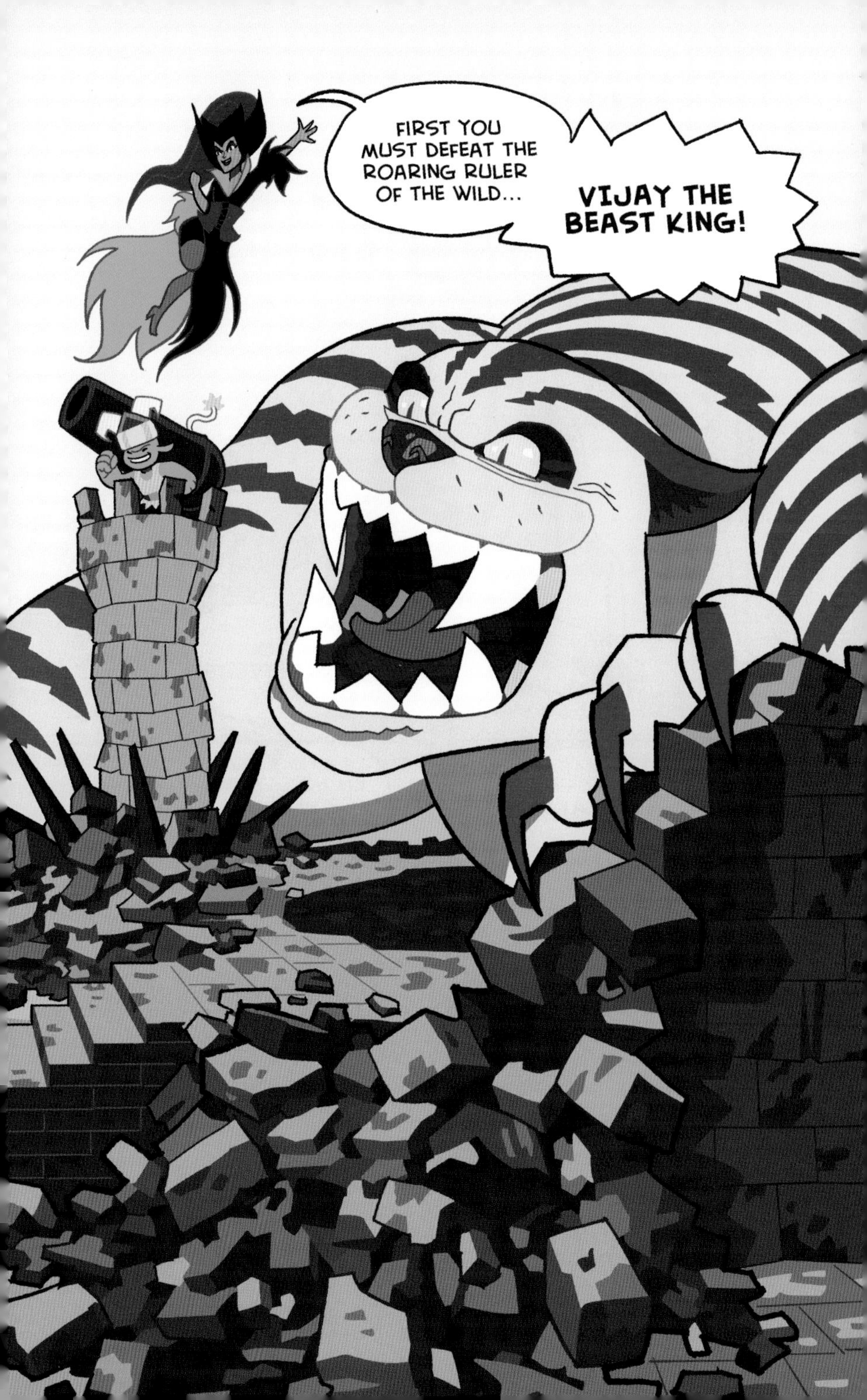
FIRST YOU MUST DEFEAT THE ROARING RULER OF THE WILD...
VIJAY THE BEAST KING!

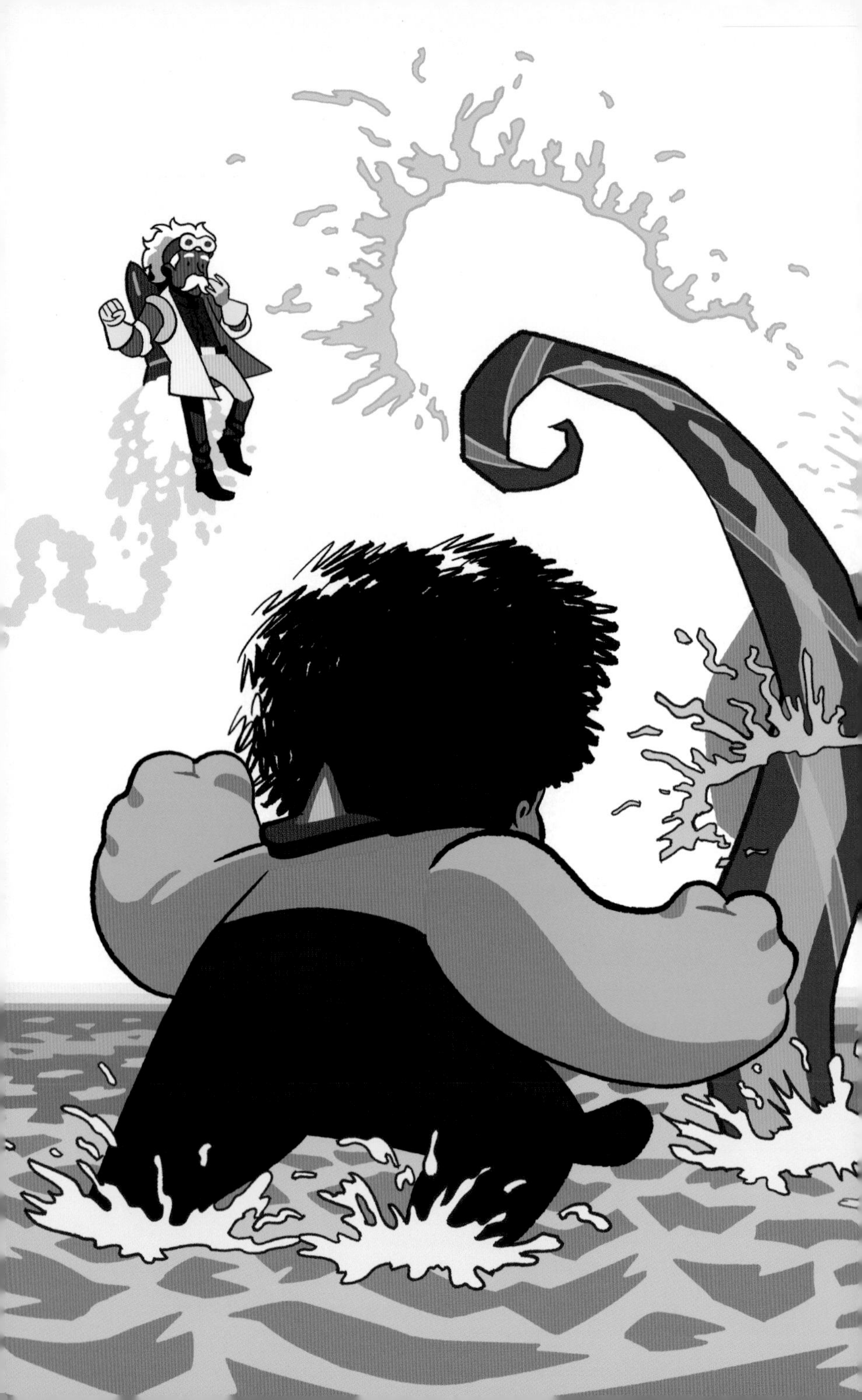

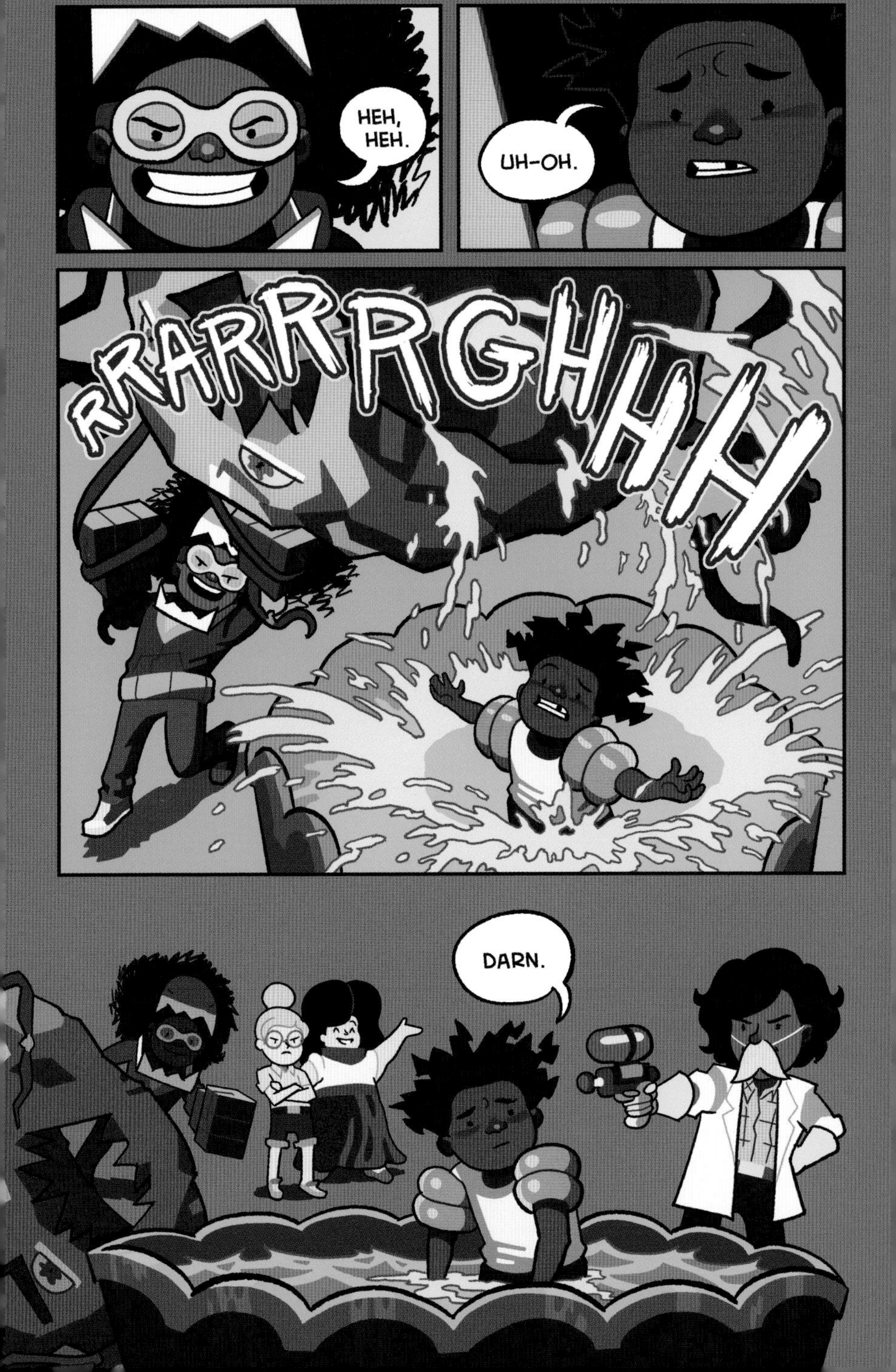
HEH, HEH.
UH-OH.
RRARRRGHHHH
DARN.

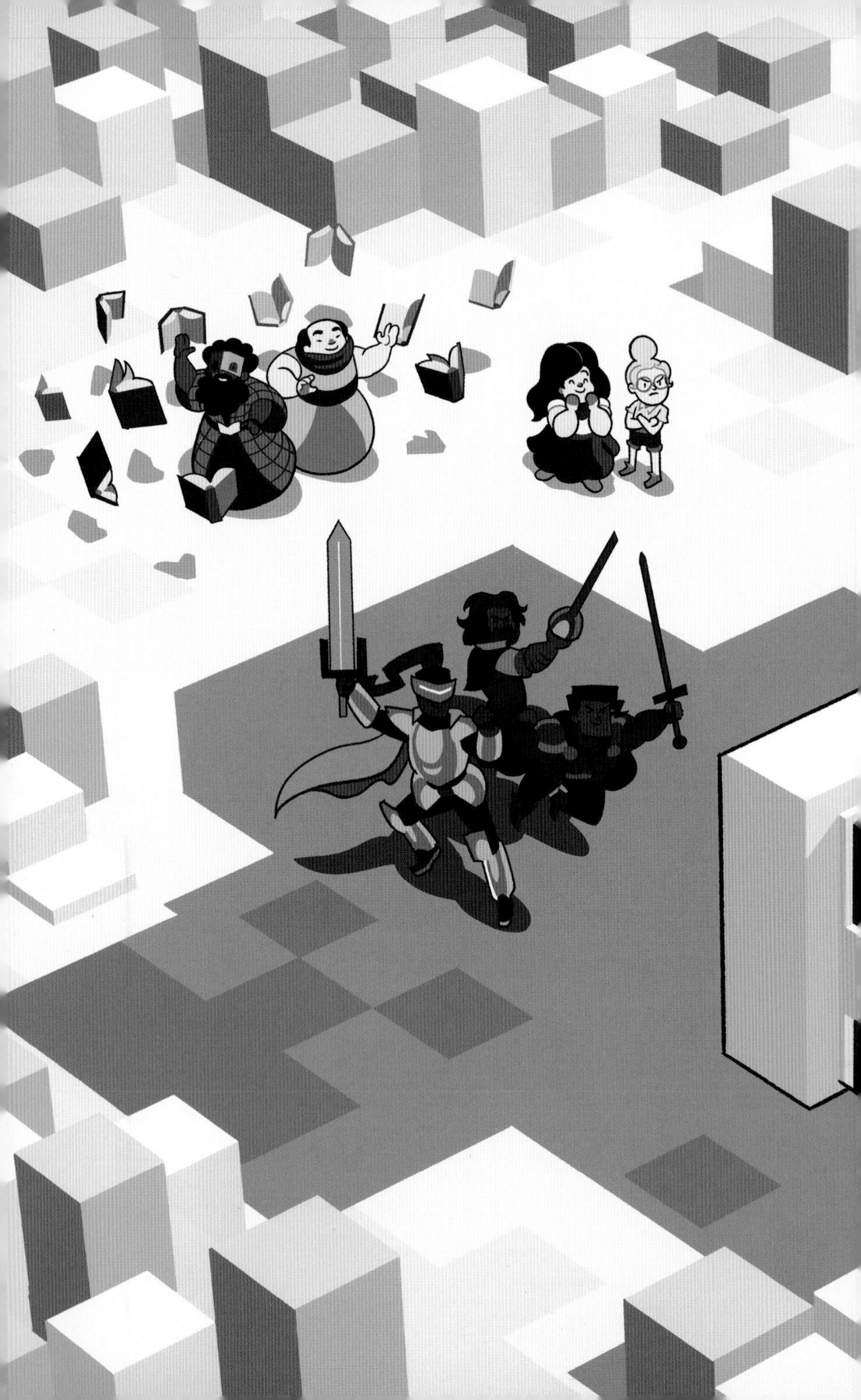

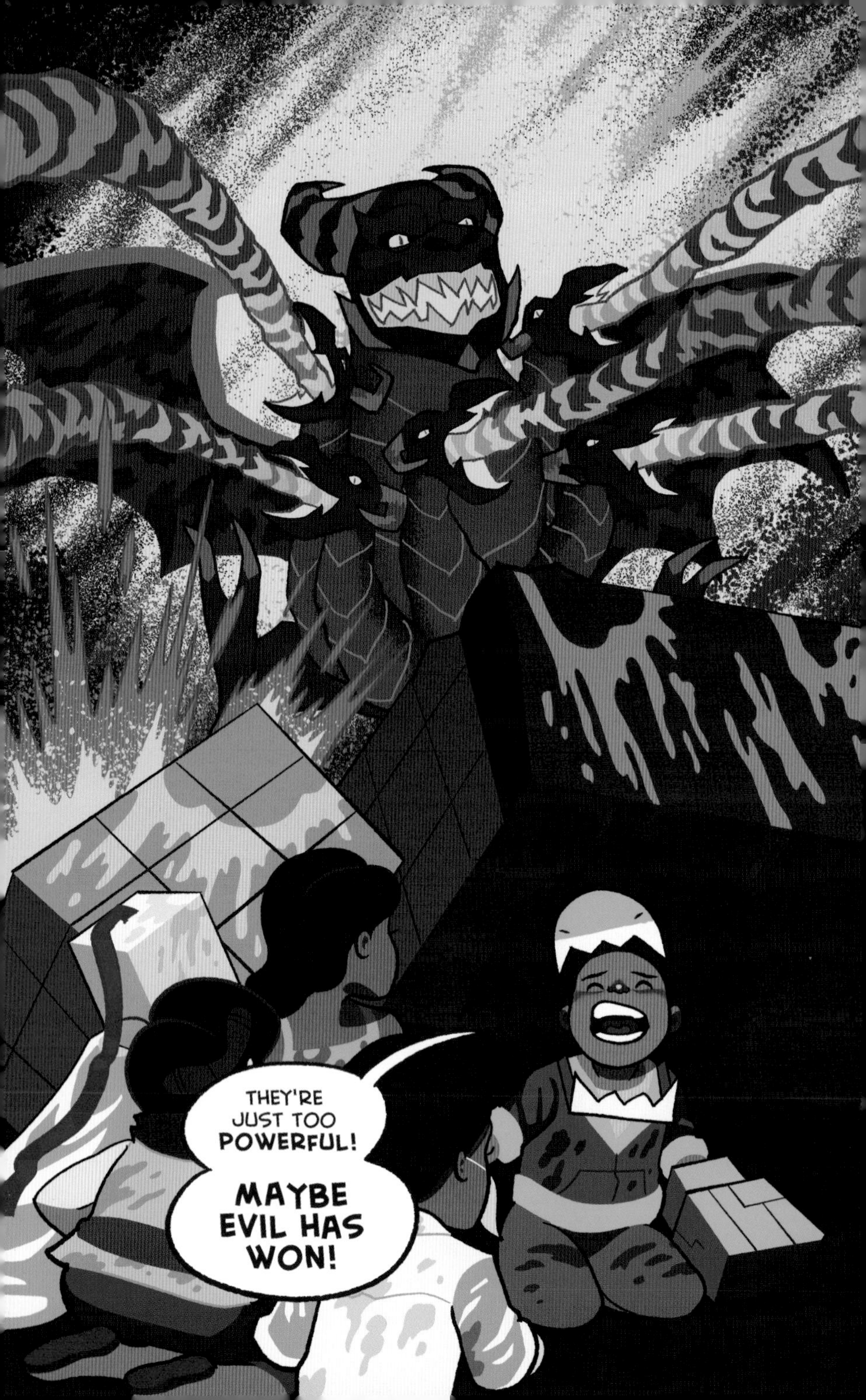
THEY'RE JUST TOO POWERFUL!
MAYBE EVIL HAS WON!

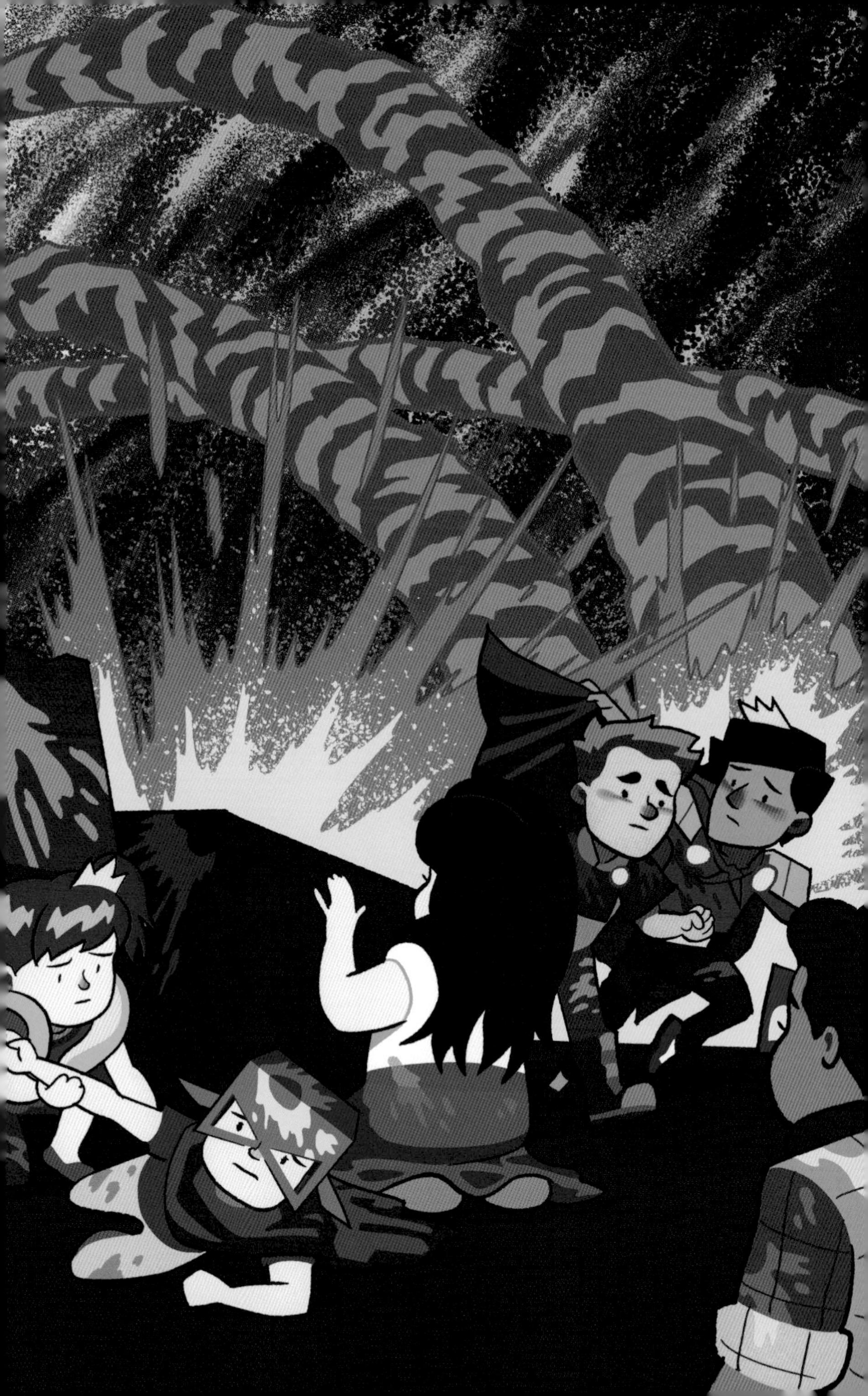

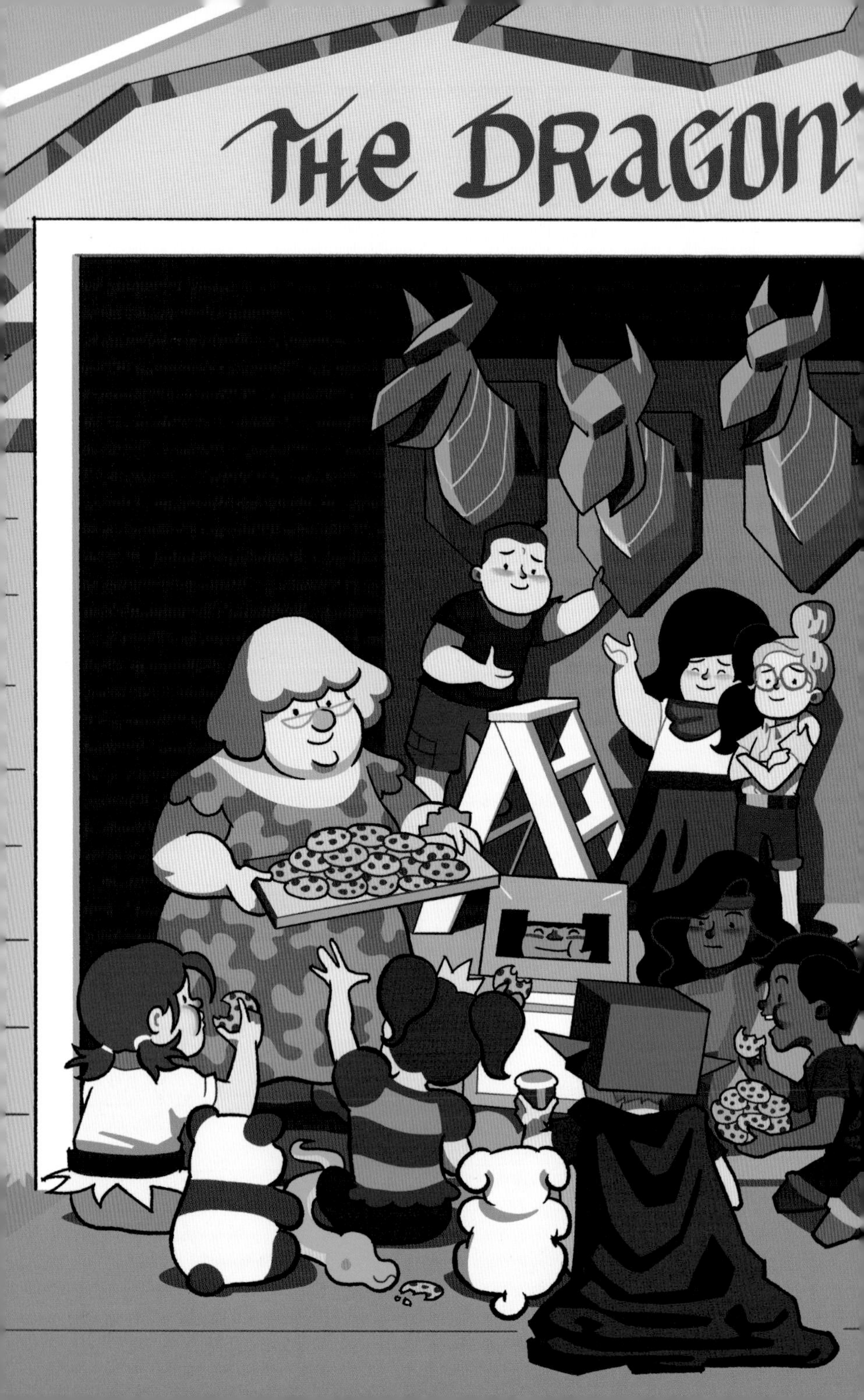
THE DRAGON'

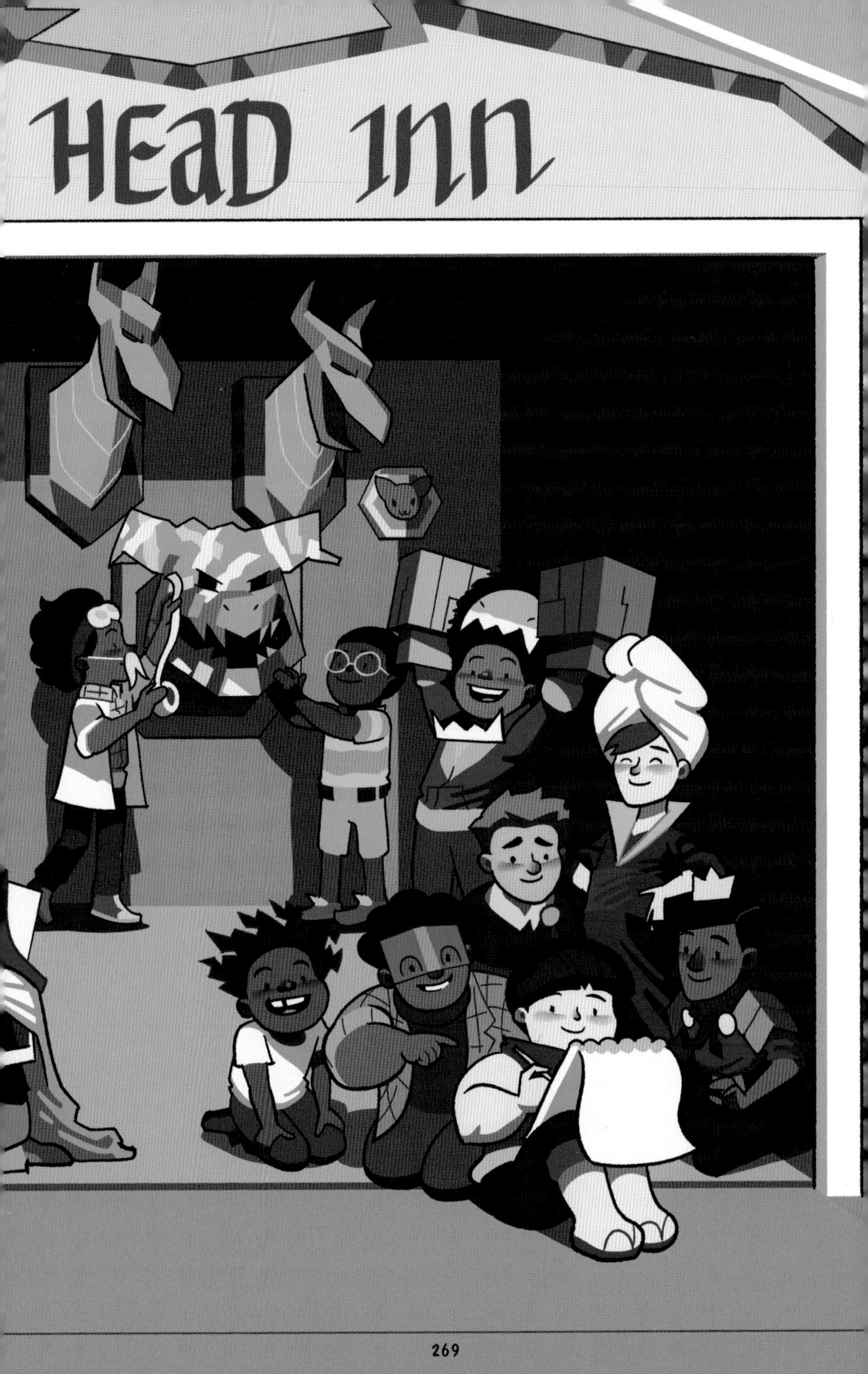
HEAD INN

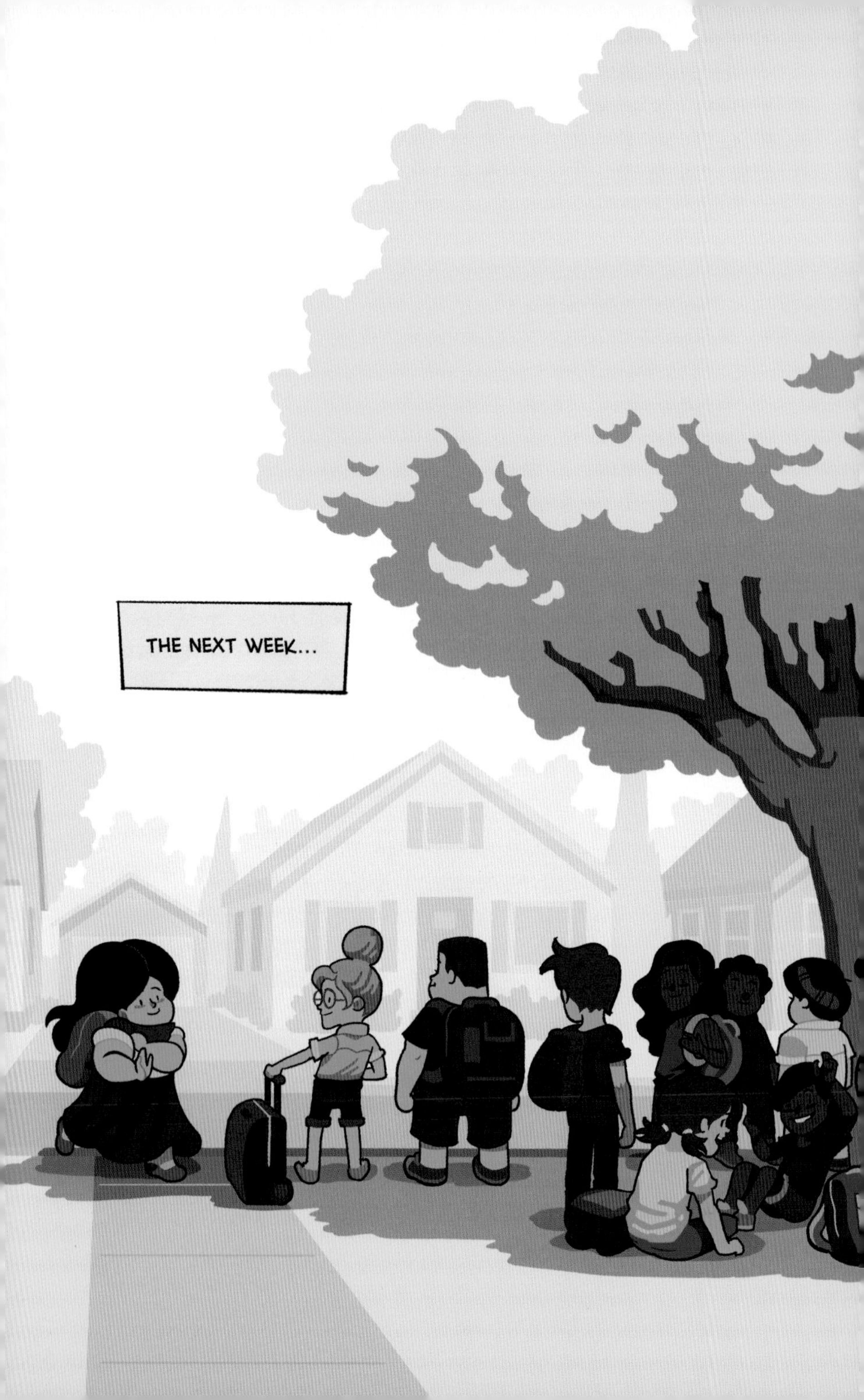
THE NEXT WEEK...

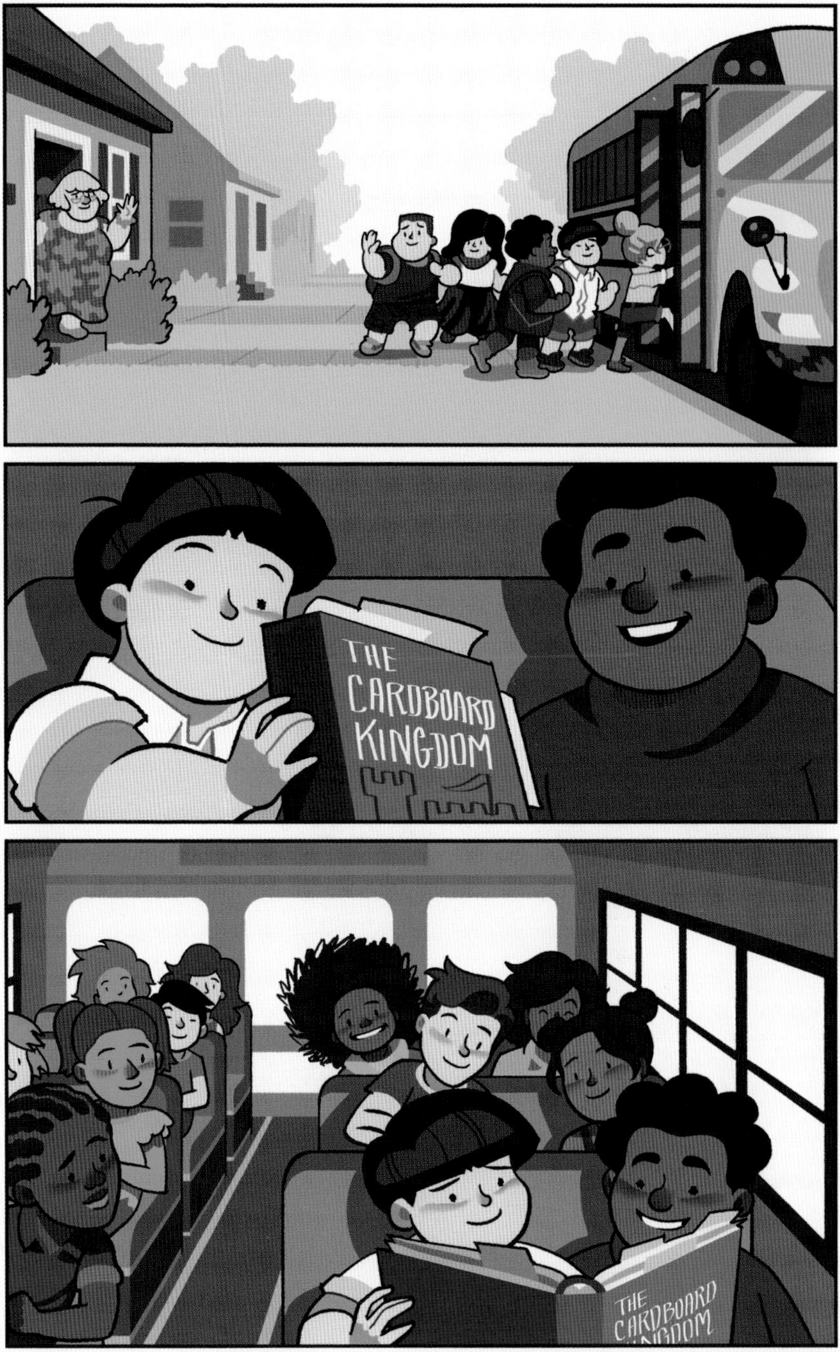
THE CARDBOARD KINGDOM
THE CARDBOARD

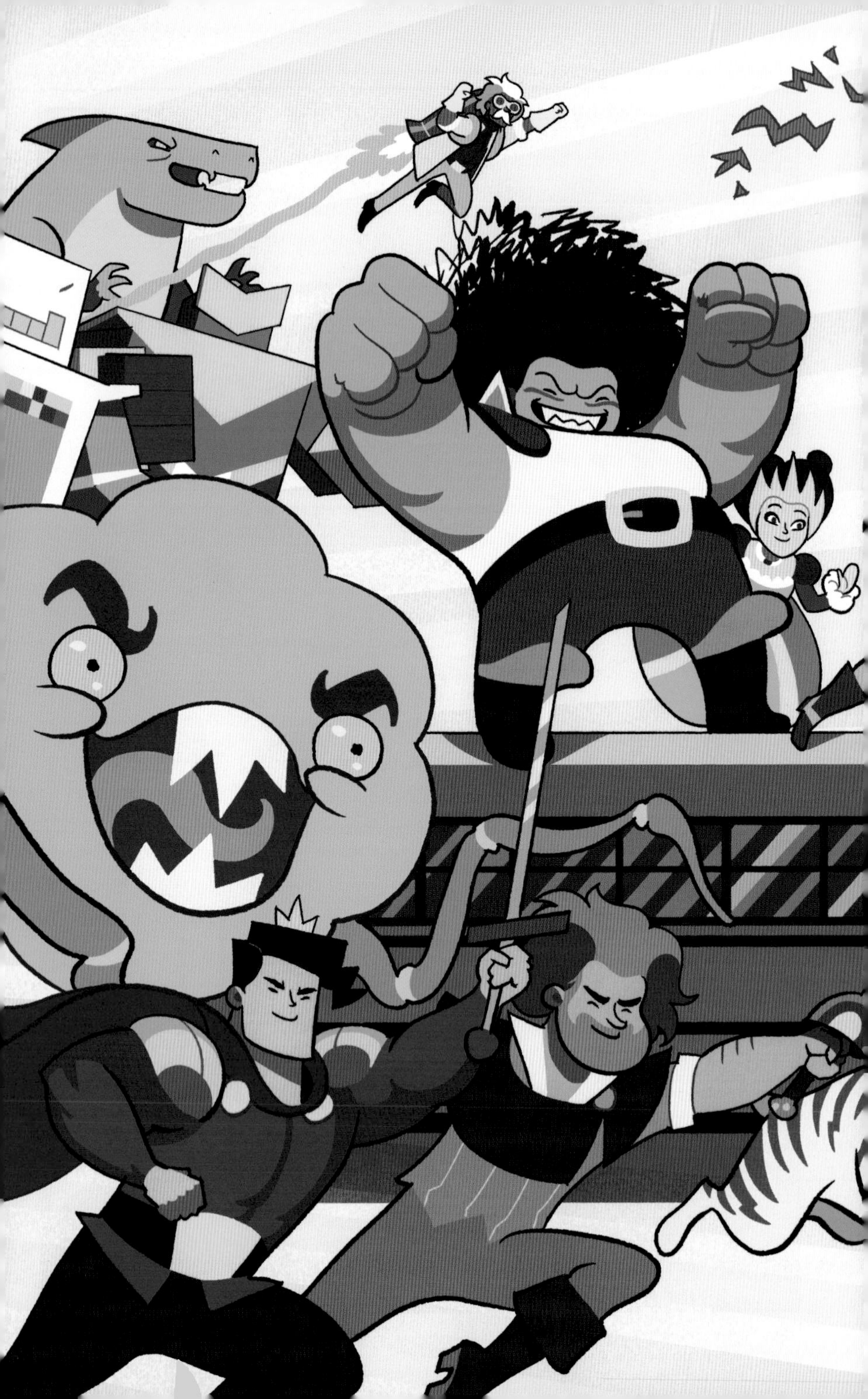

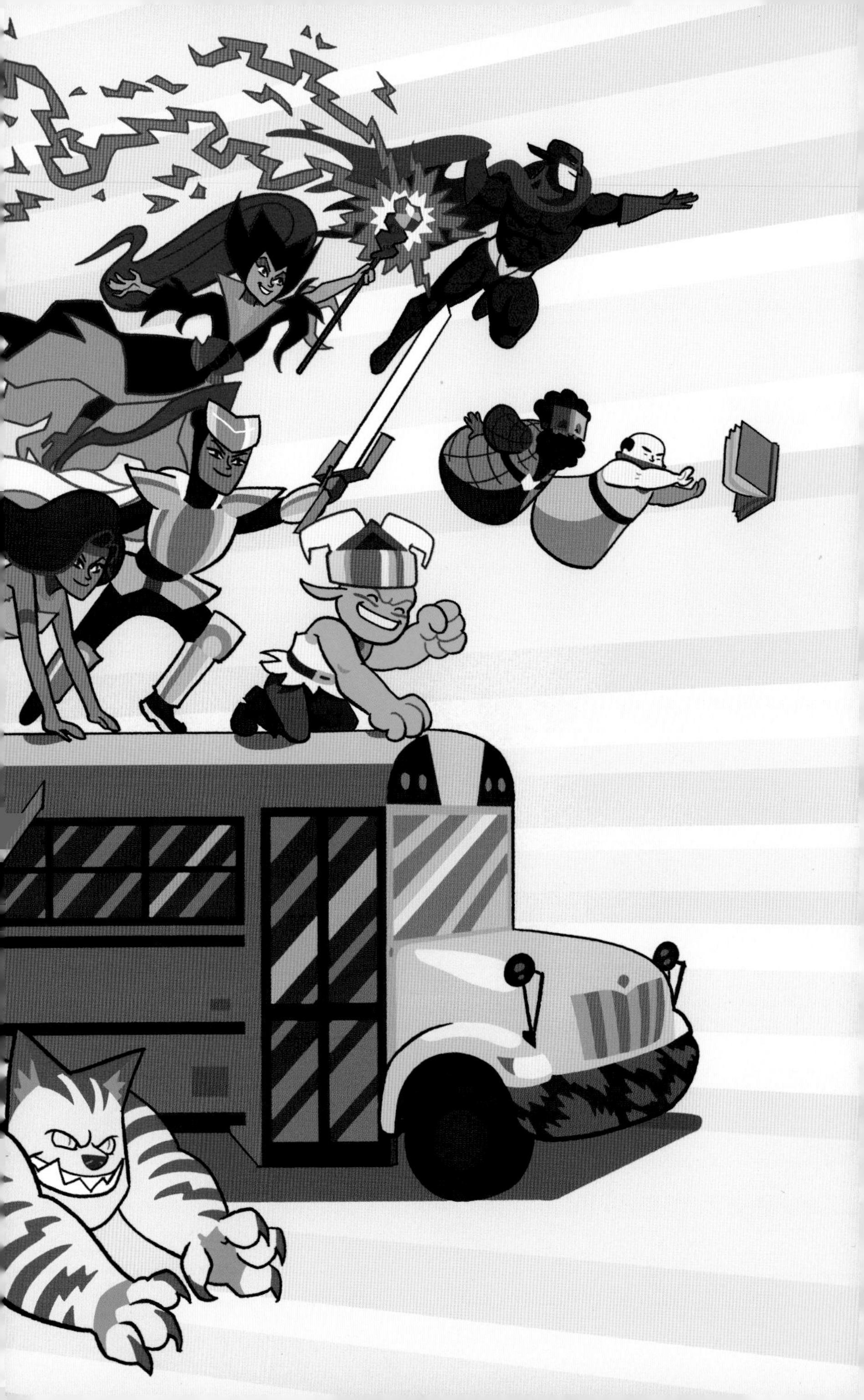

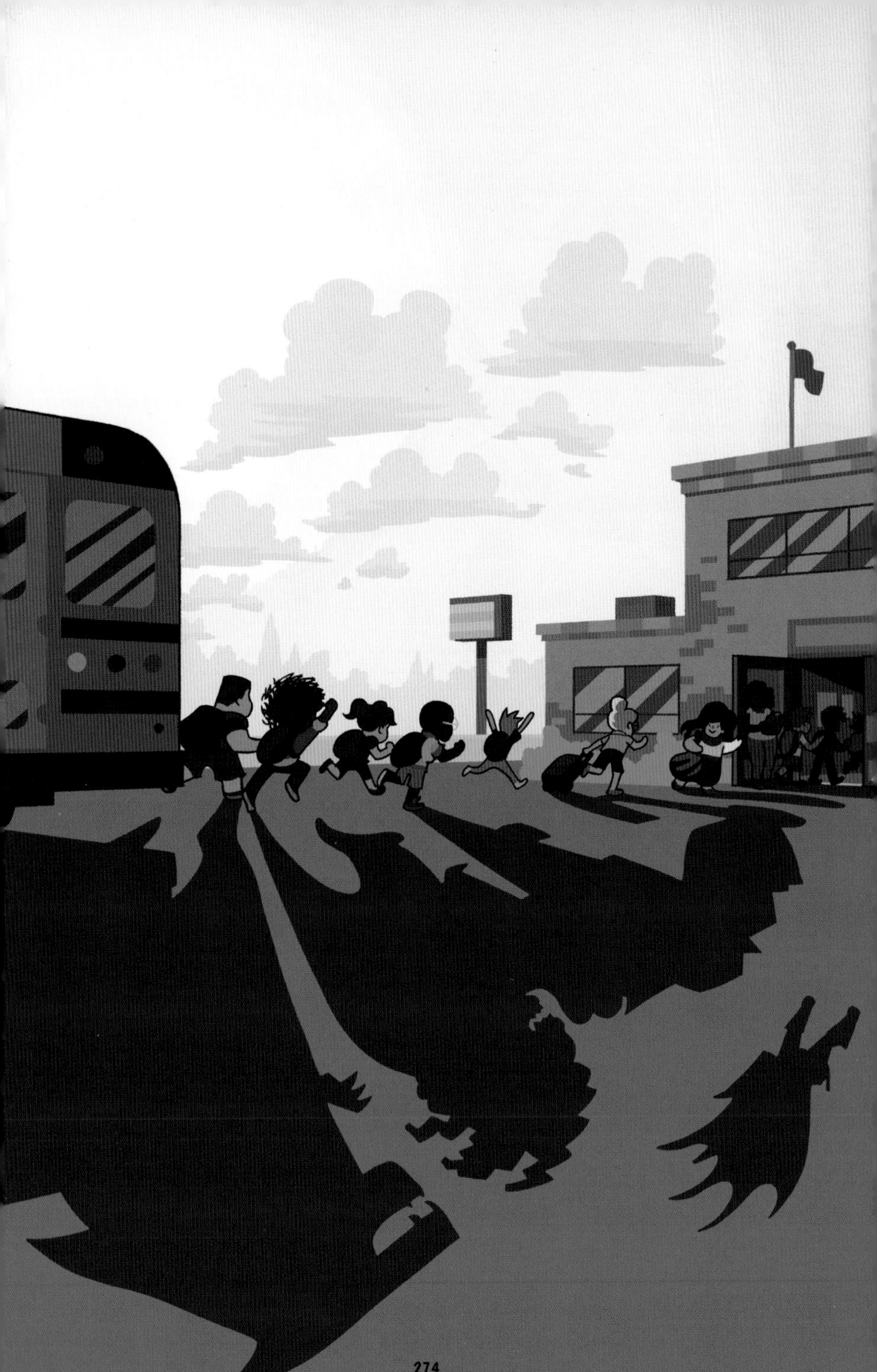

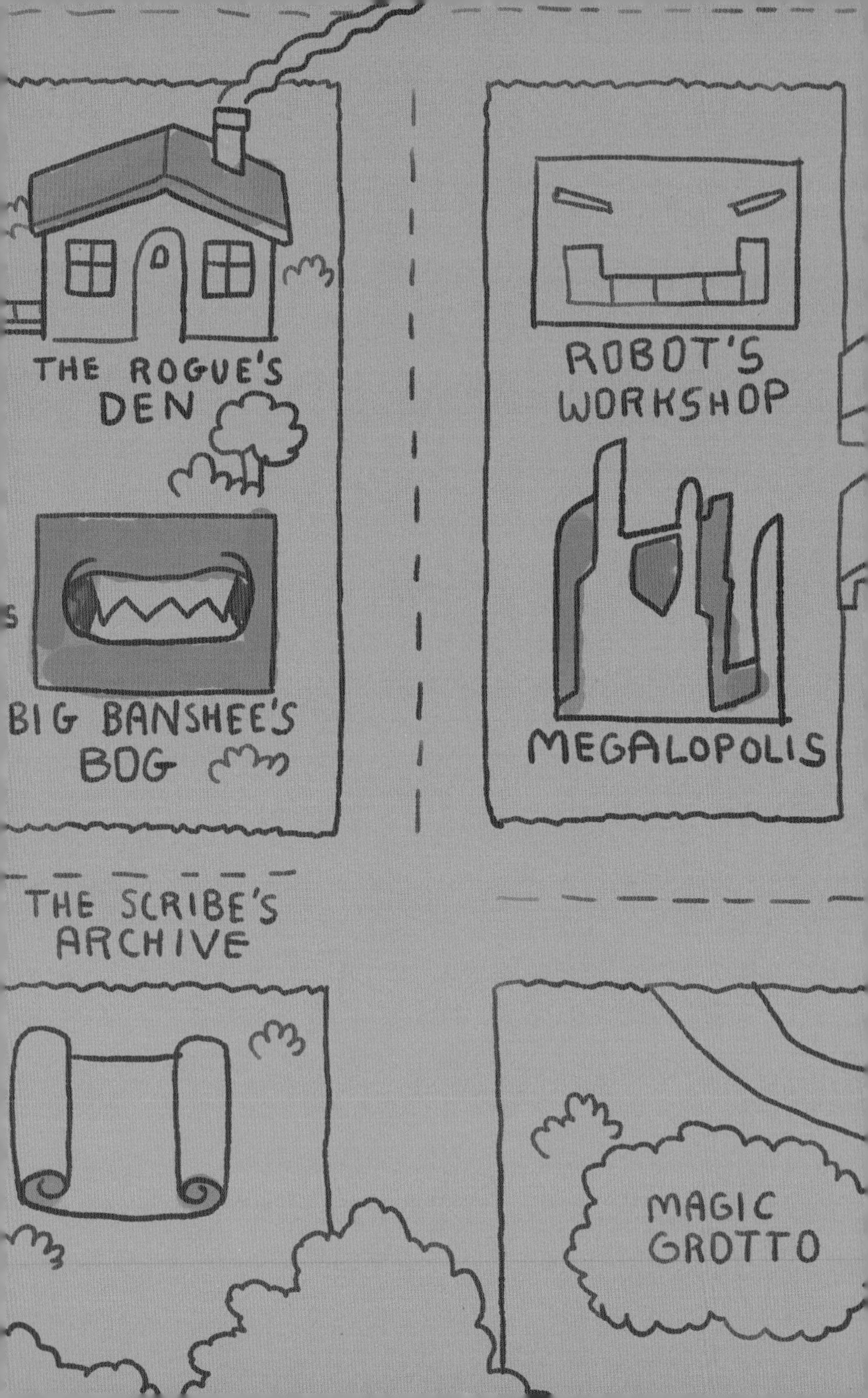
THE ROGUE'S DEN
ROBOT'S WORKSHOP
MEGALOPOLIS
BIG BANSHEE'S BOG
THE SCRIBE'S ARCHIVE
MAGIC GROTTO

HOW WE BUILT THE KINGDOM

It all began with the mysterious and bewitching magic of the Sorceress! Chad Sell developed her story with his friend Jay Fuller, which became the first chapter of this book. But like the humble Scribe character from the pages within, Chad sought to chronicle the stories of *all* heroes of the realm. So he asked for other writers to join forces and help fill the Cardboard Kingdom with the charismatic, courageous, and magical characters you've met in this book.

JAY FULLER

The Sorceress & Megalopolis

Jay is a cartoonist living in Brooklyn, New York, with his husband, Kevin, and their little corgi pup. He writes and illustrates his comic, *The Boy in Pink Earmuffs*. Megalopolis was inspired by Japanese monster movies and the little cardboard dioramas Jay used to make as a kid.

DAVID DEMEO

The Huntress & The Bully

David is a bald jewelry designer with a large variety of hats. His favorite holiday is Halloween, and even though he is supposedly a grown-up now, he still makes his own costumes and dresses up every year. David lives in Caldwell, New Jersey. The Huntress was based on David's babysitting responsibilities as the oldest of three beast brothers.

KATIE SCHENKEL
The Big Banshee

Katie lives in Chicago with her partner, Madison, and she wants to be Batgirl when she grows up. In the meantime, she's written comics like *Moonlighters* and *100 Light Years of Solitude*. The Big Banshee was inspired by Katie's memories of being the girl who "talked too much."

MANUEL BETANCOURT
The Prince

Manuel spends his days in New York City writing, baking, and watching way too many movies. He has a PhD but doesn't like to brag about it. The Prince was inspired by the many (many!) childhood crushes Manuel had on several animated fairy-tale heroes. He's happy to have finally written the story he wished he'd had while growing up.

MOLLY MULDOON
The Animal Queen

Molly is a writer, editor, and newly minted librarian who's always on the move with her pawtner-in-crime, Jamie McKitten. At the moment, they live in Portland, Oregon. The Animal Queen was inspired by Molly's childhood menagerie of stuffed animals.

VID ALLIGER
The Blob & The Robot

Vid is an aspiring writer and illustrator living in upstate New York. He's still figuring things out, and that's okay. The Blob was inspired by Vid's constant desire as a child to tag along with his older brothers, who were usually kind enough to let him play, too.

CLOUD JACOBS
Professor Everything

Cloud is a fifth-grade teacher in Stuttgart, Arkansas. When he's not reading and writing comics, he's working his way through every Star Wars book he can get his hands on. Professor Everything was based on Cloud's awkward childhood, when he would usually be reading while the other kids were playing football.

MICHAEL COLE
The Gargoyle

Michael teaches English literature at Wichita State University, where he also works as an accessibility technologist and is pursuing a master's degree in creative writing. In his free time, he can be found with his three dogs, playing *Breath of the Wild*. The Gargoyle was loosely based on Michael's childhood experiences, but if he had been a superhero, he would rather have been Jean Grey, not a gargoyle!

BARBARA PEREZ MARQUEZ

The Mad Scientist

Barbara is a Dominican American writer. She lives in Baltimore and has been writing since she was in seventh grade. Just like Amanda, Barbara was born and raised in the Dominican Republic, loves mustaches, and believes we can all experiment a little more in life!

In Memory of

KRIS MOORE

Kris grew up in the suburbs of Detroit and lived there with his partner, Weston. As a kid, all he ever wanted to do was write comics, and as an adult, he did just that with his comic anthology, *Saturday Morning Snack Attack!*, and all-ages series, *Science Girl*.

His characters, Becky and Alice, were inspired by the girls he grew up with, who were some of the most ruthless entrepreneurs ever to run a Kool-Aid stand.

His boundless creativity and unforgettable characters were essential in making this book—we couldn't have built this kingdom without him.

To my parents, who gave me a childhood full of love,
encouragement, and creativity
—C.S.

THIS IS A BORZOI BOOK PUBLISHED BY ALFRED A. KNOPF

This is a work of fiction. Names, characters, places, and incidents either are the product of the author's imagination or are used fictitiously. Any resemblance to actual persons, living or dead, events, or locales is entirely coincidental.

"The Sorceress" text copyright © 2018 by Chad Sell and Jay Fuller
"The Huntress" text copyright © 2018 by Chad Sell and David DeMeo
"The Big Banshee" text copyright © 2018 by Chad Sell and Katie Schenkel
"The Alchemist and the Blacksmith" text copyright © 2018 by Chad Sell and Kris Moore
"The Prince" text copyright © 2018 by Chad Sell and Manuel Betancourt
"The Animal Queen" text copyright © 2018 by Chad Sell and Molly Muldoon
"The Blob" text copyright © 2018 by Chad Sell and Vid Alliger
"Professor Everything" text copyright © 2018 by Chad Sell and Cloud Jacobs
"The Gargoyle" text copyright © 2018 by Chad Sell and Michael Cole
"The Mad Scientist" text copyright © 2018 by Chad Sell and Barbara Perez Marquez
"The Robot" text copyright © 2018 by Chad Sell and Vid Alliger
"The Army of Evil" text copyright © 2018 by Chad Sell
"The Bully" text copyright © 2018 by Chad Sell and David DeMeo
"Megalopolis" text copyright © 2018 by Chad Sell and Jay Fuller
"Summer's End" text copyright © 2018 by Chad Sell, Jay Fuller, David DeMeo, Katie Schenkel, Kris Moore, Manuel Betancourt, Molly Muldoon, Vid Alliger, Cloud Jacobs, Michael Cole, and Barbara Perez Marquez
Art copyright © 2018 by Chad Sell

All rights reserved. Published in the United States by Alfred A. Knopf, an imprint of Random House Children's Books, a division of Penguin Random House LLC, New York.

Knopf, Borzoi Books, and the colophon are registered trademarks of Penguin Random House LLC.

Visit us on the Web! rhcbooks.com

Educators and librarians, for a variety of teaching tools, visit us at RHTeachersLibrarians.com

Library of Congress Cataloging-in-Publication Data is available upon request.

ISBN 978-1-5247-1937-1 (trade) — ISBN 978-1-5247-1938-8 (pbk.) — ISBN 978-1-5247-1939-5 (ebook)

The illustrations in this book were created using Clip Studio Paint.
MANUFACTURED IN CHINA
June 2018
10 9 8 7 6
First Edition

Random House Children's Books supports the First Amendment and celebrates the right to read.